M000317292

When Hearts Break

Endorsements

This is a powerful and beautiful work from the hand of Jerry Eicher. With this book, he moves Amish fiction from delightful romances into the realm of realism and classic storytelling. He begins to bring the genre alongside great American works like A *Tree Grows in Brooklyn, To Kill A Mockingbird*, Faulkner's *Go Down Moses*, and Hemingway's **The Sun Also Rises**. I am not saying those books are all the same, but they have a similar style—to be more honest to God about what our lives are like. To be truthful about our world in all its darkness and its light, all its sunshine and shadows. Jerry gives us full-blooded characters in their struggles and complexities, the things they overcome by the grace of God and the things that bring them to their knees in humility and defeat. By doing this, he makes his entire novel shine. Five stars. Highly recommended.

—Murray Pura, *The Face of Heaven, Ashton Park, The White Birds of Morning, Gettysburg*

When Hearts Break by Jerry Eicher gripped me from the first paragraph. Two women, the man they both loved, jealousy, heartbreak, a young woman's shame, a grown woman's forgiveness. A dark and haunting tale that stepped into sunlight and made me cry. This is a story I will not forget."

—Lucinda J Kinsinger, author, *Anything But Simple: My Life as a Mennonite*

Foreword

When I first started writing Amish fiction ten years ago, one of the names that always came up in conversations about the genre was Jerry Eicher, an Amish man who wrote Amish fiction. We both wrote for Harvest House, but in all the following years, I never read one of Jerry's books. I have now corrected that glaring mistake.

I have just finished *When Hearts Break*, a tour-de-force into the dark side of Amish life. I had already read the two chapters included in our recent anthology, The Amish Menorah and Other Stories, but I had no idea of the depth and power I was to find in the complete book.

When Hearts Break is not Amish fiction—it is brilliant literary fiction about Amish people. Mr. Eicher takes a deep dive into the hidden secret of many Amish communities—sexual abuse and its effect on lives and families. But he does not leave you in the darkness. Instead he delivers characters who are powerful and mesmerizing, and a story that is absolutely riveting, and along the way, you will discover grace and redemption.

This book embodies all the qualities I look for as a reader—brilliant writing, incredible dialogue, picture book settings—they are all here, and when you finish reading *When Hearts Break*, Mr. Eicher will have accomplished what every great writer hopes to do—you will be forever changed for the better.—Patrick E. Craig, Author of *The Amish Menorah*, the Apple Creek Dreams series, and The Paradise Chronicles.

When Hearts Break

Jerry Eicher

ELK LAKE PUBLISHING INC
Plymouth, Massachusetts

Copyright Notice

When Hearts Break

First edition. Copyright © 2020 by Jerry Eicher. The information contained in this book is the intellectual property of Jerry Eicher and is governed by United States and International copyright laws. All rights reserved. No part of this publication, either text or image, may be used for any purpose other than personal use. Therefore, reproduction, modification, storage in a retrieval system, or retransmission, in any form or by any means, electronic, mechanical, or otherwise, for reasons other than personal use, except for brief quotations for reviews or articles and promotions, is strictly prohibited without prior written permission by the publisher.

This is a work of fiction. Names, characters, businesses, places, events, locales, and incidents are either the products of the author's imagination or used in a fictitious manner. Any resemblance to actual persons, living or dead, or actual events is purely coincidental.

Cover and Interior Design: Derinda Babcock

Editor(s): Peggy Ellis, Deb Haggerty

PUBLISHED BY: Elk Lake Publishing, Inc., 35 Dogwood Drive, Plymouth, MA 02360, 2020

Library Cataloging Data

Names: Eicher, Jerry (Jerry Eicher)

When Hearts Break / Jerry Eicher

386 p. 23cm × 15cm (9in × 6 in.)

Identifiers: ISBN-13: 978-1-64949-027-8 (paperback) | 978-1-64949-028-5 (trade paperback) | 978-1-64949-029-2 (e-book)

Key Words: Amish, relationships, family, abuse, redemption, sin and forgiveness, literary fiction

LCCN: 2020942634 Fiction

Prologue

LILY

I stared at the pages of the notebook Barbara had written. I didn't stay for the funeral, but left Walter's body washed, not a crevice of his skin untouched by my hands. As the tree falls, the tree lies. So went the familiar saying in the community. I stared at the notebooks again. Barbara left me her story. She trusted me, so I will write mine, and together we will share the tale of what came before the falling.

Section One—1903 to 1910

Barbara

Chapter 1

The community was little more than dusty, framed-wood buildings, rough and weather-beaten if you saw them during the day, or a softer appearance when outlined against the starry skies at night. This was Indiana's southernmost Amish settlement—the beginning, a mile or so below the small town of Odon, along County Road 1200 and south from there.

I am an old woman now. I rarely venture out on the roads alone without Walter driving. Automobiles whizz past making dull whooshing sounds, as if to suck the air right out of the buggy. I thought I was used to the modern world, but old age travels one backward, I have been told. I saw Lily's face in the clouds the other day—not simply a rough outline, either.

"Look," I told Walter.

"A cloud," he said.

I didn't argue with him. I know what I saw. Before the calendar turns twice again, fifty years will have passed since my sister left the community for the last time. Walter's son will be approaching the same age—a son, to replace the one I gave Walter and lost. Lily will come back when I am gone. I will leave her Walter. A shell of the man she once knew, but Lily accepted this inevitable end when we parted.

I could seek to justify myself in this telling of my tale. I will try not to, but I suppose I will. We all labor under some form of self-delusion. I wish I had always been right. I wish desperately as I see the waters of the dark river approaching I would ride triumphant into heaven. Yet, I will not. If God understands what I have done and how I have lived my life,

I will be satisfied if his hand can reach me—as I know his mercy has—for Walter has loved me. I will ask for no more.

We were born long before automobiles clogged the roads, Lily and I. Daett was a short man, while Mamm was lean and lithe. On Sundays, the top of Daett's black hat barely cleared Mamm's bonnet.

Lily was a wisp of a girl compared to my stocky frame. She had taken after Mamm and her sisters while I had inherited all my genes from Daett's side of the family. At least I thought so for a long time—about Lily getting only Mamm's genes, and me getting Daett's. Time would reveal another reason, a dark secret which had frozen the hearts of my parents into icy pillars. Lily would get the worst of the fallout from Mamm's sin with an English man, and from Grandpa's transgressions against the community by serving in the Union army during the Civil War. I wish I could use the sins of the fathers to justify my own behavior, but I can't. I never suffered what Lily suffered.

Lily looked over at me from her side of the bed one evening, "Grandpa gave me a smile today."

"I don't care," I said.

"Grandpa likes me." She looked dreamy eyed at the ceiling.

"Maybe you should worry more about what Daett thinks of you," I shot back.

"I like Grandpa," she said, as if the pleasant fact canceled out any unpleasant ones.

Lily dropped off to sleep instantly. She always did. I, on the other hand, lay awake thinking, and often heard raised voices coming from Mamm and Daett's bedroom after we had gone to bed. Mamm begging and pleading and Daett's lower harsh tones. I could never understand what they said. I didn't really want to know, or why the rapid squeaking of the bed followed these exchanges.

I awoke one morning to Mamm shaking my shoulder.

"Get dressed and come downstairs. We're leaving for Aunt Nancy's place," she whispered.

I sat up and rubbed my eyes. The world was completely dark outside the plain, dark bedroom curtains. I got out of bed and dressed by the flickering light of the kerosene lamp Mamm had left behind on the dresser top.

"Get up." I told Lily.

She groaned but didn't move.

"Mamm wants us up," I said, louder this time.

Lily finally stirred, and I helped her dress. She stayed close to me, with one hand on my sleeve, as we made our way downstairs and into the kitchen, where a meager breakfast sat on the table.

"Sit down and eat," Daett ordered. His bowl of oatmeal and toast already half eaten.

"Why are we going to Aunt Nancy so early?" I asked.

"Just eat," Daett said.

We ate, the usual prayer of thanks after breakfast skipped. Daett left for the barn the moment he had scraped the last bite of oatmeal from his bowl. We left the dishes unwashed, since Daett had the horse and surrey ready. Mamm hustled us out, holding our hands, and we climbed into the buggy. Aunt Nancy's home soon appeared in the distance. I couldn't see the line of buggies already parked in the yard until Daett whirled into the driveway. Maiden had barely come to a halt by the hitching rail before Mamm hopped down the buggy step. The barn door swung open in front of us, and soft lantern light spread across the driveway stones. Aunt Nancy's husband, John, hurried out, with Mamm's Daett by his side. Both men had their black brimmed hats pulled low over their faces.

"You should both go into the house," John said to Mamm, and placed his hand on Maiden's bridle. "We'll take care of the horse and bring the girls in when you've had a few moments alone."

Mamm made her way slowly up the sidewalk with Daett walking behind her. I was ready to climb down when Grandpa appeared in the buggy door.

"Shall I help you?" He offered his hand.

Before I could answer, Lily piped up. "What's wrong?"

"Your Aunt Nancy will soon be with Jesus," Grandpa said. I exited the buggy, while behind me Lily clung to Grandpa's neck.

"You'll be okay, sweetheart," Grandpa whispered. "Everything will be okay."

"I'm glad to see you." Lily cooed.

Grandpa patted Lily on the head. "I'm glad to see you too."

"I'm taking the horse into the stall," Uncle John hollered. "You should bring the girls into the barn for a few minutes."

We followed Uncle John. The musty odor of cows and milk greeted us, with soft bellows of the cows coming from the barnyard in the back.

"We'll wait here," Grandpa said.

He gave us little stools to sit on until they took us up to the house, where Grandma Yoder met us at the front door.

"You can't hide these things from the little ones," she said.

Uncle John set his lips and didn't answer.

"Death cannot be changed," Grandma continued.

Uncle John's face twitched. "We will say no more about this. Nancy may be your daughter, but she's my wife, taken from me in the prime of her youth. The Lord may have forgiven, but the pain stings deeply."

"You think our hearts don't also hurt?" Grandma asked.

"I said, we will say no more about this." Uncle John turned on his heels and disappeared into the kitchen.

"Come here, Lily," Grandpa said, and sat down on the rocking chair to pull Lily up into his lap. He appeared old and tired.

The other adults left for the bedroom. Their soft cries drifted out of the open door, rising and falling against the living room walls. I waited silently with Cousin Heidi as the sun began to rise outside, the first rays bursting through the window and dimming the light of the lanterns.

The adults drifted back from the bedroom one by one, and a meeting was soon called with Uncle John in charge. "My heart is broken this morning," he began, "knowing Nancy's crossing is at hand, and yes, there is anger over what is happening, yet we are still family, and we must make the best of things. The Lord will see us through this trial. Somehow he will."

"I have to speak," Grandpa said. "What you say about my sins following me home into the community from my rumspringa is not right. I have begged both the Lord and the church for forgiveness. I know I fought as a solider in the great war between the states, and so committed a great evil by killing men by my own hand. Yet, what is happening here is what happens to many a family. We cannot draw conclusions about the Lord's judgment because of the ill which befalls us. Otherwise, Job would not have been left to us as an example."

"Job was a perfect man," Uncle Mose said, "which you are not. I agree with what they are saying in the community about the Lord's judgment. These are not old wives' tales. The sins of the fathers visit the third and fourth generation. I have repented often that I was not more careful before I married into this family."

Aunt Malinda leaped up to rush from the room. Mamm stared after her sister but didn't move.

"I accept blame for what I have done," Grandpa said. "I did a great evil in my younger days, but this is not an evil I have brought on my family."

"There is no benefit in this discussion." Daett spoke up. "What is, just is. We will have to live with the past and make the best of things."

The men stirred restlessly. Outside, the sun continued to rise, pushing its warmth past the window drapes. Deacon Miller arrived with his wife, Lavina. Bishop Mast and his wife, Esther, came in the buggy behind them. They didn't question the glum faces in the house. There was a mother and wife dying in the bedroom.

More of the cousins had joined us, and we whispered together planning our escape. No one was paying attention so with Heidi in the lead we slipped outside. Lily and I hung to the back of the group, the hush from the house still on us.

Chapter 2

We crept past the long lines of buggies, where a few somber-faced men stood around, chatting. They looked at us, but no one objected to our leaving. Children were supposed to play, even when their relatives lay dying in the house.

I didn't know our destination. The release from the house was enough. In the summertime, there would have been green pastures growing on either side of us, with ragged grass growing down the middle of the cow path leading back to the creek behind Uncle John's barn. The brown grass bent and matted in this weather. There would be ice along the edges of the creek below us, the water cold to the touch. We could not wade along the shallow shores, but we still ran down the cow path.

I was panting when we reached the edge of creek and petted the nose of Uncle John's pony, named Brownie, to cover for my deficiency. Lily climbed on his back and stroked his nose. Several of the cousins pressed on down the stream bed. Their cries soon reached us. "We've found something!"

Lily climbed down from the pony and ran along the bank.

I followed more slowly, the pony staring after us. Lily was pointing towards a low branch of a tall oak tree when I arrived. Someone had tied a pair of red shoes to the tree limb. They had straps over the top and had open sides which would obviously display the wearer's bare feet. Their sheer audacity held us spellbound as they glittered in the sunlight.

"Who could have put them there?" Heidi asked.

We stared silently.

Lily was the first to move, reaching for them, and untying the strings. She held them up, one in each hand. "Aren't these pretty shoes?"

"Those are English things." I found my voice. "We shouldn't take them, even if the owner doesn't want them anymore."

Lily appeared unfazed as she allowed Heidi to examine the shoes.

"You should try them on," Lily offered, her eyes shining.

Heidi did, slipping off her boots, and sliding into the shoes in her stocking feet, their redness a stark contrast to any color Heidi was wearing.

"They are so beautiful!" Lily gushed.

Heidi turned her feet first one way, and then the other.

"Those are English shoes," I tried again. "They don't belong on our feet."

Heidi took them off and handed them back to Lily.

"Leave them," I ordered.

"I'm wearing them when we ride Brownie back to the barn!" Lily declared.

And Lily did, alone on the pony. Heidi knew I was right and wanted no part in the action Lily had taken.

We followed, and arrived at the barnyard to find Walter, the boy from next door holding Brownie's bridle. He was admiring Lily's shoes.

"Aren't these pretty?" Lily was waving her feet about.

"Were did you find them?" he asked.

"Hanging on a tree branch."

"Really? I wonder who left them."

"I wouldn't know," she said. "Can you help me down."

Lily was perfectly capable of sliding off the pony on her own, but she liked Walter, as she liked Grandpa. Walter barely noticed me, especially when Lily was around.

Walter was grinning as he took Lily's hand and helped her down.

"Lily shouldn't be wearing those red shoes." I spoke again.

Walter finally looked at me. "Be quiet, Barbara. No one else is complaining."

Which was true. My cousins appeared dumbfounded. Only Lily blossomed in his presence. I opened my mouth to object further but changed my mind. Walter was on his knees in front of Lily running his fingers playfully over the red straps.

Lily lifted one foot high in the air. "I'm wearing these for the rest of the day."

Walter chuckled. "You'll be a pretty English girl until bedtime."

"Yes, I will be." Lily beamed. "I'll be an English girl all day today."

"Why are you here?" I demanded of Walter, mostly because I couldn't stand his fussing over Lily.

He stood to his feet and didn't answer as he watched Lily disappear around the corner of the barn, with several of the cousins in tow.

"There goes nothing but trouble," I said.

He turned back to look at me. "What is wrong with you? Leave your sister alone."

"Why are you here?" I asked again.

"Daett wants me to help with the Byler's chores tonight." He was staring after Lily again.

"She shouldn't have worn those shoes," I said.

"Lily is lots of fun," he said. "Lots."

"Lily is different," I muttered.

He wasn't listening.

I turned to the pony who lingered by the fence. I felt like climbing on his back and riding furiously across the pasture with my dress pulled up well past my knees, and my head

11

scarf thrown from my head. I had beautiful long black hair. What a sight I would make with my hair blowing in the wind. Maybe Walter would see me then. Instead, he was moving towards the barn, still staring at the corner around which my sister had disappeared.

Chapter 3

When Walter entered the barn a moment later, I left the pony and headed for the house. I heard Lily's sobs halfway across the yard. They were more like wails than cries. I ran up the front porch steps and entered the front door to find a disheveled Lily lying on the couch, holding her bottom with both hands, with horrified adults staring. The beating must have just concluded, because Daett still stood in front of Lily, the thin hickory switch in his hand. There was no sign of the red shoes.

"Where did Lily get those shoes?" Daett turned on me.

"I told her not to wear them," I managed.

Daett looked at my cousins huddled in the corner. "That's what they said. Take your sister into the barn and keep her there until we're ready to leave."

I was reaching for Lily's hand when Grandpa stopped me. "Your daughter has been humbled in front of everyone." He addressed Daett. "She should stay in the house."

Rage filled Daett's face. "What have you to say about this? Will you make more excuses for what we have seen, when the blame rests squarely on your head? You are the one who brought this trouble in from the world."

"I had nothing to do with Lily's birth," Grandpa said. "She's your child."

The rage grew on Daett's face. "We will say no more about the matter. You go with her then!"

Grandpa took Lily's hand from me. "May the Lord spare us from this anger."

Daett turned to shake his finger in my face. "The next time, you stop Lily."

I knew better than to answer.

"Would to God the child had never been born," Daett roared.

Uncle John stepped forward. "This is quite enough. There is no sense in fighting amongst ourselves."

The house settled into a stifled silence as the adults moved in and out of the bedroom, and the cousins stayed in their corner. I soon had enough of the heaviness and slipped outside again to cross the yard and push open the wooden door. The rusty hinges creaked, and I paused on the threshold. The sound of voices murmured from the interior. Grandpa's mostly, with Walter and Lily's lighter lilt mixed in.

I listened quietly.

"I love you," Grandpa was saying. "Never forget. No matter what happens. You're a little girl who will turn into a very sweet woman."

"What did I do wrong?" Lily asked.

"I can't believe she was whipped for wearing those shoes." Walter's voice joined in.

"Today was a rough day, and you're not helping," Grandpa scolded. "There are things which are difficult for children to understand."

"Can I wear the red shoes again tomorrow?" Lily asked.

"No! You must never wear red shoes again." Grandpa sounded horrified.

"I can't believe this!" Walter exclaimed. "She was just wearing them for fun."

I crept away, and the barn door hinges squeaked again, but I don't think they heard me. The front porch was empty, so I sat on the swing. The cold of the night was creeping back, and I felt alone. I swung, moving the swing when my feet touched the floor. I imagined Grandpa sitting on a hay bale in the barn with Lily's head in his lap, and Walter standing in front of them. The vision tormented me.

Chapter 4

We held Aunt Nancy's funeral the following week. There was an icy rain coming down while the ditches along the road still had piles of snow. The service was held inside Uncle John's barn, the din on the roof almost drowning out Bishop Mast's voice as he neared the end of the closing sermon.

Bishop Mast sat down, and the casket opened for the final viewing. We filed past, with Lily clutching Mamm's hand. Lily didn't even glance into the casket, as if she wanted to avoid the awfulness of the truth. I did, gazing long at Aunt Nancy's shrunken face. All of Grandpa's girls were natural beauties, although there had been only girls. Death had come to remove what Grandpa had obviously brought in from the world. I shuddered and moved on. For once, I felt thankful I was not a natural beauty. We climbed into the buggies in the pouring rain, our bonnets and heavy coat-covered shawls pulled tight around us as we drove to the graveyard. There was a terrible mess of mud under the makeshift shelter at the cemetery. Lily huddled in the thick folds of Mamm's black dress, as the men with shovels filled in the grave the best they could.

After Aunt Nancy's funeral, the dark looks sent Grandpa's way at the Sunday services transferred to Lily, who didn't seem to mind, as if she didn't even notice. On many nights, after we were under the covers, the strange sounds below us grew louder than they had ever been before. I was certain I heard Mamm crying at times.

Aunt Malinda discovered cancer in her breasts the following year. She seemed dazed at the Sunday services, helpless in the grasp of a great evil. Aunt Malinda refused surgery, and no one could persuade her from the path she had chosen. The cancer advanced rapidly. Uncle Mose's grim face at the family gatherings forbade any questions. I saw no one else contesting his obvious approval of Aunt Malinda's choice. I vowed never to incur the Lord's wrath. The first leaves were bursting out of the tree branches in the spring when we gathered for Aunt Malinda's funeral service.

I couldn't stop looking at Lily and Grandpa, who sat together. Mamm didn't object. She was overcome with sorrow, or perhaps Daett considered the cause lost and didn't care. I sat beside Mamm because I didn't belong with Grandpa. I belonged with the others, with the community. I didn't blame Lily or Mamm for their prettiness or their willowy frames. Those had not been their choices. Mamm lived a humble and obedient life, while Lily had chosen to wear the red shoes. I absorbed another lesson the community was teaching us—who you were was determined by your choices. I comforted myself, sitting there beside Mamm. I couldn't imagine myself in red shoes, not even for the few seconds Cousin Heidi had tried them on.

Aunt Maud came up in the discussions after the funeral, a shadowy figure. She was Grandpa's oldest daughter, who we had never met, who seemed to flitter on the edge of our vision. I wondered what my mysterious Aunt Maud looked like. Was she also a beauty like Lily and Mamm? I figured she was.

Bishop Mast had solemnly lectured the congregation at Aunt Malinda's funeral. "We must move on from this tragedy today, while never forgetting we are right to accept the Lord's judgments and keeping a constant guard lest we incur his wrath again. War is a horrible sin, a great and deep transgression against the kindness and graciousness of our God. We must teach our men the dangers of war, and the judgments which the Lord uses to bring our attention back to his ways."

Lily nestled closer to Grandpa. Fear had crept through the room, the kind of fear one could taste.

"War is not the only sin which displeases the Lord." Bishop Mast continued. "The world also tempts us with pleasure, high-mindedness, and pride. The world is always calling at our doorstep, trying to lure us away from the quiet and peaceable life which is pleasing to the Almighty. Our only protection against the devil's wiles is to live as a humble and broken people."

Bishop Mast concluded his sermon with a prayer.

We filed through the line, past the open casket, and then Daett brought our buggy out. We climbed in to wait behind the open wagon where Aunt Malinda's body would be placed for the ride to the graveside.

"The Lord's judgments are pure and perfect," Daett intoned.

I could see tears roll down Mamm's cheeks past the edge of her bonnet.

Chapter 5

The next five years passed quickly. Lily grew slenderer and taller as she shot upwards, while I went mostly sideways. Lily and Walter were always together on our short walk to and from the schoolhouse each morning and evening. This had been their routine from the first day of Lily's school attendance. I tried to join them a few times but gave up. They were clearly uninterested in anyone but each other. On Saturdays, I was sure Walter invented reasons to stop by our place.

Daett was the one who informed us the summer of Lily's thirteenth birthday she was old enough to move into a bedroom of her own, the one across the hallway from me. Lily seemed pleased, and Daett brought home a new bed in the open buggy for the room. Mamm had nothing to say on the matter. She usually didn't when Daett gave orders. She looked grim though—and very unhappy. She must have appeared more so than usual, because I noticed. Lily found bed sheets and a quilt in the cedar chest in the attic.

Daett peeked in the first evening everything was set up and seemed pleased. Usually there was little which pleased him about Lily or anything she did. The noises in Mamm and Daett's bedroom were worse than usual for the next several nights. I pondered the matter but came up with no answers or connection between the two occurrences. Obviously, I now know why, but how was I to know back then, or do anything about the matter if I had understood.

The moon was bright in my bedroom window a week or so later, when I awoke with a start. The usual squeaking of the bed was not coming from below me, but across the hall in Lily's room. I listened for crying, but Lily wasn't making any sound. I slept little the rest of the night and was down in the kitchen when Lily appeared in the morning. She looked troubled but said nothing.

On the way to school, Lily was subdued in her usual chattiness with Walter, but he soon had her laughing and smiling. There were strange noises in Lily's bedroom again the following week. I finally got up enough nerve to creep across the hallway and listen at the door, but I didn't peek inside. I retreated to my bedroom and left the door cracked so I could see into the hallway. When all was quiet, Daett came out and went downstairs.

"Why is Daett in your room at night?" I confronted Lily the next morning.

Tears shimmered in her eyes, but she said nothing.

I didn't dare ask Mamm, but I asked Cousin Heidi the next time I saw her, "Why are there strange noises in Mamm and Daett's bedroom at nighttime?"

"Your Mamm hasn't told you?" she asked.

I shook my head.

She leaned close. "Watch what the stallions do with the mares in the barnyard."

"The stallions," I said.

Heidi nodded. "The stallions."

I pulled the quilt over my head when the noises started again across the hallway and didn't fall asleep until a long time after Daett's footsteps had gone down the stairs. Life didn't seem different or disturbed the next morning even with my new sense of knowledge. I opened my mouth once to ask Lily what the experience was like, but the words stuck in my throat. I took comfort in the sense of tranquility settling over the community after Aunt Malinda's passing. Even talk of Lily's misdeeds with the red shoes faded into the background. Lily seemed almost normal at times. She took to staying overnight at Grandpa's place, for one excuse or the other, until Daett limited the visits to once a month.

Both of our uncles remarried the year after Aunt Malinda's passing, and the visits between our households dwindled.

A year after Daett began to visit Lily's room at night, Uncle John's oldest daughter, Lois, announced her wedding date. Lois was Mamm's niece, and Lois didn't bear the feelings towards Grandpa like Daett did. We received an invitation. The wedding would be a large one, with relatives drawn from three extended families, instead of the usual two.

Mamm left the two of us on the front porch with the other younger girls. Lily leaned over the porch rail, obviously entertaining the girls, her back arched as she reached down to touch Uncle John's roses growing near the steps. The group of girls was silent, watching Lily move. I was happy, seeing Lily flaunt herself like this. Let Lily cement her reputation for flightiness into the community's mind. They valued commonality, togetherness, and working for the good of each other. Let Walter tie his fortunes to Lily, until he couldn't untie them. I would encourage Walter's affections for Lily from now on, not discourage them. Lily was going to burn out, like a meteor streaking across the sky. I felt as though I had been given a deep dark secret from beyond the stars. I gazed up towards the sky through the branches of Uncle John's oak tree, seeing traces of an open heaven beyond them. I was filled with a reason to live. My scalp prickled with my joy, as I saw guilt stand in the distance, waiting to condemn me for this pleasure. I couldn't banish the thought though. I, Barbara Swartz, the ugly daughter, could indeed become Walter's wife. I had virtues while Lily had only her beauty.

Lily lingered on the porch as the group of girls moved into the house for the start of the service. I followed them and slipped into my place on the hard bench. Lily barely made her seat before the singing began. I focused on Cousin Lois's face. She sat toward the front of the living room with her attendants by her side. From the slight blush on her face, James, her husband to be, must have just given her a wink or a smile.

After the songs, the first minister's sermon text was no surprise. He recounted the story of Abraham sending his servant to find a wife for his son Isaac.

I shifted on the hard bench, when Bishop Mast finally rose to his feet for the final sermon. "My dearly beloved," he began. "I am old and crippled in body, but those are the ways of the Lord. I give myself to them, and to the joy which these young people possess. They are rising to take our place and will continue to walk the roads we have walked. I want to speak plainly today, considering the circumstances we are in. Over six years ago, we buried a very beloved sister and her sister soon afterwards, and their Aunt Maud is today to us as if she were dead. There are some amongst us who wish to think otherwise, and to reject the judgments of the Lord. I know this is a day of joy and gladness when one of our brothers takes to himself a wife, and I do not wish to take away from our joy. Yet, let us not forget even in this, the most sacred of times, the Lord has left us a story in the Holy Scriptures whereby we may understand his ways and order our paths. Joy must be tempered with warning. Happiness is not far removed from God's judgments. I pray the day never comes when we no longer remind ourselves on wedding days of these things."

Bishop Mast paused to get a better grip on his chair. I had heard the story of Tobias and his search for a bride often on wedding days but had never paid much attention. The tale was strange enough to be confusing, and none of the bishops recounted the story in the exact same manner.

Part of the ending stuck with me at Cousin Lois's wedding. The moment when the angel instructed the young Tobias to withhold himself from his bride for three nights after his wedding to the beautiful Sara. I figured by then I could make a good guess at what withholding himself meant without asking anyone.

"The Lord was greatly pleased with the choice of Young Tobias," Bishop Mast said, his gaze fixed on Lois and James.

I was not beautiful, but Walter would stay away from my bed for three nights after our wedding, I told myself. I would also please the Lord greatly.

Section Two—August 1911 to October 1915

LILY

Chapter 6

I sat behind the haystack shaded from the warm afternoon sunshine. My legs stretched out in front of me, my thick dress pulled up above my knees to catch the slight breeze. The smell of late summer hung in the air; the corn stalks heavy with grain, the freshly mown hay fields, and the wildflowers crushed in their prime. Lazy flies buzzed above the ground and Daett's brown, heavy-chested Belgian horses pawed in the loose dirt. I could see a trail of fresh hay from the morning's feeding run across the barnyard and disappear around the corner of the barn.

Barbara and I, with Mamm's help, had put away two dozen jars of lima beans and peas today. The warm jars sat on the basement shelves to cool, and would stay there until they were needed in the winter. Mamm could grow a garden like few in the community could. Each summer, the rows burst with an abundant harvest. We gave away a lot of things to our Amish neighbors, but never to our English ones. I often wondered why Mamm didn't sell produce as most of the Amish did in the community. I didn't mind though. Running a roadside stand would only have added to our workload.

I got up at five as usual this morning, with Barbara rising ahead of me. I had placed two loads of wash on the line and helped Daett with the chores, while Barbara and Mamm prepared breakfast. I felt woozy and sleepy. Daett had kept me awake last night longer than he usually did. I didn't complain, because I had discovered long ago complaining only made things worse. I liked peace, and I liked about life what I could, which wasn't much, but there were some things.

I liked the moment I was in—this barnyard, this stillness, and the soft footsteps on the other side of the haystack. Neither Daett nor Barbara had such a quiet step. I tucked my feet under me. I hadn't been waiting for Walter. There was no reason for him to appear, but I wasn't surprised. Walter made me very happy, and he came over often. There was something deep and satisfying about him.

A dribble of hay fell on my head, and I playfully slapped the strands away.

His face appeared above me. "What have we here, a fairy in the straw?"

"Chore time is soon," I said, pretending anger.

He flopped down beside me.

"What's wrong?"

"Mamm's not well again, and Millie and Joanna are visiting at Aunt Sarah's place. Would you help us with the chores tonight?" he asked.

"You could ask Barbara," I said.

"Maybe I don't want Barbara."

I leaned towards him. "Maybe I don't want to come." He smelled of sweat and man, not unlike Grandpa's gray beard on a hot summer day.

He smiled, clearly knowing I would. "I like this," he said, "you and me, no rush, no work, just a haystack at our back, and the whole world in front of us."

"Peace comes when I'm with you." I agreed.

"I wish we could stop time, put our finger on the beat of our heart."

"Our heart has to beat," I said.

"If our heart beats, time goes on."

He placed his hand lightly on mine, and I felt suspended in the heavens above me.

"I wish things would never change," he said. "I wish we would never change."

I glanced towards the sky. "Do you think God is up there?"

He shrugged. "The preachers say he is."

My voice quivered. "Does he care about us?"

A pleased smile spread across his face. "God gave me you."

I gazed long at him. "How sweet of you to say."

"I will always be thankful for you," he said.

"Do you believe what the others believe? Aunt Nancy and Aunt Malinda dying from cancer because of the Lord's judgments."

"I don't think about such things," he said.

We fell silent until Barbara called for me in the distance. "Lily!"

I stood to my feet, and Walter sprang up beside me.

"Is Walter helping us with our chores tonight?" Barbara asked.

"I thought Lily might help us with ours," Walter said.

Barbara didn't hesitate. "Daett and I can handle things."

"So come," I said, and took his hand. "Let's go."

We went around the corner of the barn, with Walter in the lead. We left a thin trail of bent grass as we crossed the field. Walter slowed when we arrived in the Yoder's barnyard. Their place was filled with rusty implements. Jonas didn't keep his farm tidy like Daett did, but Walter isn't like either of our Daetts. I had always known this. At school, Walter kept his papers and desk in the neatest order. No matter how many assignments Mrs. Harper gave the class in our little one room schoolhouse, Walter could always find his pages with the minimum of fuss.

I tucked my loose hair back under my scarf as we entered the dimly lit barn. Walter's Daett would be around somewhere, and his disapproving gaze always took in everything about me. There was no sense in giving Jonas a reason to criticize needlessly. I was still startled when Jonas made his appearance from the back of the barn, his dark clothing dusty from the haymow.

"I'm having Lily help with the chores," Walter said. "She can spread the feed, and I'll make sure the cows are in the barnyard and throw the silage down."

Jonas glared but didn't say anything.

"See you," Walter said, sending me a wave over his shoulder as he left.

"So." Jonas addressed me when were alone. "Walter got you to help tonight?"

"You have objections?"

"Wouldn't change much if I did," he said. "You know my feelings about Walter hanging around the likes of you?"

"I'm sorry," I said.

He acted like he didn't hear. "I know what Walter sees in you. I once saw those same things in your Aunt Maud. What a wicked woman she turned into."

This was not news to me. I knew Jonas had dated my mysterious Aunt Maud, but I still protested. "You think I'm like her?"

"Of course," he said.

I tried another tack. "Do you miss my Aunt Maud?"

He turned red. "I loved the woman to my shame. How brazen of you to bring up the subject. Just like your Aunt Maud you are—the same face, the same feet, the same figure, the same deceitfulness, the same secret intentions to leave the church and dash out into the world and take my son with you."

"I'm sorry Aunt Maud left you on the night before your wedding."

He stared at my bare feet. "I wish Walter would give up this madness and settle for a woman like his Mamm. Lois is godly and has borne children in the Lord's will. Maud would have done none of those things."

"I'm not my Aunt Maud," I said.

He stalked away, and I grabbed the shovel to throw feed into the wheelbarrow. I had barely begun to spread the grain before Walter shooed the cows in.

"How are things going?" He asked.

"I was talking with your Daett." I tried to smile.

"Don't worry about Daett," he said, and left again.

I took my time filling the wheelbarrow this time.

"Not much of a worker, are you?" Jonas said at my elbow, and I jumped.

"The task is getting done," I retorted.

He studied my bare feet again. "Your Grandpa should never have been allowed back into the community."

"I'm not a wicked woman." I tried to smile at him.

"You're your Grandfather's offspring as was your Aunt Maud." He whirled on his feet and left. I forced myself to work, and had the feed spread by the time Walter came back.

"Things still going well?" he asked.

"Almost finished."

"Ready to milk, then?"

"I am." I hid my face and went to pick up the buckets in the milk house.

Jonas walked past a few times, obviously checking on our progress.

"Thanks so much for coming over," Walter told me at the barn door when we finished with the milking.

"Anytime," I said. We lingered, our gaze on each other.

"See you soon," he said.

I nodded and followed the thin line of bent grass we had left a few hours before. I skirted the haystack and entered our barn. The place was empty, the stillness stark. Barbara and Daett had finished the chores long ago. I moved deeper inside, towards the coolness of the milk house. I entered and walked up to our stone water tank where a trickle ran in from an outside pipe. From there, the water overflowed at the lower end to exit through a stone trough.

I stuck my feet into the water and ran the coldness between my toes. I turned my feet sideways to gaze downward. These were my feet. Walter didn't think them unusual, while Daett stared at them often around the house as Jonas had done tonight.

I rubbed the skin dry with my bare hands. If Walter and Grandpa liked me, I was okay. I would always have Walter. Grandpa couldn't stay with me until I was old and gray, but Walter could.

"Walter likes us," I told my feet. "He thinks we're normal."

I wiggled my toes and frowned.

Chapter 7

A few weeks later, the Sunday services were at Bishop Mast's home. Outside the house, the soft touch of the autumn breezes blew across the flat Indiana farmland. I sat among the unmarried women, trying to keep my back straight on the wooden bench and endure the three-hour worship service.

I wanted to speak with Grandpa about what Jonas had told me, but there hadn't been a chance. Grandpa and Grandma visited our place last Saturday, but Daett had hovered about.

I focused on Bishop Mast, who has begun to preach with a chair set in front of him. He thundered in a voice which belied his frail appearance. "The judgments of the Lord are ever fresh and new and hallowed as this day is hallowed. We are called to wash our hands from our wickedness and cleanse our hearts from evil. Only then can we find peace on this earth, and a day of rest not just for our bodies, but for our souls. 'Be ye holy, as I am holy', saith the Lord."

I pressed my eyes shut. I was sure the preacher was speaking about me in these moments. Likely Bishop Mast also had Grandpa on his mind. I tried to ignore the outbursts, but Jonas's words had me worried today. How was I to live in this world if Walter thought like the others did? I had not wanted to repeat in Walter's presence the awful words his Daett spoke. Once said, they might hang in the air between us, like a sword to pierce our hearts in unexpected moments.

Bishop Mast was shouting now. "We must be a holy people, because our God is holy. 'Come out from among them' God commands us, separate yourselves from the world and its lusts, and live alone unto your God."

The bishop continued for a long time before he called the congregation to prayer. I gripped the edge of the bench to turn and kneel. Walter caught my glance and gave me a bright smile. I returned his smile without hesitation, and my fears fled far away as if they had never been.

"Holy God in heaven," Bishop Mast prayed, "worthy and blessed Redeemer, righteous and pure are your judgments. Look down today upon your humble servants and find mercy in your heart for our many and great transgressions."

The prayer continued for ten minutes before Bishop Mast pronounced the "Amen."

I took my seat on the bench, surrounded by the sound of shuffling feet. A song number was given out and the hymn sung. When the service ended, I slipped through the gathered crowd. Behind me, the living room bustled with activity as the men transformed benches into tables, using wooden legs the community had fashioned for the occasion.

A light touch on my shoulder turned me around.

"Lily." Grandpa's bearded face was close to me. "How are you doing?"

"Okay."

"What's wrong?" Grandpa's voice was gentle.

"Not in here," I said.

I followed him outside. The space under the trees was empty, and we stood near the giant oak, where no one paid us the least bit of attention.

"I noticed something was wrong last Saturday," he said.

"I don't know how to explain this." I began. "But Jonas told me in no uncertain terms he does not approve of me. Walter can never be with me—like in—"

"Like in marrying you?" he asked.

I nodded.

"I can't imagine Walter agreeing with his Daett."

"He doesn't."

"I'm sorry for what you have to go through," he said. "Surely the Lord will work things out."

"I'm happy with Walter," I said. "I'm happy with you."

Grandpa managed a smile. "I'm glad, but nothing can be done about how the community sees us. I pray Walter will be worthy of you. I pray the words he speaks will bring healing to your heart. I wish there was something more I could do, but I can't. I have made my peace with the church and with God. You do the same. There is no peace out there."

"I know," I said. "You told me."

He nodded, his long gray beard bobbing on his chest, and we moved back inside, where I left Grandpa and entered the kitchen. The press of the women's bodies in the small room was heavy. I waved my hand about, and someone handed me a plate of bread and a bowl of red beets.

When I exited the kitchen, Bishop Mast announced the prayer for the first round of meals. I waited beside the doorway with bowed head until he proclaimed the "amen." I approached the men's table and delivered my plate of bread and bowl of red beets between two broad shoulders.

The men always seemed to approve of me when I served the tables, but I knew better. This kind of approval brought coldness to the heart. I caught Grandpa's gaze from the other end of the table. He appeared troubled. I left for the kitchen and stayed there. I busied myself at the counter, cutting bread. Thirty minutes later, the first round finished eating, and Bishop Mast offered the prayer of thanks. I filled a bucket with warm water to clean the utensils for the next round and set to work on the now empty men's table. Two other girls worked with me. When we finished, I handed the bucket to one of the older women who had eaten in the first round and sat down to eat with Barbara and Cousin Heidi across from me.

"Hi." Cousin Heidi gave me a bright smile.

"Hi," I replied.

Barbara didn't say anything or look at me.

"How are things going with you?" Cousin Heidi turned her attention to Barbara.

"Just fine." Barbara sounded cheerful enough.

Cousin Heidi lowered her voice. "Guess who is close to asking me for a date?"

Barbara didn't miss a beat. "Benny Stoll."

Cousin Heidi made a face. "Are we so obvious?"

"There's nothing wrong with being obvious," Barbara said.

"Why don't we know about you?" Cousin Heidi asked.

Barbara smiled and didn't answer. My sister had dreams of dating Walter even back then. She never said so in words, but rather in facial expressions when she saw Walter. She followed his movements in a crowded room. A lilt tinged her voice when she spoke his name.

Walter was waiting when I left the house after the meal. I had seen him leave the basement where the unmarried men had also eaten at the second round of tables, and I had given him time to hitch his horse to the buggy. Since we lived next door to each other, Walter used the excuse to drive me home from the Sunday church services.

"Ready?" Walter asked.

"Yep," I said.

He climbed into the buggy after me. "Nice afternoon?"

"Yes." I agreed.

"What did your Grandpa want?" he asked. "I saw him speaking to you in the yard right after the church service."

I took a deep breath. "We were talking about what your Daett told me the other evening."

"My Daett? What did he say?"

"His opinion of me."

"Which doesn't matter," he said.

I stared out of the open buggy door at the fields of ripened corn without answering. What could I say?

"Lily." His voice broke through my thoughts. "Nothing changes between us. Nothing can."

I didn't look at him.

"We'll make our way through this together, Lily." He took one hand off the reins to touch mine. "We'll change how they see you."

"How?" I asked.

"I have a plan," he said. "We'll go through our rumspringa like normal people, and we'll be baptized, and everyone will see you have left the world behind you."

"You don't think I'm from the world?" I asked.

"No, Lily. There is nothing wrong with you, but we must begin our rumspringa soon."

"Barbara isn't having one," I said.

He wrinkled his nose. "Nobody cares what Barbara does."

"Will this be a wild rumspringa?" I asked.

"I don't know," he said. "Do you want a wild one?"

"Of course not," I said.

We laughed, and I felt much better.

I soon sobered though. "What if we can't persuade them?"

"I'm never giving up on you," he said, "so let's not think about this anymore. We'll take one day at a time and enjoy life together."

We bounced into the driveway, and Walter dropped me off at the hitching post. I went upstairs to my bedroom. The quilt lay unwrinkled from where I had stretched the cloth tight this morning. I stood near the window and stared across the empty fields, thinking about Walter and his plans to spend our rumspringa together. Walter cared about me, and his plan would work. I must believe. There was no other choice.

Chapter 8

A YEAR LATER

The spring darkness had fallen an hour earlier, the last rays of the sun still in the sky above the horizon displaying a faint hue of purple, greens, and yellows. In the distance, clouds had gathered in the east, and the thunder rolled.

I clung to the side of the buggy door with Walter seated a hair's breadth away, his feet braced against the dashboard as the buggy rocked from side to side. We were driving south towards the barn where the rumspringa gathering would be tonight.

"Rough weather," I said.

"We'll have a good time though." He gave me a warm smile.

The thunder sounded again and Walter's horse, PJ, raised his head high. His nostrils flared in the brief flashes of lighting. I focused on the road ahead where lights spilled out of the open doors and windows of the bank barn. "Is this the place?"

"Yes," he said.

I leaned out of the buggy for a better look.

"You should take off your head covering," he said.

"Really?"

"Yes," he said.

I pulled the pins with no further questions and dumped the whole thing into the back of his buggy. "Better?"

"Your hair should come down."

"How do you know these things?" I asked. Had he been with another girl? But Walter wouldn't. Walter was true to me!

"I've been here before," he said.

He pulled the buggy to a stop along the fence row and waited while I worked. When I finished, my hair hung over my shoulders and streamed down almost to my waist. I couldn't look at him. I wore a night cap in bed, and Daett had never said anything about letting down my hair. This felt right though. Walter should be the first man to see me like this, before anyone else did.

"You need a comb," he said, and placed his hands on my shoulders to run his fingers gently through my hair.

I closed my eyes and drank in the feeling of pure bliss.

"Perfect," he said, when he finished.

I hopped down from the buggy, and he followed me to tie PJ to a post. The storm had moved closer, and the wind blasts came around this side of the barn. We ducked our heads for the walk to the open doors. Lanterns hung everywhere with straw bales spread along the outer walls. Several young men with musical instruments gathered toward the front.

I should have been blushing by then with my exposed hair hung over my shoulders, but I wasn't. I didn't look different from the girls who milled around me.

I searched the faces in the crowd. Most I didn't know, since there were many Amish districts to the south of us we rarely visited. A few of the young men gave me smiles, and I returned them. No one approached us though as we stood along the outer wall, listening to the musicians up front.

I jumped when Walter touched my arm.

"Sorry. Shall we go get something to eat? They have Pepsi and pretzels."

"Sounds great," I said.

I stayed close to him, my hand in his in the close quarters.

We arrived at the wagon, and Walter paid for the purchases. "Shall we sit over there?"

I nodded, and he led the way to the bales of hay stacked along the edge of the barn. Couples had begun to move into the center of the floor, swaying with the music.

"What do you think?" Walter asked, taking a sip from his drink.

"Different," I said, "and crowded."

"This is a crowd." He laughed.

"How does my hair look?"

"Beautiful."

"Thanks." I chewed on my pretzels.

"Do you want to dance?"

"I don't know how."

"You'll be a fast learner." He stood and held out his hand.

"Walter! I'll be embarrassed."

"Listen to the music and follow me."

I gave in, and his arm slipped around my waist. He pulled me close, and I allowed his strength to flood through me. Walter was different from Daett. I had always known. Somehow! I focused on the happy faces around us as we moved across the room. My feet worked, and Walter seemed a part of me. I could feel his heartbeat against my chest.

"Relax," Walter whispered. "You're good at this."

I breathed deeply, and we moved around the room for a few more songs, until Walter led us back to the hay bales, and helped me sit. "Don't collapse," he teased.

"Dancing with me was sweet of you."

He sat down beside me. "You're great company, Lily."

"You're a great teacher," I said.

We laughed and sipped our drinks.

"Try again?" he asked.

"I will." We joined hands and brought our faces close together.

The tune was faster this time, and I was breathing deeply in five minutes. We ended up against the wall watching the others.

"Are there other things we can do after tonight?" I asked.

"We could travel around on weekends a bit and see things."

"Great," I said.

"Again then?" He held out his hand.

The dance was slower this time, and I laid my cheek on his chest. We ended up back at the hay bales, where I held his hand, while we watched the dancers. Silence settled between us as another number was struck and the tempo increased.

He stood to his feet. "Time to go."

I nodded and followed him around the edge of the barn. We went outside, the starry expanse of windswept sky above us. I climbed into the buggy while Walter untied PJ from the fence post. We dashed off into the night, and I leaned against his shoulder, as the cool night air rushed over us.

He pulled into our driveway and stopped at the end of the wooden walk.

"Good night," he told me, as I slipped from the buggy.

I paused on the front porch to listen until the sound of his buggy wheels turning into his Daett's driveway had died away into the darkness.

Barbara's bedroom light still shone under her doorway when I went up the stairs, but the glow blinked out quickly. Daett's footsteps followed me a few moments later. I struggled for the first time, but my strength was no match for his. When he left, I went to the window and pulled back the drapes to let in the starlight. Darkness made things worse afterwards. There was a light on in the house across the fields, so Walter had not gone to bed yet.

I thought of Walter and our evening together. How understanding the man was. How kind. How even now

Walter was probably thinking about what we could do next week that I might enjoy. In my mind, I saw open fields of corn growing into the horizon, waving in the soft summer breeze, waiting for the threshers to enter the wooden gates and begin the harvest. Walter and I were fresh and unbroken, with our whole lives before us. Nothing could cause us harm if we were together. In Walter's arms, I would never feel pain—or this coldness wrapped around my heart.

I stood at the window in my nightcap. A sorrow gripped my heart like a vise, so deep I thought I might die. But what was death? I already felt dead. What was missing was a coffin, and the breath to leave my body.

The light blinked out in the house across the fields. Walter would soon be with me, and hold me in his arms, and never let me go. Walter would never stop loving me. Never! He couldn't, and still be Walter. We were a part of each other as the rain was a part of the clouds, as the heat was a part of a summer day, and as the corn growing in the field was a part of the earth. I listened to the silence of the house, and tiptoed downstairs to the bathroom. I didn't bother to put on my nightdress. I didn't care who saw me.

Chapter 9

Walter met me at the end of our driveway the following Saturday evening with his buggy. I climbed in, and we were on our way.

"So how's my lovely?" he asked.

"I'm with you."

"We're going to the circus in Loogootee."

"Really?"

"Everyone likes the circus," he said. "The distance is a little way, but PJ is fresh tonight."

I snuggled against him, the sun setting behind us, as we turned east. We traveled south for nearly an hour, the silence comfortable and peaceful between us. The traffic grew the closer we came to town, and Walter parked in a field off the main road. He tied PJ, and I waited for him beside the buggy.

I took his hand. "Thanks for bringing me."

"You haven't seen anything yet."

"Anything will be amazing with you," I said.

"There are other wonders in the world beyond the circus," he said. "Community, family, good food, and the love of home."

"I haven't seen the circus wonders."

"At least you've seen the others," he said.

I forced myself to nod, and we approached the outer ring of the tents. The noise level increased with rough animal sounds mixed with the murmur of human conversations. Walter paid at the gate, and we entered.

The first booth contained several giant women, who were from Germany, the sign said. They stood gazing pensively out over the crowds.

"Just tall women," Walter said. He led me across the yard to cages containing lions with thick manes and across from them striped yellow and white tigers.

"I like this," I said.

"So do I," he said. "Lions from Africa and tigers from Asia, both from the other side of the world."

"A long way to bring them."

He chuckled. "The Barnum and Bailey circus has deep pockets."

One of the lions roared, and I jumped back.

Walter grinned. "A little different from the farm."

I agreed. I had to stop thinking about Daett.

We moved on to booths containing a man who smoked through his eyebrow, another displayed the world's shortest man, squatting on a stool staring at us. There was also a display of the world's tallest man and the shortest woman, standing side by side. Across from them was a man who twirled swords holding three in his mouth at a time.

"What do you think?" Walter asked.

"I'm not sure."

"A little weird," Walter said.

When an announcer came out to proclaim the start of the evening show, we went inside and took seats in a huge tent. I had been around horses my entire life but had never seen them ridden by people standing up and jumping between the speeding horses. The women were as agile as the men, while above us, men and women swung from suspended bars, letting go to glide through the air towards each other's arms. They clasped and swung across the space, to let go again, and catch another bar.

"Quite something," Walter said, following their flight pattern.

"Do they ever miss and die?" The cold feeling I got when Daett came into my bedroom crept over me.

"They probably have safety lines attached that we can't see, or safety nets somewhere. They can't always get their flight pattern right."

I watched another amazing release and catch, the man flying in an upward arc to grasp the bar effortlessly.

"Amazing," Walter said.

"Sort of like life. You let go and hope you don't miss the bar."

"You can't practice for life, though," he said.

Again, I agreed. I always went on living until the sun came up, and a new day dawned. I was with Walter. I would seize this moment of happiness. Someday Walter would always be with me.

The wild animals were almost as amazing, the tigers jumping through rings of fire, and the elephants thundering around the ring, to bow at their trainer's feet. The big lion did what he was told, backing up, and trotting in circles.

We stayed late—until ten or so, before we set out for home. PJ's hooves beat a steady trot on the road.

"Did you like the evening?" he asked.

"Yes." I looked up at him, and the desire swept through me. "Kiss me," I whispered.

He smiled down at me, as if he hadn't heard, his face a faint shape in the darkness. "What if we leave early next weekend on a trip which includes an overnight stay?"

I stopped breathing for a moment. He was offering more than kisses.

"We don't have to," he said, "but the adventures I'm thinking about involve the whole weekend. We won't spend a lot of money. We can take a tent, hitchhike on the main roads, and camp out in a farmer's field at night."

I found my voice. "Okay with me."

"With two sleeping bags," he said. "I didn't mean anything indecent."

"Of course not." I was certain he didn't mean what he was saying. Walter loved me. He would be with me. He would make me whole.

He smiled. "Let's plan on a lovely weekend together."

I nodded in the darkness.

Walter dropped me off at the end of our sidewalk, and I stayed on the front porch to watch his buggy lights turn into his driveway. A dread settled over me when I thought of entering my bedroom and hearing Daett's footsteps following me up the stairs. Of late, he seemed to pick the nights I had been with Walter to torment me.

I focused on the porch swing, and thought of the quilt on the couch, just inside the doorway. The covering would be light and thin but would suffice in the warm night air. I retrieved the quilt on tiptoes and returned to the swing. The chains creaked as I lay down and wrapped the cover over me. I watched the stars twinkle in the sky until I fell asleep thinking about Walter.

I awoke with a stiff back, and the sky still dark on the horizon. I crept into the house and made my way up the stairs. I undressed and climbed in to fall asleep again. I woke to the sound of Barbara calling me in the hallway. "Time to get up."

I dressed and went downstairs rubbing my neck.

"Nights with Walter getting to you?" she asked.

"I slept on the porch swing for a few hours," I said.

She gave me a strange look but didn't say anything more.

Daett was already out in the barn, so I followed him to help with the chores. He said nothing when I entered the barn to begin the milking. In the evening after supper, I sat out on the swing until the others had gone to bed, before I curled up under the thin covering. I watched the stars above me, and the lights twinkling out in the house across the fields. I was beginning to doze off when Daett came out on the porch.

"Enough of this," he said. "Upstairs with you."

He followed me. I closed my eyes in bed, and imagined the hour when Walter would pick me up in his buggy.

On Friday evening when Walter came, I climbed in, after stuffing my bag in the back. The loveliness of Walter's presence washed over me.

Walter didn't seem to notice my joy. "I brought along a tent, two sleeping bags, food in cans—soups mostly—crackers, and English clothing. I hope they fit you."

"They will be perfect," I assured him. He knew I had no access to such things. Walter had made the effort to buy them himself. I was the love of his life.

We drove to his Amish cousin's place on the edge of the community, and after greeting the couple, I went upstairs to change. The blue polka dot dress fit my thin frame perfectly. I looked at myself in the mirror, thinking the most wonderful thought. Walter had chosen this dress. He knew my size. The feeling comforted me deeply and felt so right. As if this was what I had always wanted and hadn't known I did.

I went down the stairs and took a whirl for him in the middle of the living room floor. We had danced together, but I still felt shy and warm from the look in his eyes.

"Perfect," Walter said, and his cousin's wife Nancy nodded her approval in the kitchen doorway.

Out by the buggy again, the things which Walter had brought went into back packs, along with my night bag, and we slung them over our shoulders. I giggled, filled with an immense happiness and joy.

"What?" asked Walter.

"I'm just happy," I said.

We walked with the back packs over our shoulders a mile further up the road. Walter stuck out his hand and the first automobile stopped.

"Where to?" The elderly man asked.

His wife sat beside him smiling from ear to ear.

"Heading north for the weekend," Walter replied. "We're not sure exactly where."

"Hop in then," the man said.

We did, chatting until they dropped us off an hour later at an intersection near a small town.

"Do you think they knew we were Amish?" I asked Walter when we were alone on the road.

"We still look Amish even in English clothing." Walter looked up and down the road. "Where to now?"

"Anywhere with you," I said.

He grinned. "Sounds like a plan."

We did little but walk, pausing where we wished, and taking our time. We stopped for the night beside a pond with ducks swimming on the water and a thick forest around us. The closeness to Walter as we stood near the water's edge made me dizzy.

"Shall we camp here?" he asked. We had passed a farmhouse five minutes earlier, but no one seemed to have noticed us.

"I like this place," I said.

Walter started a fire, and I set up the tent. I laid the sleeping bags inside, side-by-side, close but not together. I was dizzy again. Walter would make me right tonight. He would heal what hurt deep in my soul. Yet Walter must not know what Daett did to me at home. I knew that with a certainty which took my breath away. I was using Walter, but I couldn't help myself. I wanted what he had to give me too desperately. If Walter did not want me, did not help me, I would have no hope left in this world. I held on to the side of the tent until my whole body stopped shaking.

When I came out of the tent, Walter was working by the fire going through the food he had brought along.

"Not quite like home," he said.

"Being with you is not supposed to be like home." I stood at his shoulder, and he smiled up at me. My heart was pounding in my throat.

"Are you cooking?" he teased.

"You know I am," I said, and warmed the soup on the fire in a metal bowl out of Walter's backpack. Would Walter know I had been with Daett? Could he somehow tell?

We ate, saying little, watching the ducks floating past effortlessly on the water. They moved as if nothing propelled them forward but random motion. I calmed myself by breathing deeply. I was right. This would be different. With Daett, I felt nothing but coldness and horror.

"We didn't see much today," he said. "Sorry I didn't make more definite plans."

"I'm okay," I said. "I love being with you." Could he not see how much I wanted him?

"Next week I'll do better." He wasn't looking at me.

"This is perfect," I said. "The walking, the silence, the peace, and just you."

"You're wonderful," he said.

"I love you," I said. I didn't know what else to say.

He placed his arm around me, and I nestled against his shoulder. Fear niggled at me. Could he tell? How did a man know when a woman was no longer pure? The ducks went past on the water again. They didn't appear to notice us, as if we weren't even there.

"I don't want this to end," he said.

I pulled away from his shoulder to wash the soup bowl in the water at the edge of the pond, and the ducks came closer with outstretched necks.

"I have nothing for you," I told them.

Walter walked up to throw a few breadcrumbs in the water. Their heads bobbed, and legs broke the water, churning the air, as they gobbled the morsels. Walter stood beside me, and we watched them for a long time.

"I want to stay here forever," he said.

"I know," I said. "I want our love to grow and grow and never die."

"My love for you can't die," he said.

"Yet, you're afraid. Are you afraid of me—because I—because—"

"Don't say such things, Lily. I'm not afraid."

I didn't answer and we studied the ducks jabbing in the water, searching for the last crumbs.

"I need to bathe," I said. I had never thought of such a thing with Daett, but maybe if I washed for Walter, he would overcome his hesitation. I returned to our packs for the soap and wash cloth.

He stayed where he was, while I walked a short distance away to undress and step into the water. I didn't look back, but Walter could clearly see me. I thought I heard his footsteps, but I didn't turn around. When I finished, I glanced over my shoulder, and he was sitting on the ground staring at the fire.

I joined him. "Why did you not come in with me?"

"You're so incredibly beautiful," he said.

"I'm yours," I said. "You can have me."

"You know we can't," he said.

"Why not?" A great pain welled up inside of me.

"Maybe the others do such things on their rumspringa, but we can't. You're too pure for me to defile."

"You know I'm not," I said.

"We'll wait until our wedding night," he said, not looking at me.

We slept in our sleeping bags, side by side, with Walter holding my hand. He didn't even kiss me. I had lost every hope of the day. My whole body throbbed, but I didn't dare move.

"Hold me," I whispered into the distance between us.

He held me, both of us staying in our sleeping bags, with my head on his shoulder and his face in my loose hair. I could feel his breath on my neck. Walter was wrong in how he saw me, and he would be even more wrong if he knew about Daett. I dared not enter those dark woods.

I shut out the pain the best I could. The effort became easier as time passed, and I came to believe perhaps Walter was right. Perhaps I could hide what was in my heart. Perhaps we could survive until we were married. Nothing could keep us apart then.

Walter rejected what I offered to him the summer we spent the weekends on the road. I could tell the cost on his face was fierce some of those nights when we slept side by side in the fields or in some forest or barn. He saw me bathing often, as I kept hoping despite my resolve to see things how Walter saw them, dreaming I could be clean and pure enough for him. He watched openly, transfixed, like a man caught in a dream.

We traveled to Indianapolis on an extended weekend and toured the buildings downtown. We ate in a little diner with a river flowing past the windows. We headed out of town at dusk and found a campsite in the middle of the farmland. I helped Walter set up the tent and cooked our food over a fire within a ring of stones. We sat on the ground to eat. This was the moment. I had to tell him about Daett. Our relationship would be ruined, but Walter's way wasn't working either. I tried to speak. I tried again. No words would come.

"Baptismal classes start this fall," he said.

"You've seen what you wish of the world?" I asked, surprised my voice worked.

"We have to trust the community," he said, as if he hadn't heard. "No man can live by himself or by his own rules."

We ate in silence and he held me tight in our sleeping bags. I awoke early, with the mist rising in the woods outside the tent. I reached over to touch his face, his beautiful face, so manly, so young, and yet already so weather-beaten by his work in the open fields.

"What's going on?" he asked sleepily, not opening his eyes.

"It's morning," I said.

He followed me outside and stirred the fire. I fixed breakfast, and we ate, seated side by side on the ground. We rolled up the tent and left for home. The tears wanted to come, great gushes of them, but I smiled instead.

Chapter 10

Our rumspringa ended, and we found ourselves seated in Bishop Mast's upstairs bedroom on a bright sunny Sunday morning. I kept my hands on my lap, and my gaze fixed properly on the floor. Two girls sat on either side of me, with the five young men in our class seated across from us. Walter gave me a smile from across the room, and I tried to smile back. The drone of Bishop Mast's voice filled the room, as he recited the articles of faith the community adhered to.

"There's no cleansing in the act of baptism," Bishop Mast declared. "The water is only water which washes away the dirt on our skin but cannot remove the sin from the heart. This act today is an outward sign of your inward cleanness. Now let us proceed with our final words on the lesson, and we shall be done with this."

"Amen," several of the ministers echoed.

Bishop Mast nodded in the deacon's direction.

Deacon Miller cleared his throat. "I too can give my blessing to our baptismal class. This is a great day for rejoicing as we look to the addition of new members to the church. The road to this day is not always easy and often beset with many difficulties, but this is the way of the Lord."

"Amen," several of the ministers said again.

We stood to our feet when the ministers concluded their remarks, and moved downstairs, the young men first, in line from the eldest to the youngest. We seated ourselves on the special bench set up in front of the congregation. I kept my head down, and my eyes on my thick black stockings.

My dresses had grown darker through the winter, and longer, hanging almost to my ankles. I wore thick black stocking even for our barn chores. My head covering had also grown larger, the strings longer, and they must always be tied.

The singing of the congregation stopped when the ministers filed down the stairs. The sermons began, as the clock on the living room wall ticked out the seconds. Bishop Mast had the main sermon and concluded with one final exhortation, "My dear people, the hour approaches in which the Lord shall appear in the clouds with great glory and power. Those who have not prepared themselves shall perish. Let us take heed to the warnings of Scripture. So now the hour is here. If these dear young folks are still willing to take upon themselves the sign of baptism, let them kneel."

I waited until the girls around me moved before I dropped to my knees. The questions began with the men at the end of the line. The answers were muffled, and the steps came closer. I whispered, "Yes," when asked.

Deacon Miller poured the water, which ran over my head and trickled down under my chin to puddle on the floor. Hands pressed on my white head covering.

"And now I baptize you in the name of the Father, the Son, and the Holy Spirit," Bishop Mast said, and they moved on.

When the last girl was baptized, Bishop Mast went to the front of the line, and helped the men to their feet. They exchanged a kiss on the cheek. The bishop's wife, Esther, greeted the girls, though the bishop gave us his hand upward. We sat down again, and the service concluded. I helped with the Sunday meal preparations in the kitchen as usual, where several of the women shook my hand and offered their own kiss of sisterly blessing.

When we had cleared and restocked the tables for the second serving, I ate with the other girls. The prayer of thanksgiving was offered again, and Walter slipped into the room.

"Ready?" he whispered.

I nodded and followed him outside to wait at his buggy. Twenty minutes went by before he brought PJ out of the barn. His face looked troubled.

"What's wrong?" I asked, as we fastened PJ into the shafts.

Walter motioned for me to climb into the buggy and hopped up beside me. He shook the reins and we trotted out of the lane.

"What's wrong?" I repeated.

He set his face, as PJ's hooves beat a steady rhythm.

"What happened in the barn, Walter?"

"Bishop Mast spoke with me."

"Why?"

"I'm speaking with Daett as soon as we get home," he said. "There is no need for alarm."

My hands turned cold as ice. "You had better tell me."

He waited a long time before he spoke. "Daett went to speak with Bishop Mast last week and expressed his strong objections to our planned marriage."

"We already knew," I said. "This was supposed to end your Daett's objections."

"I know," he said. His face fixed.

I pulled in a long breath. "Can't you see what they were doing? They were waiting until I was baptized. Now they think they have me under their control. I know what being under their control means."

"I'll talk with Daett," he said.

"Your Daett will not change his mind."

"We must try, Lily."

"Will Bishop Mast marry us, if your Daett disapproves?"

"He didn't say."

"The bishop told you something."

"He said we should make our peace with my Daett. Surely, if you're not like your Aunt Maud, Daett can be persuaded."

We pulled into our driveway, and Walter got out to tie PJ at the hitching post.

I called to him. "Will you marry me this fall, regardless of what they say?"

He came back to stand in front of me. "You can't force things, Lily."

"I can't wait, either. I have my reasons." I begged with my eyes.

He looked away. "We belong together. Everyone knows."

I pressed on. "They will not change their minds, and you won't go against them."

A troubled look crossed his face. "Come, we will sit on the porch swing and talk about this."

I climbed down, and the swing chains squeaked above us as we sat down. We still hadn't said anything when Daett and Mamm pulled into the driveway with Barbara in the buggy with them. Mamm and Barbara came up towards the house. They nodded and went inside. Daett soon came out of the barn and crossed the yard towards us.

Walter cleared his throat. "Could we have a moment with you?"

"Sure." Daett paused. "I assume Lily can hear this?"

"Lily knows what Bishop Mast told me today."

Daett didn't look surprised.

"Did you know Bishop Mast would speak with Walter today?" I asked.

"Not exactly," Daett said, "though Jonas came to me last week with the concern he has."

"Can you help us?" Walter asked. "Surely you know Lily is not like her Aunt Maud."

Daett thought for a moment. "I really was hoping I wouldn't have become involved in this issue."

"Couldn't you calm my Daett's fears?" Walter asked.

"We're taught in the community to listen when our brother has a concern. In this case, Jonas is your father," Daett said.

"We cannot wed if my Daett disapproves."

"You should have listened sooner." Daett shrugged and closed the door behind him.

"We have to wed this fall," I said, my voice raspy.

"Let's not quarrel, Lily. This may be a dark valley, but the Lord wants us to walk through the shadows."

"My valley is already very dark. I need this to end."

"I want to marry you, and quickly," he said, "but another year is a small matter to keep peace in the community."

"You said our rumspringa would convince them."

"I guess I was wrong," he said. "I'm sorry."

Walter soon left, and I confronted Daett when he came to my room after Barbara's bedroom light was extinguished.

"Why are you doing this to me, on top of everything?" I asked.

"I'm never giving my permission for your marriage to Walter," he said, "and neither will Jonas."

"What if I tell Walter about you, and what you do to me?"

He laughed. "Walter won't believe you, and neither will anyone else. If they do, Walter won't wed you. Not if you've been defiled."

I didn't want to believe him. I knew Walter was different, but those long nights of Walter lying beside me in the tent, not touching me, haunted me. They could only mean one thing. Walter thought I was pure and the world would never be the same after he knew I wasn't. If only Walter had done what I wanted. We would be armed to defeat them all, but

Walter hadn't. I beat my pillow with both fists until they hurt and cried myself to sleep.

I saw Walter next when he walked across the fields to see me later in the week. I couldn't look at him for fear I would burst out in tears. He knew I had been upset about our threatened wedding, so I assumed he figured my troubles went no deeper. He was wrong about so many things.

"I spoke at length with my Daett," he said, trying to comfort me. "We have to wait and pray."

"I can't live like this," I said, still not looking at him.

"We have to. The Lord will give us strength."

"You should have taken me when you had the chance," I said. "Now—"

He seemed not to hear. "Our wait may seem long, but in the larger scheme of things the next few years will pass quickly."

"Your Daett will never give his permission."

"We will have to trust the Lord," he said.

Walter left me with only a quick goodbye, and in my agony, I harnessed our horse to the buggy, and I drove down to Grandpa's house.

Grandma opened to my knock. "Hi, Lily."

"Is Grandpa around?"

"In the barn," she said.

I nodded and retreated.

Grandpa must have heard me push open the squeaky barn door, because he called down from the dusty hay mow. "Up here, Lily."

I climbed the familiar wooden slats, to find Grandpa leaning on his fork.

"I need to talk with you," I said.

"Sounds serious." He motioned towards the stacked hay bales. "Shall we sit?"

I seated myself, and he did the same. "Jonas has gone to Bishop Mast with his concerns about Walter marrying me," I began. "Apparently, my baptism did not calm them."

"Surely Jonas will change his mind."

"Daett told me he won't support us, either. Like in never!"

Grandpa stroked his white beard for a long time. "I'm sorry. I sincerely believed this day would never come."

"I should never have imagined things could work out," I said. "I put up with too much, too long."

Grandpa stood and paced the floor.

"I know what must be done," I said.

"I will speak with Jonas," he said.

I shook my head. "I need Aunt Maud's address, and the money to get there. Will you help me?"

He sat down and held his head in his hands.

"I have to go. There is no choice."

"I cannot bear this, Lily. This one last burden I cannot carry."

"Do you want me to head out on my own?"

Grandpa groaned. "Okay. Your aunt had cancer surgery this past year, so perhaps there is a small comfort in your going."

"Cancer!" I exclaimed. "The kind Aunt Nancy and Malinda had?"

"Yes. Breast cancer," he said. "The doctors think they got everything."

"Then I'm leaving tomorrow."

He said nothing more, and I left. When I went up to my bedroom after supper, I barred the door with a chair and the edge of the dresser. I was ready to scream and create a terrible racket, but Daett didn't come up all night. I walked out of the house and down the road the next afternoon. I packed nothing, so Mamm didn't ask questions. I figured I needed English clothing anyway. Mostly I didn't care. Grandpa drove me to the train station in our local town and purchased my ticket for Richmond, Virginia.

"May the Lord go with you," he said.

"You will write?" I asked.

"I will," he said, and I saw the tears before he slipped away.

I left the community as Aunt Maud left, without a goodbye. I was proving them right after the long years of protesting I wasn't like her. The train clattered south and east, and every dream I ever had of life improving crashed in on me. I thought I knew what darkness was, but this was a soul-crushing blackness.

"Are you okay?" a lady asked from across the aisle.

The tears trickled down my cheeks, and she came to sit beside me on the empty seat.

I closed my eyes, and she was no longer on the train when I awakened in the dim light of the dawn. We were riding through open fields, similar to those at home. Walter would be busy at this hour with his chores, and Barbara would have had to cover for mine. In my mind's eye, I saw Barbara smiling. She didn't mind the extra work. Barbara was looking beyond me, as if seeing a vision of a bright future. Someone would have to tell Walter of my departure. I hoped they didn't send Barbara.

I was still in my Amish clothing when I arrived in Richmond, Virginia, two days later.

Aunt Maud gave me a hug at the station. "Lily." She said my name softly and in our mother tongue. "I'm so happy you came."

"You look like Mamm," I said.

She smiled. "I'm her sister. Where's your luggage?"

"I walked out," I said.

Alarm filled her face. "You need a place to clean up and good food."

I managed to smile. "I guess I'm hungry, but how is your health?"

She looked at me strangely.

"Grandpa told me," I said.

"I'm perfect." She smiled again. "Let's say no more about my health."

She took me through the city to her apartment where she made sandwiches while I bathed and slipped into an unfamiliar dress. We packed the food and walked a short distance to the bank of a wide river. On a grassy knoll with the water rushing over rocks below us, we sat and ate. The tears started again, until sobs racked my body.

Aunt Maud held me close. "I understand," she whispered.

I wondered how I would continue to live, while the river spoke to me with murmurs of lives gone before, of joy, of pain unspeakable, of agony, and of life bubbling upward and onward towards the great sea.

"Come. You need sleep," Aunt Maud finally said.

"Why did you leave the community?" I asked.

She thought for a moment. "I loved Jonas, and almost convinced myself I could live his life, but with the wedding date looming in front of me, I had to face the truth. I was trying to live my Daett's life, conforming to his wishes while deep down there was this longing for something else, for what Daett had seen and turned his back on. I knew the desire would never leave me. I would break under the duties of a farmer's wife, having babies every year, endless laundry twice a week, and a man who would order me around my entire life. I tried to explain to Jonas, but he said my feelings would go away once we were married. I knew better. They would only have gotten worse. In the end, I had no choice but to leave, and I have not regretted the decision."

"So, you didn't leave because—because of—?"

"Because of what?"

"Nothing," I said. "I'm tired and weary."

"I will help you get started up with your new life," she said.

"Thank you." From somewhere I found the strength to stand.

Aunt Maud gathered up our lunch scraps, and we returned to the apartment. The tears came again when I was alone in the bedroom. I kept my sobs muffled in my pillow. I eventually dropped into a sleep of utter and complete exhaustion.

Aunt Maud was there for me when I awoke. She was there for me in the weeks which followed, as I made the transition from an Amish farm girl to a woman who lived in the city and worked at her Aunt's restaurant.

Down Home Cooking, Aunt Maud called the place.

"Amish cooking," she told me. "We just don't tell them."

I fell into the routine of restaurant life easily. I already knew most of the recipes by heart. At night, the crying spells became less, but Walter's face grew no dimmer. He had been ripped from my life, but no one could ever take him from my heart.

Section Three—November 1916 to September 1925

BARBARA

Chapter 11

The bonfire burned on the shore of the small pond the week after Thanksgiving, lighting the ice and snow and the darkness along the shore. I leaned into my skates, the icy pond in front of me open to the far shore. I was both tired and exhilarated tonight. The work on Daett's farm was heavy since Lily left, but my sister was gone—really gone. There were times late at night when I thought I heard Daett's footsteps squeak on the stairs, and Lily's heavy presence settled over me, but I was always imagining. My sister would not come back, and the world I had imagined was open in front of me. The greatest prize my heart had ever longed for was within my grasp. Walter acted as if he didn't know I existed, but he knew. He knew I belonged to him.

I took a deep breath and left the fire behind, to speed across the ice, and glide to a halt at the shadowy pasture grass. I turned to look back at the forms of the young people clustered along the far bank, their voices echoing on the chilled air. They were busy with preparations for a game of tag. Life for them had moved on, but no one had forgotten the scandal when Lily left a year ago. First Aunt Maud, and now Lily, had forsaken their blessed lives in the community for an existence in the wild evil world. I had escaped any association with my sister due to the exemplary life I'd lived, and physically I did not resemble her. For once my stout farm body, inherited from Daett, was a blessing.

Walter had been heartbroken. I understood. Lily mesmerized the man, as she did half the community's men. I needed no further evidence of my sister's evil influence. The community with its large and hopeful heart tried to offer Lily redemption, but I had figured the effort wasted from the beginning. Lily did not follow any rules. Walter should have known better. There was a part of me which wished he would have known, but I would not hold the transgression against him. If Walter had not fallen for my sister, he would be married to a proper community woman by now and settled down with a child on the way. Instead, he placed his bets on Lily. Walter had lost and was left with nothing. Lily was beautiful. I will be honest there, but Lily tortured Walter. My sister would have left him after their wedding. Walter should be thankful. He had been spared an awful future. As a married man, Walter would be without recourse, cursed to a life without a woman, and I would live my life knowing I could never have him after my sister had discarded him, as she discarded most of the other wonderful opportunities which life offered her.

Maybe Walter wasn't dating because there were no girls his age available. I must face the question, even while I tell myself no one will take him after the way he fawned over my silly sister. Walter's Daett, Jonas, found a wife after Aunt Maud left him on the eve of their wedding, and a man's broken heart is a heart only a woman can heal. Some girl will wake up any moment, so I must make my move soon.

He will be happy with me, and I will be more than happy. How can any woman not be happy with Walter? I could never have been picky, yet here I am getting a shot at the best. The thought took my breath away. The glory of Walter overwhelmed me.

I skated closer to the others, my skates a hiss on the ice.

Their voices grew louder. "We'll stay on this end of the pond tonight to save the ice on the other end for next week's party."

"There's a thaw coming tomorrow, so our tearing up the ice doesn't matter," someone else said.

I saw Walter on the far side of the pond, standing alone. He still showed his face at these gatherings. The man was tough, but he was in way over his head. The day would come when Walter would see what I had done for him and be thankful. I skated closer, and glided to a halt in front of him.

"Good evening." He acknowledged me.

"Walter," I said. "How are you doing?"

"Getting ready to skate on this nice evening."

"Yes, a nice evening," I agreed. I had noticed the moon earlier, but seeing Walter was better than any moon.

"Taking an early spin on the ice?"

"Yep." I laughed. "Loosening up for the game."

"How are things going at home?"

I shrugged. He wanted to know about Lily, and I wasn't telling even if I had known. "The usual. Chores, housework, getting ready for the Sunday church services tomorrow."

"I'll have to stop by sometime."

"Why don't you?" I gave him my best smile.

"The bonfire is warm," he said.

"They'll be starting the game soon." Getting Walter to talk to me had always been akin to pulling hens' teeth. "You ready?"

"I'm not young anymore." He forced a laugh. "Working all day in the barn and skating at night. Sports are for youngsters."

"Ah, you're still young," I said. "A veritable spring chicken."

He pushed back his stocking cap. "Is there news from Lily? A letter to her Grandpa perhaps?"

"I wouldn't know," I said. "You should be thankful things turned out like they did."

"An awful thing for you to say."

"You were always going to lose her."

71

He turned from me, as anger flashed across his face. "I failed her."

"No one could have changed Lily," I said. "We all tried."

"Stop talking, Barbara."

"I speak the truth," I said. "I know what you went through, what you're going through. Your pain is deep. I understand more than you think. Lily was my sister, but she's impossible. You should have lived with her like I did—her obsession with foolishness, her hunger for the things of the world, her despising of our way of life. If you had married her, you would be a forsaken husband right now, and a single man your entire life."

"She's your sister," he said. "Why are you talking like this?"

"Because the time has come to say the words," I said. "I know you loved Lily, but it's not right what she did to you, how she used you for her purposes, and cast you away like a dirty rag."

"You've said enough." His face hardened.

"You will not shut me up," I said. "I'm here for you. I've always been here for you. Look around and see for yourself what your reputation has become, what Lily has done to you. What do you want? Years spent waiting for this scandal to die down? The husband of some young woman you passed up to die? Lily has destroyed more than herself, she has destroyed you. Your father was caught by surprise with Aunt Maud, so the community overlooked things, but everyone has known since Lily was a girl and those red shoes, what she was like. I, on the other hand, accept and understand you. I know what Lily is like."

He stared at me. "You can't mean—?"

"Why not?" I said. "I have desires like any woman has. Why do you find my loving you so strange? In fact, I have always loved you?"

"Barbara! Listen to yourself," he said. "You're saying crazy things."

"Lily is not coming back."

"Now you're saying horrid things."

"I speak the truth." I said. "This is unfixable."

"So, you would pick up the pieces of my heart your sister left behind her?"

"If I could," I said, "but I know you don't love me, and you don't have to. I will still take you. Will any other woman make you such an offer?"

He stared across the pond and said nothing.

"I'll be there for you. I'll work on your farm as a woman should. I'll keep your house. I'll make your meals and wash your clothing. I'll bear your children. I'll be an honor to you. You will have the community's respect again. The shame of my sister will be forgotten."

"If Lily comes back?" he asked.

I gritted my teeth. "She's not coming back. Has Aunt Maud showed her face in the community again?"

"We should join the others," he said, and skated away.

I watched him leave. I had said nothing of which I was ashamed. I was doing what was right for Walter. If I succeeded, I would have one of the best men in the community as my husband. I deserved the Lord's mercy and grace showered upon me as an obedient and faithful servant.

I followed Walter, and the game began. We joined in. Our forms raced in the flickering shadows across the ice in wild pursuit of each other. I lost myself in the passion of the game and in the knowledge Walter was almost mine.

An hour crept past; the cold grew bitter. Bright stars twinkled above us, with the flames of the bonfire burning lower. A few of the young folks began to gather at the perimeter, their arms outstretched to warm themselves. The game dribbled to a halt. Wooden sticks were brought out, and hot dogs roasted. There was laughter in our voices, our faces turned away from the glow of the heat. I found a stick, and carefully attached my hot dog, to hold the meat over the coals. Walter sat down on the other side of the bonfire, and I walked over to squat down beside him.

"Roasting going okay?" I asked.

"Mine's about done," he said, but he didn't look at me.

"You're a little close to the flame," I said, and meant more than bonfires flickering beside icy ponds.

He retracted the stick and studied the hot dog in the dancing firelight. "I guess you're right."

"Maybe you like them black," I said.

"I don't." He returned his hot dog to the glowing embers.

We sat in silence with voices murmuring around us.

"Your hopes were a dream," I said. "Lily was never going to stay."

His voice turned bitter. "Lily was the purest, most beautiful and virtuous woman I will ever know."

"Most men think so of their first love, and Lily was beautiful."

"Just be quiet, Barbara."

"I've been quiet long enough. You've sown your wild oats, and now the time has come to settle down. I can live with how you acted with my sister."

"Lily was a saint," he said.

"Says the man who lost her to the world."

"You're not making anything better."

"Why would Lily leave if she really loved you?"

His hot dog dropped into the embers.

I wanted to ask a thousand questions. Why was he so devoted to Lily? Why did beauty have such a powerful effect on a man? Why did he let my sister do this to him? "Is the hotdog okay?" I asked instead.

"I'm fine," he said, but he had stopped eating.

"You're a good man," I said. "Just not in picking a woman as your wife."

"Hush, Barbara."

"Lily was not worthy of you."

"I lost her."

"Most men would not have tried."

"But I did," he said.

"I've always admired you. I have since I was a little girl. The Lord has not left me without virtues."

"Don't repeat yourself," he said.

"I'll always give you the highest place in my heart. I'll honor you. I will."

He said nothing, contemplating the fire.

"I would be yours, unlike my sister."

He sat unmovable.

"Am I such an unpleasant creature?"

"I don't want to talk about this."

"Can you take me home at least?"

"Why?"

"A few short moments with you would be heaven on earth."

"I don't like this," he said.

"I'll tell my cousins I have a ride home."

"Barbara, no."

"Please. Just this once."

He gave in with a quick nod of his head.

I looked away, for fear I would scare him. He drifted to the other side of the fire with his hotdog still uneaten. I didn't care. Ten minutes later, I followed him into the shadows beyond the fire. I knew where he had parked his buggy and climbed in while he untied PJ.

I was sitting in the very place my sister used to sit on her exalted throne. I gloried in the moment, in the conquest of good over evil. Lily had not succeeded, and I was glad.

Walter climbed up beside me and sat down, staring straight ahead. PJ made his way out of the field and onto the snowy gravel road. We drove quickly, with a long line of buggies behind us. He turned into our lane, his horse blowing white breath from his nostrils, to park at the hitching rack.

"Can you come into the barn for a few moments?" I asked. "We should talk."

"I don't want to talk," he said.

"Riding home with you was such an honor."

He gave in and climbed out to tie PJ to the hitching post.

I slipped my hand in his for the short walk to the barn, and he didn't object. I wondered how my hand felt compared to Lily's long slender fingers. He seemed lost in his own world as I pushed open the squeaky barn door and lit a lantern. The soft glow spread out across the straw strewn floor.

"I'm not staying long," he said. He looked restless.

I motioned towards a hay bale. "Sit down."

"There is nothing to say," he said, but he sat down.

"We need to talk about our wedding date."

He looked at me "You have your nerve. A few words you said."

"I only used a few words. You need me."

"I'm doing fine." He held his head in his hands.

"You're not being truthful." I kept my voice soft, trying to speak with Lily's sweetness.

"How will marrying you help?" He removed one hand from his face.

"I already told you."

"Why are we having this conversation?" His hand went back into place.

"Because you're going to marry me."

He rubbed his forehead. "Have you lost your mind, or have I lost mine, sitting here talking with you?"

"You're talking with me because you know I'm right."

He didn't say anything, staring at the shadows dancing on the barn wall.

"I adore you, Walter. I'll be exactly what you need in a wife."

"Be quiet," he said. "I can't think."

"Then don't. Let me set the date."

"You don't want a proper courtship?"

"What has been proper about your life with Lily?"

"I'm having a nightmare," he said. "I was having this beautiful dream."

"We awaken from our dreams," I said, "but I don't hold the dream against you. The others do."

His eyes glistened in the light of the flickering lantern.

"You're a community man," I said. "In your heart, you always have been. My corrupt sister distracted you. I'm the one who knows and accepts you. Lily tried to change you. I am right for you. Lily never was."

"How can you say such wicked things about your sister?"

"Because they're true."

His eyes still shone. "Lily is the most lovely and gracious woman to ever walk this earth. I wasn't worthy of her."

"I disagree."

Sadness crept across his features. "I have failed—utterly and completely failed her."

"My sister has failed you and deceived you. She is wicked, Walter."

His face changed and blazed with anger.

"I forgive my sister and I forgive you, but the truth has revealed itself plainly. Face reality, Walter. I'm here, and my sister is not."

He didn't answer.

"Be honest," I said. "Admit Lily betrayed you as she betrayed us. The girl didn't even say goodbye, just like Aunt Maud didn't say goodbye to your Daett."

"Enough," he said, and jumped up from the straw bale.

I watched him leave the barn and waited until the sound of his buggy wheels died away before I got up from the straw bale. I turned off the lantern and found my way outside. The dark winter sky above me rolled with clouds, but I ignored them. I pulled my coat tightly around my shoulders and hurried up to the front door. I had made a lot of progress tonight. Walter had engaged me in conversation about marriage. My first miracle had happened.

I peeked into Lily's room at the top of the stairs. The bed was made, the quilt stretched tight. No one had slept here since Lily left. Mamm used the guest room across the hall when visitors came. I stepped closer and lay down on the bed without removing the covers.

I lay there for an hour or so, wondering how you felt when a man came into your bed. The mechanics of the act I understood. The passion and fury of the stallions in the barnyard took my breath away. I had never had a man desire me with such fire in his loins. Lily had been with Walter, and I was bothered by the knowledge. I wished I had been first in his arms, but I would have Walter as my husband, while Lily would only have a memory.

I got up and tiptoed across the hallway to climb into my own bed. In the morning, after breakfast had been eaten, and Daett was in the fields, I cornered Mamm in the kitchen. "I want the truth about Lily."

"I'm not talking about your sister," Mamm said.

"You don't know what I want to know."

Mamm stirred more vigorously, the wooden spoon beating the cake batter.

"Maybe you do know what I want to know."

There was still no response, but beads of sweat were visible on her forehead. Mamm was sweating from more than her work.

"Is Daett Lily's father?"

Mamm froze. When she spoke, her voice quivered. "What do you mean?"

"You know what I mean."

"Why would you ask such an awful thing?" The spoon still wasn't moving.

"I want to know," I said.

Mamm's flushed face had drained of color, so I knew I was right. "If I have to, I'll ask Daett."

The quiver was gone from her voice. "Why are you asking this?"

"For a lot of reasons. Daett going to Lily's bed so freely and you not objecting. The simplest to understand perhaps is my shortness and Lily's tallness. How did she escape Daett's genes?"

Mamm spoke slowly. "There was an English man—one summer—a long time ago, who bought produce from our garden. I—I couldn't resist him."

"But we don't sell from our garden."

"Before Lily—before she was born, we did."

"Is this English man Lily's Daett?"

"How do I know? Your Daett was also coming to my bed."

"Thanks for telling me," I said.

"Will you ruin us?" She was staring at me.

"I won't," I said, and I didn't in the next months as I continued to put pressure on Walter. He gave in steadily until one summer night in late June he told me, "Let's just get this over with, Barbara."

"Get what over with?" I asked, not daring to believe the end of the road was really in sight.

"Set our wedding date this fall," he said. "I no longer care one way or the other."

"You will never regret this," I whispered.

"Let's hope neither of us does," he said almost under his breath.

Chapter 12

The blush of dawn was still in the sky on the morning of my wedding day. I had my dress laid out on the bed, and my underclothing laid off to the side. The bedroom mirror was in front me with the flame from the kerosene lamp flickering on the dresser top. The shadows danced on the old glass, and I reached over to turn the wick up. When a wisp of smoke curled up the glass chimney, I turned the knob back a notch. I turned to study the image of the woman in the mirror.

I wasn't Lily, and would never be Lily, but I was a woman. I looked like a woman, even if the shape was heavy. I could satisfy a man and bear his children.

I would disrobe for Walter tonight after the last guests had left, but he would have to wait for the prescribed time before he lay with me. Those were the instructions from the holy story of Tobias. I couldn't imagine Walter objecting. He had yet to touch me willingly anywhere. We held hands, but I was the one who initiated contact. Walter would see me like this tonight. After Lily, He probably needed a few nights to adjust his expectations. I was superior to Lily in other ways. I would comfort myself with the thought.

I studied my length and width in the mirror. I had longed for Walter since my earliest memories. I wanted him near me, at my side. This was where love led.

I moved closer to the mirror. There was no use wishing I was taller or more graceful. My body could bear children. I would carry them low on my hips with the minimum of fuss. I could bear a dozen children and still work in the fields until noon. I would give Walter a son, our firstborn. Walter would be proud. He would laugh as he used to when Lily's presence was in the room. I could give Walter what he needed.

I pulled on my undergarments, taking my time. The flush of dawn was still in the sky and the first buggy wouldn't be here for another thirty minutes, unless Walter came early. He might. I walked to the bedroom window and pushed aside the drapes. The driveway was empty, the hitching post beside the barn a dim frame in the light of the rising sun.

I held up my dark blue wedding dress. I had worked late at night, after Mamm was exhausted from my rushed wedding preparations, to complete the dress in time. We were marrying in September, way before the usual wedding season in November, but I was in a special circumstance. I couldn't let Walter change his mind. Bishop Mast had looked surprised when we showed up at his doorstep on a Saturday evening to request our wedding announcement in church the next morning, but he hadn't looked displeased.

I shook out the dark folds and turned to the mirror. I slipped the dress over my head and began placing the pins. Walter owned his farm, but I had insisted on tradition. A bride must spend the first night in her bedroom, the man an invading force into unfamiliar territory. After he watched me undress, I figured he could sleep in Lily's bed. He could crawl under the quilt where Lily had been and mourn for her. The quicker I could banish Lily's ghost, the sooner we could get on with our lives.

I punched in the last pin and blew out the light. The sound of buggy wheels was coming up the driveway. I pushed the drapes aside again to peer out. Walter was climbing out of his buggy, with his black hat pulled over his ears. I smiled. He had come early. I watched him unhitch and lead PJ into the barn.

With quick steps I left the bedroom and made my way down the stairs.

"Walter's here." Mamm greeted me in the kitchen.

"I know."

Moments later, Walter's form appeared in the opening between the kitchen and the living room, his hat pushed back on his head, and his dark suit glittering in the flickering flame of the lantern. "Good morning."

"Hi." I gave him a bright smile.

"You have your wedding dress on."

"Don't you like the fit?" I turned around once for him to see.

I knew what he wanted, but I wasn't going to give him the satisfaction of knowing I knew. He had imagined a much prettier dress for his wedding day, worn by a much prettier girl. What foolishness the man had once entertained. The brilliance of having him spend the night in Lily's bed looked better with each passing moment.

"Sit down and I'll fix you breakfast," Mamm said. "We haven't eaten, either."

"I'll wait," Walter said. "The others will be here in a moment."

"Barbara shouldn't have put on her wedding dress so early," Mom said.

"I'm sure Barbara knows what she's doing."

"I do what's best for you," I said.

Mamm bent over the stove. "If more guests arrive, they can eat with us. You, Barbara, change out of your wedding dress before you help with the food."

I left the room and called over my shoulder. "I won't be eating."

I had been skimping on food the last few weeks. From the looks of the figure in the mirror this morning, my efforts had shown little progress. My body kept its form stubbornly with or without food. Walter was sitting on the couch when I returned. He glanced up but didn't say anything. I entered the kitchen to take the utensils out of the drawer and spread them on the table.

There were footsteps in the living room. Walter was walking about, probably checking the road for further arrivals. I placed the bacon slices in the pan, and the vapors rose quickly to the ceiling, followed by loud sizzling. I stirred the pieces, as the bacon curled in the pan from the heat.

I heard buggies come into the driveway, and voices raised at the front door. More footsteps came into the living room. Mamm went to greet them, but I stayed at the stove until the food was ready. Several of the arrivals had eaten, but the ones who hadn't, I served, and smiled while I filled plates . Walter ate heartily. The man couldn't be too disturbed. I comforted myself with the thought.

"Bride's not talking much this morning," someone teased.

I forced a laugh. "I'm delirious with happiness."

More buggies poured into the driveway.

I began to wash the dishes when Mamm stopped me. "The cooks are here. Go change."

I retreated up the stairs. The pins went in faster this time, and the wedding dress was soon secured. The mirror taunted me, and I turned away. I wondered what kind of dress Walter was expecting. Lily would have chosen a light green dress, or perhaps light blue. Both would have broken the ordnung fence. I, on the other hand, the faithful girl, wore dark blue. For a moment, I wished I had done otherwise. Yet, I had never owned a light green dress in my life. I would have felt completely unlike myself, like I was giving in to everything Lily represented, like I was supporting the complete wreck she made of her life. No! I had Walter. Lily with her beautiful dresses had not accomplished what I had. Walter would see the value of me someday.

The stairs were a blur on the way down, and I steadied myself with a hand on the wall. Faces moved past me in the living room, and murmurs from conversations were a buzz in my ears. Mamm was organizing the table waiters, and the cooks had charge of the kitchen. The idle guests went out onto the lawn.

Walter came to stand by my side with a smile on his face, but his attention was directed at the others. I comforted myself. I would his wife by tonight. The witness couples soon gathered on either side of us. We watched through the living room window as the men formed a line by the barn, and Bishop Mast led the way into Daett's pole barn. From there, each age group followed them until the yard was empty.

"The time has come," Walter intoned. He sounded as if he faced his execution. I comforted myself with the thought of how wrong he was.

He led the way out of the front door, and across the yard, to our chairs set up in the barn loft. I kept my gaze on the dusty floor as the songs began and the ministers filed out for their usual morning meeting. In the community's tradition, the couple went with the ministers for their final marriage counseling. Walter rose to his feet and I followed, the minister's silent forms in front of us as we walked back across the yard.

We went up to my bedroom for the session and sat on chairs someone had placed there since I had last changed. Walter and I were on one side of the room, and the ministers sat across from us. The instruction began about things I already knew—housekeeping, submission, and bearing children as the Lord gave them.

The lectures ended, and the walk back across the lawn began. Walter had nothing to say. We took our seats again, and the sermons began once the ministers filed in. Bishop Mast had the final sermon and told once again the familiar story of Young Tobias. I kept my head down. I had listened to the story with great attention for many years. I knew what must be done.

"Would the couple please stand." Bishop Mast addressed us. The first question came quickly. "Do you, Brother Walter, believe this, our Sister Barbara, has been ordained from the Lord to be your wedded wife?"

Walter said, "Yes," and I said, "Yes," to my questions, and the deed was done, which could not be undone, except by death, and I was not dead, and neither was Walter.

We ate our wedding meal together, seated in the corner of the barn, and Walter even laughed a little, but he did not touch my hand under the table as I had seen many newly wedded couples do. I comforted myself. In four nights, I would lie in Walter's arms.

The afternoon was a busy affair of chatting with relatives who had come from near and far, and who wished us well on our wedded life. We smiled and nodded, and I was happy. I really was. Walter pretended well, and I felt a little sorry for him, even though I knew he was thinking about Lily.

The evening hymn singing did not close until a quarter after nine, and the older guests lingered for a long time. The hour was past twelve before I led Walter back up the stairs to my bedroom, my body aching from tiredness. I lit the lamp and smiled up at him, his handsome face silhouetted in the dim light. I touched his face, tracing the firm lines of his jaw. He didn't draw back.

"We're man and wife," I said.

"We are," he agreed, but there was no happiness in his voice.

I touched the pins on my wedding dress. "I hope you like what you see."

"What I like makes no difference now," he said.

"I want to please you."

"You can keep your dress on," he said.

"I knew your expectations were low, but …"

His jaw drew tighter as I removed my clothing.

"You will have a few nights to adjust," I said.

"What do you mean?"

"The Tobias Scriptures. You can sleep in Lily's bed."

"In Lily's bed?"

"Yes. You've been thinking about her the entire day, and you're thinking about her now."

"What are you talking about?"

"I don't want to explain," I said, and climbed under the quilt.

The coolness of the cloth burned on my skin. I would put on my night dress when he left the room.

"I'm not sleeping in Lily's bed," he said.

"Don't you believe in Tobias?"

"Lily didn't believe in Tobias."

"Lily is gone, so go think about her if you must, but you're not sleeping with me."

His voice turned bitter. "I'm having none of this Tobias nonsense or your manipulations."

"Go to Lily's room. Give yourself a chance to properly mourn my wicked sister."

He seemed not to hear me; his gaze was fixed out of the darkened window.

I waved my hand. "Go."

He came closer instead. He was at my bedside when I pushed my hand against his chest. His response was to grasp my wrist and propel me out of bed. His strength was amazing. When I grabbed for the edge of the dresser, he caught my hand in mid motion. I felt myself lifted out of the door and propelled across the hall. He pushed aside the quilt on Lily's bed, and threw me in. He climbed in and there was an awful lot of pain. I couldn't believe what was happening, but I refused to cry. I would not begin our married life with tears.

I lay awake for a long time after Walter left, not moving under the quilt he had thrown over me. I couldn't fall asleep in Lily's bed, but I would not humiliate myself by voluntarily climbing into my own bed with Walter. I had heard the bedroom door shut across the hallway. I finally dragged the quilt down on the floor, and with Lily's pillow under my head, I fell asleep. I awoke in the middle of the night cold and aching. My resolve slipped away, and I crossed the room to my familiar bed, inhabited with the form of a man. I slipped in, but I took care not to touch him.

When I awoke, Walter was standing at the window in the morning light. I stared. I couldn't help myself. He saw me looking at him and pulled on his clothing to leave the room.

Chapter 13

Walter wasn't around when I had dressed and arrived downstairs.

"He's helping Daett with the chores." Mamm answered my unspoken question.

"I expected as much." I replied.

"You made plenty of racket last night," Mamm said, but she didn't smile.

"He's a strong man." She didn't respond, and I was glad. Mamm must have her own secrets from her wedding night.

Walter seemed cheerful enough when he came in with Daett from the barn. We left right after breakfast to drive over to Walter's place, and I proceeded to set up house. I had Walter as my husband, but I didn't have him in my bed when night came.

"You want your three days, you can have them," he said.

The three days stretched into weeks and Walter spent his nights in the guest bedroom upstairs. When we had visitors and he had to sleep with me, he didn't touch me.

I soon noticed my belly growing, along with my need for Walter. A piece of something was missing from my soul. His eyes didn't have to glisten like they did for Lily. I could make peace with reality, but I still wanted to be wanted, in some basic mechanical way at least. Didn't I deserve a little? If the other women in the community knew I couldn't keep Walter in my bed, my disgrace would rise to the heavens. Such a thing was unheard of in our world. Walter had not forgotten my sister, and from what I could see would not forget her anytime soon. My growing belly saved my reputation, while my desire for him kept rising. I lived with the hope a son would open Walter's heart to me. I would please him, and Walter would begin to see my true worth.

The months passed, and by August I paced the floor of our home with more of a waddle than a walk. The pains began late in the morning and took over with a vengeance. I sent Walter to notify Sarah Yoder, the midwife, and Mamm. The day was hot and sultry, the air moving through the house in slow motion. My belly protruded from my middle with a bulk heavy on my hips. I had conceived on our wedding night, but I did not feel blessed.

I turned from my pacing to approach the bed. I had stretched the white linen tight this morning, not knowing the birth pains would grip me today. I pulled the Texan Star quilt to one side, but the urge to lie down left me when another spasm began. I walked to the window and hung on to the frame. The noon sun was high in the sky. There would be no rattle of dishes in the kitchen tonight or food laid out on the table—at least not by me. Mamm might bring a casserole with her. By morning, I will have given birth to Walter's son. I groaned and imagined the joy filling me when Walter sees what I have given him.

I lifted my head when a buggy pulled into the driveway. The midwife had arrived. Walter must have gone to the Yoder's place first and from there stopped in to notify Mamm. Sarah had visited several times during my pregnancy. There had been no signs of complications. I knew I was tough, and Walter was not concerned about me. He knew I would survive anything.

I waddled through the living room and opened the front door. Sarah had tied her horse to the hitching post and called out, "How are things going?"

"Coming along," I said.

Sarah pulled her satchel out of the back of the buggy and trundled the load up the sidewalks. I reached down to help, but Sarah waved me away. With a bounce, the woman was inside, her weathered beaten face a blaze of smiles. "Came right on time, I would say."

"I think he did." I searched for joy to accompany the words, but there was none.

Sarah's gaze centered on my middle. "How close are they?"

"Ten minutes or so, and they hurt."

Sarah chuckled. "You'll do well. You're built for these things."

"I know." I tried to smile.

"Shall we check?"

I nodded, and Sarah dragged her satchel into the bedroom with me in tow. The linens on the bed crinkled as I lay down.

"Measures a three." Sarah announced a moment later. "A little way yet. Shall we go for a walk?"

"For a waddle." I quipped, and we laughed.

I followed Sarah outside and up the lane.

She moved slowly matching my progress. "Have you heard from Lily since she left?"

I winced. "I haven't, but I suppose she's been in touch with Grandpa."

"What happened with your sister was a great shame," she said. "At least Walter found out before he wed her."

"I know." I scrunched my face in pain with the onslaught of a contraction.

Sarah touched my arm briefly. "We must pray for all lost souls—and forgive."

I stopped short. "You think I haven't forgiven Lily?"

Sarah didn't answer. Walter's buggy appeared in front of us. He stopped and leaned out of the door, "Are you okay?"

"Your son is okay," I said.

He nodded. "Don't overdo yourself." I knew when Walter was pretending.

"What's going on between the two of you is not good," Sarah said, once Walter was out of earshot.

"What do you mean? We're wed, and I'm giving my husband a son."

"This is just an old woman talking," she said. "I know how the community feels about Lily and your Grandpa. I don't say I disagree, but you're a troubled woman. Giving birth is risky with turmoil in your soul."

"I've done what's best for both of us," I said.

She smiled slightly. "Yet you have a spirit which torments you?"

"I have my sister who torments me." I retorted.

"I see," she said, and we turned back towards the house.

Sarah said no more on the matter, and I was giving birth to Walter's child. No one could prevent me.

Before we arrived back at the lane, Mamm passed us in her buggy. She waved but didn't slow down. Mamm was bustling about in the kitchen when I made my slow way back inside the house.

"There's plenty of food on the table if either of you are hungry." Mamm called to us.

I lay down on the bed again, and Sarah checked my progress.

"Why don't you come out and sit on the front porch swing. Nothing is happening yet," she said.

I did, and when we had seated ourselves on the swing Mamm brought a chair to join us. The chains squeaked above us.

I made a face, and Sarah glanced at me. "Does the sound bother you?"

A savage contraction gripped me, and I clutched my side.

"Okay. Back inside with you." Sarah ordered.

She held the front door open for me. I maneuvered through and made my way to the bed. I lowered myself, and Sarah contemplated me for a moment. "Stay as comfortable as you can and conserve your energy. I'll be in the kitchen with your Mamm. You can call, if something unexpected comes up."

Darkness settled outside the bedroom window, and the kerosene lamp was lit. The minutes ticked passed, followed by the hours. Midnight came and went.

I heard Walter whisper to Sarah at the bedroom door before he left for one of the bedrooms upstairs. I wondered if Sarah or Mamm noticed someone had been sleeping in the room regularly. Maybe they figured I had been trying to avoid bothering Walter with my late pregnancy thrashings. I tried to doze off between the heavy contractions, but they came too quickly. Sarah stayed by the bedside and wiped my forehead with a washcloth. The room grew hazy at times. I heard laughter and saw forms running, and knew I was dreaming while I was wide awake. I saw Walter reaching for Lily, and her slipping from his grasp to disappear into the night. I saw his face, lifted in a storm, tormented as lightning split the sky from horizon to horizon. I had never seen the face of a man so grief stricken. I added my own cries to the tumult, and Sarah's washcloth wiped again and again on my forehead.

"Is she okay?" I heard Walter's voice at the bedroom door. I knew he wasn't inquiring about me. He meant Lily, and Lily wasn't here.

Sarah didn't answer, and Mamm's voice mingled with the sound of my agonies. They hovered over me, with Walter's broad shoulders in the doorway. I trembled and shook violently. I dug my fingernails into the palm of my hands, the pain unfelt with the fire burning between my legs.

"Push!" Sarah called. "Push hard!"

A cry filled the bedroom. I drew quick breaths. Sarah was wiping the child in a towel and laid the infant on my shrunken middle. I could feel the legs and the arms waving about.

"Hold your daughter." Sarah ordered.

An icy sword cut through me. "My daughter."

"The Lord has given, and His ways are always right," Sarah said.

I saw Walter's face come close, rapturously looking at the child. He held her. "My Lily," he said. "She's my Lily Joy."

"She's a pretty baby." I heard Mamm say.

"No." I screamed into the room.

Walter didn't seem to hear me. "We will call her Lily Joy," he said.

The room grew hazy again, their forms moving above me. Walter was holding the baby and fussing over her.

"I hate you, Lily." I whispered under my breath. "I really, really hate you."

Chapter 14

Walter was in our bedroom six weeks after Lily Joy was born, fussing over the sleeping child. I couldn't wait until the time arrived to move the child upstairs or somewhere out of our bedroom.

"How are you little one?" Walter cooed.

He leaned low to brush the blanket with his fingers. His eyes were soft and filled with joy when he looked at me, but I knew who he was seeing.

He closed the bedroom door and began to undress. I opened my mouth, but decided against speaking. He hadn't been sleeping in here since we moved into the house.

He climbed into bed and studied me.

"Why are you here?" I asked out of the corner of my mouth.

He didn't answer but climbed out of bed to pull the drapes shut.

"You haven't touched me since our wedding night."

He looked at the crib and his face softened. I knew the answer. The tears wanted to come, but I held them back. I was expecting a repeat of his furor, but I should have known better. The child in the crib had changed him and softened his anger towards me. I had my sister to thank for my husband's kindness.

He lay looking up at the ceiling afterward.

My chin quivered, but I forced myself to speak. "Did you have to think about her while you were with me?"

"I wasn't thinking of Lily," he said.

"You're lying."

"Just hush," he said and went to sleep.

At least he was in my bed. I should be happy, but I wasn't. My sister lived with us. The child looked decidedly more like Lily with each passing day.

Mamm noticed quickly. "Doesn't she … I mean … look like?"

"I know," I said.

Walter was mesmerized, like a man awakened from a long sleep. I soon figured out why he was in my bed each night. He wanted another child. He wanted a house full of children who looked like what he had lost. I should have dissuaded him, but I didn't. I wanted a son. I clung to the thread of hope a son would impress Walter with me.

My hatred for my sister blended with my dislike for my daughter. I told myself the baby was not to blame. The innocent child had been caught in this fracas through no fault of her own, but there was no convincing my heart. I didn't abuse her, but my efforts to bond with Lily Joy went nowhere.

I tried to find pleasure with Walter in bed, but I hadn't conceived after a few months. I expected an objection from Walter, but he said nothing. His attentions were taken up with Lily Joy. He couldn't spend enough time with her in the evenings, playing on the floor, reading stories to her on his knee. I was tormented by memories of Lily seated on Grandpa's lap. More than once I thought I would lose my mind and run screaming from the house. I waited for things to get better, for the bitterness to ooze away, but nothing improved.

There were evenings after supper when Walter's gaze would linger on me, and a wistfulness would creep into his expression. I figured he wished my sister was sitting where I sat, with a face and form to match his daughter's.

The patter of small feet sounded on the hardwood floors behind me. I forced myself to turn and smiled down at the small face, a smudge of oatmeal from breakfast on the corner of her lips.

"Mamm," she said, so sweetly, so similar to Lily's voice.

"Go play." I ordered.

She tottered away. The Lord had smitten me. I could find no other answer. One more stroke of His wrath, and I would lose my mind. I endured the unspoken questions from the women at the church services. They were not surprised Lily Joy looked like my sister. What they wondered was why I had borne so quickly the first time, and now the months were passing with no sign of another child.

After the life I had lived in the community, they shouldn't suspect me of shirking my duty, but I am Lily's sister. I am not escaping the shame of her reputation. I am being blamed for what Walter did with Lily.

I gazed out the living room window to think about the matter. The fields were hazy beyond the barn with the morning mist still on the ground. I stepped behind the drapes when Walter's team came out of the barn. He was cutting hay today. His handsome face turned toward the house. I am filled with an unexplainable desire to be with him, in the same way Lily was with him out in the open fields, under the starry heavens in a tent.

The rattle of buggy wheels in our driveway interrupted my thoughts. Walter waved before he moved into the field with his team. Mamm's face was outlined in the buggy door. I opened the front door, and the patter of small feet followed me outside onto the porch.

I picked up the child, and we crossed the lawn.

"I've volunteered to prepare lunch for the women's sewing this month," Mamm said. "I need two of your cooking pots."

"I'm helping Walter in the fields today." I forced a smile. "Could you do me a favor and take Lily Joy with you?"

Mamm frowned.

"I have to live with her every day," I said.

Mamm nodded. "Bring me the satchel, and I'll be on my way."

Mamm followed me inside, and I prepared Lily Joy's things. She found the cooking pots she needed and led the way out of the house. I watched them drive out of the lane, before I returned to the kitchen to fill a small jug with ice and add squeezed lemon, water, and sugar. Walter had the larger water jug with him in the field. I made sandwiches and took a thin blanket from the bedroom closet. I placed the items in a paper bag. With the jug in one hand and the bag in the other, I headed across the fields. The mist had melted away, the sun a globe of redness through the thin clouds. The heat already pressed down, the coolness of the night driven back to the earth.

Walter saw me coming and paused, his hat pushed back on his forehead. The team stopped, their nostrils sending out blasts of hot air, and their necks trickling with sweat.

"You're pushing the team too hard," I said.

His smile was tight. "I thought you left with your Mamm for the sewing. I saw the buggy go by."

"Lily Joy went with her. I stayed to help you."

"Help me!"

"You need help. The sewing isn't important."

He appeared relieved. "I can get another team going. The old blades on the mower are still sharp."

"I'm sure they are," I said. "You wouldn't have put up dull blades."

He hopped down from the seat and offered me the reins. I climbed on after I left my lemonade jug and bag in the shade. He slapped the horse's necks and they were moving again. I keep my gaze intent on the field ahead. He had the other team out the second time I came around, and we cut together, half a field apart. We were good together. I timed myself to his movements, something which Lily could never have done. In a thousand ways, I was his match, and yet my sister would not leave us alone. I yearned for one thing, for peace to enjoy this man in my own right, unclouded by my sister's presence, or her memory, or the smell of her lingering in the recesses of our brains.

The sun rose higher and I drove down to the stream to water the horses. I waited a moment in the shade for the heave of their sides to settle. I drank from Walter's water jug and moved the lemonade further under the tress. Walter took the exit when I returned to the field. We paused to rest the horses twice more before noontime. I had the blanket spread on the grass when Walter finished washing his hands in the creek.

"You wouldn't have had to do this," he said.

"We'll finish early." I gave him a smile.

He nodded and picked up the sandwich to bow his head for a moment of thanks before he ate. We sat silently across from each other. I gathered up the crumbs when we finished and folded the blanket. The horses' harness tinkled in the distance.

"There's a pool around the bend," I said. "No one will see us swimming. The horses could use the rest."

"You would go for a swim?" He looked surprised.

"No one can see us back here."

He was baffled, but not displeased. Walter followed me, and I pressed the undergrowth aside. I took off my dress at the water's edge and waited. He had his shirt off, watching me with the strangest look on his face. I ignored the expression to undress and enter the water. He followed a moment later. I turned to splash water on his face. We swam deeper, two forms with water sprays behind us from our kicking feet. We didn't have much time. He would soon remember his duties. I returned to the far bank and lay out the blanket. He came out of the water, to stand on the bank dripping wet, not moving. If men could be called beautiful, Walter would break every scale of measurement.

I closed my eyes and prayed to heaven Walter would be pleased with my offering. I heard the rustle of the grass as he dressed. I opened my eyes when he walked past me back to his team. I had been rejected. The pain burned deep inside me. The tears wanted to come, but I resisted. I dressed and arrived back at my team to see him working halfway around the field. After we retired in the evening, he climbed in the bed and drew me close. I decided to count my efforts of the day a victory even though they tasted like defeat. I tried not to remember why I was rejected lying there on the grass, exposed and naked. I looked nothing similar to Lily, or the memories he must have of the nights spent with her under the stars of the open heavens.

There was peace in our house in the weeks following. There were moments when I forgot Lily, when I felt like I belonged to Walter, to the flow of his life, to the rhythm of those who had gone before us, who loved out of necessity without the luxury of choice, like us, like me.

I conceived again, somewhere in there. Elsie was born the following spring, and baby Mary two years later. Neither of them had Lily Joy's looks, and I began to feel a little happiness in my heart.

"Our next child will be a son." I told Walter.

"Looks like you can only bear girls," he said.

Walter was wrong. Baby John was born in late December. I invited the extended family over on a Saturday evening to celebrate. Grandpa hadn't been well, but I made a point of encouraging him to come. He stood over the crib looking down at the new infant.

"He's mine," I whispered close to him.

I couldn't resist the chance to rub Grandpa's nose in the fact I had given Walter the son Lily would never give him.

Chapter 15

My son grew and my measure of happiness with Walter lasted until September when Grandpa passed.

"Lily is coming for the funeral," Mamm told me when she broke the news. "Grandma sent her a telegram, and the answer came back immediately."

"Lily." I felt the blood drain out of me.

"I don't want to see her either," Mamm said.

"At least she'll look like an English woman." I comforted myself.

Only my sister didn't. Lily arrived and stayed at Grandma's house, who must have helped her procure Amish clothing. Lily came to the viewing in an Amish dress and sat brazenly through the funeral on a chair the ministers supplied her, set off to one side since Lily was excommunicated. I managed to avoid her at the viewing by hook or crook. Halfway through the ceremony, I realized the dress Lily was wearing looked familiar. My sister was wearing her own clothing. Lily's figure hasn't changed a bit. I knew the dresses were still in the closet in her bedroom, and Grandma would also know this.

Baby John stirred beside me on the hard bench, but I couldn't focus on his face with the rush of my emotions. Lily was here, and Lily was going to tear down what I had built. I was certain I was right. How? I didn't know, but Lily had not given up on Walter.

Walter kept his eyes on my sister for the entire service. I wished I was the one in Grandpa's casket. At the gravesite, Walter made sure Lily had a special place to stand near the open grave. I hadn't seen Lily cry earlier in the day, but she wept plenty when the men shoveled dirt into the hole. Walter moved towards Lily to comfort her, but I hung on to his arm in protest. Holding him back would not have stopped him, had Walter dared make a spectacle of himself in front of everyone.

I balled my fists when Walter had the audacity to approach me in bed. "She's not your wife."

"You know how I feel about Lily," he said. "I will always have such feelings, so get over your sister."

I gritted my teeth and endured his attentions. This was one advantage I had over Lily. I slept with Walter and she didn't.

The funeral passed, but Lily stayed over at Grandma's house. A week had gone by. She was tending to Grandma, Lily claimed. I knew better. Lily never did anything unrelated to a personal benefit. I felt a horrible foreboding of what might lie ahead of us. Did Lily hope to lure Walter away from the community? Would I awaken one morning to find the house and the barn empty? Walter gone? Slipped away in the night with my sister? The shame would be greater than I could bear.

In the meantime, Lily Joy picked up a nasty flu bug—I assumed at the funeral. She missed school two days this week, but the girl was determined to get out of the house this morning. To show her fitness she was washing dishes in the kitchen.

I joined her. "You don't have to do this," I said. "You can stay home another day or so and get completely better."

"I'm better." The voice was grim. "Mrs. Camille doesn't want us to miss any days of school."

I nodded. "I can understand. My teacher, Mrs. Harper, was the same way, but you didn't want to get sick."

"I've been resting since Sunday. I want to go back."

"Okay." I gave in. "Walk slowly to the schoolhouse, and don't overdo things once you are there."

Lily Joy smiled, a weary smile. "Give Baby John a good morning kiss for me."

"Okay," I said.

On this, we had bonded. Lily Joy shared my delight in the child. Walter never took to his son as I figured he would. Walter's daughter was his sunshine and total delight. No one objected in our family other than me, but I had my revenge to comfort me. If Walter could have a favorite, so could I.

I watched Lily Joy's form walking up the road towards the schoolhouse, framed against the rising sun in the east. At eight years of age, the girl was beautiful like my sister, who was a glorious being hiding a great evil. My sister had haunted Walter's life, and was trying to lure him away from me with what he could never have. Lily Joy appeared different, but the harm just hadn't started. I saw my sister looking at Baby John the day of the funeral with a look of longing in her eyes. I didn't let Lily get close to the child, but nothing had ever stopped my sister from getting what she wanted.

I turned away from the window to find Elsie and Mary seated on the couch, as still as mice. They had my looks and character. I stopped short when I noticed their flushed faces. They had appeared well at the breakfast table.

"We're feeling sick," they said together.

I touched their foreheads, the heat rising against my hand. I took them in my arms and pulled them close. "You poor things. You must have the awful flu. Go back to bed and rest for the day."

I helped them upstairs and settled them on their beds, fully clothed, and darkened the room by pulling the window curtains. I kissed their cheeks and left. The crib squeaked in our bedroom, and I entered to find Baby John standing at the rails, his face aflame through the wooden trestles. I rushed forward and pulled him out of the crib. He whimpered in my arms. I stared at him, horrified. Lily Joy never looked this afflicted, but the suddenness of the onslaught was the same. Babies apparently were stricken the hardest with this flu.

"You poor child," I whispered in his ear, and rocked him gently against me. "Everything will be better soon. Mommy promises."

I made a bed nest for him with a quilt on the living room floor, but he cried when I set him down. I carried him into the kitchen with me and paced the floor. The day's duties stared me in the face. I had two buckets of dirty diapers sitting in the basement, and the breakfast dishes were unwashed. Walter would bale hay this afternoon and needed my help. I could see him through the living room window come out of the barn door with his team, headed towards the fields. I hurried out of the front door, with Baby John still in my arms. Walter pulled back on the horse's reins.

"Whoa there," he called to his horses, appearing displeased.

I ignored the look. "The children are sick in the house. I thought you should know."

"They just have the flu," he said. "Lily Joy went to school I noticed."

"I know, but I think this might be something serious."

He frowned and looked at Baby John. "You're just worrying. He's tough and hardy like you are."

I didn't answer, and he jiggled the reins. The team stamped forward. I returned to the house. The upstairs was silent, so I climbed the steps and peeked into the bedroom. Their eyes are closed, their faces flushed. I touched their skin and pulled back my hand. Joy had not been this stricken. Something more was going on, and I needed help. Mamm might have some advice. She would come, if Mamm knew of my need. Daett might even consider coming along and helping Walter this afternoon in the hayfield. I felt desperation rise in me. I walked to the window to ponder my dilemma. With Walter's disapproval, I didn't dare hitch the horse to the buggy and drive out of the lane with three sick children inside. My actions would belie my serious assessment of the situation.

I would have to make the best of the situation, and Baby John would have to cry himself to sleep on a quilt while I worked. I went downstairs, my attention drawn to an automobile pulling into our driveway. Probably some salesman here to see Walter. He would have to find his way out to the fields.

I had turned away from the window when I noticed there was a child sitting on the front seat. I took Baby John with me for a better look. The sight of Lily Joy had me running out of the house and across the lawn.

"Mrs. Yoder," the man said in greeting.

"Yes."

"I'm Principal Wellborn. Mrs. Camille sent for me. Can I speak with you and your husband?"

"I'll go fetch him," I said.

"How are your other children?" he asked.

"Sick," I said.

"Hurry then." He looked angry.

"Go into the house and watch Elsie and Mary," I told Lily Joy.

I hurried across the barn yard with Baby John in my arms. In the distance, Walter had stopped the team and turned towards the house.

"What's going on?" he hollered, when I got close enough.

"Principal Wellborn brought Lily Joy home from school. He wouldn't tell me why."

"Meddling English people," he muttered and tied the team to a fence post.

I followed him back to the automobile, staying back a step. Baby John lay quiet in my arms.

"I have bad news for you," Principal Wellborn began. "Your daughter has diphtheria, as do the rest of your children, I assume. Thankfully, Mrs. Camille was on her toes this morning and knows more about this sickness than some people." Principal Wellborn's glare took in both of us.

Walter cleared his throat. "How do you know this? Mrs. Camille isn't a doctor."

"Mrs. Camille's a sharp woman, Mr. Yoder. We've sent for Dr. Whittaker. He'll be here before long and confirm the diagnosis. He'll also visit the other two Amish children who are down with this illness. What is wrong with you people, sending your children to school with diphtheria? Now the whole neighborhood has been exposed. This will not be looked upon kindly."

"I'm sorry. I'm to blame." I stepped forward. "Joy's fever was down this morning, and I thought she was getting better."

"I'll let the doctor explain things to you folks," he said. "I have other errands to run. Just listen to whatever instructions the doctor gives you."

"Of course." Walter agreed. "We have done the best we know with our children, and we have prayed. The Lord will be with us."

"One would hope." Principal Wellborn climbed back into his automobile and roared up the driveway.

"Diphtheria," Walter said. "Our children have diphtheria?"

"You should go get Mamm," I said.

I looked down at Baby John, and my legs went weak. I was certain of one thing. My sister brought this illness in from her world.

Walter headed across the yard back towards his team.

"Ask Daett to come along," I called after him.

He didn't answer and I returned to the house. I took a seat on the couch with Baby John in my lap. He was whimpering with his face buried in my chest when Walter drove past in his buggy. There was silence upstairs, where Lily Joy must be on watch beside her sisters' bed. The reality burned through me. Diphtheria! Fever, sore throat, blocked airways, a barking cough, and in severe cases, death.

I sat unmoving as the clock ticked on the wall. I had work which must be done. I tried to stand but sat down again at Baby John's anguished cry. The automobile chugged back into our driveway, and I went to the door. Principal Wellborn made the brisk introduction. Dr. Whittaker was the new doctor who tended to our area.

"Sorry to hear the news, Mrs. Yoder," he said.

"Do you think this is diphtheria?" I was grasping at straws.

"My opinion is, yes," he said, his bag spread out on the living room desk. "Teachers usually gets these things right." He motioned for me to come closer. "Let's start with this one."

Baby John turned his face away and I held his neck in place. Dr. Whittaker peered down the throat, his face grim. "Is this the first morning of his illness?"

"Yes."

"We'll have to move fast then. I already sent for the antitoxin, but we will need more. Are there other children in the house?"

"Three girls."

We moved upstairs with Baby John in my arms.

Lily Joy met us at the bedroom door, and I woke the two younger ones. Dr. Whitaker examined the girls then said, "All of your children are down with diphtheria, Mrs. Yoder. Aren't you people aware of the serious illness in this country. I'm sure Mrs. Camille mentioned the fact."

I winced at his sternness. "I'm sorry."

He grunted, packed up his bag and I walked with him to the door. I wished he would stay, as the darkness swirled around me. I felt helpless and alone. Mamm and Daett's buggy pulled into the driveway ten minutes later, and Mamm took charge in the house while Daett went out to help Walter in the fields. I stayed with Baby John, his condition worsening as the day progressed.

Lunch was quiet. I tried to eat, but couldn't swallow around the lump in my throat. Mamm managed a few bites. Dr. Whittaker returned and administered the medicine.

"I'll be by in the morning," he told me. "Just keep them comfortable. There is not much else you can do."

"Will the baby be okay?" I dared ask.

"We'll have to see," he said. "I'll be back this evening to check on the children."

Mamm stayed in the bedroom with me after Dr. Whittaker left.

"This is Lily's doing," I said, quite loudly. "She's jealous because I gave Walter a son which she couldn't give him."

"The children will hear you," Mamm warned.

"If anything happens to Baby John, I will …"

"Go do some work," Mamm said. "I'll watch the children."

I found my way to the darkness of the basement. The coolness soothed my burning body. I worked with great plunges of my arms across the washboard, turning the soiled diapers white again. My muscles cramped in my arms, and I paused to massage them. The emptiness where Baby John's head laid throbbed. The handwriting on the wall was there for me to see. Lily was taking my son.

The hours crept past and I worked, hanging out the diapers in the bright sunshine. They dried quickly. Mamm had Baby John laid on a blanket beside the stove, when I entered the house again. He was sleeping but his breathing was shallow. He awakened when I looked at him and whimpered. I gathered him in my arms and carried him with me while I checked on Elsie and Mary. They had flushed faces, but didn't fight for air like Baby John. Below me, I can hear Mamm in the kitchen beginning the supper preparations.

Walter and Daett ate when they came in from the fields, but I still couldn't swallow a bite. We gathered around the couch in the living room and Walter prayed for us. He beseeched mercy for the girls' sake but said nothing about Baby John.

"Lord help my son." I hollered towards the ceiling.

Walter's mouth gaped open, but he said nothing. Mamm left to work on the dishes, while Walter nestled the girls down on blankets beside the couch. I stayed on the rocker with Baby John, his head cradled on my shoulder.

Dr. Whittaker came again just before nine, his automobile lights bright in the driveway.

"I don't have good news for this one," he said of Baby John. "The others are doing okay, though. I don't dare give the baby more antitoxin. He's a big boy, so let's hope. The youngest usually take this the hardest."

There was no sleep as the night advanced. I paced the floor with Baby John until Mamm sent me into the bedroom for a few hours of rest. I drifted off to a storm of torment, wild wanderings in the night through forests of trees growing so close together I could barely slip between them. Above me, Dr. Whittaker's automobile lights played in the treetops, like ghostly movements of light.

Mamm awakened me with a shake of the shoulder. "Come. Baby John's getting worse."

I rushed out to the kitchen to find Walter with the child. The girls were sound asleep on the floor of the living room. Mamm had a fire burning in the stove, and a pot of water heating. We kept our voices down as we applied moist warm towels to Baby John's chest. Walter tried to help, but Mamm finally shooed him away. He sat on a kitchen chair with his head in his hands and watched us labor. Our best efforts failed. As the sun came up, Baby John breathed his last with a shudder through his whole body.

I stifled my cries with a warm towel stuffed into my mouth. Mamm took the body from my arms, and I raced out of the house, to run across the yard, and around the corner of the barn, before I wailed my agony to the open heavens. Walter found me there.

"How dare you come out now?" I shouted at him. "This is the hour of my greatest shame."

"You should not be carrying on like this," he said. "This is the Lord's will, and we must submit."

"You wouldn't say such things if Lily Joy had died from this awful sickness."

He hesitated a moment. "I would struggle, yes, but I would submit, as you will submit."

"I will bury my son," I said, "then I will have everything which belongs to my sister out of the house."

"We don't have anything of your sister's," he said.

"You have Lily Joy."

"She's my daughter." Walter had lowered his voice, trying for patience with me. "I'm disappointed in you, to say the least. You sound like an insane woman."

"Lily Joy is leaving my house after the funeral," I said. "She can go with my sister, or to one of your relatives who live out of the community, but she will not live in my house."

"You need to calm down," he said. "Other people have lost children. I can give you another son."

"Leave me, now!"

"Lily Joy is not going anywhere," he said.

"Then let me tell you what I will do." I lowered my voice. "I will spill the beans on the sordid details of my sister's birth. Tell the whole community who her father really is."

Disdain filled his face. "I know you hate your sister, but she's a shiny angel compared to your misdeeds."

"My sister was conceived by an English man," I said.

He didn't even hesitate. "You're lying."

"Do I lie?"

"Then you are insane," he said, but the shock registered in his face, along with the confusion, and the denial.

I turned my back on him. "Go inside and ask Mamm. If Lily Joy isn't gone after the funeral, I will expose your sweet, beautiful, pure little angel to the stark light of our world. You will be married into a family who never lives down their disgrace."

I heard him leave, and when silence returned, I screamed my agony towards the dawning horizon, and heaven answered not a word. I really didn't expect one.

Section Four—September 1925 to June 1926

LILY

Chapter 16

I stood looking out of Grandma's kitchen window, where low clouds scurried across the horizon with more following behind them. The morning had dawned blustery with a feeling of upheaval in the air. I had lingered at Grandma's house for two weeks already, following Grandpa's funeral. I was in no hurry to make the trip back to Aunt Maud's home in Richmond, Virginia where I had lived these past ten years. Mamm came across the fields to check on me almost every day, and sometimes twice. From her disapproving looks, she isn't happy I'm still here.

"You know she's in the Bann?" I heard Mamm whisper to Grandma, loud enough for me to hear.

"I'm too old for those things," Grandma replied.

Grandma ate with me at the kitchen table, after making sure there were no buggies pulled up in the driveway. There were obvious limits to Grandma's defiance, but she always did live a brave life at Grandpa's side bearing the disapproval of the community's opinion.

"How did he go?" I asked. "I mean, I know Grandpa died in his sleep."

"Peacefully," she said. "I heard no sound. I awoke, and he had a slight smile on his face, his eyes still open."

"What do you think he saw?"

"The promised land," she said.

"I think he saw the angels. The ones who came to carry him home."

She smiled. "Your Grandpa did awful things in war, but I never saw any of them in him. He was the kindest, most gentle man I ever knew. What a shame the community couldn't forget his past. Maud might have changed her mind if they had."

"Aunt Maud didn't come because she isn't well," I said.

Grandma clearly didn't believe me.

"I guess she wouldn't have come anyway." I admitted.

"Bitterness doesn't seem to have taken a hold of you," she said.

"I guess I had Grandpa."

"So did Maud, but the pressure became too much."

"I didn't want to leave," I said.

She didn't believe me, again.

Grandma was still asleep this morning in the main bedroom, and I lit the wood stove. I heated water in a bowl and poured in the oatmeal when the water boiled. This was the food of my childhood, a part of my earliest memories sitting at Mamm and Daett's table.

Now Walter belonged to my sister, to conniving, manipulating Barbara, who picked his grieving heart like one would take a ripe peach from a tree branch.

I added milk and brown sugar to my oatmeal bowl and sat down at the kitchen table. The stillness of the house hung heavy on my shoulders. I had become accustomed to the noise of the city. Aunt Maud would be at work this morning. She had several older women who filled in part time at the restaurant, so I was not placing an undue burden on her with my absence.

I paused and savored again the memory of Walter, standing just inside the front door when I walked in the first evening for the viewing. The look on his face brought my heart pounding to my throat. He remembered me. He remembered our times together. He remembered what we had been through. He had not forgotten our love. Walter was Barbara's husband, but she had not taken his heart from me.

I came close to stumbling over the couch in the living room. I could see anything but Walter's eyes, his immense sorrow written on every feature of his handsome face. They led me into the bedroom to view the body. They thought I was crying for Grandpa, and I was, but I was also crying for what once had been and no longer could be. For what was lost, for what we once held so tightly in our hands, and so close to our hearts.

I stood in front of the casket and whispered, "Grandpa."

I touched his kind, wrinkled face.

Walter wasn't in the living room when I left. He had fled to avoid seeing me again. I didn't blame him. Moses parted the waters of the red sea for the children of Israel to walk through, but no man on this earth could part the troubled waters between us. We couldn't flee from each other at the funeral in the morning, though. I was seated near the coffin, off to the side in a separate chair, but in plain sight of the men's section. Walter sat on the second bench, his blue eyes as blue as I have ever seen them. He seemed to have abandoned any effort to avoid me. I couldn't imagine Barbara gazing into his eyes as I did or feel the torrent of emotion ripping through my chest.

Walter made certain I was given a privileged place to stand near the open grave. Bishop Mast gave Walter a sharp look but said nothing when Walter returned to Barbara's side. She took Walter's arm, and managed to smile up at him. I made my escape back to Grandma's house the second the graveside service closed. The torture was useless, and yet here I was waiting. For what, I had no idea. Perhaps a few more days with Walter's closeness so near, and then I would return to my world and never come back.

"I am no longer Amish," I told my heart, who remained unconvinced.

I placed the frying pan on the stove, and pulled my thoughts back to the present, just as Grandma appeared in the kitchen doorway with a warm comforter wrapped around her shoulders.

"Making breakfast." Her lips parted in a smile which didn't reach her eyes. "Something smells good."

"Sit down. I'll have something ready soon."

"Oatmeal would be enough." She took in my bowl.

"Bacon and eggs will be ready in a minute," I said.

"You—uh—leaving today?"

"Maybe." Much as she cared about me, my presence was a burden she shouldn't have to bear.

Grandma stared out of the kitchen window. Tears dotted her cheeks. "I feel so lonely with him gone, especially mornings like this."

"I know," I said.

"I thought I saw him this morning lying beside me in bed, but he was gone the moment I reached over to touch him."

I walked over and gave her a hug. "I'm so sorry for your loss."

She smiled through her tears. "He loved you too."

"He did." The tears came to my eyes. "I could never thank him enough."

"I imagine he's happy this morning on those mountains in glory. I'm sure they are using him better than he was ever used down here."

"They are," I said. "Grandpa had such a kind heart."

I returned to my pan and dropped in the bacon. A sizzling filled the kitchen and occupied my attention.

"There's someone at the front door," Grandma said.

I startled, and the pan slid.

"Keep going." She motioned with her hand. "I'll answer."

She tottered out of the kitchen and I heard voices on the front porch.

"You had best sit down," Grandma said, when she returned.

"Why?"

She didn't answer, staring out of the window again.

I waited. Perhaps some community news, but I was no longer affected by community news.

"Barbara's son passed last night." She spoke abruptly, her voice disemboweled.

I gripped the edge of the counter. "Baby John?"

"Baby John," she said.

"I didn't know he was ill." The bacon burned to a crisp in front of me.

"Apparently, no one thought to inform us in the rush of things. Diphtheria struck the community last week."

"Barbara's going to blame me."

Grandma appeared not to hear. "I'm glad your Grandpa is there to greet Baby John. A child should awaken to a face they know."

The smell of the burning bacon captured my attention, and I yanked the pan from the stove. The meat was a total loss. I took out the pieces and forced myself to fry the eggs. We bowed our heads for a short prayer of thanks, and I pretended to eat. Nothing was going down my throat. Grandma ate the burnt bacon and I didn't protest.

"I'm glad you stayed," Grandma said.

"You want anything more for breakfast?"

She shook her head, and I helped her walk into the living room and settle on her rocker.

"We must see the body this afternoon," she said. "The family will gather."

I hesitated.

"You must come."

"Maybe," I said.

"Surely you're going to the funeral?"

"Depends."

She didn't press the issue, and I returned to the kitchen.

Chapter 17

Two days later, the upper barn loft was crowded, and rain lashed the wooden siding outside. Benches were set so close people's knees nearly touched the backs of those in front of them. I sat on a short bench along the back wall, with my legs tucked under me. I was the outcast, but I was there.

I caught Walter's eye across the crowded room. His face was full of pain and anger, and he looked away quickly. I wanted to scream into the crowded room. Had I lost him, after these long years? Stabs of pain went through my whole body.

Few people seemed to notice me, their attention focused on the small casket under the hay mow window. Everyone was in funeral clothes, and I wore my black Amish dress for the second time within three weeks. I shifted on the hard bench, as the first minister rose to speak. I knew him, an older man, Emmanuel Esh, who had been ordained since I could remember.

Minister Esh bowed his head for a few seconds before he looked up and began to speak. "My dearly beloved people, a great sorrow is laid upon us today. A child has been taken from our midst. I know this has been said before, but the Lord rebukes many for the sins of the few. This judgment has come to afflict our community. This is the truth which we must face. Yet Scripture tells us there is also the Lord's mercy. Today we must mourn with those who mourn, and not point the finger. Death is no stranger to any of us. My own wife passed away a few months ago. My heart weeps afresh this morning along with the bereaved, as do those who have not suffered such a loss. Together we can rise up and comfort this family. Let us put our arms around them and speak words of hope and blessings into their ears. The Lord's hand is still with us, even as his staff is upon us heavy with discipline. His judgment will guide us through this valley of sorrow and death and give us protection from evil. If we put the wicked ways of the enemy from us, and beseech the mercies of the Almighty, he will come and heal us. He is the Lord most high, the Holy One, the everlasting God of Israel. Blessed be his name, says the Psalmist, and worship him all the lands in the earth."

I listened, and I studied Minister Esh's face. I had not known his wife passed, but there would be no reason for anyone to tell me.

I looked at Lily Joy who sat on the front bench beside Walter. She gave me a smile, and I sent one back. The girl was so sweet, which was probably why Barbara disliked her. Barbara hated everything about me, and Lily Joy did bear my resemblance, and had Walter's affection. My heart throbbed with pain again. I should have followed Aunt Maud's example and stayed away from this place.

I distracted myself by looking further down the bench. Barbara's other two girls, Elsie and Mary, were not in attendance. They were still ill, as were many others from the community.

I returned my attention to the small casket, as Minister Esh finished speaking, and Bishop Mast stood to his feet.

"This is indeed a day of mourning and sadness," he began, "a day of clouds and rain. The weather outside reflects our hearts, which is how the Lord in his divine wisdom has decreed we should react. Deep sorrow grips us at this young life snatched so cruelly away from the arms of his parents, doomed because of the sins of others. Death is a great enemy, and a terrible avenger in the hands of the Lord. We tremble when innocence is cut down before a baby has time to take more than a few breaths. This child, this promise given to us, this first son of his Daett, a precious child in the eyes of a man, has fallen, has been wrenched away from the arms of those who loved him. Oh death, how cruel, the grave a darkness we cannot comprehend, and the wickedness of man without boundaries."

Bishop Mast's gaze swept over the packed room. "We bury a child today who never grew into adulthood. He never learned to run, or play at school, or listen to the voice of the Lord. He never became a young man who took a wife and bore children with her. Baby John never grew old in this world. We know in heaven he will always be young and fair, nestled in the arms of the Lord. We must not forget, and we must not forget our duty, our need to search our hearts, to find repentance after this tragedy has been visited upon God's people."

Bishop Mast lowered his voice. "I know this is not the only home in which this sickness has come. Tomorrow we bury another one of our precious innocent ones. We must ask the question, even if the answer tears at our hearts. Have we all sinned, as some among us have sinned? We know the world always sins around us, but this is not the plan for the people of God. We must ask. How has calamity been allowed to pass through our doors? Have our hearts strayed from the holy will of the Lord? Have we taken thoughts into our minds which are against his commandments? We must ask, and we must find the answers. We must cleanse ourselves. The world suffers and they continue in their suffering, because they do not ask why. We must not be like the world. We must profit from the smiting of the Lord's hand."

Bishop Mast's gaze was fixed on Lily Joy. "There are even those among us who carry with them the smell of the world. We must take this opportunity to send the world back with those who have rebelled against the Lord and against his Church."

I turned my head. Lily Joy was an angel, innocent and pure as the sun in the morning sky. Had the community found another target for their anger? I clasped my hands together and didn't move.

The sermon finally concluded, but I remained seated on my small bench, until the last person had been past the casket. Grandma came for me and we took our turn in front of the still body. The baby's face was small and white, a handsome boy like his father. I lingered, until Grandma tugged on my arm. We moved outside. Grandma let go, and I helped her climb into the back of a buggy. The line of buggies lurched forward to creep along the edge of the road. The graveyard appeared ahead of us, the stones silhouetted in the distance. I pulled up to a fence post along the ditch line and climbed out to help Grandma down. We gathered again by the grave, an open wound gaping towards the heavens. Bishop Mast spoke, his voice rising and falling in the open air. I willed the words to silence and heard nothing. Bishop Mast finished, and men lowered the casket then took turns shoveling in the dirt.

Walter stood there, straight as a ramrod. Barbara was crying into her handkerchief and ignoring him. I focused on the shovels rising and falling in the still air. Soon the mound of dirt rose high above the grass. Grandma led the way back to the buggy. The horse was untied and the clopping back towards Walter's place for the meal began. I should have fled over to Grandma's place, but I didn't. Instead, a small table was set up for me in the corner of the living room. I filled my plate, ignored the table, and went out on the front porch swing to eat. The young girls hanging on the chains, saw me coming and ran into the yard to play. I sat as a pariah, the outcast with no shame left. The front door squeaked. Lily Joy peeked out. She smiled and joined me on the swing.

"Hi." I gave her a warm smile.

She wiggled beside me. "I'm sorry you had to sit by yourself in church again."

I slipped my arm around her. "I'm sorry about your brother's passing."

"I'm too," she said, and the tears shimmered. "He was a sweet baby."

We sat in silence, contemplating the horizon.

"Baby John is in heaven," she said. "Things are much better up there, although down here is also nice."

I pulled her close. "It is, sweetheart."

She looked up at me. "Mamm says I am to leave with you tomorrow."

I stared, speechless. What was the child saying?

She didn't seem to notice. "I like my home here with Daett and Mamm, but I suppose living with you would also be nice. Mamm says so."

I still couldn't find words. Had my sister lost her mind?

"Do you live far away?" she asked.

"A little way." The words came out, but I still wasn't understanding.

"How do we get there?"

"By train. Do you want to live with me?" I might as well play along. If Barbara had fed her these things, my correcting her would do no good.

"You're my aunt." She smiled. "I like you."

A lump formed in my throat. The child sounded totally sincere. I stuck the food with my fork repeatedly, and finally got a bite to my mouth. I chewed slowly.

"You're not eating much." Lily Joy stated the obvious. "Shouldn't you get your own food?"

"I already ate, and I have my suitcase packed. I'm to come over to Grandma's to spend the night with you."

"I don't have to leave tomorrow," I said. My head was still spinning.

"Mamm said you did."

"What else did your Mamm say?" I tried another tack.

The shoulders came up again. "Not much. I'm to live with you for a while. Will there be a school for me to attend? I like school."

"There's one, I'm sure," I said. "Aunt Maud will know."

"I've never met Aunt Maud. Is she one of your Mamm's sisters?"

I nodded. "Aunt Maud will be very happy to see you." I hoped I wasn't lying.

She retreated into the house, and Grandma came out to leave again. I confronted her in the buggy. "What is going on with Lily Joy being sent off with me? She's eight years old!"

"I don't know," Grandma said, driving out of the lane. "But Walter said he's coming over tonight."

I fell silent, and Walter did come. I waited until he was on the porch before I went to the door. He had a small suitcase in one hand, and Lily Joy in the other.

We gazed at each other for a long time.

"Lily," he finally said. "How good to see you."

"Why are you here?"

"Go inside." Walter motioned for Lily Joy to enter the house.

"Grandma will take care of you until I come in." I gave her a hug and closed the door behind her.

We sat on chairs across from each other. "What's going on, Walter?"

"Why did you leave without a goodbye?" he asked. "I have the right to an answer."

"There is no use explaining," I said.

"Were you pretending you loved me? Those years we had—those sweet times we had together?"

"No."

"Then why?"

"I tried to explain once upon a time. Now it is too late. You would have made me right, Walter."

"How?"

"Your love would have driven away my darkness," I said. "We had to marry. I couldn't wait."

"I don't understand." He sighed. "I guess I never will, but will you help me now? Take Lily Joy for a while?"

"Where is this coming from?"

He appeared not to hear me. "I have to let things cool off at home with Barbara, but this may work out for the best. This is your way back. You can repent and join the community again."

"Why would I want to?"

He looked at me. "You can't be happy out there. I want you here."

"I still wouldn't be married to you."

"I know," he said, "but you would be here, and they will accept you if you marry someone else. We would be near each other, as near as we apparently ever could have been—at least with the community's approval."

"I can't come back," I said. "Tell me more about why I'm to take Lily Joy."

"There's great bitterness between Barbara and me over our children. With Baby John dead, Barbara wants the girl out of the house."

"Why have you nothing to say about this?"

"Barbara tells me if I do not agree she will spread about your family's secret."

He noticed my struggle for breath.

"I'm not trying to shame you about your birth, Lily. Nothing changes for me, but I don't want this thrown on top of everything else you have endured."

"My birth?" The air came back into me with a gasp.

"You don't know."

"I don't know anything about my birth."

"You don't have to know."

"Tell me, Walter!"

He hesitated for a moment. "Your Daett is an English man. Your Mamm had an affair one summer with a garden customer."

"Are you sure?"

He looked away. "Sorry to be the one who breaks the news."

I felt nothing but intense relief. He didn't know about— "I guess this explains why we never sold produce from our garden."

"Now you know," he said, "but this need go no further."

"I don't care," I said, "Barbara can say what she wishes."

"But I care," he said. "Like I said, this may turn out for the best. Lily Joy is all I have of you. Barbara will send her off to some other relative if you don't take her. If you do, you can also bring her back. I will have you both, or have you as close as I can have you."

"Why are you settling for this, when—?"

"I know." Pain filled his eyes. "I'm so sorry for my failures, but I'm still a selfish man. I want you near me."

"What makes you think I will return?"

"You will," he said, "because we belong together. Nothing can change what was meant to be."

I leaned forward. "Walter, listen to yourself. You speak nonsense. I'm shattered. We are shattered. We can never be un-shattered."

"We can try," he said.

"I'm through trying. You could have made me right once. You still can, if you leave with me."

Torment filled his face. "I promised you and I failed. Breaking more promises will not help either of us."

"Sorry." I covered my face with my hands. "I know you can't."

"I can't," he agreed, "but I will always love you."

"You don't love Barbara, do you?"

He appeared startled. "Your sister doesn't require such a thing."

"My sister is lying."

"Barbara doesn't lie," he said. "Nothing in heaven or earth can undo what I did."

In desperation I tried again. "In my world, it can."

"You are not from out there. I know you better, Lily."

"Maybe I always was from out there."

"You're not," he said.

I let the sound of his voice soak through me. "Is Barbara kind to you?"

"She takes care of me."

"I would have loved you, Walter. There is a difference."

"Barbara does in her own way," he said.

"You know what love is. I offered you my love."

He stood to his feet. "I will write and stay in touch about Lily Joy. I pray the day will come soon when you can return together."

With his shoulders slumped and his head bowed, he made his way back to the buggy. I dug my fingers into the palms of my hand. I wanted to run after him, and drag him away from this place, to a land where we could be together, but I didn't. I stood and watched the last of his buggy lights disappear into the darkness as if they had been swallowed up and never existed. I bent down and picked up the small suitcase. The weight was light. Barbara obviously hadn't sent much. She wanted me to quickly make Lily Joy a person of my world. My sister was wicked. We were both wicked, but she had Walter and I had nothing.

Chapter 18

The following day the train blasted eastward, the steady rattle of the tracks brought sleep and stirred the mind to irreconcilable conundrums at the same time. I sat unmoving; my eyes fixed on Lily Joy's small form. The girl was beautiful, her arms willowy, and folded tightly in her lap while she slept. There should be complaints coming from her, after being sent off with strange relatives, but there was only resignation written on her face, underlined by a deep weariness. She hid her sorrow well when awake.

I looked away as the thought crossed my mind. The girl was suffering enough, and I hated to broach the subject, but something must be done about Lily Joy's clothing before we arrived at Aunt Maud's place. My aunt's hostility towards the community went deep. I was bringing a child of the community to live in her house. If Lily Joy arrived dressed in English clothing, the shock would be blunted.

Across from me, Lily Joy stirred in her sleep.

I leaned over to touch her arm and whispered, "Sweetheart."

The eyes opened instantly.

"How are you doing?"

"Okay." She tried to smile. "I must have been sleeping."

I took a deep breath. "As you know we are going to my Aunt Maud's to live. You've never seen my aunt, but she's a very nice person."

The sober look didn't leave her face.

"This will be another world for you." I plunged on. "A different world, but—"

"I understand," she said.

"Life will be very different."

"You live in the English world," she said.

"Yes, English. We wear different clothing, and—"

"You're still dressed Amish."

"I haven't changed yet, but I will soon. Would you wear English clothing if I bought some?"

The conflict showed in her face, but she nodded solemnly.

I reached over to hug her, and she clung to me. I expected sobs, but none came.

"I'm so sorry about this," I whispered.

"I don't blame you."

"And another thing," I said. "What if we begin calling you Joy, without the Lily in front? I'm also Lily. Simply Joy would be less confusing."

"Fine." She brought up a big smile from somewhere.

"You're such a sweetheart." I gave her another hug. "Aunt Maud will love you."

She said nothing, her gaze fixed out the window at the passing landscape.

"You started school this fall, didn't you?" I stated more than asked.

"I love school," she said.

"We'll get you enrolled at once when we get to Richmond, Virginia. Aunt Maud will help us."

Her gaze was steady out of the train window. I held her close. Her small frame shivered. "Mamm let me go back to school the day Baby John died."

"Baby John's death was not your fault, sweetheart."

"Maybe I should have stayed home and taken care of him."

"Did your Mamm say Baby John's death was your fault?"

She shook her head.

"Do you like my Daett?" she finally asked.

"He's a wonderful man," I said. "He had a wonderful little girl—you."

"Do you think I will like your world?"

"I don't know. I like where I live." I wondered if I was lying, if Walter was right? I almost wished he would be.

"Then I will like living with you." She put on a brave face.

She leaned into me and slept again. I ran my hand over her forehead and tucked the strands of hair under the white head covering. I gathered my courage and loosened the pins to slip off the cloth. I undid the hair ball and brushed the long hair free with my fingertips. She muttered and awakened. Joy's hand searched her head and came up empty.

I waited for the protest, but none came. Joy laid her head back on my shoulder and closed her eyes. I pressed back the tears, as we slowed for a small-town station. The clatter of the tracks ended with a leap backwards at the stop.

I took Joy's hand. "Shall we peek out the window?"

The town was small, with horse traffic moving through the streets, and the occasional automobile chugging along. We kept watch as the train rattled and moved forward again.

We soon left for the dining room. Eating was a distraction, but the questions hung in the air. I didn't know how to answer them. I was doing this for Walter—for myself, but I couldn't tell Joy.

We returned to our seats, and she mercifully fell asleep until we pulled into the Washington, DC, station. We stepped outside, the station a frame of roof and steel stretching overhead. The blast of the train engines filled our ears as I led Joy forward. She stumbled, caught off balance by the step downward. She laughed and righted herself, but her face could not hide the pain.

Anger rose inside me at my sister, at her conniving, manipulating ways. The Lord had given her a beautiful child, and Barbara had thrown the gift out of her house.

I set the suitcase down, once we cleared the station, and flagged a carriage. Joy tossed in her satchel and hopped in without my assistance.

"Where to?" The driver asked.

I gave him the address of the hotel, and the lurch forward came quickly. We clung to our seats, our luggage behind us.

Joy stared at the passing streets; at the clutter, at the high red brick buildings reaching skyward, and the clouds above us scurrying past and soon gone.

"I have never seen a city before," she mused.

I didn't ask if she liked the city. I already knew the answer. We settled in for the night and went shopping the next day. I bought clothes, and back at the hotel, Joy didn't object when I dressed her in English clothing for the first time.

Joy wanted to see herself in the mirror. I stood behind her while she contemplated herself. "I look English."

"You're still the same girl." I tried to comfort. "Only the outside has changed."

Joy didn't appear persuaded, but she forced a smile. We ate in the cafeteria downstairs and settled in for the night. Joy lay on the bed with her eyes closed, but neither of us fell asleep for a long time. I dozed off first, and she was crying when I woke, the streetlights dim in the windows. I held still, and the weeping went on for a long time, before she turned over and pulled a pillow over her head. I pretended to awaken, but she had fallen asleep.

We took the train out in the morning, and by noontime arrived in Richmond, Virginia. Another carriage took us to the apartment, which was empty this time of the day. The hinges squeaked as I opened the door.

"Is this your home?" Joy asked.

"Yes. Aunt Maud and I live up there." I pointed towards the stairs rising before us. Joy went first, her small satchel in both hands. I followed and found the girl on the landing, unmoving.

"Where is your Aunt Maud?" she asked.

"At the restaurant. We'll go down once we're settled in."

"Where am I sleeping?"

I led the way to my room, where the large bed filled the center across from the window. "We're sleeping there."

"I'll make a little nest with blankets." Joy pointed. "Over there under the window."

"I want you comfortable, sweetheart. You can sleep with me."

"I'll like the bed down there," she said. "This is a little like the window at home."

"Okay then." I gave in quickly. "You can put your things in the closet."

"I can keep my Amish things in the satchel." She offered.

I nodded. Better if Aunt Maud never laid eyes on Amish dresses. I checked the time on the kitchen wall. Three o'clock. There was time to help with the evening crowd if we left soon. I waited while Joy settled down in the bedroom. When I peeked in, she was standing in front of the closet door, her satchel on the floor in front of her, and holding one of her Amish dresses. I retreated to wait ten minutes or so before I approached again, making sure my footsteps made noise this time. "We need to meet Aunt Maud at the restaurant."

Her face was tearstained when she turned around, but she followed me out of the bedroom without protest. We walked the three blocks to Lafayette Street, the upscale buildings which also housed Aunt Maud restaurant. The place served some of Richmond's oldest families and drew businessmen from across the city.

Joy stared as we entered the double doors. A few customers sat at the tables but paid us scant attention. I clutched Joy's hand to lead her into the kitchen.

Aunt Maud was waving her hands about, lecturing the cook. "You should know this customer by now, George. She's Mrs. Emmett who stops in every time she's in town, especially for our mashed potatoes. She's due in tonight, and this dish is a disgrace. The potatoes taste like plastic. I want them whipped up until they are frothy, with just a touch of cream. Get this done at once."

"Yes, ma'am," George muttered.

I stepped forward, and Aunt Maud noticed me. "Lily, you're back. I was beginning to think you had stayed."

"You know I wouldn't." I cleared my throat.

"And this would be Lily Joy?" Aunt Maud's gaze traveled up and down Joy's attire, and to my relief no displeasure showed. She opened her arms, and Joy hurried into them for a hug.

So far so good.

"You have a very beautiful restaurant here," Joy said.

Aunt Maud couldn't have looked more pleased. "Thanks, child. Can you cook?"

"A little."

Aunt Maud clucked her tongue. "I was teasing. You're very welcome here."

Joy smiled. "Thank you."

"Let me take care of the potatoes tonight," I told George, who was diligently peeling a fresh batch of potatoes at the table.

"Thank you, ma'am." Relief swept his face. "You know I try, but your version of mashed potatoes is a difficult task to master."

"You'll learn eventually." I comforted. "If an Amish woman can make mashed potatoes, you southern cooks should be up to the task."

"Yes, ma'am." George's face was pained again.

"Joy can help peel the potatoes." I offered.

"As you wish, ma'am." George made room at the table, and Joy hopped up to sit beside him. He handed her a peeling knife, and Joy went to work without further ado.

Aunt Maud motioned me towards the back of the room. "You want to fill me in on the details of why this girl was sent back with you?"

"Community troubles," I said.

"Is she your sister's girl?"

"Yes."

"She looks like you."

I gave her a glare. "Lily Joy is eight, and I've been here for ten years."

"Just checking." Aunt Maud smiled. "I'm fine with her staying."

"Thank you."

"You're welcome. Now for my confession. I went to the doctor while you were gone. The cancer is back and quite advanced. Too late for an operation."

I stifled my gasp.

"I'm dying," she said. "Let's not have drama."

I attempted valiantly to collect myself. "How long are they giving you?"

"No one knows, but I've begun arrangements to sell the restaurant, so don't worry. You can have the money, work here if you wish, travel the world, return home to the community. What I have is due to my father."

I was having trouble breathing.

"Your Grandpa supported me those first years. I wouldn't have made it any other way, so don't object."

"Why did you not go to the doctor sooner?"

"The early diagnosis would have made no difference."

"I don't want to lose you," I whispered. "I can't lose you."

Aunt Maud moved away without answering, waving her arms at George who had set up at another table. "Mrs.

Emmett will be here in an hour, and I want the bread made to perfection."

I forced my feet to move. I had to get the potatoes on the stove.

"What's wrong?" Joy asked.

I shook my head, but I couldn't stop the tears. Joy patted my arm, and asked no further questions, as if she knew the answers had been exhausted for the night.

Chapter 19

The red brick school building towered above me, the street cluttered with debris and carriages. The distant drone of voices hung in the background, drowned out by the clanging of the passing streetcar. I slipped inside the courtyard and stood unmoving in the shadows of the columns. This was where Joy had gone to school since her arrival in September of last year. I walked the streets from the apartment with Joy, whenever possible. Today, I had begged off early from my waitress duties at the restaurant. The new owners gave their permission without a fuss. I hurried and managed to arrive before three thirty when school lets out, and the children spilled out of the doors. I needed a distraction from the grief which still gripped my heart at unexpected moments. Aunt Maud had left us last month, buried in the Riverview Cemetery. I was alone in the city with Joy, and neither of us was happy with our lot in life.

I focused on the children flooding out of the school yard. Joy would be among the others, but there was always something different about her, something in the way Joy walked and held herself, in the look of maturity on her face. She came from another world. She had grown since her arrival in the city. Her slender body stretched higher with each passing month. I waved when I caught a glimpse of Joy's face. The head bobbed above the others for a moment then was lost in the crowd. The mass of little ones moved past me as I waited until Joy reappeared with her arms outstretched. We embraced and clung to each other for a long time.

"You came," she said. Her face looked up at me. "How are you doing?"

"Okay. My boss let me off early, but I have to put in extra hours tomorrow night." I gave the slender shoulders a quick squeeze. "You'll be alone until midnight."

"I'm okay." The answer came quickly.

"Should I take you shopping today, maybe for a new dress?"

"I'm fine with what I have," she said.

I fell silent. The loneliness of the city gripped us. With Aunt Maud gone, everything had changed. I had begun to suspect Joy would never succeed in her efforts to adjust. I held her hand, and we set out, dodging carriages and the occasional chugging automobile. We crossed the street with the press of the crowd on either side of us. Joy pulled out the key I had given her well before we arrived at the apartment and unlocked the door. She grabbed the mail, a single envelope with a familiar postmark.

"Daett!" Her hand held the item high.

"Come." I took the envelope. "Let's read this, and then, we should talk."

We climbed the stairs together and seated ourselves at the table. I tore open the top and unfolded the page. Walter's strong handwriting with the rising loops on his letters had become familiar to me. I lingered a second on the sight before I handed the paper to Joy.

She read out loud, "Dear Lily Joy,

Greetings from home. Summer is almost upon us, with a beautiful spring just past. I miss you as terribly as always. I think I hear your footsteps in the kitchen sometimes, but I know I'm imagining things. You're far away, but in good care. I comfort myself with the thought.

Here in the community, the diphtheria epidemic is long over, stomped out in part by the diligent efforts of Dr. Whitaker who has been tireless in treating our sick children. The tragedy is, three of the community's children died before this could be done, but the Lord knows best, and we should not complain, much as I miss my son.

I pray each day you might be restored to our family. I hope you bear no bitterness in your heart against us. There are things happening in the community which you're too young to understand, but which affected you unfairly. I want to assure you of my love, and even of your Mamm's love.

I'm sorry to hear of your great Aunt Maud's passing. I never met her, but I'm sure she was a lovely woman, who was kind enough to take you into her home, along with your Aunt Lily, of course. Please tell Aunt Lily if there is any chance things have changed since your great Aunt Maud's passing, I greatly long for both of your returns to the community. Tell her I know nothing can be made completely right between us, but I feel things could be made much better than they currently are. I would welcome you and your aunt back to the community. I pray this will be the Lord's will, as I long to see both of you again."

Joy paused in her reading and looked up at me.
I wiped away the tears. "Go on."
Joy continued.

The breath of late spring is in the air. There is a last lingering coolness early in the morning when I go out to begin the chores. The stars are so bright in the sky, like a million twinkling dots of lights. Remember last year when you got up extra early and were waiting for me on the front porch? The stars were out in their full glory. You wanted to help with my chores, but Mamm couldn't spare you from the breakfast preparations. At least I got to hold you close for a few moments with the day dawning around us. I imagined you were with me the other morning, when the stars were bright. I could almost feel your hand in mine and see your beautiful smile in the dim morning light. I love you so much, Lily Joy, even if we can't be together.

Your Daett, Walter."

Joy laid down the letter, her gaze fixed on the far wall.

"We should make supper," I finally said.

I had come past the market last night on the way home from work, so there was plenty of food in the house. We worked quietly, side-by-side, our faces intent. We made fried potatoes, corn on the cob, green beans, tossed salad, and had donuts rising while we ate the first course.

The fat was heated by the time we finished, and we managed to laugh while we dunked the donuts. Outside our apartment window was the usual street clatter, the unceasing traffic, and the smells. Inside, we could feel the emptiness of Aunt Maud's presence. I glanced at Joy's face. The sorrow was written there, ever plainer with each passing day. I would not succeed in removing the influence of the community from Joy's heart. She might look like me, but Joy was not me. I had tried and I had failed, as Walter knew I would. Joy would succeed in the community if I helped her. Walter could fully be Joy's father, even if he could never fully love me. I would have to settle for second best.

We made frosting for the donuts, the page to the cookbook open in front of us. I measured, and Joy stirred the ingredients. We dipped together, one on either side of the bowl, and ate with fingers dripping the delicious whiteness, the gooey goodness melting in our mouths. We laughed and forgot our sorrows for a moment.

We cleaned up afterwards, moving slowly, taking our time, talking in low tones about nothing in particular until sleepiness arrived, and I tucked the slim form under the covers. Sadness crept across her face as Joy slept.

I slipped back into the living room and gathered up pen and paper. I sat and wrote, "Dear Walter,

We received your letter today, and I had Joy read the pages aloud. Thanks for every word you write to your daughter. She lives for news from you and the community. Our hearts are like each other in so many ways, yet I have failed. There is hope though for Joy, and through her, perhaps for me. You knew this well before I did. Which means you have faith in me? Perhaps your heart even believes there is goodness left in me. Do I dare hope? Even if I can never have you as my husband, knowing I still have a small place in your heart where real affection for me can exist would be a great comfort.

Joy must come home. I am convinced of this, and I must do what must be done. The girl pines for you and the things she has lost. She is wasting away here in the city yet is not complaining. How golden her heart is. She's trying to do what is right. I can't take her suffering anymore. I could bring her back and leave her with you, which we both know wouldn't work. Which leaves us with the option you proposed before I left. Perhaps the time has come to make peace with the community in the way the community wants.

I sit here thinking about the matter. I could say I want to come back, but I don't really when I know what my arrival will mean. There were too many years of dreaming of the day when I would be in your arms. If the choice was up to me, I would choose this loneliness, this hopelessness, rather than face the agony of letting go of the memory we had. I cannot seem to dissuade my heart from believing we belong together. You're married to my sister. I say the words to myself, but Barbara married to you is not the same as me married to another Amish man. The thought brings me awake at night with a cry of alarm. There was but one man I needed, and I was found unworthy. Yet there is Joy, and her life. I have to remind myself that everything has been taken from me, the cupboards are bare, my heart is empty of everything but the longings. Perhaps the pain would be less if I lived close to you, even in the same district? If I saw you each Sunday? Would another man know where my heart belonged? Would he care? Barbara once said sarcastically in reference to you and me, 'a man can ignore much for a beautiful woman.' She may have been right. I almost hope she was.

I must say the bitterness in my heart towards my sister concerns me at times. Perhaps another reason to consider my return and eventual marriage to a community man—peace between Barbara and me. Barbara would be overjoyed to see me safely in the bed of an older Amish man, or any man but you. She would consider the cord which binds my heart to yours severed for eternity. Barbara is wrong. I feel certain enough to take the risk and return. I would do anything to have you, but I know the impossibilities of our situation, so perhaps I can do what is right for Joy at least?

As always, with all my love,

Lily.

Walter's letter arrived two weeks later, full of breezy pages for Joy, and a sealed note for me. "Bring Joy home," he said. "I will clear the matter with Bishop Mast before you arrive, and you will be accepted back into the community. What Barbara thinks, I don't care."

We paid a visit to Mrs. Emmett the following weekend at her home outside Amelia Courthouse, and told her of our plans to return to the community. Mrs. Emmett responded by inviting her nephew Robert for supper the next evening. Her last-ditch attempt to bond us, I suspected. Robert spoke little during the meal eaten at the formal dining room table and left the minute he finished eating.

Mrs. Emmett frowned at his back, before she turned to me. "When are you leaving for the community?"

"In a few weeks," I said. "Joy can't wait."

"If you ever decide to return and want out of the city, my home is open to you."

"How kind of you," I said, "but I don't think I'm returning."

"Remember you're welcome." She sent a quick glance towards the door through which Robert had departed.

Why did everyone see me as belonging in the arms of some man? While the man I wanted I couldn't have.

We sat up late on Mrs. Emmett's back porch, listening to the cricket's chirp in the fields below the mansion, and the fireflies flicker on the lawn.

"This is like home," Joy said.

"I know," I replied, but I didn't speak the truth. There was no Walter and no community. There was the resemblance without the soul of the matter.

"Shall we settle down for the night?" I asked.

Joy stood to her feet and followed me into the bedroom without protest. We dropped off to sleep quickly and left for Richmond in the morning. Mrs. Emmett had Robert drop us off at the train station in the buggy carriage. He was as uncommunicative as he had been the evening before.

Robert unloaded our suitcases, nodded, and drove away.

"He's a nice man," Joy said, but her eyes had a faraway look in them.

She was thinking what I was thinking. We would soon be being seeing Walter.

.

Chapter 20

The carriage rocked on the dirt road pocked with ruts the driver made no attempt to dodge. I assumed the potholes had been freshly filled with water from an early summer shower. Ten minutes into our drive, the town houses around the train station had given way to open fields of planted corn. The stalks were hand high in places, the leaves reaching for the heavens.

I steadied myself on the carriage seat and looked down on Joy's rapturous face.

"We're almost home," she whispered.

"We are," I agreed and looked away.

A vision of Minister Esh preaching at Grandpa's funeral flickered in front of me. I could see each line on his weather-beaten face, the long sweep of his graying beard down his chest. The scene changed and I could see him in the buggy seat beside me, in the place where Walter was seated for so many years. The ministers knew I was returning to the community. Walter wrote after speaking with Bishop Mast, the letter arriving two days before we left. The Amish ministers were willing, and Minister Esh was willing. His home had been empty for too long, the letter said. Minister Esh meant his bed, but no one put such things on paper. I told myself I didn't care. A man was a man, if he was not Walter. This would be legal at least and serve a purpose.

"The men are working in the fields," Joy said.

I tried to compose myself as we passed an Amish man with two horses hitched to his wagon. He had been in the same group of Amish young people I grew up with. He waved, and Joy leaned out of the carriage to wave back.

I couldn't tell from the look on his face if he recognized us. I would have dressed Joy this morning in one of the two Amish dresses Barbara packed for Joy before we left the community, but they no longer fit. I was wearing my plainest English dress, but I still looked English. Everything not made with Amish hands was English in this community. Which included me. Walter had claimed I had been birthed from an English man's unholy union with my Mamm. Barbara wouldn't make the claim, unless she had the truth on her side. My sister always had her facts straight. I wondered if Minister Esh would be told? Not likely.

Joy was studying each passing home, waving when a face appeared in the window, oblivious to my internal turmoil. This was home to her, the place of happy childhood memories, of young years lived in bliss, comfort, and safety. Death had disrupted Joy's life and cast her adrift. The dark specter had brought immense suffering to her young heart, and yet Joy had remained sweet and kind. I couldn't say the same for myself. Death had not been my enemy. What had come in his place had stolen my innocence, deadened my dreams, and stifled my delight in life with a grip I couldn't loosen. The least I could do was assist Joy in attaining what measure lay within her reach.

"Are you happy to be home?" I asked, already knowing the answer.

Her words startled me. "Are you?"

I lied. "Of course." Had not Joy pretended for almost a year while she lived with me?

The carriage bounced through a rut on the road, and we held on to our seats. Both of us fell silent as the familiar sights increased. These were homesteads we both knew, the countdown repeating itself for me from two years ago. When we approached the old home place, Jonas appeared in his barn door, his beard parted in the wind, his hair white and long over the ears.

"Grandpa!" Joy leaned out of the carriage door and waved with both hands.

The distant figure raised one hand in greeting and shaded his eyes with the other.

"Grandpa," Joy repeated. "He likes me."

"I know." I held the girl's hand. "I'm glad he likes you."

She wiggled away and continued to gaze at the retreating figure. What I saw was the faded paint on the barn wall which rose high above Jonas, the red chipped away in spots, the rough sawn boards exposed beneath. How little the young knew of the world. Enough for them that the sun rose and set at the proper time. A great longing swept over me. The desire ached with a furious intensity—for the days of hay tickles in my hair, the feel of my back pressed against the softness of a hay mound, and the sound of soft footsteps from the boy I loved so desperately. Those days were no more, and never could be again. The task fell to the young to carry on, to dream once more, and to hope if they could. They did not know enough to imagine the road might end in shadows, the day in storms, or the heart torn by the wind, against which there was no strength to resist.

If Joy was to succeed, the poison from my past must not pollute her present. I would not destroy innocence, or clip Joy's bud before the blooming. I would give and not take. This would be my redemption.

We were coming up on our homestead, and Mamm was standing at the hitching post with her horse and buggy ready. My original plans had been to arrive at Grandma's place, but Mamm had insisted in a letter I come here first.

The carriage slowed, and we came to a halt near the buggy. I climbed out to pay the driver. Once he was gone, the barn door opened behind me. Daett came out. I froze. This was the reason Mamm had insisted I come here first. Daett wanted to speak with me.

"Lily," he said. "Did you have a good trip?"

Joy gave him a hug, but I stayed silent by our suitcases.

Daett came closer. "I need to speak with you."

"I'm not speaking with you," I said.

"Come out to the barn." He motioned over his shoulder. I didn't move.

"Take Lily Joy to the house," Daett ordered, and Mamm scurried away with Joy in tow.

"Leave me alone," I said.

"Why are you here?" He studied me carefully.

"You know why I'm here."

"How would I know?"

"I'm not explaining myself."

"Are you finally going to redeem yourself?"

"You made me what I am."

"I did not," he said. "Your Mamm did."

I knew for certain from his words—Barbara had her facts straight. I glared at him. "Why are you objecting to my homecoming? Isn't this what you wanted before I left?"

"I did," he said, "and I'm glad if those are your plans."

"I just told you."

"You can't have Walter," he said.

"Do you fear your sins will see the light of day?"

"I saved you from the world, didn't I? Look at you! You're here ready to marry a proper Amish husband. Left to yourself you would have destroyed Walter's life along with your own."

"Can't you be a little sorry for what you did? For the mess you made out of my life, and Walter's?"

"Your Mamm made the mess, I fixed the problem."

"You used me," I said. "You took advantage of a helpless girl. You should be shamed and excommunicated by the community for the rest of your life."

"You know the community doesn't agree."

"Then why are you afraid?"

He turned on his heels, and I stared after him for a long time. I wanted to run away and never come back. I wanted to leave this world forever, but I knew I couldn't. The ache, the terror, would only follow me. I must make my peace, somehow, somewhere, and with Walter's help. He was on my side again.

Mamm's voice broke into my thoughts. "You're finished talking with Daett."

"I was finished with him a long time ago," I whispered.

Mamm didn't answer as she helped Joy into the buggy. We lurched out of the driveway and onto County Road 1200, going in the opposite direction from where we had come.

"I want to visit Grandpa's grave," I said.

Mamm turned the horse towards the south at the next crossroads without protest. We clopped along in silence. Joy was watching the passing homes again but saying nothing. We tied the horse to the fence row when we arrived and walked across the grass to the mound at the end of the graveyard. Mamm stayed back, holding Joy's hand, while I knelt at the head of grave. No flowers adorned the length of broken ground. Such things were forbidden by the community. The only color was the faint purple of a creeping thistle in the undergrowth. The single head reached towards the heavens and would be cut when the grass was mown next, but for now stood like I did, my existence a bold defiance to bishops and deacons.

"Grandpa," I whispered. "I'm trying to do something you would have wanted, and my strength is failing me."

I didn't hear a voice, but I felt the comfort of his presence as if I were a child again, sitting on his knee in Daett's living room. The wind stirred my loose strands of hair, bringing back memories of his fingers on my forehead.

"Come!" Mamm said loudly behind me. "I have to get back."

I stood and walked across the graveyard without answering. I paused in front of a smaller mound, also grass covered, but with no thistle to adorn its peaceful existence.

I motioned for Joy to join me, and Mamm let go of Joy's hand. We looked downward together.

"He was so sweet," Joy said. "He's in heaven with the angels."

"He is," I agreed.

"Come!" Mamm said again. "We must go."

We took a moment longer, standing there motionless, before we joined Mamm for the drive north again. Grandma was out on her front porch when we arrived. She waved and came towards us. Joy jumped out and ran to meet her. I watched the two embrace, not moving on the buggy seat.

"This is not wise," Mamm said.

"You could help things by admitting your own part in what Daett did to me," I said.

"I did the best I could."

"I was supposed to marry Walter," I said.

"You were supposed to obey," she said. "Don't mess things up again."

I climbed out of the buggy and removed our luggage from the back.

"We'll see you later," Mamm called to Grandma before she drove out of the lane.

Grandma took us into the house and fed us supper. We settled in for the night. I dreamed of Walter and of water running in a brook. I was bathing again, with the warm embrace of the summer night around us, trying to make myself pure enough. Walter was on the bank, looking at me with utter delight written on his face. I came out of the water, and in my dream, he opened his arms. I ran into them, and I felt his strength wrapped around me, the hunger of his fingers pressed into my back. I awoke with a start, the bedroom dark and empty, and my pillow wet with tears.

Section Five—November 1926 to March 1927

Barbara

Chapter 21

On Thanksgiving morning, I poured hot water into my teacup. The steam blinded me. I winced and turned my head. The pain stung from more than the heat. My whole body ached, and I knew why. My sister lived down the road at Grandma's house, and nothing was happening. The weeks crept past and had grown into months. Baby Jane had been born, and no one was doing anything about my sister. I knew matters in the community moved slowly, but this was beyond reason. I couldn't take much more of Walter and Lily staring at each other at the church services.

"Breakfast," I called.

There was the patter of small feet, and the children quickly settled in place.

Walter had been in the living room for some time. He took his time responding to my call, while I waited with teacup in hand.

"Let's pray," he said, after he took his seat.

We bowed our heads in silence, until Walter pronounced, "Amen."

I passed the plate of eggs before I asked. "Exactly what did Bishop Mast promise would happen when Lily came back?"

"No one promised anything," he said. "They said they were willing."

"You know they promised." I shot back.

He helped himself to the eggs and said nothing.

I waited until we had finished eating and I had shooed the children out of the room. I faced him. "You know exactly what I mean. My sister sits there by herself in a chair set up against the wall each Sunday. You can't take your eyes off her."

"Excommunicated people sit where I can see them," he said.

"She's no longer your girlfriend."

"As if I didn't know that!" He stood to his feet. "When is the company coming?"

"Ten or so," I said.

I didn't have the courage to tell him who was coming for Thanksgiving dinner besides the expected guests.

Walter left the kitchen, and fear niggled at me, deep down, like a worm in an airless can who wouldn't die. Lily had been out in the world for over eleven years. She knew the ways of the English, while I could only imagine such things. Walter wouldn't give in to my sister's charms again. Surely not! He was a man of the community. He was strong in his faith, in his roots, and in his calling as a Daett to our children. Walter would not abandon me.

Small footsteps pattered behind me, and four-year-old Elsie's voice called out, "Can we go outside and play?"

"Yes." I patted her on the head. "Go ahead and take your sister with you."

I walked into the living room. "I invited Minister Esh today," I said.

Walter shrugged. "Don't blame me if your schemes don't work. Minister Esh was willing, but he has his standards."

"You know those standards can be adjusted in the face of other standards which my sister has in abundance," I said. "Standards which men find tantalizing. Even an old Amish minister isn't exempt. You knew this when you brought Lily back to the community."

He didn't answer.

"I don't live in a dream world, Walter."

He turned away as a buggy drove in the lane. The front door slammed on his way out. I put the last of breakfast dishes away before Mamm's footsteps came into the house. Baby Jane chose the moment to cry out from the bedroom, and Mamm kept going past the kitchen doorway. She appeared moments later with the baby in her arms.

"Good morning," I greeted her.

"At least none of your other children look like Lily," Mamm said.

The front door slammed behind us, and Lily appeared. "Good morning," she said.

I kept on working at the sink.

"Why are you wearing such a dress?" Mamm asked, and I turned to face Lily.

I stared. Lily had on a dark blue dress, but the make wasn't Amish. There were frills on the collar and the sleeves. "How dare you? I've invited Minister Esh."

Joy had followed Lily in and looked at me with a worried expression.

Lily didn't act inhibited in the least. "Don't you want me to look pretty for the occasion?"

I turned to Mamm. "Take her upstairs and change her into one of my dresses."

"I'm not a child," Lily said.

"You're acting like one."

"Come." Mamm took Lily by the elbow.

"None of Barbara's dresses fit." Lily protested.

"You should have thought about that earlier," I said.

They disappeared up the stairs and I tried to compose myself. Joy was cooing to the baby, smiling and clucking her tongue at Baby Jane. Elsie would have been reduced to tears by the tone of our voices. I moved Joy and Baby Jane to the living room and faced my sister in the kitchen when she returned robed in one of my dresses.

"Do I look ugly enough?" Lily asked.

I ushered her into the kitchen. "You look Amish."

"I can go back home."

I glared at her. "You want Walter, and you're not getting Walter."

"Is there a chance I could?"

"Of course not!"

"Then why are you scared?" she asked.

"I'm tired of Walter gawking at you," I said, "sitting on the little bench by yourself each Sunday."

"You can take Joy back, and I will leave."

"I'm not taking the girl back until this matter is settled."

"What if I get what I want some day?" she asked.

"You won't." I said. "I'm married to the man, and I'm not dying anytime soon."

"Maybe the Lord is on my side."

Buggy wheels were coming in the driveway again.

"Just don't do anything stupid today," I said.

Lily joined Joy in the living room, and I took Baby Jane from Mamm to nurse her on the back-kitchen bench. Mamm worked at the stove, the heat rising to the ceiling.

"You can't help us," I told Lily when she came back into the kitchen. "You're in the Bann, but you can watch the children." I handed the baby to her.

Lily left the room with the child.

I finished beating the mashed potatoes and poured in the milk. The men drifted into the house around eleven, and Walter seated Minister Esh on the rocker, while Daett took the couch. Minister Esh and Daett divided up the week's Amish Budget between them. From what I could see, Lily kept herself occupied with the children and her head down. Minister Esh sent her furtive glances over the top of his newspaper.

"Feels like snow in the air," Daett said loudly, his piece of the Budget rustling as he turned the pages. "Michigan had their first dusting last week."

Minister Esh grunted. "I think I should head south for the winter. Sarasota, Florida, has temperatures in the eighties."

Daett chuckled. "Do you think you could handle the traveling at your age?"

"Most certainly!" Minister Esh declared. "These old bones become limber at the very thought of warm weather."

The chatter continued in the living room, with Lily's voice mixed in at times. I carried the turkey from the kitchen to the dining room table and caught Lily's eye.

My sister mouthed. "Are you happy now?"

I lifted my chin and hurried back to the kitchen for another dish of food. Daett and Minister Esh had their noses in the Budget again when I came back, but Walter was looking at Lily.

I gave him a glare. He ignored me.

When the last of the food was transferred, I approached Walter to say, "The meal is ready."

"Let's get to the table then," Walter said, but he didn't smile.

The adults seated themselves at the main dining room table, and I motioned for Lily to sit at the end amongst the children. Lily's excommunicated status must be maintained in some form. Everyone bowed their heads, and Minister Esh led out in the prayer of thanks without being asked. After the Amen, I passed the dishes, and plates were heaped high with food.

"How are things going for you since you came back into the community?" Minister Esh asked Lily, sending a smile towards the end of the table.

"Okay." Lily ducked her head. "I clean houses for some English people. Grandma was kind enough to give me a few leads."

Minister Esh piled his plate higher. "A wholesome occupation for a woman, I would say. How's Lily Joy doing?"

Lily reached over to give Joy a hug. "We call her Joy now, and I think she's very happy to be home in the community."

"Bringing Joy back from the English world, and coming back yourself was a right honorable thing," Minister Esh said.

Lily kept her gaze lowered. "I'm trying to do what is right for everyone."

"The Lord blesses those who seek his will," Minister Esh said.

"He does." Daett agreed.

"I noticed you at Baby John's funeral," Minister Esh said. "A sad time indeed, but you conducted yourself well, and now you're back."

"Yes, I am," Lily said.

Walter cleared his throat. "How's the fall plowing going, Minister Esh?"

Minister Esh shifted to face Walter. "I started this week. I see you're about done."

"I got an early start." Walter sliced off more of the turkey breast. "Is everyone getting enough to eat?"

Minister Esh chuckled. "This dinner is delicious, Barbara, especially to a man who has no wife in the house."

"Thank you." I tried to smile, but my face felt frozen.

"Did Lily help make any of this?" Minister Esh asked.

"She didn't," I said. "Though Lily is quite a decent cook, let me assure you."

"Good," Minister Esh said.

I didn't appreciate the look on Walter's face.

"Have you been to speak with Deacon Miller about getting your Bann lifted?" Minister Esh asked Lily, still smiling.

"I haven't," Lily said, "but if you think the time is right, I can visit this Saturday. I didn't want to appear inappropriate."

Minister Esh was beaming. "I would encourage your visit to Deacon Miller at your earliest convenience."

"I will stop by this Saturday," Lily said.

Minister Esh cut a large piece of turkey. "I must say I am very happy things are finally moving forward."

"Do you expect snow this week?" Walter asked.

"My bones tell me the weather will change for the worse!" Minister Esh declared. He dished out more mashed potatoes and gravy.

The conversation continued, lighthearted and cheerful, and the men sat around in the living room again, while we cleaned up after the meal.

Minister Esh came to the kitchen doorway before he left, where Lily was sitting beside the stove holding Baby Jane. "I will be awaiting news of your progress," he said.

My sister kept her head down, fussing over the baby.

"Thanks for the meal," he said in my direction and left.

"Looks like you got what you wanted," Walter told me in bed.

"Getting my sister married had better be what you want," I retorted.

He didn't answer, and the sounds of his heavy sleeping soon filled the bedroom.

"Let this end quickly." I breathed a prayer towards the ceiling.

I felt nothing, but why should I? The Lord had stopped listening to my requests a long time ago.

Chapter 22

Christmas Eve had arrived. We were on the road to Mamm's place for the evening's celebration. The snow swirled around our buggy, and PJ's hooves beat hollow on the gravel road. The drifts had formed in the ditch during the night, long shadows blown sideways with the steady wind gusts. I pulled my coat tighter around my shoulders and adjusted the blanket to cover Baby Jane's head. From the surrey's back seat came the whispers of Elsie and Mary's childish conversation.

I looked over at Walter. His gaze was fixed straight ahead, his hands taut on the reins.

I shifted on the buggy seat and stated the obvious. "Lily never went to speak with Deacon Miller."

"This is Christmas Eve," he muttered. "Leave a man in peace."

"Thoughts of Lily's continued disobedience and broken promises should disturb you."

He didn't answer.

"Why does Lily still have a place in your heart?" I wanted to hit his arm, wake him to his senses.

"I'm not talking about this."

"Minister Esh has not been invited to Mamm's place tonight, but Lily will be there with Joy. I don't want you mooning over her."

"I will mourn my loss," he said.

I took a long breath. "My sister has bewitched you. Can't you see?"

"This is a pleasant bewitching," he said. "Be quiet."

Baby Jane wailed and I lifted the blanket to hush her.

"You're disturbing the whole family on Christmas Eve," he scolded.

"My sister disturbed us a long time ago."

He didn't answer, the drifts heavy along this portion of road.

"My sister is not right for you." The bitterness filled my voice.

"Stop complaining," he said. "I have said my vows, and I have been true to them."

Weakness swept over me at the thought of what Lily might still do. "How much comfort can I take from your promises?"

He jiggled the reins and didn't respond.

I forged on. "You know you have to make peace with Lily's marriage to Minister Esh."

"I'm at peace," he said. "Lily is here."

"I love you," I muttered, "more than my sister ever can."

"Then hate me," he said, "if this is love."

Despair swept over me. "Lily will always have you, won't she?"

He didn't answer as the buggy bounced into our old home place. Walter came to a halt by the barn door and hopped out without even a glance in my direction. I laid Baby Jane on the buggy seat to climb down. Once on the ground, I helped Elsie and Mary down the step.

"Go to the house." I ordered. "The temperatures are too cold to play outside."

They didn't object but raced hand-in-hand toward the front door. Walter had PJ out of the shafts and left with his face grim. Somehow Walter must see the seriousness of our situation and do everything in his power to help.

I had Baby Jane in my arms when another buggy appeared on the road. The clip of the horse was familiar and so was the buggy. Lily had arrived with Grandma.

Joy climbed out when they stopped in front of us. Lily was helping Grandma out of the buggy, while I unfastened the first tug clip. Maiden neighed, the sound piercing in the stillness of the winter air. I heard Walter's footsteps approach from the barn, and saw Lily send him her warmest smile.

I hid my anger and held the shafts while Walter lead Maiden forward by the bridle. Lily was gazing at him with one hand on Grandma's shoulder.

"Go," I said, and Walter left with the horse.

"Good evening, Barbara." Grandma was smiling at me.

"How are you doing in this cold?" I asked.

"Lily is taking care of me."

"Shall we go?" I took Grandma's arm and we went up the sidewalks with Lily on the other side.

"Grandpa would have wanted you two to live in peace," Grandma said.

Neither of us answered as the wind blew a blast across the yard and stirred the snow drifts.

Mamm ushered us inside to a dining room table spread with food; ham, steak, salads, pies, corn, and puddings. I was going to lose my mind if I didn't stop thinking about Lily and Walter. Mamm didn't look in much better shape.

We settled around the dining room table after Walter and Daett came in from the barn. The food was delicious as usual, but I barely swallowed anything. Walter noticed, but he noticed Lily more.

We finished the dishes after the meal and stashed the leftover food in containers and carried them down to the root cellar. Lily was playing with the children on the floor, when I walked into the living room.

"I'm going out to get the buggy ready for Grandma," Walter said.

I found Grandma's winter coat behind the stove and helped her into the sleeves. On the other side of the table, Lily and Joy readied themselves to leave.

"I'll take her out," Daett offered, and I let go of Grandma's arm.

Lily had Joy's hand in hers, as they went out the front door. Their buggy lights soon drifted out the driveway. I collected the girls and Baby Jane. Walter had our buggy ready when I arrived at the end of the sidewalk.

We drove along at a steady trot towards home, the buggy blankets pulled tight up around our chins. PJ's nostrils sent out long plumes of white breath against the dark sky. They looked like angel wings, but there were no angels. I felt nothing of their brush on my heart this Christmas.

Chapter 23

Over a month later, the winter weather had fastened its grip on the countryside with a vengeance. On a Friday evening, the wind blew across our yard driving the snow drifts high up the side of the barn and even higher against the house. I tended the stove but paused for a brief glance out the kitchen window. Walter was hard at work with his shovel. He had cleared a narrow path from the house to the barn, and a larger parking spot at the hitching rack. Things were finally moving forward, though still at a snail's pace, not unlike the grip the weather had on the land. Bishop Mast and Deacon Miller had requested a meeting with Lily to talk about her broken promises and lack of a proper repentance.

I turned the chicken over in the pan and took another quick peek out the window. Walter had placed his shovel up against the barn and was deep in conversation with Bishop Mast as they unhitched the horse from the bishop's buggy. Esther was almost at the front door, and I had to greet her. I wiped my hands on my apron and hurried out of the kitchen. Esther, with her winter coat tightly wrapped around her shoulders was on the front porch when I opened the door wide.

"Good evening. How good to see you."

"And good to see you," Esther said. She stepped inside and caught her breath. "I told Ben we should have chosen another night for this meeting."

"I could have made any evening work." I assured her. "I'm sure Walter could have done the same."

"Poor Lily," Esther said. "The girl has been through so much. I can perfectly understand why she didn't want to come until after supper, this thing with the Bann and having to eat at the children's end of the table—how embarrassing. I'm hoping things can be worked out soon for her."

"Do come into the kitchen. I have the fire going." I gritted my teeth at Esther's naïveté concerning my sister. She's known Lily forever. Why can't she see what's in front of her eyes?

Esther followed me and lowered herself into the offered chair.

The front door slammed, and I returned to the living room. Walter was escorting Bishop Mast inside, and I hurried over to take his coat. "Good evening, Bishop."

He smiled. "Good evening, Barbara. I smell good things cooking in your kitchen."

"Just fried chicken," I said, "but do come in. The kitchen is warmer near the stove. I have a chair beside Esther for you."

"I think I will," he said, as Walter left again.

I took his coat into the bedroom. Bishop Mast appeared comfortable when I returned. He had produced stick candy from his pocket and had charmed Elsie to his side and Mary into his lap.

"I hope I'm not spoiling their supper." He grinned up at me.

"You know you are." Esther chided.

"I'm not objecting," I assured him. "One piece of candy never hurt anyone."

"Exactly how I feel!" Bishop Mast declared.

I transferred the last of the food dishes to the dining room table and checked the kitchen window again to see Deacon Miller's buggy in the driveway. Walter was busy unhitching the horse at the deacon's side, so I left to meet Lavina at the front door.

"Awful chilly tonight," Lavina greeted me.

"I agree," I said, and gripped Lavina's arm. "Have you prayed for this evening? There is so much at stake for Lily and Joy."

"I have." Lavina took off her shawl. "I have only to remember the distress on Lily's face at Baby John's funeral to cause me to send up many prayers. The last thing we want is for the girl to leave the community again."

I forced myself to say the appropriate words as I led the way into the kitchen. "Thank you for praying and understanding my sister's delays."

Bishop Mast looked up with a smile. "Well, look who's here, the deacon's wife herself."

"You know I had to come and keep Dennis straight," Lavina teased.

They laughed and I joined in.

"Supper is ready," I told Walter when he appeared with Deacon Miller.

We gathered at the dining room table, and everyone bowed their heads while the bishop led out in a prayer of thanks.

"Almighty heavenly Father, creator of heaven and earth, look down upon your helpless and humble creatures gathered tonight around this table, and extend your great mercy and grace towards us. We are weak and feeble and give our thanks to you for every breath flowing into our bodies. Bless now this evening," Bishop Mast concluded. "Let your will be done. Amen."

I began to pass the dishes.

"Excellent, excellent chicken," Deacon Miller declared. "If I had chicken like this every day, I'd get fat for sure."

"You already are," Bishop Mast said.

Laughter filled the dining room.

Walter cleared his throat. "Perhaps we should discuss the evening's planned event, before Lily arrives?"

"Why do you think so?" Bishop Mast asked, his mouth full of chicken.

"Perhaps we could say some things easier by ourselves instead of in front of Lily," Walter said.

Bishop Mast chewed for a moment before he nodded. "I think I agree. What about you, Deacon?"

"Sounds good to me."

Bishop Mast turned to Walter. "Okay. What do you wish to say?"

"Barbara and I are not in agreement on this matter," Walter said.

"Is this true?" Bishop Mast turned in my direction.

"I think Lily should stop breaking promises," I said.

"And you don't believe this, Walter?"

"We should stop asking her to make promises she can't keep. Why can't she make her things right with the church, live in the community, and Joy can come home again?"

"I see," Bishop Mast said. "You would make a change from what you told me when you asked permission to invite Lily back into the community?"

"I would," he said, "but I can see Lily is hesitating, struggling even, suffering. Why can't we have mercy on her?"

"Having her marry Minister Esh is not a punishment," Deacon Miller said. "Marriage to any Amish man is an honor."

"I agree," I said, and they looked at me.

Bishop Mast cleared his throat. "I see we were wise to speak of this before Lily arrives.

"This was your decision in the first place," Deacon Miller said to Walter. "We trusted your judgment."

"I think I made a mistake," Walter said. "I don't want to make another one."

Bishop Mast thought for a moment. "I would not have agreed to this meeting if Minister Esh had not assured me he is ready and willing to take on the task of loving and bringing Lily back into the fold of God, a task worthy of any man. I don't think your objections can override our plans."

"Maybe you are mistaken in how you see Lily," Deacon Miller said.

"I don't think so," Walter replied. "She isn't coming tonight."

"You knew this?" Deacon Miller asked.

Walter shook his head. "I just know Lily."

"Has she made peace with you, Walter?" Bishop Mast asked.

"I think so," he said.

"But you're not sure?" Deacon Miller studied Walter's face.

He didn't wince. "Maybe she hasn't? And maybe I haven't?"

"Well, so we are back to base one," Bishop Mast said, "unless Walter is wrong, and Lily is coming tonight."

Silence fell over the house as we listened. The wind stirred outside and rattled against the windows. There was no sound of a buggy pulling in the driveway or the sharp whinny of Lily's horse.

I got up to serve cherry pie for dessert. The men spoke in soft tones, discussing the snow forecasts for the rest of the winter, and expressing their hopes of breaking into the fields before the first of April.

They finished the food and gave thanks again. The men moved to the living room, while the women helped me with the dishes.

The clock on the living room wall struck eight. I sent the girls upstairs to bed and the men went out to prepare their horses for departure an hour later. Walter went with them. Esther and Lavina wrapped their winter coats around their shoulders. They gave me hugs at the front door, their faces somber.

I waited until their forms were swallowed in the darkness before I checked on the girls upstairs. They were sound asleep, as was Baby Jane in our bedroom. I returned to the living room window and waited, but Walter didn't come in. Around ten, I lay down and fell into a troubled sleep. I awoke to the sound of the wind on the windows panes, but the bed was empty beside me.

I went to the front door and called into the night. "Walter."

There was no answer. I searched the rooms upstairs and down, but there was no sign of him. I returned to the bedroom and fell asleep to dream of Lily, of baptism, of water, and bare feet. I was soaked with sweat when I awoke. Darkness still veiled the bedroom window and the storm had increased.

I slipped out of bed and tiptoed into the living room. The house was empty of Walter. I lifted the lid on the closet cedar chest and tugged out a quilt. With its thick folds pulled over my shoulder I sat on the couch and waited for dawn.

Chapter 24

The sun hung low in the March sky, and its rays danced on the drifts in the snowy windowpane a few inches from my arm. Winter this year refused to release its stranglehold on the land. A month had drifted past, of waiting for what, I did not know. I forced myself to concentrate on the stitches of the quilt I held in my free hand. My finger had needle pricks from earlier in the day, the blood staunched with a quick touch to my lips. The room around me was filled with women, but I felt alone, lost, and forsaken. I stared out of the window past them, at the shifts of the snow when the wind stirred. The formations moved sideways, while others took shape behind them. Each was new, and yet somewhere, I had seen every one of them before.

The scene was not unlike Walter and me. We were heaps of snow formed into familiar shapes by the dictates of winds we could not control. Walter had slept in the basement since the night of the meeting with Bishop Mast and Deacon Miller.

If Walter did not give in, Lily would have to leave the community. I was ready to settle for her absence, even if her shadow would forever drape over our lives. Better a fear unknown, then a certainty staring in your face. Every day, I faced the reality Walter loved her, and Lily was close by.

I pulled my gaze away from the window. From across the room, Esther's concerned face looked quickly away from me. Did I dare leave early? The day of the woman's sewing had been a long one, begun soon after the sun came up. They wouldn't stop working until the time had arrived for supper preparations at home. The quilt was set up in the middle of the room, with chairs placed around the frame. These were expert quilters and we took turns at the available spots.

I finished another stitch before I laid down my needle and thread. I slipped from the chair and smiled when one of the women looked up. The buzz of conversation didn't halt as I passed. Elsie and Mary were not in the kitchen, but one of the older girls had Baby Jane in her arms.

"Thanks for taking care of her," I said, and took the child.

"She's been good for me." Hannah smiled.

"Can you run upstairs and see if Elsie and Mary are there? Tell them I'm ready to go."

Hannah vanished up the stairs. I opened the basement door and listened for a moment. There were no children's voices rising from the dark depths. I waited, thinking about Walter in our basement each night instead of in my bed. My sister had pushed him there. Our family could be a happy one, filled with happy chatter and good cheer, if my sister would leave us alone. Instead our hearts were frozen in place, like ice formed a yard thick over a winter's river.

"Time to go home," I whispered to Elsie and Mary when Hannah reappeared with them in tow.

They followed me out into the hallway where Esther met us. "Leaving already."

"I should be going." I shooed Elsie and Mary toward the front door.

"I hope things go well this evening when Minister Esh visits," Esther said.

I collected myself in time to hide my distress. Walter had said nothing about Minister Esh stopping in.

Esther took my arm. "Come, I'll go out with you and help you hitch your horse to the buggy. The community cares about you. Don't doubt."

I tightened their coats and tossed Baby Jane's blanket over her face. Esther had PJ out of the barn and beside the buggy by the time I had the girls bundled inside. I turned to raise the shafts for Esther and fastened the tugs.

"Thanks for helping," I said.

I climbed in and jiggled the reins. The snow squeaked under the buggy wheels as PJ broke into a trot. Baby Jane wiggled under the blanket beside me, until I pulled the cover back to expose her face.

Walter must have known about this visit since the last Sunday services. Grandma's house came into view, and both girls perked up. I made a point to stay away from Grandma's house. They cracked the door open to wave together, even though no one was visible.

I jiggled the reins, and PJ fell into his steady trot again. I had noticed the pause and my fingers dug into the palms of my hands. PJ had passed a familiar turn, and I hadn't pulled into Grandma's driveway since Lily's arrival. I willed the fear in my heart to settle down. PJ was an old horse and he had a long memory.

I urged him on, and the next mile rolled past quickly. Minister Esh's buggy was parked in front of the barn when I pulled in our driveway. His horse was not in sight. The man had unhitched and must be in the barn with Walter.

Our buggy came to a stop, and I sat still frozen in place. Elsie and Mary had no such compunctions and climbed down to race for the house. Little puffs of snow rose from each plunge of their small boots. The barn door remained closed. Walter must be in deep conversation with Minister Esh not to notice my arrival.

I climbed down and unfastened the first tug. Baby Jane wailed on the front seat. I was ready to check on her when the barn door opened, and the men appeared. I hurried back to the buggy door and stuck my head inside. I grabbed the baby in my arms and turned to face the approaching men.

"You will get this thing taken care of then?" Minister Esh was saying.

"I'll think about what I can do," Walter replied.

"You will do more than think," Minister Esh said. He turned to me. "Sorry for keeping your husband while you had to unhitch by yourself, but we were almost finished with the conversation."

I tried to smile. "You're staying for supper?"

Minister Esh chuckled. "I couldn't impose on you, since you didn't know I was coming. Walter said he didn't tell you. I can understand how a husband could forget such things."

"You're still welcome to stay," I said.

"Maybe another time." Minister Esh turned sober. "I'm sorry about the stress this fuss with your sister is putting on your family, but at the same time I know problems left to their own are rarely solved. Perhaps this is the Lord's way of healing old injuries in your family. I know the road gets rough at times, but I don't hold anything against either of you, and the rest of the ministry feels the same way. We want the Lord's will done, and I hope we can obtain Walter's full support for Lily's welcome back into the community."

"You really have to stay for supper," I said, "with no wife at home to fill your empty stomach."

"You're tempting me." He grinned.

"Then in this case, give in to temptation."

"I believe I will," he said. "Let me help Walter in the barn with the horses, and we'll be in before long."

"Okay," I said, and he moved away, a stooped figure in the fallen snow, with his white beard slung over his shoulder by the wind.

I took a deep breath. Lily deserved a husband like Minister Esh. Lily knew she did and was extracting her pound of flesh before she caved. I pulled the blanket tighter around Baby Jane's head and hurried toward the house. I had supper underway when the men came in from the barn, shaking the snow from their coats and boots in the washroom.

I called them to the table when I had supper ready.

"What a spread," Minister Esh proclaimed, "and after your long day at the sewing. I don't deserve this."

"Just eat," I said. "I only have meatloaf, vegetables, and a salad. We have peach pie for dessert. I would have made mashed potatoes and gravy, if I had known you were coming."

Minister Esh beamed at me. "Look at the food she can prepare so quickly, and the kind of godly woman she is. If a thousand women were like my wife was, and Barbara here is, we would never lack for virtue and honor in the community."

We had a prayer of thanks, and I passed the plates of food.

After the main course I served the dessert, cutting the pie into wedges.

"This is just totally unnecessary!" Minister Esh exclaimed, but he helped himself to a large piece, and Walter did the same.

I fed the girls, and Minister Esh left for home immediately after the final prayer of thanks.

I faced Walter in the living room. "Have you been stopping by at Grandma's place?"

"What do you mean?"

"I mean stopping by to see Lily."

"I stop by to see my daughter," he said.

"This is how you know so much about my sister and her state of mind."

He didn't look the least bit guilty.

"Are you sleeping with my sister?" I asked.

Rage filled his face. "Lily offered herself to me many times those long years ago, and I was too stupid to accept what only the Lord can give. Now the case is closed. Lily knows. I know. I will die wishing Lily was in my arms."

"How can you be so hateful, after what I've given you?"

"Hateful is marrying Lily to Minister Esh, condemning her to a loveless marriage with an old man, when your sister is so full of life, so full of joy and happiness."

"Why have you always hated me?"

"As heaven is true," he said. "You make things dark, Barbara. You make life dark."

I left him and finished the dishes. Elsie and Mary worked on either side of me, their faces sober. They couldn't have helped overhear some of our conversation. What we said could have made no sense to them. I put them to bed at eight and settled Baby Jane in her crib afterwards. Walter was still in the living room.

"Are you coming in?" I asked.

He didn't answer.

"I want you," I said.

"You don't know what you want," he said, not looking at me.

I walked over to face him. "We can't go on like this. What if people find out you're sleeping in the basement? I want you in bed with me."

"I don't want you," he said.

"You can't have my sister."

"I know, but I don't have to sleep with you," he said.

"Sleeping with me is right, Walter. You know."

"Then may God spare me from what is right."

"You're blaspheming," I said.

"Your existence is a blasphemy to both heaven and earth," he said. "Now, one last time, leave me alone."

I did, and the bed was cold even under two quilts. My whole body was cold, thinking about Walter's words. My sister was not going to stop until she destroyed us completely, until there was nothing left but ashes where beauty had once been. I felt like I would wash away, like I was a leaf on a raging spring stream, rushing out to the sea, out to the roaring ocean where home would never be found again.

I tossed and turned, and when the clock stuck twelve, I got out of bed, wrapped the quilt around me, and made my way down the basement steps. The stillness was heavy, and Walter's breath came shallow from the corner. I felt my way with my feet and found the edge of his foam. I lay down beside him, and his breathing didn't change. I listened to the sound until I fell asleep and awoke to the first blush of dawn on the basement window glass and the bed empty beside me.

Chapter 25

I rushed upstairs to begin our breakfast preparations. I had seriously overslept. I was losing every structure and dignity life afforded me. The girls were awake, sitting on the kitchen chairs with puzzled expressions on their faces.

"Sorry," I muttered. "I'm going to change."

They were staring at the basement door when I rushed out of the kitchen. I entered the bedroom, and Baby Jane stirred in her crib. I hushed her with a touch of my hand and dressed. I rushed through the breakfast preparations and cut corners where I could. Walter was in the washroom long before I was ready.

He stared at me. "Why were you—?" he left the words hang in the air after a glance at the girls.

I placed the plate of eggs on the table.

We bowed our heads in silent prayer. Elsie and Mary soon had their heads bent over bowls of oatmeal. The steam from it rose into their faces. The two smiled at each other, the tinkle of their spoons soft as they ate. I forced food down my throat, but Walter appeared to have no such problem.

The minutes ticked past, counted by the clock in the living room. We finished and bowed our heads again for a thanksgiving prayer.

"Girls, go play," Walter ordered.

They left the kitchen quickly.

"What if I follow Minister Esh's advice?" Walter asked.

I tried to collect my thoughts. "I don't know what he advised."

"Minister Esh wants me to make peace with Lily."

"Exactly what do you mean?"

"He wants Lily and me to talk about our past," he said.

"I don't want you speaking with my sister alone."

"Are you wiser than Minister Esh?" he asked.

"In this case, I think I am."

"I want to meet with Lily for whatever time we need, and somewhere other than on Grandma's porch with her listening in the living room."

Bitterness swept through me. "Too bad you can't have two wives."

"If I do speak with Lily—" He ignored my barb. "I may not be able to tell you what we said."

"You would take me into the gutter, wouldn't you?"

"I think the gutter is your home," he said.

"How dare you?" I faced him. "You're the one living in sin."

"Will you cooperate or not?"

"Okay." I screamed. "Speak with her, but nothing more!"

Section Six—March to June 1927

LILY

Chapter 26

The sun hung high in a cloudless April morning sky, with a warm breeze moving across the open fields. The first sign of spring had arrived after the long and wearisome winter. I stepped out on the front porch when I heard hooves beating in the distance. Walter hadn't stopped in to visit Joy for some time. I hoped this would be him, and my hopes were correct. Exuberance surged through me, enough to make me dizzy. I sat down to await his arrival.

"Hi." He greeted me still sitting on the porch. "I need to speak with you."

"You're speaking with me."

"Like somewhere alone—when we have some time."

"Grandma's barn works," I said. My mind raced. He couldn't be ready to give me what I most wanted.

"Minister Esh wants us to make our peace." His smile was pained.

"You know what I want," I said.

He winced. "We have to let go."

"Do you want to?"

"No."

"You're saying we have no choice?"

"We don't," he said.

My mind was still racing, but I spoke firmly. "I will still want something from you, even if you don't give me what I really want."

"What, Lily?"

"I don't know," I said.

"This has to end." He was staring at the ground. "What time can we meet?"

"I have time tomorrow evening—well, anytime really."

"We just have to talk," he said, and left.

"How are things going?" Grandma's soft footsteps came up behind me.

"Okay." I forced a smile.

"Did I hear something about Walter coming back to speak with you?"

"Tomorrow evening," I said.

I was surprised she didn't object. She must have heard the part about meeting in the barn. I stared after Walter's buggy which had vanished around the wooded bend in the road.

"Your Grandpa had a hard road to walk," she said, "but I think he's looking down, and hoping you will succeed in following his footsteps."

"I expect you're right."

"I know I'm right," she said. "He would have wanted you to make your peace with both Walter and the community."

"Will marrying Minister Esh bring me peace?" I asked.

"Only God knows," she said.

"Why does the right choice not guarantee peace?"

"I don't know, Lily, but your Grandfather had his share of rough waters and he made the right choices."

"Do you think I can be fully accepted into the community?"

"As Minister Esh's wife, I'd say there should be no further problems."

"I can't see myself as his wife," I said. "He will not heal my pain."

"When you're with a man you become part of him."

"Sleeping with Minister Esh won't help," I said.

"Why? Because you were with Walter first, and you think no man can take his place?"

"I haven't been with Walter," I said.

She looked both surprised and pleased. "Then you have yet to experience the wonder of becoming part of a man. You can look forward to the experience."

I kept staring after the empty space where Walter's buggy disappeared. "Did Grandpa change you?"

"I became alive when I was with him," she said.

"I want Walter," I said.

"You can't have him." She reminded me.

We ate early, and I retired to my bedroom upstairs. Joy slept across the hall from me, as Barbara had in our younger years. I climbed under the quilt and thought long and hard about the meeting tomorrow night with Walter. There must be something he would agree to. Something he could do which would fit his rules, would heal a portion of the hurt inside of me.

I lay on my bed and allowed some of the memories to come back—Daett's footsteps on the stairwell, coming ever closer, and the sound of the doorknob turning. I blocked the scene from going further. I lay trembling for a long time. The thought flickered on the edge of my mind for awhile until I paid attention. I remembered the staring at my feet which Daett often did when he came up to my room. Jonas had done the same thing when I visited his farm with Walter. My feet had become the focus of my uncleanness in my mind, the permissible part of my body I could think about without total revulsion. Perhaps Walter felt the same? I lay staring at the ceiling. Did I dare? Could I say the words? Could I ask and hope for agreement. I had nothing to lose. I would ask. The men and women washed each other's feet during the communion service. Why could Walter not wash my feet?

Peace didn't come to my heart exactly, but a measure of peace. Maybe this was everything Walter could give me. I could and would be satisfied. I had no choice. Sleep came sometime later, a light sleep in which I awoke at every sound.

The morning found me at the window, gazing out on the brightening horizon, not knowing if I dared hope or if despair would be my only reward tonight with Walter.

I cleaned the basement after breakfast that morning and baked three cherry pies.

"Is Walter coming for supper?" Grandma asked. She didn't look like she approved.

"No," I said.

"You'll make Minister Esh very happy."

"I can cook," I said.

"You will like him." She smiled.

I didn't answer and put the pies away in the cupboard. Walter arrived soon after we had eaten supper and I met him on the front porch. He looked weary and old.

We walked side by side across the lawn. The late sunlight was faint in the window when we entered the barn. I lit the lantern before we sat down on bales of straw.

"Does this remind you of something" he asked.

"Our first rumspringa outing?" The memory came back in a rush.

He nodded. "We need a band tonight."

Through my pain I forced a laugh. "What? To take our minds off ourselves?"

"Maybe."

"You did your best," I said. "You were very kind to me."

"My best wasn't good enough." Agony flickered across his face.

"Maybe there was nothing you could have done to change things."

"Do you wish there would have been?"

"Of course," I said. "I wish with every breath I breathe."

"So do I." He buried his face in his hands. "I've lived those weekends over again, minute by minute, a thousand times. If I had them again, I would … "

I waited for him to finish, then asked, "You would what?"

"I would have given you what you wanted. We would at least have the memories."

"I wish you had," I said, trying not to scream the words.

He seemed in a daze. "I wanted you too much, Lily. The Lord must have decided I didn't deserve you."

"I don't think the Lord was involved."

"The community then," he said after a pause.

Bitterness surged through me. "They believe they are the Lord."

"Then why are we giving in to them?"

I felt the hopelessness of dealing with him—with them, flood through me. "Maybe the Lord is on their side?"

"I know." He groaned.

"I was being sarcastic." I almost shouted.

He looked puzzled.

"Go on," I said. "We're not going to agree on the subject."

"I want us …" he stalled quickly.

"I don't want to live without you." I said, and almost reached for him, but he would only have pulled away.

His eyes looked feverish. "Yet the Lord seems to think we should."

The bitterness rushed through my body again. "Stop bringing up what keeps us apart. I know I belong to you in the Lord's eyes. I've always belonged to you and should belong to you now."

"I'm married to Barbara."

"I know my sister lies in your arms at night."

"I'm sorry, Lily. I'm so very sorry."

"I'm sorry for you," I said, "and myself. I need you, Walter."

"There must be more to life, Lily, than ourselves and what we want. There must be."

"More than you? Not for me there isn't."

He stared at the straw strewn barn floor. "Okay. I'll be honest. I try to submit, but I can't stop the whys. I try, but I can't. Why have I not known you as I wanted to know you, in a thousand different ways, in a thousand dreams? Give me a million agonies, I don't care. Take all my children from me. They are nothing compared to the loss of you. I admit missing your face awaking beside me each morning. The years without you are swept away, as if they never existed."

I almost screamed. "This is not helping."

"If Barbara should pass?" He continued, not seeming to notice. "Are you sure you want the door to our wedding closed?"

I said as loud as I could. "My sister is not passing. She will die a withered old hag."

His laugh was choked. "How do you know this?"

"Barbara and I are doomed to live our lives together. I must marry Minister Esh, and you must be my sister's husband. The will of God, according to you, has spoken."

"You don't believe a word of what you just said."

"Yet I must marry Minister Esh. There is no other way, Walter."

"Shall I come with you?" He waved his arm vaguely. "Like you asked?"

"And leave behind what you are?"

"I would leave anything for you," he said.

"You would leave yourself for me, and I would no longer have you."

"Maybe," he said, looking unconvinced.

"You don't even know yourself."

"Perhaps not." He admitted. "A true mess indeed."

"I suppose we have always been a mess." I tried to calm down and remember what was possible from this moment. "I do have one request of you before we leave tonight."

"What?" He turned to face me. "You know I can't—."

I let the pain show in my face. "I have given up hope you would love me so much. Can you wash my feet at least? Can you stoop so low?"

"Wash your feet?"

"Yes. We wash each other's feet at communion. Give me a sacred moment, Walter."

"Why?"

"Can you not touch me?"

"You know how much I want you, Lily."

"Then will you? I'm not going to explain further. Can you for once give me what I want? This one small thing?"

The struggle was immense on his face. Relief flooded through me when he stood to his feet. "Where?"

"The milk house," I said, and led the way.

The inside door squeaked on its hinges when I pushed it open. The dust stirred on the concrete floor. The milk house was in the back, the cobwebs high above us from disuse, but the sound of water still ran fresh through the cooling tank. I sat on the stone edge to remove my shoes and socks. He studied my face, not looking at the rest of me. My tears came. He had seen me bathing those long-ago days. Why was he afraid of me? I pulled my dress up to my knees. The sharp intake of his breath stopped me from pulling further. I dipped my toes into the water and waited. He came around to stand beside me. He took my foot in his hands. He didn't move for the longest time, his rough callousness pressed against my skin.

"You have beautiful feet," he said, the old transfixed look in his eyes.

His words were the same, but his touch moved me the deepest, radiating up my ankles and into the rest of my body.

"Your beauty is from the Lord," he said. "Even your feet are heaven come down to our sin-cursed earth."

The tears tickled on my cheek, and I brushed them away.

His fingers traced the depth of my arch, gentle and burning with fire at the same time. He reached for my other foot and held them together. The tears streamed down my cheeks.

"How pure and lovely," he said, "so right in every way."

He dipped his hand into the water and rubbed the coolness on my skin. He wiped my feet with his handkerchief. I looked up into his face, his cheeks also wet with tears. He let go and opened his arms. I flew into them. He held me for the longest time, as I drank the smell of his chest with each breath.

"We should go, Lily," he finally said.

"Thank you," I whispered.

I found my socks and shoes, my eyes stinging from the tears.

"Let me," he said, and knelt to slip them on my feet.

I embraced him again, but he didn't hold me long this time.

"Goodbye, Lily," he said. "I will forever love you."

He turned and led the way outside. I waited by the side of his buggy while he untied PJ. He climbed in and drove away without looking back. I stared after him until his buggy was a small blip in the distance.

Chapter 27

I left the following week on a Saturday evening right after supper for the trip down to Deacon Miller's place. I pulled into his driveway and tied up at the hitching post.

The deacon met me on the lawn. "Good evening, Lily."

"Good evening." I returned the greeting. "I'm ready to make things right with the church."

"And with the Lord?" he asked.

"I am."

"Did Walter come to see you?"

"He did," I said.

"Can you come up with the baptismal class tomorrow morning?" he asked.

"I can."

"Minister Esh will be glad to hear this."

He looked very pleased with himself. They had conquered me. The deacon helped me untie my horse and turn the buggy around. Joy was waiting for me when I returned, seated on the porch swing.

She came running across the lawn. "Did everything go well?"

"Everything went very well," I said.

I didn't feel well, but I was doing what must be done.

The morning dawned bright and cheerful, and I managed a smile on the way to the Sunday services. Deacon Miller met us in the barn yard and helped us unhitch.

"How the community cares about you," Grandma whispered on the walk up to the house.

Joy was ahead of us, already tall and beautiful in a dark Amish dress. I didn't respond.

"You're making the right choices," Grandma said.

We greeted the women in the kitchen, and the services began twenty minutes later. The ministers stood to file up the stairs for their regular Sunday morning meeting, and the baptismal class followed. I went to the end of the line, feeling every eye from the congregation fixed on me. I had worn my black dress, as if I were at a funeral.

We took our seats upstairs. The ministers sat on one side of the room and the baptismal class on the other, with a large space between the boys' and girls' chairs. Their young faces were filled with hopes, with dreams, their faith placed in the future. I had no faith. I didn't need faith for this future. I only needed to act, and Walter had given me the strength and healing last night. Enough for this. I was here to learn, to repent, and to acquire anew the teachings of the community before I was granted repentance.

I looked up to see Minister Esh's gaze fixed on me. He smiled and nodded a greeting, but I felt no happiness, just a coldness settling in the pit of my stomach. The morning's instructions for the baptismal class began. These were familiar words I heard before, explaining the doctrines of the Lord and His Holy Church. They felt as distant and meaningless to my life as they had felt those long years ago.

I didn't look up again, but I felt the intensity of Minister Esh's gaze on me. I wanted to cry out. I silently begged the floor to open and swallow me, until I felt Walter's touch again; his hands moving on my feet, and I calmed down. I had been given strength for this journey and I would not fail Walter, to say nothing of Joy. To Joy belonged the future, not to us. We were doomed to fill out our days with whatever measure of happiness was left in our broken buckets.

I was expected to name my sins, after the morning instruction class was completed and the others filed downstairs. These were not ignorant men, sheltered though they were by the community's cocoon. They knew what men did with their wives. They were married and knew the beauty of a woman's body. They could imagine what I had done out in the English world. They were wrong, but I would have to say something to satisfy them.

In the meantime, I forced myself to listen.

"Our responsibility lies towards each other," Deacon Miller was saying, "not just to ourselves. You will soon be part of the community, as we are a part of each other. As such we are to care for each other. We are to watch for dangers the others might be in and give warning, supply care, and offer comfort where needed. You will become responsible for burdens which are not your own."

I had tried to believe these words once, but I didn't try this morning. They were empty as my heart was empty. The only love which touched me had come through my sister's husband last night. They had told Walter to speak with me, but I doubt if they had imagined what Walter would do for me. I knew they would not have approved.

Joy would never sit where I sat, because Joy was different. The girl had one desire—to stay in the community. Her heart became alive here. Joy was the girl I never had been. I never would be. Joy was Walter's daughter, and I felt peace settle over my troubled soul. With the help of Walter last night, and the knowledge I would give fresh life and hope to his child, I would stay in this room and say what I must say. I would climb into Minister Esh's bed after our wedding. Willing or unwilling would not matter.

Deacon Miller's voice stopped, and Bishop Mast spoke again, "Our baptismal class can now leave, but Lily will stay with us a few moments longer."

They stood to their feet, seven boys and three girls, their backs to me as they filed out of the bedroom door. The ministers seated on the bench, waited with heads bowed. Even Minister Esh had his gaze on the floor.

Bishop Mast cleared his throat. "We come to this hour with joy in our hearts. I'm glad Lily has consented to make her things right with the Lord and with His church. Are you ready, Lily, to join the community again through a renewal of your baptismal vows and with a full confession of your sins?

"I am," I whispered.

"You may begin confessing your sins," Bishop Mast said.

From somewhere I found the words. "I've been sinful," I said. "I left the faith of the community and lived in the world. I gave up hope I could change when I should have hung on. I was unfaithful to my baptismal vows. I deserve the punishment the community has seen fit to place on me. I wish to repent and make things right and return to what I used to have."

Bishop Mast coughed. "You and Walter have made peace with each other."

"We have," I said.

"Have you confessed the wrong between you and asked his forgiveness?"

"I have."

I waited while the ministers consulted with each other in hushed tones.

Bishop Mast finally spoke. "We are in agreement. We can accept your repentance and receive you into the church fellowship again, not without some doubt in our hearts, but with Minister Esh's strong support I believe we can move forward today. Are you satisfied with our decision?"

"I am," I said.

"You will renew your vows today then, and repent in front of the church on your knees?"

"I will," I said.

"You're dismissed." Bishop Mast gave me a quick nod. "The blessing of the Lord be with you."

"Thank you," I whispered, and slipped from the room.

I took the stairs slowly. The eyes of the seated men below me rose to take in my progress. I felt nothing, no emotion, no hope. I wanted to find Walter's face, but I didn't dare search the length of the benches. I took my usual chair set apart against the wall. The singing continued until the ministers filed down from the upstairs bedroom. They walked with solemn faces, beards pressed against the chest, and hands clasped across the heart. These were the leaders of the flock, the humblest of the humble, and I would soon be a wife of one of them. I always thought Walter would be a minister. Now I felt only horror and dread grip my soul.

The sermons began, followed by the Scripture reading. Bishop Mast stood for the second and final sermon. I tucked my feet under the chair. An hour later, Bishop Mast finished and approached me. I slid to my knees without being asked.

"Lily Swartz." His voice rumbled above me. "Do you promise once more to forsake the devil, the world, and your own lusts?"

"I do," I whispered.

"Do you confess you have sinned greatly against the Lord and against his people? Do you promise to return with your whole heart and seek the will of the Lord and the council of his people? Do you promise to live in obedience to the Lord and to His church?"

"I do," I said, a little louder.

"Then stand and be accepted back into the blessing of the Lord and the graces of his people." Bishop Mast offered me his hand.

I stood, and Esther came forward to welcome me and planted a kiss on my check followed by a long embrace.

"Welcome home," Esther whispered into my ear. "I'm so glad you're one of us."

The service concluded and the usual meal was served—peanut butter sandwiches, coffee, red beets, pickles, and a meat the family had hand-smoked from their own livestock.

I helped serve the unmarried men's table in the basement. They gave me strange looks, but I was from another generation and another man's problem.

Minister Esh found me in the front lawn after the meal, where I tended several of the small children.

He could not have looked more pleased. "This is the day of the Lord, Lily. Let us rejoice and be glad."

"This is a nice day," I agreed.

"Glad to see you helping out today. Such a great spirit, getting right into the swing of things."

"I try," I said.

"I sense no bitterness of spirit in you, just a sweetness rising from your presence. You have been humbled and broken, now is the time to be exalted and filled with good things."

I knelt to straighten a child's diaper.

"Are you busy this afternoon?" he asked.

"Nothing more than usual."

"Let me drive you home then. You have eaten, and I have eaten. Yah?"

I hesitated. "Grandma is a little old to drive by herself."

"Joy is here," he said. "She is quite mature for her age. Someone will help them hitch up."

"As you wish." I forced a smile.

"Be a minute then." He nodded and headed for the barn.

I collected my shawl from the washroom. A few of the women gave me encouraging smiles.

Esther made a point of squeezing my arm. "You're getting a very good husband. Minister Esh is a kind man."

"He does seem so," I agreed, and hurried back outside.

Minister Esh had his horse in the shafts, and I helped slip in the tugs on my side. He was clearly pleased.

We climbed in. He shook the reins and his horse trotted out of the driveway.

"What a joy, Lily." His whole face beamed. "I cannot tell you how my heart is filled with happiness. Not once since my beloved wife passed from cancer did I dare hope the Lord would so bless me again, in fact, bless me above my first marriage. I didn't dream such a thing was possible."

"I have done things I shouldn't," I said.

"They have been forgiven and forgotten." He assured me. "Mention them no more. As the Lord says, they shall be cast into the sea, into the depths, and never found again."

"Not exactly a direct quote," I said.

He laughed. "I see you were listening to the sermons of your childhood. What a joy rises in my heart. Since the beginning the Lord has been preparing you to make peace with the past."

"Must we speak more about this?" I asked.

"You're right," he said. "You've made your peace."

We turned in Grandma's driveway, and Minister Esh climbed out to tie his horse to the hitching post. "I guess I can stay a few minutes." He grinned.

"I have time till supper must be made. Are you staying for the evening meal?"

"I don't think so. Can we sit on the swing?"

I nodded.

"So peaceful this afternoon," he said, "as if the Lord is being extra kind to us."

"Peace is good," I said.

He was quiet for a moment. "There is something I must tell you before we go much further."

I waited, not daring to look at him. Was he going to tell me he knew about my unsavory birth, or worse?

"I have known for some time I have heart trouble." He continued. "An inherited weakness, the doctor said. There was a fancy name which I didn't care to remember. I discovered the problem when my wife was ill with cancer. I had the doctor look at me, and the issue is there. I have some years left, he said—if I don't overdue things."

I was breathing again. "I'm sorry to hear the news."

"There's really no problem." He was smiling again.

"Am I supposed to worry?"

"Not worry, just be warned. You're a beautiful woman, Lily. There's a life in front of you after I am gone. I will have no objections."

"I don't know what to say."

"I just wanted to tell you," he said.

"Do your relatives know?"

He shook his head. "I'm a bachelor. Privacy comes as a privilege at my age. Why bother them with what can't be changed. Now I should be going, but when can I see you again?"

"You can come for supper some night next week, maybe Thursday?"

"Perfect." He stood to his feet.

I followed him out to the buggy.

"Thank you, Lily," he said, his hand on the wheel. "Thank you for everything." He climbed inside.

He looked old, I thought, as he drove away, and tired. I had not noticed before, but I had not been looking. A few years of married life together was what Minister Esh envisioned for us. Long enough to have several children with him. They would remain, when he left this earth. I would be a widow but accepted in the community. He would have had me for those years. I was too numb and cold inside to care.

Chapter 28

Thursday evening arrived, along with Minister Esh's visit. We ate supper and sat on the porch swing afterwards while Joy helped Grandma with the dishes.

"What a meal, and such a lovely evening." He stroked his long gray beard. "The Lord is pleased, I believe."

"What did you do with your day?" I asked.

"Cut the hay for the first time, fixed a couple barn boards blown loose this winter."

"When is the hay going up?"

"Monday, if there is no rain over the weekend."

"Care if I come over and help you?"

He looked startled. "I was expecting no such thing."

I shrugged. "I would like to help."

"Nice," he said. "I can see you're serious about our relationship."

He left an hour later, and I arrived early on Monday morning with Joy in the buggy beside me.

"He has a nice place," Joy said, looking around.

"You won't be living here with me after the wedding," I said. "You'll go back to your Daett's place."

Tears trickled down her face. "Thanks for keeping me during this time and for helping me."

The barn door swung open, and Minister Esh hurried towards us. I climbed down from the buggy to greet him.

"Good morning." His smile was bright.

"Good morning," I said. "Have you eaten breakfast yet?"

"I'm afraid I haven't quite gotten there yet," he said.

"Then I'll have breakfast ready by the time you finish the chores."

"You will." He looked quite pleased. "What a treat this is, and Joy has come along today. Welcome."

"Come, Joy," I said, and headed up to the house.

We entered to find a well swept living room, but a kitchen without signs of any breakfast preparations.

"What do you think he eats?" Joy asked.

"Or when," I said.

We had the eggs and bacon fried by the time Minister Esh came in from the barn.

"Chores finished?" I asked.

He seated himself on a kitchen chair before he answered. "They are, and I'm having a hard time believing my eyes. Here I have two lovely women in my kitchen fixing breakfast for me."

I ignored the compliment. "Do your daughters stop by from time to time?"

"They do."

"I saw a casserole in the ice box."

"Mary was here last night," he said. "She takes some time out of her Sunday evening to visit Grandpa."

"And make sure he is fed?"

He laughed. "I never learned much in the way of cooking."

We set the table for him and laid out the food. He ate hardily, as if he had been hungry for a while.

"Will you be in school today?" he asked Joy.

Joy glanced up from her plate. "Mamm said I should help with your hay."

"We can't keep children out of school for work on my farm." He protested. "My nephew is coming over, and with Lily's help we can manage."

Joy furrowed her brow. "How do I get to school from here?"

Minister Esh glanced up at the clock. "There's a buggy going by in about thirty minutes. I will flag them down and send you along. Agreed?"

"I do love school," Joy said, "but I can also help today."

"Breakfast is enough," he said. "You're an excellent cook."

Thirty minutes later, he did what he promised and had Joy on the buggy bound for the school. The stillness of the farm crept over me. I was alone with the man. I didn't fear, which was good, but the coldness inside of me didn't leave.

"Joy is a very decent girl," he said, staring after the departing buggy. "I'm trying to remember why she was sent away from the community."

"I would rather not speak for my sister," I said.

He nodded. "If you wed me, I will ask for no more."

"I will wed you," I said.

He smiled. "Your Mamm would normally host the wedding, but things are a little different for us. How about having the wedding here on my farm?"

"I have no objections," I said.

"Good, then we should speak soon of a date. In the meantime, there is the hay which must be baled. My nephew should be coming soon."

"I'll clean the last of the dishes." I forced a smile.

He hurried towards the barn, and I returned to the house. The dishes were done quickly. I worked in a daze. My eyes wouldn't focus. I steadied myself on the edge of the counter. I was not going to think about our wedding night in this house. There had been a man in my bed many, many times, and I had survived. This was legal, at least—in Barbara's way of doing things. Maybe legal translated into better? For once, I hoped my sister and her ways were correct.

I heard Minister Esh's wagon clatter outside the kitchen window, and I left the house to join him. He slowed the wagon and gave me a hand upward. I hopped on to steady myself on the back wooden rack.

"Come up front," he hollered.

I did, and we bounced down the lane standing side by side. We looked like what we were not, a husband and wife, bound for a day of work in the fields. He wrapped the reins around the middle board, and we jumped to the ground.

"Work with me," he said, when I made to head towards the other side of the wagon.

I grabbed a fork and we pushed a line of hay together to toss upward.

On the third heave, he leaned on his fork to catch his breath. "I'm okay," he said, when I showed my concern.

I lingered close, skeptical.

He caught his breath and spoke. "I have been thinking about our earlier discussion. In special cases like ours, the couple doesn't always have a wedding during the week. They get up on a Sunday morning after the sermon and say their vows to the bishop."

I didn't hesitate. "I have no problem with the arrangement. We're a special case."

He seemed to struggle with believing me. "You would be willing?"

"Yes. When?"

"Maybe in a few Sundays, after we've spoken with Bishop Mast?"

I shrugged. "How is not a big matter to me."

He touched my arm. "I will be kind to you, Lily. I promise."

I nodded but didn't look at him. "Thank you."

We worked silently until the nephew, Markus, arrived, a stout young fellow, with a clean-shaven face.

"I figured you'd have the entire field done by now," he teased.

Minister Esh leaned against the wagon to rest. "There was the day when I would have had the entire field done by myself."

"I was teasing. You're not really old," he said.

"Old enough." Minister Esh forced a laugh.

We set to work and had three wagons of hay in the mow by eleven. "Should I fix lunch?" I asked.

"I was hungry an hour ago," Markus said.

"There's your answer," I said.

Minister Esh didn't object, and I left for the house on the next round.

I had sandwiches ready when they came in from the field, still wet around the edges of their hair from the wash at the outside water pump. Minister Esh ate sparsely, I thought. Maybe breakfast was his large meal of the day?"

"Another sandwich," I asked.

"I'm fine," Minister Esh said, but his face was pale.

Markus grinned. "A little nap under the shade tree will perk the old man right up."

"I think a nap is exactly what I need," Minister Esh said, and retreated to the living room. I heard him moan when he lowered himself on the couch.

"I see you're helping him out for the day?" Markus was looking at me.

"You object?"

"No, just wondering."

"You shouldn't believe everything you hear," I said.

He looked sheepish. "I suppose so, but you were living with the English for a long time."

"I'm back now."

"What is life like out there?"

"Aren't you about ready for your rumspringa?"

"He ignored my question. "They say you had quite a wild one, you and Walter."

"Like I said …"

"Don't believe everything you hear," he finished.

"Exactly."

"Things are changing in the community." He eyed the two remaining sandwiches.

"You can eat them," I said.

He hesitated only a moment before his mouth was full.

"How are things changing?" I asked.

He swallowed twice before he spoke. "We seem to live pretty tame lives compared to yours. Wasn't your Grandpa a soldier in the Civil War?"

"He was."

"We don't do such things, or what you did." He snuck a look at me.

"What things?" I asked. I might as well indulge his fantasies. Perhaps dissuade them if I could.

He grinned. "They say you wandered around the countryside one summer with Walter. We wouldn't dare."

"We didn't do what you think," I said.

He obviously wasn't convinced. "Are you really going to marry Minister Esh?"

"Do you want the other sandwich?" I asked.

He laughed and took the last one.

"Have you dated yet?" I asked. Time to move on to safer subjects.

"Not old enough," he said, "but I like someone."

"Does she like you?" I raised my eyebrows.

He didn't look too happy. "She smiles at me, but she also smiles at a few other boys."

"Come now," I encouraged him. "You can win her affections."

"I doubt." He swallowed the last of his sandwich.

"Girls like confidence," I said.

Marcus made a face and left for the living room. He was back in a moment, his mouth open. "He's not moving."

"Who?"

"My uncle."

I followed him. The form on the couch was still. I touched his face. "Call a doctor," I whispered.

"He's dead," Markus said.

"You still have to call," I said.

Markus rushed outside and ran across the lawn towards the neighbor's home.

I stepped back from the body on the couch. There were pieces of hay on his collar which he had missed from the wash at the pump. I moved closer to pick them off with my finger. I dropped them to the floor. His shoes lay on the floor, the socks on his feet askew. I pulled them straight. I paced the floor. An automobile finally raced into the driveway. I had the door open, when the doctor brushed past me to kneel by the form on the couch.

"He's gone," he said within minutes. "What was he doing this morning?"

"Putting up hay."

"Are you his wife?" He stood to his feet.

"No."

"Do you know if he had any medical problems?"

"There was a heart issue," I said. "I don't know the name, but he was expected to live a few more years."

"Only God makes such judgments," he said and picked up his bag.

The doctor left, and I returned to the kitchen until Deacon Miller's buggy came into the driveway.

"What happened?" Was the first question out of his mouth.

"His heart problem, I suppose."

"What heart problem?" The deacon stared at me.

"The one they found when his wife was sick."

I could tell from the look on Deacon Miller's face he didn't know about Minister Esh's heart condition, and apparently no one else did either. Their logical conclusion was not difficult to anticipate. I was told to return to Grandma's house for the evening, and at the funeral was told to sit in the back with the women who were not related to Minister Esh.

I didn't protest. Two Sundays after the funeral, I was excommunicated again.

Deacon Miller spoke with me after the service. "We request you leave the community at once and take Joy with you."

"I can't," I said.

"There is no use staying around," he said. "The door to reconciliation for you has closed."

"I will go, if you let Joy stay."

"This is not a negotiation," he said.

"This is a sad day." Grandma told me on the way home. "When will you be leaving?"

We unhitched at the house and I asked Grandma once Joy was out of earshot. "Does leaving her with you work—if I go?"

"You know the answer," Grandma said. "I will pray. Perhaps the Lord will yet have mercy on us for your Grandpa's sake."

Grandma did. I heard her cries during the night, and early in the morning. I wept, hearing the agony in her voice. I couldn't imagine how this would change anything, but, in Grandma's voice, I heard Grandpa's love, and some of the bitterness oozed out of me. I would wait. As long as Grandma prayed, I would wait.

Chapter 29

The weeks passed. Despite the uncertainty of our existence, the sun shone warm overhead. The fields lay open with swaths of fresh cut hay, the sweat beading on weathered brows with the straw hats pulled low.

I no longer attended the church services and was not welcome at any community activities. I didn't care, I told myself. I also didn't care what anyone would think about my visit to Minister Esh's gravesite. I left for the short trip on a Friday afternoon right after lunch. As usual when I left the house for any reason, Grandma didn't ask where I was going.

I drove Maiden southward and brought the buggy to a stop along the wire fence. The graveyard stood stark in the mid-afternoon sunshine; the tombstones highlighted with shadows on their sides. Along the far fence the dirt was fresh, cast up in a mound and unwashed by the rain. I climbed down from the buggy and tied Maiden to the fence post.

There was a soft breeze stirring the graveyard, warm from the day's sunshine. I still wore my Amish clothes. There was no sense in causing undue conflict with Grandma. I took off my bonnet and opened the fence gate. A far away clip-clop of horse's hooves drifted towards me. I paused. Getting caught red handed wouldn't be fun. While I waited to see which way the buggy would turn, the starkness of my change swept over me.

A month had passed since the date when I had told Minister Esh I would marry him. I would be his widow by now—if the wedding had happened. Instead, I was the woman who had brought death into the community.

I had slain, not with my hands, but with my past. In the community's eyes, I deserved what had been dished out to me—an utter casting out. There would be no repentance offered to me again, and yet here I was visiting Minister Esh's gravesite. I walked closer, across the grass growing between the tombstones and knelt, my dress pulled above my knees. The dirt was warm on my skin. I reached down to touch the earth. The tears came and dripped on the ground.

I cried. Why? Marriage to Minister Esh would have been difficult, but I had been willing. No unkind word had passed my lips. I had not spoken evil of the man whose body lay below me covered in dirt.

I lifted my face to the heavens and wept. Joy did not deserve this. She was not to blame. Joy was a child of the community. She was not like me. She had done no wrong."

There was silence around me, broken only by the wind in the trees. The idea came to me while I was kneeling beside the grave. I would not say Minister Esh spoke to me from beyond this life. I heard no voice, and yet this was when both the thought and the courage flooded into me. I knew what must be done. I rose to my feet and returned to the buggy. Maiden's hooves beat a steady trot northward and then to the west. Grandma sat on the porch when I pulled into the driveway. I tied Maiden to the hitching post and approached the house.

"How are things going?" Grandma asked.

I leaned against the porch railing. A great weariness swept over my body at the thought of the task ahead of me.

"You know this can't go on forever," she said.

"I know." I stood upright. "I think I know what must be done."

"What?" She asked.

"Let's just say I'm taking Joy with me right now. You can start packing her things. She won't be coming back with me today."

"Where are you taking her?"

"First to Daett's place and then I'm leaving her with Walter where she belongs."

"How is this possible?"

"The time has come to speak the truth," I said.

She looked at me, but didn't say anything more.

I went into the house and found Joy.

"Come with me," I said.

Joy didn't ask our designation. We arrived at my home place, and I tied Maiden to the hitching post.

"Wait here," I told Joy, and went straight to the barn.

The hinges squeaked with their familiar sound and the odors inside were from my childhood. The coldness crept through me, but I forced myself to move deeper inside. I was no longer a child, and I would not tolerate another innocent child's destruction. This time, there was something I could do with my pain.

I peered through the dusty haze towards the back of the barn. Daett appeared with his pitchfork in hand. "Lily," he said. "Why are you here?"

I faced him. "I'm tired of what the community is doing, first to me, and now to Joy. I've had enough."

He didn't look impressed. "And what exactly is your plan? You've killed one of our ministers. No one cares what you think."

"I'm telling Walter what you did to me while I was growing up. For once, Barbara's honesty will work in my favor."

"No one will believe you." He smirked.

"Walter will, and Barbara won't lie," I said.

"Like I care?"

I ignored the barb. "I'm not asking you to admit anything—like you would, but I don't want one objection from you on Joy staying in the community."

"Sounds like you're threatening me," he said.

"I am. I will go to the law if you say a word to the ministers against Joy."

"Seems like what I did to you was a long time ago. I'm thinking the law will agree."

"I don't know what the statute of limitations is on raping your underage daughter," I said, "but my guess is there will be questions at least, from the authorities. Questions you will wish to avoid, so keep your objections to yourself."

"Protesting has always been useless, Lily."

"Shut up," I said, and left him. He appeared small to me, withered, as if his frame had shrunk. His smirk was no longer on his face.

I climbed back into the buggy and jiggled the reins. Maiden trotted out of the driveway. I caught a glimpse of Mamm in the kitchen window, but I didn't pause. I felt nothing but sorrow for Mamm—for her silence, for her coldness, for what her soul must look like. Maiden trotted westward. Walter came out of the barn door when I drove in. He approached the buggy. I let the reins hang limp in my hands.

"Lily." His voice was filled with tenderness.

"Walter," I said, and the tears came.

"What is wrong?" The alarm showed on his face.

"Give me a moment please." I struggled to speak.

"What happened?" he asked.

"Go into the house, and stay there," I told Joy. "Tell Barbara I said you could."

She looked puzzled but obeyed.

"What is this, Lily?"

"I know how to get Joy back into your home," I said.

"You do?" Delight lit up his face, before vanishing again.

"I just came from speaking with Daett," I said.

He couldn't have looked more perplexed.

"Daett will no longer object to Joy's return to your home."

"You're making no sense, Lily."

"Go get Barbara," I said. "Please."

"She won't come out."

"I think she will," I said.

I was right. Barbara walked a few steps behind Walter, but she came back with him.

"Why are you here?" There was fury in her voice.

"The time has come to settle this matter," I said. "Joy belongs in your home, and there is only one way to get her there."

"You should have listened to the ministers and left a long time ago." She raged.

Walter stood there, bewildered, saying nothing.

"I'm not arguing with anyone anymore," I said. "You're here to tell Walter I'm speaking the truth."

For once she was silent.

I couldn't look at Walter. My fingers dug deep into my palms, as I spoke the words. "Daett came to my bed from my early childhood until I left for Richmond."

Walter was staring.

"Tell him this is true," I said to Barbara.

Rage still filled her face.

"Or say nothing," I said.

"Is this true?" Walter's voice croaked. He had turned to stare at Barbara.

My sister was silent.

"You knew of this?" Walter reached for Barbara's arm, and she pulled back sharply.

"Don't take your anger out on her," I said.

He was facing me. "Your Daett came to your bed? Like in …"

"Yes, Walter. He raped me."

"All those years?"

"Yes. I told you I wasn't pure and holy, but you wouldn't believe me."

"I didn't …" His voice gave out.

"No one did," I said, "but now you know. Use this if you have to, but don't let anyone drive Joy out of your home again."

"Lily," he said. "I had no idea. I am—I am the most horrible, awful human being on this earth not to have suspected."

"You were a man of honor," I said, "and you still are. Now I'm going. You can tell Joy she's staying, and Grandma will bring over her clothing tomorrow."

I left them standing in the driveway, two figures frozen in time, unmoving when I glanced back a half mile down the road.

"How did you do this?" Grandma asked after I had Maiden unharnessed and came alone back into the house.

"I'm not explaining," I said. "I don't know how much Walter will tell you."

She looked completely confused. "Joy is home? She's staying?"

"She is," I said. "I'll be leaving soon."

Only I didn't. I waited. I waited because there was hope in my heart, because I was hanging on by my fingernails. I didn't believe Walter would come. Yet I didn't leave either.

Anger smoldered on Grandma's face when she drove in from the next Sunday's service. Walter had apparently told her plenty.

Her hand trembled on my arm. "I'm so sorry this happened to you, Lily. I had no idea. Certainly, Grandpa didn't. He would have—"

"I know," I said. "Let's say no more on the matter."

She didn't ask questions when Walter's buggy pulled into the driveway in the afternoon, and I went out to speak with him.

I stood there looking up into the buggy.

"There is a small stream a half mile from here," he said. "If the weather is clear, walk down to the large sycamore tree by the road, and cut across the fields. I will meet you there on Wednesday evening after dark by the creek."

"Walter," I said.

"Please, Lily? I want to."

"Are you sure?"

He nodded.

"I'll be there," I said.

He jiggled the reins and drove out of the driveway again. Grandma didn't say anything when I came back into the house.

Chapter 30

"I'm going for a walk," I told Grandma, late Monday morning, even though she usually didn't ask.

Grandma didn't respond. She was waiting, I figured. For what she wasn't sure, but she wasn't interfering.

I headed down the road on foot, and found the large sycamore tree around the bend, set along the fence row among the smaller trees, with branches sprawling towards the heaven. There was no break in the wooden fence, but I was an Amish girl. I clambered over easily. The field was open before me, the hay fresh cut. I strode downward to the small line of trees. A stream lay hidden behind them, where the water tinkled past, musically dancing over the small rocks.

I sat down on the bank, and the memories flooded back. I saw days gone by. Walter and I camped out in the open fields at night, with water in front, and the silences of the open heavens above us. I lay back on the grass with the sound of the water in my ears and wept for what we had lost.

I sat up and composed myself. This was a dream. This couldn't be real. Walter didn't want to meet me here, yet I had heard the words come out of his mouth. I hadn't imagined a thing.

I wiped away the tears. Maybe Walter only wanted to spend the night here. We had done that so many times before, lying close beside each other, not touching more than our hands, his eyes fixed upon me, gazing with longing and passion, until the starlight dimmed the vision, and there was only the outline of his face, the steady breathing of his breath across from me.

This must be what he longed for, as I had longed for a few hours spent together to say our farewells. We had thought our goodbyes were said in the barn when his hands touched the skin of my feet, but we had come to know differently. Our hearts had their own mind divorced from the dictates of men and the councils of ministers. Along those long ago streams, our hopes and our love were brought to its highest existence, and here they must die by the tinkle of the water, washed downstream past the open hay fields and on to larger waters, till they were swept into the vastness of the ocean itself. There to mingle with the tears of others who had loved and lost, who had lived and who had died.

I had dared stand up to Daett, and Walter had responded with a daring which took my breath away. No one would ever find us here, but Barbara would know. In her heart, she would know where Walter had been, but the issue didn't seem to matter anymore. I could not continue to give my sister what belonged to me. She had taken, and I had only this left. This once, I would live, and then I would die.

I lay on my back and drank in the sight of the sky above me. The clouds scurried past on the soft wind blowing up from the south. This was a summer from my childhood, encapsulated and offered on a silver platter for my healing and comfort. I would drink this cup—whatever Walter had to offer. I would not object or complain. I would not reach for what he could not give. I would hold him with open hands for these few hours when we were once more young, and had dared look each other in the eyes as if tomorrow had no goodbyes.

The sun was high in the sky when I rose to my feet and walked back across the fields. I prepared myself a sandwich in the kitchen and was eating on the porch when Grandma came out to sit with me.

"How was Joy on Sunday?" I asked.

A smile crept into Grandma's face. "She looked happy. Your sister doesn't though."

"Barbara's time of getting everything she wants is over."

"I'm so sorry again for what happened in your childhood," she said. "Neither Grandpa nor I had the slightest idea."

"I'm okay," I said.

"What happened was not okay, but there's not much I can do now."

"Don't be so sure," I said.

She looked at me but didn't say anything. Grandma thought I wanted her to push for Daett's punishment. I didn't enlighten her. She would find out what I meant soon enough.

"I'm going out for a walk," I told her again as the sun was setting.

"In the dark?" She questioned this time.

"Not quite dark," I said. "I'll be back by the time the stars are out."

On Tuesday night, I did the same but didn't return until eleven or so. She was sleeping and didn't awaken when I entered the house. On Wednesday evening, I left again to climb the fence line this time. I saw no signs of a horse and buggy tied along the road. Walter was at the stream when I arrived, with PJ tied to a small tree trunk.

"How did you get in?" I asked.

"There's a gate around the bend." He had a small fire started and stirred the flames with a stick.

I sat down a short distance from him. "I came here on Monday."

"You did?" He didn't sound surprised.

"How's Joy doing?"

"She's home," he said. "Barbara raged for a while, but I told her Deacon Miller knew everything. I also told your Grandma."

"I know," I said. "What will happen now?"

"Nothing, likely. They're leaving us alone."

"My plan worked." I smiled. "I was right."

"You're always right," he said. "Come closer. Sit beside me."

I did and held his hand.

"You haven't aged a bit," he said. "Your beauty and charm grow with the passing of time."

"I haven't birthed children like Barbara did," I said, "and you exaggerate anyway."

He looked at my figure, with longing in his eyes. "You'll always be beautiful, young, and so full of life and joy."

I swallowed the lump in my throat, daring to hope. "There have been plenty of sorrows, you know. Our hearts have ached deeply."

"Always together." His voice sounded dead.

"I know," I said.

We sat silently listening to the sound of the water running beneath our feet, the flickering of the flames casting wild shadows across the ripples.

"We were always meant to be," he said. "You knew the truth before I did."

I wanted so much not to cry. "I did and I do," I managed, "but what is, just is."

"You should be back with me at the house, instead of your sister."

I drew a long breath. "Stop talking like this, Walter. I never will be."

"I know," he said, "yet you should be."

I sighed, the hope draining out of me. "Is this what you came to tell me?"

"No." He stirred in the dark. "I came to make right what I did wrong, to give what you wanted those long ago years. To love as I should have, and never did."

226

"Do you really mean what I think you mean?" My heart pounded in my throat.

"I do," he said, his eyes on my face

"You will pay."

He hung his head. "The price kept me before—not my virtue, not my honor, not anything but my fear of dishonor."

"You're the most honorable, virtuous man I have ever known." I protested.

"Then why did I not give you what you wanted?" he asked.

For the first time I spoke freely on the subject. "You didn't know who I was. I was the one who was the most wrong. I should have told you."

"I didn't want to know," he said. "This is the bitter truth."

"Now you know. Are you really going to love me?" My voice trembled.

"I'm so sorry, Lily. I can't believe … I simply can't imagine what you went through."

"Let's not speak of Daett at this moment." I reached for his hand, daring to touch him.

"I love you, Lily." His fingers were tight on mine. "You know I do."

"I do," I said, gazing into his eyes.

The stars twinkled on the horizon, an exceptionally bright one in the line of my vision. I sat in silence. I waited. This was Walter's moment, and he was in charge. He let go of my hand and stood to walk over to the buggy to pull out several blankets. He spread them out on the grass. "Come."

"Do you really mean this?"

"I do," he said.

He embraced me, and I clung to him. I had never known such belonging in his arms before, as if I had been made for this moment, for this man.

"Will you come again next week," he asked well over an hour later.

"You know I will," I whispered.

I climbed into his buggy for the drive out to the road.

"You can't take me any closer," I said.

I didn't check if Grandma was asleep when I snuck into the house, and she didn't say anything the next morning. I made a point to take another walk later in the week, and again on Monday night. Grandma must have suspected as the weeks of the summer crept past. She must have remembered what I said, and decided to remain quiet. How Walter explained his absence to Barbara, I didn't ask, and I didn't care. I was lost in a haze of joy unlike any I had ever walked in before.

Walter's touch healed me in places I didn't know existed. All the years of agony, of pain, from being Daett's helpless victim slowly washed away. I didn't want to awaken from this dream. I saw Walter's face when I woke in the early morning hours, and he flickered before my vision when I lay down on my pillow to sleep.

"Have you made your peace with the community?" Grandma asked some two months after our first meeting by the river."

"Why?" I asked.

"You seem happy. You almost—I don't know, glow. I thought perhaps a miracle of the Lord had happened and you hadn't told me."

"A miracle has happened," I said.

"I see," she said, and we continued to wash the dishes.

I knew our time together was ending when Walter asked to see me twice a week. I wept, and he comforted me. "You are so beautiful, so exquisite."

"How am I going to live without you?" I asked.

"I don't know, but we had our time together. If I die tomorrow, I will pass from this world satisfied."

"You will live a long time," I said, sitting upright, "and you will have a son."

"I suppose so," he said, "but let's not speak of Barbara."

"I'm not speaking of Barbara," I said.

He didn't ask what I spoke of, but Walter must have known. He asked to see me each night the following week. Those hours are still a haze in my mind, as if I walked in the shadow of heaven and knew I must soon return to the agony of another world.

Walter left me at the end of Grandma's driveway. I thought I would cry my eyes out, but I didn't. Calmness came over me, as if water was still tinkling at my feet. I had been given a great gift, a gift I thought had been taken from me forever. The ache was still there, deep down inside, as an old scar throbbing with the weather clouds on the horizon, but the stars were out tonight, brightly shining above me. I turned to look for his buggy. Walter was gone.

I was English now. The feeling crept over me. I was loosed from my past, from my obligations to this place. I could walk away and live, no longer looking back. Walter had given me freedom. We could have been so much more, but what could have been had not come to pass, and now what was, had been, and we were finished.

I smiled. What a strange thing, my smile, so gentle as if the feeling came from the skies above to flood my being. We would always have these nights, no matter the miles between us. We had been one, as our hearts had always been one.

"Thank you," I whispered, into the dark. "Thank you very much, Walter."

Grandma was sitting on the front porch swing in her night gown when I walked up to the house.

"Come sit with me," she said.

I did, and the chains squeaked above us in the starlight.

"This has to stop," she said. "You know seeing your sister's husband can't go on."

"I'm no longer seeing him," I said.

She looked skeptical.

"I'm not going out again."

Grandma stayed up a few nights to make certain, but she could have spared herself the effort. We had let go, because we had never been apart to begin with. I didn't explain to Grandma, or to anyone else.

There was Barbara though. She was my sister, and I would speak with her before I left. The time was not yet. When the moment would come, I didn't know, so I waited.

Section Seven—June 1927 to May 1928

BARBARA

Chapter 31

The hot summer sun blazed down outside our kitchen window, and the hay field stretched out behind the barn until the woods rose to meet the back fence. I leaned against the kitchen sink and took in the scene. Walter had cut the grass yesterday, and by midday on Monday, they would drive the wagons across the mown ground to gather in the hay. Our place looks like a normal Amish place, run by a normal Amish couple, bent to their farming duties, and living a contented and fulfilled life. Yet I was not living such a life.

I stood by my kitchen window stunned and immobilized by the events which had swirled around me these past three months, since Lily had dared drive into our place brazenly while I worked upstairs. She had ordered me down to speak with her. I think Walter would have dragged me out if I hadn't gone willingly.

The whole sleazy story is out. Grandma will barely speak to me at the Sunday services. Our justifications seem to mean nothing. No one else had to grow up with Lily or see what she was really like. In my wildest imagination, I could not have conjured up Lily's plan. My sister turned the tables on me. I hadn't even known she was capable of such scheming, and I know why. Lily was successful because she did not see her actions as scheming. More like a reaction to events. I should have anticipated what Walter and Lily would do, but what would I have done to change anything? Looking back, I knew there was nothing I could have done. Things were out of my hands. In the past months, Walter headed down to the basement each evening where he supposedly slept. I knew better. Walter was out many nights until late in the morning hours. I didn't hear the basement door open and close, but I heard his buggy coming and going. He must have known I knew.

I had seethed with rage one moment and fallen into utter hopelessness the next. I finally went over to speak with Deacon Miller about what Walter was doing, but barely got two words out of my mouth before the deacon turned on me.

"Where we had better start, Barbara," he said, "are with these terrible accusations against your family. After we have answers for them, we can talk about any complaint you may have against your husband."

"These are more than complaints," I said. "Walter is seeing my sister."

"As I said." The deacon barely heard me. "Tell me about what supposedly happened in your home while you were growing up. Are the accusations true?"

"What does Daett say?" I sidestepped the matter.

"To tell you the truth, Barbara, I'm tired of this awful subject. I always thought of you and your Daett as among the most up-building members in the community. The very thought that you might have been hiding such terrible secrets makes me want to hang my face in shame. Perhaps we should depend on the Lord's mercy and beg his forgiveness for what may or may not have happened. We're all sinners and in great need of his grace. On those points, everyone can agree."

Lily had done her work well. I fell silent and protested no more. Minister Esh was dead, and no one was doing anything lest the scandal spread further. At least in the past week, I had no longer heard Walter drive his buggy in and out of the lane. Had he stopped seeing Lily? I lay awake at night and wondered. Could he have grown tired of her, as he had grown tired of me? I couldn't imagine him growing tired of Lily.

I moved back from the kitchen window when a buggy pulled into the driveway. I didn't want to see who had arrived, and I didn't want to know what their errand was. Walter could deal with them. Walter's steps have become those of a young man these past months. I saw his face increasingly glow with utter happiness. I caught him often in the evenings, absentmindedly looking over his copy of the Budget. I sat in the rocker beside him, and he glanced over at me, but the joy disappeared at once, replaced by a studied hardness. He was a man of two faces, one for me, and one for my sister. Lily didn't live at our house, but I had grown up around my sister and Walter. I knew what their love looked like.

Most women would have sobbed themselves to sleep at night on their pillows, but I didn't. I wouldn't stoop so low. I wondered often if Lily would take Walter with her when she finally left the community. They both must know this couldn't go on forever. Walter was willing to leave, I assumed. He had a gleam in his eye I had never seen before, so the matter would be decided by my sister. I didn't like the choice, but the thought was comforting in a way. The truth was I trusted my sister more than I trusted my own husband.

There was a soft knock on the front door, and I jumped.

"Grandma," the voices of the younger girls called out.

I hurried out of the kitchen to find Mamm hugging Elsie and Mary. I waited until they finished.

"Run off and play," I told the girls. "Grandma will be here for a little while."

"I will?" she asked me, as if in a daze.

"Mamm." I took her hand. "I'm sorry I didn't notice you driving in. I was …"

"We all are …" she said. "How did this happen?"

"I don't know," I said. "Come sit." I helped her to a kitchen chair.

"Daett is in the barn talking with Walter."

"Why?" I leaned against the counter as weakness washed over me.

Mamm's voice lacked the usual strength. "Those two must make their peace or this will never go away."

I sighed. "You know everything has changed."

"I'm having nightmares," Mamm said.

"Aren't we all," I said, with great bitterness.

She didn't seem to hear. "I mean real ones. I wake and I think I hear horrible noises upstairs. How did we …? How could we, Barbara?"

"Do you want some hot chocolate?" I turned to the stove without waiting for Mamm's answer.

"There's nothing which comforts me these days," Mamm said. "Everyone knows, even if they pretend not to. What can we do?"

"Nothing," I said. "I went to speak with Deacon Miller. They won't be doing anything about anything."

"I wish they would," Mamm said. "I wish they would put us both in the Bann for a year, or maybe two years."

"You know the Bann wouldn't help make you feel better."

Mamm didn't seem to hear me. "I'd go to Deacon Miller and confess everything, but Daett won't let me. He hardly lets me out of his sight. He wouldn't let me come over here unless he came along."

I poured milk into a pan and stirred the fire.

"I go out of the house at night," Mamm said, "so I won't hear the noises."

"There's nobody up there."

"I can hear them plain as day," Mamm said. "Daett's footsteps creaking on the stairs, and then … Why did I, Barbara?"

"You'll just have to forget about this," I said. "There's nothing we can do."

Mamm stared at me. "You're not doing much better, are you?"

I stirred the milk and didn't look at her. "Walter has been going to see Lily at night. A few weeks ago, he went almost every evening."

"You didn't tell Deacon Miller this?" Mamm's voice filled with horror.

"No one wants to hear more awful things about our family."

Mamm stared into her cup. "I think I'm going to lose my mind."

The cup of chocolate steamed on the kitchen table, its tentacles rising upward and disappearing towards the ceiling. Loud voices came from outside the kitchen window, and Mamm leaped to her feet. We looked at each other before we tiptoed over to peer outside. Daett and Walter were talking beside the barn door, with Daett waving his arms around.

"I should be going," Mamm said, and bolted from the kitchen.

I continued to watch from the window. Daett walked away from Walter when Mamm's figure appeared and hurried across the yard. Mamm climbed into the buggy, and Daett untied his horse. They drove out of the lane without a backwards glance at Walter, who went back into the barn.

Soft footsteps behind me broke my reverie. "Where's Grandma?"

"I'm sorry, she had to leave," I said.

"She didn't drink her hot chocolate." Mary eyed the cup on the table.

"Grandma didn't want her hot chocolate," I said.

"Can I drink it?"

"Why not." I really didn't care if she drank the whole pot.

Her eyes shone. Mary took a sip, then gave the cup to Elsie.

"I'm going out to the barn," I said, and left the kitchen.

I followed Mamm's steps across the yard, my mind filled with the vision of my two girls savoring Mamm's forsaken cup of hot chocolate. Would my children make a better go of community life than Mamm and I had? Would this be my comfort? Where I had failed, they would not? I grasped for straws, I knew, yet I clutched the feeble strands with both hands.

I pushed open the barn door and entered.

Walter had buckets of feed in his hands and set them down. "Did you ask your Daett to come over?"

"He came because Mamm came, and he isn't going to give in to you."

His face was filled with anger. "Says the woman who tolerated his evil doings."

"I was a little girl," I said.

His anger changed to scorn. "When are you going to stop making excuses—for him and for yourself?"

"What do you want to happen?" I asked.

He hesitated only a moment. "Confession and repentance. We could start there."

"How would words change anything?"

His face darkened again. "How dare you say such a thing?"

"You can't start seeing Lily again," I said.

His eyes gleamed. "We're going to visit the Mennonite church on Sunday. I have had enough of this nonsense."

"The Mennonite Church?" Now horror gripped me.

"We're going," he said, and picked up his buckets to walk away.

"What if I don't go?" I called after him.

"You're going," he said, without looking over his shoulder.

We ate supper with a heavy silence between us. The girls didn't seem to notice, as they chattered amongst themselves. I understood why. We had lived this way for a very long time.

The girls and I cleared the table after supper and washed the dishes. The girls went up to their rooms around eight, and Baby Jane settled down nicely in her crib. Walter was still in his rocker when I came out of the bedroom.

"I'm not going with you to the Mennonite church," I said."

He didn't look up from the Budget he was reading. "We're going as a family."

"I'm not getting in the buggy with you."

"You're going to listen," he said.

"Why should I?" I asked.

The pages of the Budget rustled. "Because you don't have a life left, Barbara. At least the one you've built."

"Have you really been sleeping with my sister?"

"You're going with me," he said.

"Joining the Mennonite church isn't going to get you Lily. Not as your wife. They believe what the community believes. You can't leave me for her."

He studied the page his eyes blank. "You don't think I know?"

"Then what is joining their church going to help?"

The anger came back. "Because they don't tolerate people who do things your Daett did."

"You wouldn't know if they did," I said.

"I know they don't." His gaze went back to his paper. "You're coming with me."

"What did Daett tell you today?"

He didn't answer at once. "I don't want to speak about your Daett."

I tried for a contrite tone. "I know we were wrong about things. Mamm knows we were. She came over today to talk to me."

"Are you going to Deacon Miller and asking him to excommunicate your Daett for his sins?"

"They wouldn't excommunicate Daett, even if we asked."

"Don't avoid my question," he said. "Why won't you stand up to the man?"

I sighed. "There are things we can't change, Walter. This is one of them."

He glared at me. "Neither can my love for your sister change, yet I have to live without her."

"I live with my own sorrow, as does Mamm."

"You know nothing of sorrow!" He exploded. "You know nothing of pain which comes from loving and losing the most precious thing in life. You only know your selfish, self-centered desires, which burn your heart out like a flame, and scorch everything you touch."

I kept my voice steady. "Why are you destroying everything we built so carefully?"

"What you built." He rose from his rocker and I stepped back. "You build empty structures from rules and laws and fill them with your cold calculating heart. Why I ever gave an inch to you, I can't imagine."

I nearly tripped over a chair, my eyes on his face. "Seems like you didn't think so once or see much value in the destruction my sister leaves in her path."

"I'm telling you," he warned. "You're coming with me to the Mennonite church."

"Will you not go to her at night again?" I begged.

"You're bargaining with me?" His voice rose.

"There's no use giving in if you haven't stop seeing her."

"You're going," he said, and went down the basement steps.

I stood by the window until the stars were bright in the sky, but no dark form crossed the yard, and no buggy drove out of the lane.

I didn't understand any of this, or where Walter intended to lead our family. I was not a Mennonite woman, and I never could be one. Driving with him to visit the Mennonite church would not change anything. Walter was serious in a way I had never seen him before. I felt like a widow already, and yet I wasn't one. Widows had a place of honor in the community, but a woman forsaken by her husband, with a house full of children would be looked at as the epitome of failure. Sympathy would be the best I could expect.

I was no longer the strong woman I once was, determined and certain I could bend the events of life to fit what was right. I had failed. Mamm had failed. We had all failed, as had my sister. Yet Lily had Walter—at least his heart.

I cried for the first time. I stuck a kitchen cloth in my mouth to quiet my sobs. I couldn't control the dam which broke inside of me. Tears had never helped anyone, and they weren't helping me now. I felt weak, helpless, and miserable to the core of my being when the torrent settled down. I climbed into bed, and the tears came again. I laid awake until the storm passed, like thunderclouds moving into the distance. They stayed in my dreams during the night with tumbling, tumultuous emotions, undefined and terrifying.

I awoke with a start to the sound of Walter's footsteps going through the kitchen and out of the house. I crept out of bed to push aside the drapes. The faint outline of dawn was on the horizon. The tears stung again, and I wiped them away. I would not cry anymore. Tears did no good. They never had and they never would.

Chapter 32

We drove southward on Sunday morning. The corn stalks in the open fields had crept out of the parched ground, their feeble arms reached heavenward as if in supplication for rain. Not unlike myself, who sought to breech heaven despite my certain knowledge the Lord was not going to give me anything.

I had a grip on the side of the open buggy door with one hand while I held Baby Jane on my lap with the other. Joy, along with her two sisters, was in the back seat of the surrey, silent, as if they knew what everyone else would soon know. We were headed for a Mennonite church service. Walter hadn't spoken on the matter since our conversation in the living room, but his determination hadn't waned. This was a disaster for everyone, a public display of the devastation our lives had become. At least I hadn't cried again.

We couldn't have hidden our dismal situation must longer anyway. Walter's dark face at the services and his grunted good mornings to the other men made the matter clear enough. Walter had lost hope in the community, along with his confidence in our goodness, and now the faith of his childhood was threatened.

"There's still time to turn back," I whispered. "Everyone will understand and praise you for having withstood temptation."

"Something has to change," he said. "They all believe lies. All of them."

"This is not the answer," I said.

"I don't want to hear what you think, Barbara. Do I make myself clear?"

I fell silent, the strength going out of my body. I couldn't believe this was me, sitting in our buggy headed towards a Mennonite church service.

The tears wanted to come again when Walter turned into the Mennonite church parking lot. A few automobiles sat along the far fence, but mostly I saw buggies. The sight was a small comfort, but this was not home. I had not been born to worship the Lord in a strange land.

"Don't just sit there," Walter ordered. "Come out."

He was already on the ground and gave his hand to Joy and the two girls. He never acted this way at the Amish services, where Joy and her sisters hopped down on their own.

"Barbara!" His voice was sharp.

I laid Baby Jane on the buggy seat and climbed down. Walter had Elsie and Mary by the hand with Joy beside him. Together they moved toward the double doors of the church house. I forced myself to follow with Baby Jane in my arms. I felt like the whole world had turned to look at me, a straggler who walked behind my husband and daughters, rejected and spurned for the love of another. They had to see into our hearts. We had been ripped and torn apart with nothing hidden anymore.

Walter took off his hat when we walked inside, and a bearded stranger was there to greet us and shake our hands. He was young, with a bright smile, and a cheery voice.

"Good morning, folks." He stuck out his hand. "Glad to have you come out and worship the Lord with us."

I felt dizzy and disoriented, as if I were a fish out of water gasping for air.

"Thank you," Walter said, and the young man motioned us on inside.

Others directed us to a seat. They were strangers, their faces from another world. Doubtless these people had left the community years ago, or their parents had. They were drifters to me, people who had forsaken their Amish heritage for one reason or the other. They had longed for the world and its ways and sought comfort outside the will of the Lord.

I kept my gaze on top of Baby Jane's head. They had to know who we were. The harsh rumors must have circulated and spread their noxious fumes abroad. Didn't Walter know he was a marked man? They might not know about his nightly visits to see my sister, but they knew he was associated with a big mess. I hadn't thought to remind him. I was glad I hadn't. Better the impact be fresh and untarnished. Hope began to stir inside me.

The form of a woman appeared in front of me and she offered her hand. "Hi."

"Hi." I managed.

Her bearded husband stood smiling beside the woman. "Good morning," he said. "Aren't you the Yoders?"

"Yes," Walter said. "Barbara and Walter." He didn't seem to know what the greeting meant.

"Levi and Silva Raber," the man said. "I'm one of the ministers here at the church. I suppose we're related somewhere." He laughed. "Seems like everyone is around here."

Silva studied us, while she pretended not to. "We were sorry to hear about your community's loss awhile back. Minister Esh was known to us, although not personally. I hope the Lord has been ministering grace to your broken hearts."

"My sister-in-law Lily is doing the best she can," Walter said, "as is everyone under the circumstances. Thanks for your concern."

"The Lord is a great healer," Levi said. "We have to keep this truth in mind, but enough talk on tragedy. Perhaps we'll be seeing more of you after the service? You're welcome to come to our house for dinner. There's always a place at the table for visitors."

"Thanks. Sure," Walter said.

He sounded desperate. I put my head down, as the couple moved on, shaking hands as they went. Out of the corner of my eye I saw Walter had a smile on his face. He thought things were going his way with the minister's dinner invitation. I knew better.

A song was given out, and the singing began. The numbers were in English, of course. I tried to join in, but the notes stuck in my throat. A great longing swept through me for the joyous German words I was used to, sung in unison by the congregation. This was my first Sunday service when I had not heard them. I glanced over at Walter. He was singing, with his smile still present. How could anyone smile in the face of this shallow nonsense? Our songs had been written by men in dungeons, with chains bound to their feet. These were English songs, likely written by the same people who had persecuted our forefathers. Before the day was done, Walter would see his mistake. There were no answers for us in this church house.

After the songs, the Sunday school hour was announced.

"Sunday school is from the English people!" Bishop Mast had often warned our congregation. "Why would men and women who love the truth subject themselves to questions, suppositions, and wrestling with Scriptures? These things belong to those who seek the Lord outside of his will."

The crowd broke up, and I was directed into a room with the other married women. I held Baby Jane close to me, while a younger woman took charge of the class and began the session with a prayer.

"Help us, dear Lord," she prayed. "Help us find your will in the Holy Scriptures today. Give us enlightenment by your Spirit and draw our hearts together in our study of sacred things. Amen."

"Amen," several others echoed.

Chills ran up and down my back. They were so bold in speaking of God and His word, and the woman in charge was so young. She had prayed out loud as if she talked to the Lord standing right here in the room, instead of seated in the heavens high above us.

The discussion began after the prayer, with Bibles opened on their laps. When someone noticed I didn't have one, a Bible was slipped into my hand. I found the Scripture they were talking about and opened the pages. I felt as if I should have refrained myself, as if I was sitting there with my Bible, approving of their audacity and presumption by my participation. Women could not understand the Scriptures without the ministers present in the room.

An hour later, we filed back to our seats where more handshakes and whispered names were exchanged. I could see the comprehension dawn on faces, followed by quick downward glances. These people knew who we were and what had happened. Walter still didn't seem to notice.

The preaching began, but I didn't listen. I had reached the limits of my endurance. The instructions of the Lord should be spoken in the German tongue, not in the language of the world which had swallowed up my fallen sister and threatened my husband. The sermons didn't last long, which was another atrocity. The service closed with a song and a prayer. Handshakes were again offered in parting, along with a few dinner invitations.

"Minister Raber has already invited us," Walter said, and they would nod and smile and move on.

No one seemed disappointed, but Walter didn't notice, either. He led the way outside and we climbed into our buggy.

Minister Raber waved to us from across the parking lot, with his automobile already running. "Second house on the left." Minister Raber was off in a puff of smoke.

"You can't really want this," I said.

"Be quiet." Walter ordered, and PJ lunged forward.

We trotted down the road and pulled into the Rabers's driveway. Minister Raber and his wife had vanished, but their automobile sat in the driveway. Walter helped the girls down again. I didn't say anything, our march to the front door silent. Walter knocked.

"Come in. Door is open." Minister Raber hollered from inside.

We entered to find him at Silva's side deep in the bustle of dinner preparations. Walter looked a little uncomfortable. Men working in the kitchen were not an Amish staple. I felt happiness stir inside of me. This was another sign Walter's plan wasn't working out.

"Please take a seat." Minister Raber motioned towards a large dining room table with ample seating space. "As you can see, we can handle a dozen guests, but you're special today."

"Thank you," Walter said, and pulled out a chair.

"I'm so glad you folks stopped by this morning," Minister Raber continued. "I hope the Lord ministered to you. Perhaps something you can take back home with you."

"Careful. You were the one preaching," Silva teased.

"I didn't mean to toot my own horn." Minister Raber laughed. "The word of the Lord is alive and powerful whoever says the words."

Walter nodded, as if he understood this fancy talk.

"Can I help you?" I asked Silva.

"Just sit and relax," Silva ordered. "We don't have much, but the meal's almost ready."

248

Silva proceeded to take a meat roast out of the oven followed by a bowl of corn. A salad must have been prepared earlier, along with the cherry pie on the counter. They soon joined us at the table, and we bowed our heads. Minister Raber led out in a lengthy prayer of thanks.

The food was passed, and I filled my plate and managed to swallow. Joy and the girls appeared to have no such problem. They ate with abandonment. I joined in the conversation where I could. Walter looked happy.

We finished the meal, and I helped clear the table and wash the dishes. Walter followed Minister Raber into the living room and sat down across from him with Baby Jane at his feet. I couldn't overhear the conversation, and I didn't want to. I wanted this to end.

"How is your mother?" Silva asked.

"She still gets around," I said.

"Your baby's growing."

"Yes. I'm thankful for good health."

"You lost one a couple years ago."

I nodded, a lump forming in my throat.

"The ways of the Lord are difficult to understand," she said.

"They are," I agreed.

Walter was ready to leave when we finished the dishes, which I took as a good sign. He was silent on the walk back to the buggy. We climbed in and drove out of the lane.

"Well, you got your way," Walter said out of the corner of his mouth. "We're not going back."

I didn't say anything, but my heart pounded in my chest.

"I suppose you know why."

I still didn't answer.

"Minister Raber thinks we shouldn't change church membership at the moment. Seems they have heard things about your family. No details, he said, but people should fix things at home before they make a major church move."

"They know about us," I said.

"They know about your Daett," he said.

"They know about you and Lily," I said.

He didn't say anything, his face grim.

Chapter 33

If Deacon Miller was informed of our disastrous visit to the Mennonite church, he chose to ignore the information. Maybe he figured we had learned our lesson. We did show up for the Amish church services as usual the following Sunday, and families did visit around. Everyone knew we were under considerable pressure. They gave us tight smiles before the services began, and life went on.

Two weeks later, on a Saturday evening, I set up the wash tub as usual in our bedroom, with the door locked and the drapes drawn. The girls had bathed an hour earlier. They were relaxing with Walter in the living room in preparation for their bedtime after our long hard day of Saturday labors.

I stepped into the water, first one foot and then the other. I reached for the washcloth laid out with the soap on top of the upturned water bucket. I caught sight of my form in the dresser mirror and paused. I turned sideways for a better look. I had lost weight these last difficult months, but my hips were still broad and my legs stout. I had been born with those features and would die with them. At least my breasts were full with minimum sag. I pushed beneath one with my fingertips and stopped. The lump under the skin was unmistakable, hard and traveling length wise. I stared at the figure in the mirror. A lump! The judgment of the Lord! I was not Aunt Maud or my sister Lily!

I felt a numbness creep over me. I wanted to call out for help. I wanted Walter to hear me. I wanted him to rush into the bedroom, wrap his arms around me, and overwhelm me with his strength. I wanted him like I had never wanted him. Walter was right out there in the living room. He would come if I called. He knew what I looked like. Walter had seen Lily long before he had seen me, but I didn't care anymore. The Lord had smitten me.

This was cancer. I pressed again. The lump hadn't gone away. I reached under the other breast. The lump was smaller there, but there was a lump. So suddenly! Perhaps they had been there a long time and I hadn't noticed. They must have been and I had been occupied with concerns I thought more urgent, while my body prepared me for destruction. I felt myself leave this world, sucked right out of the bedroom window into the gathering darkness. I was going to die.

Walter could have Lily. As in really have her living in the same house, calling her his wife. I could let go. Just open my hands to this blackness where there was no struggle, no agony, and no grief.

A sense of relief filled the empty spaces on my skin until I burned with heat. The wisps of steam rose from the water tub and coiled upwards around my thighs. I no longer knew myself. I was cold and I was hot. Was this death, a clash of two worlds, a mixing of fire and the cool breezes of heaven? I took the soap and washed my body. I did so without thinking. Nothing mattered. I had no choice. I could have my breasts removed and stay on this earth awhile longer. Yet, I could not live without them. Not if I wanted Walter. The shame would be too much. I had never been what my sister was, but I had still been a woman. I still had something. This would leave me with nothing. I would rather die than face the surgeon's knife.

I understood Aunt Malinda's choice, and I had reasons to reject surgery a thousand times greater than any Aunt Malinda possessed. Uncle Mose had adored her, while Walter despised me. Walter had always despised me. He had married me because he hated himself for what he had done to Lily. I was his punishment. I had been wrong about everything. I had imagined my virtues could compete with my sister's lithe form and beauty. I had failed, and the Lord was agreeing. This was his judgment. The earth was better without me. Walter, the girls, and yes, Lily would find their lives improved by my absence.

The washcloth moved on my body, and the tears came. Sobs choked me. I held the bar of soap between my teeth to silence myself. The soft voices from the living room had become still. They were listening, but they didn't believe their ears because I never cried. I splashed water about and sloshed my arms with the wet cloth. The murmur of sound resumed outside the door.

I dried myself with the towel and dressed in my night clothes. Walter looked up when I walked out of the bedroom with a bucket of water in my hands. I ignored him and deposited the contents outside the washroom door.

"Time for bed," I told the girls, and they scurried up the stairs.

I finished transporting the rest of the water outside. Walter didn't look up when I sat in my rocker.

"Aren't you going to her tonight?" I asked.

He scowled at me. "Just be thankful I'm here."

I wanted to tell him. I wanted to scream I had cancer. I was dying, but I didn't. I would go down in silence. I would leave suddenly, perhaps in the nighttime alone on my bed. Aunt Malinda had been bedridden for a few weeks, but I was different. I was not loved. I had a strength Aunt Malinda didn't have. I would die in the fields while I worked, and they would never know why.

We sat for an hour in silence. I watched the swinging of the pendulum on the grandfather clock, the ticking growing louder and louder in my ears. Walter ignored me, as if I wasn't there. He couldn't be enjoying this anymore than I was, but maybe I no longer existed to him. Maybe I was already gone from his mind. I certainly was out of Walter's heart. I probably had never touched the door like I had imagined I had, let alone entered the room of Walter's inner most being. I had comforted myself with the rightness of my ways. I had held firm through the years in the belief good prevailed and evil lost. Yet here I was with the Lord's judgment in my breasts, and my sister living in my husband's heart.

My failure was my greatest sin. I could die from cancer, but I would not suffer a worse calamity than what my existence had become. Before me, Aunt Nancy and Aunt Malinda had opened the way. They had been good people. The dying did not make me bad; the living did. Maybe life was my redemption. The comfort of the thought did not steal over me. The emptiness only grew. I did not want redemption. I wanted to live. I wanted Walter. Dying would only accentuate my failure. I wanted something deep inside of me, with an ache which burned and left me icy at the same time.

Around eleven, Walter rose to his feet and without a glance went down to the basement. I could hear his heavy footsteps clunking on the stairs and fading away. If I hadn't lost Walter, he might have found the lumps months ago with his probing fingers. The tears stung again. I lived in a dream world. Walter had never explored my breasts or anything else on my body. I fantasized. I imagined things he should have done, things I wanted desperately to have done. I hadn't known how desperately. Things he had doubtlessly done to Lily. I was seeing what should have been, because with Lily they were real. I wanted for the first-time what Lily had. My throat hurt, and my mouth went dry. I thirsted for Walter. I didn't know a woman could so thirst for a man.

This was what Lily must have felt for Walter those long years of her draught, her yearning for his arms, for Walter's comfort. I had played my part, a big part, even a very large one in keeping my sister from her oasis. For this I was given my dues, the Lord's judgment. Dying would be to cheat the punishment, both for me and for Walter. I could never give him Lily back. Perhaps I never could have given him such a thing. I was a small clog in a great wheel turned by the fate of our lives, yet I had played my part. I must drink my cup.

I saw clearly the path I must choose. There was no putting back together what was broken. I didn't know exactly why, but I saw the pieces of our lives on the ground and the judgment hanging over me. I must choose the judgment. I might still die as Aunt Malinda and Aunt Nancy had died, but in the brief moments left in my existence I must bear my shame. The Lord had willed this, and I must accept.

I went to bed but slept little. The desire to lie beside Walter was so intense the longing consumed me. I wanted him to see me, to hold me for a few nights yet, before I faced the end, the brutal truth of what I was to become, a woman who was not a woman. There would never be a reason for Walter to want me again, not as a man wanted a woman.

I moved in a daze the next morning, fixing breakfast, and assigning the girls their tasks.

"I need the buggy," I told Walter, a moment before he left the kitchen.

"Okay," he said, but the horse wasn't harnessed when I entered the barn an hour later.

I had left Baby Jane wrapped in a blanket on the buggy seat, with no one in charge. I returned to the barn door and called for Joy. "Can you watch the baby while I harness the horse?"

She ran out of the garden towards the buggy, and I retreated inside. I expected Walter's snub to hurt after what I had been through last night, but it didn't. It seemed right in a way, like he was agreeing with the Lord I should be punished.

"Where's Daett?" Joy asked when I came out of the barn with PJ.

"In the back fields," I said.

She didn't ask why I had to harness my own horse, but the girl knew.

"Are you okay, Mamm?" Joy asked before I climbed into the buggy.

"I'm okay," I said. I wasn't lying, but Joy's face told me I was. "I'm going to see the midwife."

"Oh," she said, and her face brightened.

"Not a baby," I said, "but I'll be okay."

She didn't probe and stood back while I drove out of the lane. Joy was still standing there when I glanced over my shoulder at the main road. My daughter! Joy was my daughter. I had given Walter Lily, in the version I could, in the only way any of us could make right what had been done wrong. I saw with the same clarity I had seen when I saw the road I must travel last night. Walter would make right what had been done wrong to Lily. Joy would have the father Lily never had, a man who protected her, cherished her, and gave her a life unmarred by evil. These must be the ways of the Lord who casts judgment without consulting me or any man. I gave in, and I wept.

I was still crying when I knocked on Sarah's front door.

"Dear, what is the matter?" she asked. "Have you lost a child?"

"I wish," I said, and hated myself for the words.

"Then what?" Sarah took my arm and led me to the couch.

I laid Baby Jane down and reached for Sarah's hand. "This."

She could obviously feel through my dress, what I had felt last night. "Since when did you know?"

"Last night."

"Let me examine you in the bedroom," she said.

Sarah did her examination and went with me to Dr. Whittaker's office. We had to wait awhile, but the conclusion was foregone.

"You have told your husband?" Dr. Whittaker wanted to know.

"I didn't yet," I said.

"Then you must tell him. We must have the surgery at once."

"How much will you take?" I asked.

"Both of them, and everything. I'm sorry."

I nodded, unable to speak.

"Your husband will take the news hard, I suppose, but he will still have you. I think we've caught the cancer early enough."

"I wish I hadn't," I said.

He frowned. "I can understand how you feel, but your husband will still love you."

I wanted to say, he won't if he never did, but I didn't.

An attempt would be made to save my life, and the effort would succeed, precisely because I didn't want to live. I would survive, disfigured, but alive.

I left the office with Sarah and an appointment for the next week. I dropped Sarah off at the end of her driveway.

"I'll be with you next week." She promised me.

"Thank you," I said, and drove away with Baby Jane on the seat beside me.

There was no sign of Walter when I arrived at the house. I parked beside the barn and unhitched. Joy came out to take Baby Jane into the house.

"Everything okay?" she asked.

"I'll tell you later," I said.

"Daett came up for lunch," she said. "I fixed some sandwiches for him."

"You're a good girl."

"I told him you had gone to see the midwife," she said.

I nodded, and Joy left with Baby Jane. I took PJ into the barn. I didn't want to enter the house yet. Duties called, and I should get busy, but a great weariness swept over me. Walter must be told. In a normal situation, he would already know. He would have gone with me to see Sarah and Dr. Whittaker. He would have been by my side, but I was a failure, a complete one. If I needed further proof the evidence stared me in the face. Why hadn't I kept my mouth shut and never told anyone. Which was impossible, of course, and would only deepen my humiliation. I didn't care, and yet I did. I hated myself for caring, for wanting to walk back to Walter, and tell him the truth. I wished things had been done differently. I wished he had taken Lily as his wife and not me, which wasn't true, either. I wanted him as badly as I ever did.

I left the barn and walked across the fields. The summer breeze stirred across my flushed face, and the dust rose in the distance where Walter drove along the edge of the corn with his wagon.

"Whoa," he called to his team when I approached.

I stood there, unable to speak.

"I don't have time for this," he said.

I swallowed the lump in my throat. "I have cancer. I just came from Dr. Whitaker's office."

"Cancer." The reins dropped from his hands.

I forced myself to look at him, but there was no flash of joy on his face as I had expected.

"Both breasts have to go next week," I said. "Dr. Whittaker has scheduled the surgery."

"You're not dying," he said, and again there was no joy in his voice.

"Why?" I couldn't keep the wail from my voice. "Don't you want me? Don't you want what we don't have? I do. I want … I don't want to live like we're living."

"Hush," he said. "There's no use talking."

He clucked to his team and they took off, leaving me standing alone in the dust and the heat of the day. I had always been alone. I saw the vision clearly. Lily had Walter, and I would never have him.

Chapter 34

The smell of fresh mown hay drifted in through my open bedroom window. Outside, the loud clatter of a wagon rose above the beat of the team's hooves.

"Whoa, there," I heard Walter shout.

The call seemed removed from reality. I stirred on the bed and opened my eyes. I tried to sit up. The sun was high in the sky and I had household duties to perform. I pushed on the quilt, but the pain stopped me. I remembered then, the drifting off before the surgery, my abrupt return in Dr. Whittaker's recovery room with a pain which burned inside of me, and the empty spaces on my chest. I was no longer a woman, yet I breathed like one, and I hurt like one. I held still as my body turned cold from the horror of what I was.

"Barbara." Mamm called from the hallway and stuck her head in the bedroom door. "Dr. Whittaker said getting out of bed by the third day would be wise."

I turned my face to the wall and ignored her.

Mamm forced me to turn over in bed. "Barbara, life goes on."

"I can't go on," I said.

"Do you want me to raise your children?" she asked.

I forced myself to sit and took Mamm's offered hand. Together we moved slowly to the couch, the pain in my chest a dull fire, which only subsided when I sat down. Mamm disappeared into the kitchen and returned with a bowl of warm oatmeal. She seated herself beside me and proceeded to feed me with the spoon.

I opened my mouth without objection. This indignity was nothing to what I had already suffered. My womanhood had been taken from me. The little I had with which to delight Walter, the Lord had removed. I deserved his judgment which did nothing to release the agony of what I had lost. I had thought myself prepared for the Lord's judgment, but I wasn't. Like my life, so in my failure, I was found wanting.

Elsie and Mary's concerned faces appeared in the kitchen doorway to watch us, and Mamm paused with the spoon half lifted. I pushed the food away. Mamm gave in and returned to the kitchen.

"Come," I told the girls, and they crept up to me, to sit on the couch. Their gaze was tender and filled with compassion. They had not changed. I had.

"Mamm is very sick," I said, and they nodded.

I let them sit there until exhaustion threatened. "You should go play," I told them, and they left with quick backward glances.

Mamm appeared in the kitchen doorway. "Lily wants to see you this morning. I told her you weren't well. Whatever she has to say can wait, but the woman insists."

I tried to sit up straighter. "I can't see her."

"I'm afraid Lily's coming. You know how your sister is."

"When is Lily coming?" I asked.

"I think she's here now." Mamm glanced out of the living room window. "Her buggy just pulled in."

"So, you wanted me up so—?"

Mamm didn't answer, and I straightened the pillow beside me, while Mamm went to open the front door. I couldn't hear their muffled greeting. They stepped inside, and I gathered my strength to glare at my sister.

Lily stood by the door, unmoving.

"I know I look awful," I said.

She tried to smile. "I'm sorry I'm bothering you at a time like this, and of course for what happened, it's just … well, I had to come."

"Why are you here?" I asked.

"Can I sit?"

"I'll be out in the kitchen," Mamm said, and disappeared.

I motioned to the empty seat on the couch beside me.

Lily sat down stiffly. "How are you doing?"

"They're gone," I said.

"I'm so sorry."

"I don't see why you should be."

"Barbara, please, I'm leaving the community. I'm not coming back." She winced.

"Are you taking Walter with you?"

Agony filled her eyes. "With all my heart I wish."

I tried to hide the relief which flooded through me.

"We're sisters," she said. Her smile was pained.

"The reminder is supposed to make everything right?"

She seemed not to hear, as a soft glow crept over her face. "I wanted to speak with you—tell you I'm carrying his child."

My throat went dry. "You're carrying Walter's son?"

"I don't know for sure—the son part." She made no attempt to hide her happiness.

"But you do know?"

"I think I do." She ducked her head and her cheeks burned red.

"You expect approval from me?" My anger burst from my mouth.

She rubbed her face with both hands. "Of course not."

"Then why tell me?"

"I had to," she said. "We're sisters."

"You're gloating over my failure?"

She met my gaze. "I know what I did, but I'm not gloating."

"Yet you have no regret."

She lifted her chin. "Don't blame me, Barbara. I have accepted what life gave me. I did during those long years when we were at home with Daett. You know I speak the truth. I did what was best for others, and now I have done what is best for myself. Will you hold my happiness against me?"

"Walter is my husband." I tried to sit up straighter.

She ignored me, staring out the window. "I love him, and he loves me. I'm simply telling you. I will not shame the child I carry. I know the rules—your rules, but they have only brought me agony and pain. The Lord gave me Walter for a short time. I needed healing for the pain in my heart."

"I will not offer you comfort by pretending I understand your wickedness," I said.

Her gaze turned on me. "You should have considered a long time ago what your rules were doing to me—what they are now doing to Walter."

"Maybe I'm more than rules? Maybe there is a higher purpose?"

"I didn't come to blame you," she said. "I'm doing what is right for Walter's child, not for you."

"You're really leaving the community?" I touched my chest. "Don't you want to stick around and see if I'm leaving the world. Give you a chance at Walter?"

"If I could have Walter, I would have him," she said, "and you're not dying."

Coldness crept over me. "I suppose I'm not. We both want my death too much."

"I thought so," she said, "but thank you for not interfering. I needed those nights with Walter, but I'm still sorry you were hurt in the process."

"Saying sorry changes nothing."

"Yet, I wanted to say the words, because I mean them. Walter is your husband."

"A fact I have never regretted." I glared at her.

She smiled. "I understand. We're talking of Walter."

I looked away and didn't answer.

"You couldn't have changed things at home even if you had tried," she said. "I wanted to tell you. I don't blame you."

I couldn't resist the question. "Why aren't you taking Walter with you? He would follow you to the end of the world."

She looked out the window at Walter standing beside the barn door waiting. "I have considered the option often, but I can't."

"Why not?"

"The man does not belong out there. He would die away from his community."

"You wouldn't have him either," I said. We had come to the same conclusion.

She nodded.

"You're leaving him to me?" The bitterness stung.

Lily tried to smile. "You can take care of him. I can't."

"You realize what you're doing? You can never come back."

"I know," she said.

"I'm not dying for a very long time. Not with these gone." She looked at my empty chest. "I thought so."

"I will try to leave you a few years. He'll be old by then, so you being with him won't matter anymore."

"I wasn't asking," she said.

"I know, but I'm saying. Isn't this a day for saying?"

"I agree." Lily stood to her feet. "Goodbye then and thanks again. You could have taken those moments from me. You could have kept him away, but you didn't. I'm grateful. I can't say how very much."

"Don't try to soften my anger for what you did."

Tears shimmered in her eyes. "This is the end for us. I shall never see you again."

"Do you expect me to cry?"

"No, but can we part in peace?"

"Goodbye," I said. "Is a goodbye good enough?"

She nodded and hurried out of the door.

Mamm's face appeared in the kitchen doorway. "What was she up to?"

"She's leaving," I said.

"You think." Mamm hurried over to the living room window. "Walter's at the buggy."

"Let him see her off," I said.

"They're kissing!"

"Let them say goodbye," I said.

I lay down on the couch. A deep weariness swept over me, like I had passed through the night running over open fields and reached the door of my home. Mamm helped me up and we slowly moved back into the bedroom. She left and the front door slammed followed by heavy footsteps. Walter appeared with his straw hat pushed back on his forehead. He came up to stand at the foot of the bed.

"She told me," I said.

He stared numbly at me.

"She's carrying your son," I said.

Walter looked away.

"How could you?" I whispered. "You told me this would never happen."

He shifted on his feet.

"Lily always gets what she wants, doesn't she?"

He turned on his heels and his footsteps faded away. The front door slammed. I waited in the stillness with the window open. I pressed my fingers against my forehead and willed my anger to cease.

Chapter 35

The early morning fog hung on the lowlands behind our barn. A slow dawn undimmed by clouds rose on the horizon and began to burn away the mist. My fingers slipped on the wooden clothes pins. The wire line sent a sting through the palm of my hand. I clutched for a better hold and lifted the heavy denim pants into place. They stayed and I stood back to catch my breath.

The darkness and the cold between Walter and me continued. First the days had flowed into weeks, and now they were months. Eight months since Lily left, and Walter still slept in the basement. Dr. Whittaker had done what he could with my breasts, but they were pitiful specimens of what they once had been. In their absence, I realized they had been the most beautiful part of my body. The cancer wasn't back. Life went on. I was alive.

Lily would have given birth to Walter's child by now, somewhere out there on the other side of the fence, well outside the reach of the community. Lily had given Walter a son. The unexplainable stared me daily in the face. I, who had been so convinced the world spun on reason and the laws of the Lord, had failed to give Walter a man child.

We lived in our stillness, our numbness, and our nothingness. A threshold had been crossed between Lily and me, bridges had been burned which could not be rebuilt. My girls' laughter filled the house, but there was the empty space in my bed each night to remind me things were not right. In the meantime, the farm must be tended, the clothing washed, the house cleaned, the meals made, and the dishes put away.

We moved on, as the community moved on. Sunday followed Sunday. Walter said nothing further about the Mennonite church or attending again. I assumed his will to escape, or perhaps his need, had been sapped. Lily had taken more than she had given, as usual. For this, I was angry, and, just as quickly, I wasn't. I could understand Lily's desire for Walter. We were sisters, and I had found comfort in the Scriptures a few months ago. I had heard the story mentioned a few times in the minister's sermons on Sundays, but the reality of the tale had never gripped me.

Leah and Rachel had been sisters and they had fought over Jacob, the chosen man of God. I had only to look at Walter striding from the barn to the house to see a vision of Jacob, and my heart pounded. The preachers claimed we no longer lived in the Old Testament, which we didn't, but the Lord had once allowed two women to love one man. I felt a peace slip over me. I had found my rule again, and I grasped for a hold like a drowning man does the rope tossed to him. I could hope with a clear conscience Lily's child would be healthy, strong, full of life and vigorous, because he belonged to Walter.

I would never bear Walter another son, and not because he no longer visited my bed. Something had died inside of me, and I had no breasts to feed the infant. There was only emptiness where life should have been. I reached for another of Walter's trousers from the clothes hamper, the weight heavy in my hands. The water dripped cold on my bare feet. My fingers didn't slip this time, and the wooden pins were soon fastened securely.

"Let me help you."

I jumped at the sound of Walter's voice behind me.

When I didn't answer, he lifted the final trouser, his grip unerring, as if he had grown up placing denim on clothes lines. I had lived next door to him, and Walter didn't hang clothes on wash lines.

He turned to leave, as if his duty was done, when I stopped him. "Walter."

"Yes," he said, his face frozen.

"Don't you think we should make our peace?"

"How would we?" he asked.

I looked down at my bare feet. They appeared ugly in the rising light. I forced the words out. "We're married."

He shrugged. "Which didn't seem to help much with Lily and me."

"She's not coming back. Are you waiting?"

"I know she's not coming back." The bitterness was in his voice.

"Do you think we are to live in the same house, sleep on the same property, and ignore each other like we don't exist? I know I no longer have these," I swept my hand over my bosom, "but I'm still a woman."

The bitterness was still there. "What do you want from me?"

"I don't want solutions and answers which are lies. I want to be your wife again. The best I can be. I know I am asking a lot, but I know what I want."

He studied me for a long time. "Maybe you're right. Maybe someone should be told what I did. Deacon Miller probably wants a church confession, maybe a few weeks in the Bann? I guess I'm willing, if my humiliation helps."

"I want to be your wife," I said. "Nothing more."

"And what about what I did—what Lily and I did? Don't you want punishment?"

"Lily's not coming back," I said. "I'm angry, yes, but she's giving me the rest of my life with you. I would be stupid if I didn't take her offer. My sister could have stayed and done with you what she wanted, or she could have taken you with her wherever she went. You would have gone. You would have left all this behind, and I can't say I would have blamed you. What am I? My womanhood is taken from me, but Lily is my sister. We've always been sisters, and always will be. I want to start over with you."

He hesitated. "I don't know, Barbara. I don't think in those terms. I think I should do something first. Try to make this right with you, but I don't know what. I've thought long and hard. How does a man make things right with his wife when he's gotten her sister pregnant?" Walter looked away. "I'm sorry, Barbara. I guess I've never said the words because they've seemed useless really. What is sorry, when you've done what I did?"

"You're not hearing me," I said.

He shook his head. "I guess I'm not."

"I only want you."

"You're saying there will be no church confession, no dragging my name through the mud, no months of excommunication, no—?"

The tears stung and I clung on to the wash line. "I want you to love me, Walter. Nothing more. Love me with all of your heart, like you do Lily."

"How would I love you?"

"You're a man. You should know."

"I don't," he said.

I forced a smile. "You can start by eating breakfast with us as a family."

"We've never stopped."

"Eat with us, as if you were there," I said. "Pray again and read us the Scriptures after breakfast. Be a father to our girls. They need you."

He looked away. "I don't deserve any of this."

"I didn't say you did, but I'm asking you anyway. Be with us. Be with me. Maybe for the first time, I don't know."

"You don't ask an easy thing."

"Perhaps not, but do you think being with you will be easy looking like I do? Knowing you know how beautiful Lily was and is. You have been with my sister in the way a man knows a woman."

He took a deep breath. "I will try. Okay?"

I nodded. "I cannot ask for more, but come, Joy is working on breakfast I'm sure. You can sit with us while we work. I need you with me this morning, if we are to walk this road together again."

He followed me and took a seat at the kitchen table. Joy stared for a moment before a smile filled her face. "You will be here while we fix breakfast?"

"Yes, if you don't mind," he said.

Joy rushed over and gave him a hug. "I don't mind in the least."

"You can wake Elsie and Mary," I told him. "Jane can sleep awhile yet."

He stood and tiptoed up the stairs, to return with Mary in his arms and Elsie hanging tightly to his elbow. He seated them at the table and brushed the curls from their faces. Joy glowed with happiness. The bacon fat splattered landing high on her arms, but the girl didn't seem to notice.

I finished the eggs and stirred the oatmeal. The steam rose in the air when I transferred the kettle to the table. Walter leaned forward for a long sniff.

"Is this the last week of school?" He looked up to ask Joy.

"Yes. The picnic is on Saturday."

"I'll be looking forward to the day," he said, and Joy took her place beside him at the table.

We bowed our heads, and Walter prayed the familiar words, "Our Father which art in Heaven, hallowed be thy name ..."

After the meal I brought our weathered Bible to him, and Walter opened the pages and began to read, "Blessed are the poor in spirit, for theirs is the kingdom of heaven. Blessed are they who mourn for they shall be comforted. Blessed are the meek for they shall inherit the earth. Blessed …"

I listened and I wept, yet no one seemed to notice. I felt as if the long winter was past and the spring rains were gently falling. The girl's faces were fixed on Walter. He finished and closed the Bible to gather each of them in his arms and hold them close. "You be good now," he said. "Off you go to school, Joy and Elsie. I'll be seeing Mary at lunch time. Help your mom get the sandwiches ready."

They nodded; their faces full of happiness.

"Don't get too many one-hundreds at school," he called out.

Joy giggled and the other two joined in. Fellow conspirators in what? They didn't know, and they didn't care.

I followed him to the doorway and whispered, "Thanks."

He turned, his lips light on my cheek, and I wrapped my arms around him. I pulled him close. I had forgotten how strong he was, and how much I wanted his strength, yet the emptiness between us was a fire burning brightly. I knew he had to feel my lack and sense the shriveled things on my chest which were a sham at best.

"Can you help me with the spring harrowing like you used to," he whispered into my hair. "Once the dishes are done?"

"I will," I said, without looking up at him. "Mary can sit under the trees and watch Jane. I'll bring lemonade."

He smiled and left. I scurried about. I helped Mary with the last of the dishes and wiped the table clean. I sent her to fetch the lemons in the basement.

"Fill the pitcher with water," I told Mary. "I'll fix the sandwiches."

Mary squeezed the lemons, caught up in the spirit of things. We worked together and left the house with blankets, a basket, and a thermos filled to the brim.

The shadows of the trees were still long beside the fence row, and I deposited the girls there. The seat of the harrow was familiar, and the reins comfortable in my hands.

"You can still do this," Walter said, and off I went.

The sun rose high in the spring sky, the long shadows giving way to shorter ones. We ate, seated under the trees, with the wind in our faces, and the blankets spread wide on the grass.

I worked on, until the time arrived to prepare supper. We left the field with Mary's hand in mine, her face weary, but joyful. I began the supper preparations, and Joy and Elsie joined in when they came home from school, listening mostly to the chatter of their sister about her day in the fields.

"Working with Daett is fun," Joy commented, once every angle of the day had been fully covered.

"You can help Daett all summer," I told her, and the tears stung again.

We finished the meal preparations well before Walter came in from the fields, and ate by the light of the lantern, the hiss soft above their heads. After the meal, Walter gathered the girls around him in the living room while I cleaned the kitchen, his voice soft as he told them a story. He was making up the tale apparently, as he went along. I had never heard such a story before, of angels dancing in the sky on sunbeams, and smiling at the antics of little kittens in the barn.

The younger ones played afterwards, and Joy came in to help me finish the dishes. The darkness grew thicker outside, the spring sun setting quickly in the sky. The girls grew sleepy and I tucked them in upstairs. Joy went to her own bedroom and the light under the door blinked out. I crept downstairs, barely daring to breathe. Walter was coming into my bedroom. He hadn't said so in words, but the promise had been unspoken between us. He was still on the rocker, his hands in his lap.

I approached to stand in front of him. "Thank you for this day."

"You're welcome," he said.

I reached for his hand. "You promised."

"I did," he said.

I led him towards the bedroom, and he grabbed the kerosene lamp on the way. Once inside, I let go of his hand, and turned to face him. In the soft flickering light, I undid the pins, and opened my dress. I lowered my undergarments and let them fall to the floor. His gaze lingered on me.

"You're right," he said. "You're still a woman."

"Ravish me, Walter," I whispered. "Ravish me, like you ravished Lily."

Baby Susan, our last child, was born nine months later.

Section Eight—September 1928 to November 1942

LILY

Chapter 36

The houses of Amelia Courthouse were built low on their foundations. Dirt lanes crept along the sides and correlated into streets deeper into the town. This is the place where I had landed in the middle of nowhere, far from the cities, and the large communities, where scrutiny and blame could not descend on my head. I had accepted Mrs. Emmett's invitation, but had asked not to live at the big house. My return was not what either of us had anticipated or even thought possible those many months ago when I had been here accompanied by Joy. Regardless, Mrs. Emmett had welcomed me and would have welcomed me into her home, but I wanted a place of my own, a place befitting where I had fallen.

The town had taken my appearance in stride. They were strangers who had given me grace even as they must have wondered about this single woman who had shown up pregnant in their midst. Maybe they didn't scorn me because of Mrs. Emmett, who obviously had taken me under her wing. I didn't try to think about these questions too often, or about the community. I missed Walter terribly. I lay awake at night with a hunger for his arms which consumed my body. I knew I couldn't go back, and yet I wanted to more than I ever thought possible. I must accept who I was, or what I had become. From somewhere the strength always came, and I went on breathing and living in this place.

Mrs. Emmett cared, which helped, but she had her reasons. I was not innocent about the matter. Robert was not unattractive, and he was single. I wanted to know why.

I never had before, but on the other hand I had my secrets. Why shouldn't he have his?

I got up to walk out on the small front porch and willed the early evening breeze to move across my face. Summers were ferocious down here. The heat clung to every pore of my body. I thought I was used to the high temperatures after my years with Aunt Maud in Richmond. The country should be cooler, but perhaps this building was what bothered me. Aunt Maud's apartment in town had been a palace compared to this shanty I could afford to rent. The paint had shed on half the boards, and the outhouse was in worse shape, tilted on the rotted foundation, the odors no less even with the unintended ventilation. Living here felt honest in a way, but Mrs. Emmett wanted me out of the place at the earliest moment possible. She had wanted me to stay at the big house from day one. The time would soon arrive when she would officially approach me on the subject. Enough hints had been dropped. I knew what was coming.

In the meantime, I didn't complain. I was thankful for a roof over my head. I had arrived here pregnant, and I was used to making the best of things. I had successfully given birth to Walter's son. Beyond the momentous occasion, I had not allowed my mind to think.

I sat on one of the old chairs on the porch. They were rickety versions of their former grandeur. I could imagine they once graced the front porch of the big house up on the hill. I felt a kinship with their weather-beaten condition. I was still young, and I looked young, but I felt aged inside, as if I had lived a thousand years as Methuselah of old. Strange what I remembered from the sermons preached in my childhood. I heard the minister's thundering of doom as the distant sound of storms, but I couldn't distinguish the words. They were referring to women like me, I was sure, and here I was with a child and no husband. Yet I had Walter's son. I would live for him, and surely life would have pity on Walter's son.

A cry came from inside the shanty, an insistent voice raised in objection to some real or imagined wrong. I got up and gathered the bundle in my arms to sit once more on the chair. He regarded me with open eyes, fixed on my face, his cries silent for the moment. I smiled down at him, this wiggling mass of utter sweetness. Walter must have been like this when he was a child, assertive, but wrapped in tenderness, with little fingers moving on one's skin soft as silk. I touched him and I cried. I wanted his father so much. I almost named him Walter, Junior, but I didn't. I wrote Jackson on the birth certificate. The name fit the land, the trees, the town, and the heavy southern accent most of the locals spoke.

The choice brought a smile to Mrs. Emmett face. "I see you're making yourself right at home."

Marie, Mrs. Emmett insisted I call her. One of the maids at the big house, Miss Wauneta, took care of Jackson during the day when I worked at the restaurant. I didn't get paid much by the hour, but the tips were good. Joe Harley would never have given me the job in my pregnant condition, if Mrs. Emmett hadn't introduced us, and stood there with an approving smile while Joe asked me a few questions.

"I'm sure Lily will fit right in with our southern cooking," she told him. "Maybe she can even teach you a few things about cooking. Her Aunt Maud fed us well in Richmond for many years."

Joe had grunted but hired me. He hadn't let me near the kitchen though, at least not yet. I hadn't minded so far. I had Jackson. We ate and we lived. Walter had deemed me worthy. He had given me his son to raise. Poverty could bring no shame after such an honor.

I traced my fingers over the tiny forehead in my lap. He puckered his lips and smiled. I wiped away the tears as Mrs.

Emmett's automobile bounced into view, headed down from the house on the hill. She often came down in the evening to chat and see how I was getting along. I pulled Jackson into a sitting position as Mrs. Emmett turned in and came down the dirt lane. She swerved to avoid the potholes and popped to a halt across from our small shack.

I stood to my feet to greet her, but Mrs. Emmett waved me back down. "Sit, child, please. I don't want to disturb you in the least."

I obeyed because everyone obeyed when Mrs. Emmett spoke.

"How are you this evening?" Mrs. Emmett seated herself on the edge of the porch boards.

"You don't want a chair?" I stood again.

"Those rickety old things! You ought to get rid of them."

I didn't respond. The words were not intended to produce action.

"How's the little one?" Mrs. Emmett beamed towards Jackson.

"Growing bigger each day, and more handsome. Precious, of course."

"They all are, dear. Is Wauneta taking care of him properly while you're working at Joe's place?"

"She is." I didn't hesitate.

"The woman can find a wet nurse for the baby if you wish," Mrs. Emmett appraised me, "but babies do best on their mother's milk."

"I know," I said. "My tradition taught me."

Mrs. Emmett nodded. "I surmised as much from knowing your Aunt Maud, although the woman didn't want to speak of her past. Must have been hard."

"Leaving the community is always difficult."

"Is Joe behaving himself?"

I laughed. "I don't think I have to answer. The man is a gentleman."

Mrs. Emmett seemed pleased. "Men can draw the wrong conclusions, but you're right. Joe is a gentleman."

"He hasn't let me cook yet."

"You're not insulted surely."

"No, just happy with life," I said. "I have my baby."

"Is there any chance the father will be by someday?"

I shook my head.

"You sure?"

"He's my sister's husband."

"I see." Mrs. Emmett didn't appear too shocked. "You're staying long term then."

"If you will have me around."

"There's no question there, dear. We're honored to have you. These things happen, for one reason or the other."

"I'm thankful for what you have done for me, and for Jackson."

"There are no plans to stop, dear. I like you very much. I always was close to your aunt, and you seem to fit the place she carved out in my heart very well."

"I'm still grateful."

"How does your sister feel about the child?"

"Barbara?" I took a deep breath. "I can never go home again while she's alive. I wouldn't, for Jackson's sake more than anything. He deserves a life free from condemnation and accusation. He's not guilty of anything."

"He's not." Mrs. Emmett agreed. "A fresh start is best sometimes, otherwise the ghosts never quite settle."

"Thank you." I lifted my burning face into the breeze drifting across the open porch.

"Now on to another subject—Robert. Surely you knew I would go there eventually."

"I suspected."

"Robert is a fine man. He has consented to speak with you."

"I don't have objections."

"Are you going to make this easy for me?"

"Would you have me protest?" I asked.

Mrs. Emmett studied me for a second. "Take this as my opinion, but I think this could work."

"Does Robert have his secrets?" I asked.

Mrs. Emmett pursed her lips. "A fair question, I suppose."

"He's not …?"

Mrs. Emmett laughed. "No. Robert has his secrets, but not because he likes men. He once loved a woman, too deeply I would say. The wrong kind of woman, and his heart was broken. He will be kind to you though. Whether you heal his heart is another matter."

"Am I supposed to ask who this woman was?"

"Do you wish to know?"

"Perhaps he should tell me, when the time comes," I said.

"I agree," she said. "Robert needs a wife. Every man does, whether they think they do or not."

"I'll try," I said.

"You're exactly what he needs," she said. "Believe me. I raised the boy after his father, Gerald, died in the Great War, and his mother, my sister Heady, from a broken heart."

"I'm honored you think I can fill your shoes."

She snorted. "I'm an old woman. I won't be here forever."

"Jackson needs a father," I said.

"Robert assured me the child would be no problem. He plans to adopt the boy."

"Seems you have the bases covered."

"I try, dear, and you're worth the trying. Both of you are."

"I should say this," I said. "My love for Walter—our love goes back to our youth, to our childhood even. I would be Walter's wife today if life had not interfered. Walter's

282

acceptance of me—his love, I will never regret what I gave him."

Mrs. Emmett's voice was tender. "I would never ask you to, dear, and neither would Robert. I promise you. I believe in you, Lily. If knowing would help, give me the location of this community where you and your Aunt Maud came from, and I will have someone keep tabs on your relatives, keep you up-to-date on the news."

"You would?" The tears stung.

Mrs. Emmett got up to take me in her arms for a long hug. "There's a lot not right in this world, child, and you've seen plenty of the ugly side of the picture. Let's see if we can turn the frame over. Shall we?"

"I may never be able to love Robert."

"He understands, because he feels the same way," Mrs. Emmett said. "But don't close your heart, and I told Robert the same thing."

I watched from the porch as Mrs. Emmett climbed back into her automobile and drove up the hill again.

Robert visited the following week. He was nervous. Why, I don't know. I wasn't intimidating.

"Good evening." He seated himself stiffly on the chair across from me.

I had Jackson in my lap and I fussed with his hair. Jackson cooed up at me, but I didn't dare respond, with Robert so close.

"Nice evening," Robert said. Jackson jerked his head around trying to follow the sound of the voice.

I forced myself to look in Robert's direction. "I know. Quite pleasant."

"How's the child doing?" He sounded interested.

"Okay. Not too fussy for a baby, I think. He's my first."

A wry smile crept across his face. "I had hoped so."

I felt the heat race up my neck. If he belittled me, I would ask him to leave.

"How's the restaurant work going?" he asked in a perfectly neutral tone.

"Okay. Joe's very nice." He had to notice my red face.

"Knew him since I was a boy." He continued, even smiling, obviously attempting to put me at ease. "Not a finer man in town."

I relaxed a little, trying to get into the conversation. "He gave me work, and he let me cook today for the first time."

"Joe's a steady one," he said, "and a good man."

"You work at the bank, don't you?" Wasn't inquiring about him the proper approach to break the ice between us?

He nodded.

"Like the job?" Getting him to talk was like pulling hen's teeth.

"Makes do," he said. "Not very adventurous."

"Had you planned to have adventure in life? Travel perhaps."

"No. Dad traveled plenty with us during the war. Sort of made me want to stick close to hearth and home."

"You don't look like a banker."

He laughed. "What does a banker look like?"

I couldn't help smiling. "A little pudgy perhaps? Double chinned and heavy around the middle."

Robert laughed harder. "Then I'm not a banker."

"Maybe in your old age."

"Maybe," he allowed. "Let's hope not."

"Did you ever dream of doing something else?"

He shrugged. "A soldier perhaps? Boys wish to emulate their fathers, I suppose, but I'm not a warrior."

"You look like a warrior."

"Not very fierce or brave," he said.

"You could be fierce and brave."

"I don't know." He turned quite sober. "I gather my aunt filled you in on why I came down."

"She did."

"The proposal is kind of sudden I know, and you haven't known me long."

"I've been here awhile. I did stay with my Aunt Maud once, by myself and with Joy."

"I remember. I suppose I ignored you mostly."

"How could you know things would end up like this?"

"I could have been more of a gentleman. I'm sorry."

"Do you want to know more about me, about my secrets?" I motioned towards Jackson.

"I have my own," he said. "I'm fine."

"Is there a child?"

"I wish," he said. "Just secrets."

"Sorry for asking."

"I'm okay. Shall we proceed?"

"I'm ready," I said.

"The ceremony can be quiet, and small, and soon."

"I have no objections," I said. "Getting out of here would be nice."

He nodded. "We would live at the big house with my aunt. Well, at the one end. The place is huge."

"I know," I said. "I remember."

"My aunt will make the plans, inviting the relatives, and schedule the food service."

"There won't be any relatives on my part."

"I see," he said.

"You object?"

"Not if you're happy."

I forced a smile. "You are very kind, taking me in like this."

"Believe me, I'm getting the better part of the deal."

"Glad you think so."

"I am," he said, "and I'm thankful."

We had the wedding a month later, outside on the front lawn of the big house. A preacher was there in a fancy suit, and Robert was attired in the same manner. I wore a long, flowing, flower-strewn dress, which Mrs. Emmett had brought from Richmond and tailored to my figure. We said our vows simply and directly, without smiles or tears. I couldn't leave Jackson, so we boarded the afternoon train for Richmond, bound ultimately for Virginia Beach where Robert had planned a weeklong honeymoon. We had a private double bunk on the train for the night.

"We can wait," Robert said, with the clacking of the tracks beneath us. "There are two bunks, and there is the child."

I shook my head and soon had Jackson sleeping in the upper bunk. He seemed pleased when I finished undressing. He didn't move though, so I went to him. He looked like a man awakening from his sleep. I pulled his face close to me and kissed him—to discover his cheeks were wet with tears.

Chapter 37

The cool early morning breeze from the open window wafted across the room. I stirred in the bed with the covers pulled tight under my chin. The heavy quilt on the other side was tossed aside, and Robert's clothing was gone. I never saw him sleep late. We haven't been married for long, but this seemed a settled habit. I stretched luxuriously. What a change this was from living in the shanty at the bottom of the hill. I had been happy there, but I felt like I belonged here, almost as if I had been in the big house since my arrival.

I had a man in bed with me each night. I hadn't been sure how I would feel about the experience, since he wouldn't be Walter, but Robert had been tender and loving with me since our first night together on the train. I could give myself to him with a light heart. I was happy I could, after I had wanted Walter so desperately for so many long years. I had been given a precious time with Walter which was more than I dared hope would happen. I loved Walter passionately and still did, but I had also let go. Those days down by the riverbank were like pleasant dreams never to become reality again. They came to me gentle in the night with visions of kerosene lamps burning and light bouncing against white kitchen walls. There was Daett also, but he was not the horror he had once been.

I had Walter to thank. And Barbara. The Lord had blessed me with Walter's child. I felt wrapped in grace. Nothing else explained the splendor surrounding me, or the tenderness Robert showed me. He could have used me harshly. I would have understood, and there wasn't much I could have done.

Complained to Mrs. Emmett perhaps, but I wouldn't have. I would have accepted my lot, as I always had, but the Lord had chosen to favor me.

There was a soft knock on the door.

"Yes?" I called out.

The face of my young maid Bessie appeared. "Sorry if I woke you, but you said you wanted breakfast early."

"Thank you. I'll be right down."

I left the bedroom in my robe to walk down the hall and into the dining room. The place was empty except for Bessie. "Everyone still asleep?"

"Mr. Matthews left the house," she said, "but Mrs. Emmett is still in bed."

I sat down to the table laden with bacon, eggs, toast, and grits. "Breakfast looks very good. Thank you."

Bessie disappeared while I ate. When I finished, I stepped out into the garden, the early morning light still soft, and the air brisk with the scent of autumn. The summer's heat was already a distant memory.

A soft step turned me about. "Robert."

His smile was gentle. "Bessie said I would find you out here."

"Are you back for the day?"

"No, retrieving some papers, before I head into Richmond. Want to come with me?"

"Richmond?"

"Wauneta has Jackson covered for the day, I'm sure."

"I know nothing about your business," I said.

"You can sit and look pretty at the warehouse. My time there won't take long, and we can walk the river afterwards."

"The river?" I brushed the hair back from my face.

"There's a lovely spot along the banks. We can buy our lunch and eat by the tinkling waters."

"I didn't know you were into rivers."

"I've always loved the water." He laughed. "Though there isn't much out here in Amelia Courthouse."

"I'll come, then."

He reached for my hand. "You're very lovely this morning."

"Thank you, Robert."

"I'll be ready to leave in an hour," he said.

"Then I'll put on something more appropriate."

"See you then." He squeezed my hand and let go.

I went through the nursery and kissed the sleeping Jackson. I chose my yellow polka dotted dress from the bedroom closet and changed. I thought of Barbara and Walter. I wondered if Barbara had made her peace with what I did. She had understood, somehow, even during those nights I had spent with Walter along the creek. I had expressed my thanks, but Barbara had to live with the aftermath. I had Jackson, and Barbara had a husband who had loved me. At least she had him. She would find a way to take Walter back into her heart. Barbara had her rules, but she was not a fool.

The bedroom door opened behind me, and I turned around.

"I'm ready." He stood waiting. "You're more stunning than you were a moment ago."

"Do you like me in yellow?" I did a quick turn.

"I like you in whatever color you wear, or don't wear."

"Robert!" I scolded with a smile.

He returned my smile but didn't answer. The carriage waited for us at the front door and deposited us at the train station thirty minutes later. We didn't wait long before the train arrived, and we were on our way.

"Reminds me of our honeymoon," I said, once the steady clacking of the wheels was in our ears.

"I know," he said.

"You were very kind to me."

"I should have been," he said. "You're a beautiful woman."

I looked away, out the train window where the scrubby fields drifted past us. Beauty didn't always invoke kindness. I knew from experience.

"There's another stop we could make today," he said.

I looked back.

"The lawyer's office—about the adoption of your son."

"Jackson is the reason you asked me to come along?"

"No, but I've been meaning to speak about the matter."

"You don't have to."

He frowned. "I want to."

"You're very kind, thank you." I still was not used to his gentleness.

He reached for my hand. "We'll talk to the lawyer, but there is no shame in what you did. You must have had your reasons."

"You don't know." I almost added, I haven't told you about my sister's husband.

"I know you," he said.

"Is knowing me good enough?"

"For me, yes," he assured me, "but I want Jackson to know who his real father is—someday."

"I'm not taking him back for visits. Not until he is an adult, at least."

"I'm not saying you should."

"Do you want to know what happened?" I had kept secrets from Walter which had destroyed us—the keeping more than the secrets.

He shook his head.

"I'm sorry if this hurts you."

"I'm okay. I may not love you like he did, but I do love you. As much as a man such as I can love a woman."

"You love me plenty," I said, and the tears threatened.

"I couldn't help loving you. Thanks for loving me."

"I wish I could do better." I meant this with all my heart, but he could never be Walter.

"Am I like him?"

I must be honest, and I met his gaze. "No."

"At least you're truthful."

"Sorry," I said. "I didn't want to tell you."

"How am I not like him?"

This was too much. "I'd rather not say," I said.

"You won't hurt me."

I didn't believe him. "I'm happy now. Please, Robert."

He gave in with a nod. "Sorry for pushing."

The tracks clicked under us, and we leaned against each other. Was he okay with me? Did he mean what he had said?

"Do you want to visit your Aunt Maud's gravesite today in Riverview Cemetery?" he asked. "My aunt told me of her passing from cancer."

Relief swept through me. We would be okay. I smiled up at him. "I hadn't thought."

He smiled back. "We have time, and you should."

The train slowed, and I nodded. He recovered from pain well. Perhaps we were kindred spirits?

We left the car hand in hand, and Robert hailed a taxi. We climbed in, and I waited for an hour in a comfortable waiting room while Robert transacted his business at the tobacco warehouse. We went to the lawyer's office next, and had a thirty-minute wait there, seated side by side, until the secretary gave us the nod to proceed inside.

"Robert," A well-dressed man greeted us, "and ..."

"Lily, my wife, and this is Mr. Egbert."

"What a beautiful woman, but I didn't know you had wed."

"Lawyers don't usually get wedding invitations."

They laughed heartedly. "Surely my post-nuptial services are not needed so quickly?"

"Of course not. I wish to adopt Lily's son."

"Of course." Mr. Egbert turned to me. "My condolences for your loss."

"I wasn't married," I said.

Mr. Egbert didn't miss a beat. "Either way, adoption would be in order. Robert's heart is known for its largess."

"He has been very kind to me." I said.

Mr. Egbert appraised Robert. "You have been kind to him, I would say."

Robert dismissed the compliment with a wave of his hand. "Let's proceed with the details."

"Certainly." Mr. Egbert shoved papers towards us. "Give me names and dates."

While Robert watched, I wrote down Jackson's name, the date of his birth, and Walter Yoder, as father. Not married.

Robert handed the page to him. "Everything looks okay."

"Great! I'll put this on the top of my stack."

"Good to see you again." Robert stood to his feet.

Mr. Egbert gave me a bright smile. "Glad to have met you, Lily."

"And you too," I said, and we left the office.

Robert hailed a taxi again, and we arrived at the grave site ten minutes later. He paid the driver and together we approached the tombstone.

"I didn't know her well," Robert said, "but my aunt loved her."

"Aunt Maud had a sad story."

"I suspected," he said.

"Why do people do what they do to each other?"

"I don't know." His hand tightened in mine. "I stopped asking questions a long time ago."

"Is the silence less painful?" I asked.

"The world is dark enough without questions. I had my aunt. I don't know what I would have done without her."

"I had Walter," I said, and glanced up at him. He didn't appear angry.

"He was a good man, this Walter of yours."

"He was. Thank you." I meant thank you for a lot of things, but I didn't want to explain.

We left the gravesite and walked down the river hand in hand, to sit on the bank and watch the water rush by below us. Two bald eagles with their white heads stretched out straight in front of them circled above us.

I leaned against Robert. "I came here, still bruised and broken, with Aunt Maud the first day I arrived in Richmond."

"She must have come here often herself," he said.

"I think so, but I don't know."

He seemed not to hear. "We all need our place."

"Do you have yours in Amelia Courthouse?"

"The railroad tracks," he said. "I used to sit and watch the trains go by."

"I didn't have a railroad track."

"A river is better. We should come here more often."

"Perhaps we don't need the river anymore?"

"Or the tracks," he said. "Your coming was what I really needed."

"My coming cost me everything," I said.

"But you came," he said. "I'm glad."

We caught the late afternoon train and arrived in time for supper. Mrs. Emmett didn't inquire into our day, but I could tell she was pleased. I played with Jackson after supper and put him to bed at eight. I took my bath, and was in bed when Robert came in. He kissed me and held me tight for a very long time.

Chapter 38

I took Jackson with me, seated on the buggy seat, with his small hand clutched in my free one. With the other, I held the reins of the horses. Lamar, our chauffeur, could have driven Jackson down to the schoolhouse in the spare automobile for his first day of school, but I had plans beyond dropping Jackson off at the schoolyard.

How quickly the years had passed, the summer wind blowing across the dry grass of this land each year. We were flourishing, unlike the ground which often turned parched and dry. I could never love a man as I had loved Walter, but I did love Robert. I couldn't help myself.

I glanced down at Jackson's upturned face. "We're almost there, sweetheart."

"Will you leave me by myself?" he asked.

"Sweetheart, there will be plenty of other children, and the teacher, Mrs. Summers, is very kind. You'll like her right away."

Jackson's face relaxed a little. "I suppose I will."

We fell silent, the steady beat of the horses' hooves on the dry dirt surrounding us. I drew comfort from the familiar sounds of home.

"I used to go to a small school like this myself," I said.

"Really?" His face lit up.

I tousled his hair with my free hand. "Yes, sweetheart, you'll love school like I did."

Jackson's adoption had been completed six months after our visit to the lawyer's office in Richmond. He was now

Jackson Matthews and grew taller with each passing month. Walter would be proud.

I wiped away the tears with a quick wipe of my hand. Robert still didn't laugh much. There was a shadow lurking in his life. There were moments in the late hours of the evening when he sat in his study alone. I walked in, and he looked up and smiled, but the sadness didn't leave.

"What are you thinking, dear?" I asked more than once.

"About you," he would say, but he wasn't telling the truth.

I would kiss him on the forehead and hold him tight.

"I'm so thankful you're with me, Lily," he whispered in my ear.

"You're very precious to me, dear." I always told him.

I pulled back on the reins and the horses came to a stop by the small one-room schoolhouse. I hopped down to help Jackson find the step.

"Can you run in by yourself?" I asked. "Or shall I tie the horses and come in with you?"

"I'm okay." He drew himself up tall.

How similar he was to Walter, so brave and so bold.

"Run along now." I smoothed his hair with my fingers.

He clutched his small lunch pail and ran across the school yard. I waited until he reached the schoolhouse. The door opened, and Mrs. Summer's ample frame bent towards the small form. Mrs. Summers offered her hand. Words were exchanged. Jackson disappeared inside, while Mrs. Summers waved toward me. She waited while another child ran up. I climbed back into the carriage and turned the team around to drive back up the dusty road. The tears trickled on my cheeks. They grew so quickly. Staying or leaving, they were always tearing at your heartstrings.

I hesitated at the junction before I turned the team to the right instead of the left. Today was my chance to visit Joe at the restaurant—if he still ran the place. I hadn't dared ask

Bessie, lest my interest inspire suspicions. Better to make the quick trip into town to see an old friend—if anyone asked. I wanted to know something, and Joe would have the answer to the question burning in my heart.

I pulled back on the reins and turned the team down a side street. A short five-minute trot brought me to the restaurant. The sign still hung outside, "Joe's Small-Town Eatery." I tied the team and entered the back door.

A young waitress I didn't know looked up in surprise. "Can I get something for you?"

"I used to work here. Can I see Joe for a minute?"

"I'll check," she said, and disappeared into the inner office.

He came out at once. "Lily. What a pleasure. Are you buying the place?"

"Is the place for sale?" I teased.

"Not yet, although I'm old. Come back in." He waved me through the office door.

I seated myself across from his desk.

"So how are things going?"

"Fantastic," I said. "The downside is I don't get to cook or serve tables."

"I would hope not." He faked a look of horror.

"Robert is a dream, of course."

"Well, what man wouldn't love you, given the chance?"

"Thanks, Joe." I gave him a smile. "Those words mean a lot coming from you."

"Thanks again for the invitation to the wedding. I enjoyed the occasion, and you two looked great together."

"I'm the one who owes you a debt of gratitude," I said. "You took me in and gave me a job when you didn't have to. I know Mrs. Emmett forced your hand, but you could have said no."

He chuckled. "I would have given you a job any day, with or without Mrs. Emmett."

"How kind of you to say."

"I speak the truth, Lily, every word."

"Could you tell me about Robert?" I asked. "What happened before I came?"

His face darkened.

"What happened was bad, I assume."

He met my gaze. "I don't know what your comparison table is."

"Jackson's father is my sister's husband." I might as well tell him the truth.

"I see," he said. He didn't look too horrified.

"Now you know. Will you hold my transgressions against me?"

He shook his head. "I don't hold anything against you, and I hope you will give Robert the same favor."

"I already have," I said.

"You could ask anyone else in the community. This is not a secret. Why me?"

"I figured you would give me the kind version, the story of the heart."

He looked away for a moment. "Okay. Here goes. Robert fell in love with a local black girl. Lots of men around here have flings with them, but this was the real deal. I'm sure Robert thought of marriage, but around here marriage between whites and blacks is taboo, especially for the Matthews family. For everyone really, but you know what I mean?"

"I hadn't known mixed marriages were forbidden."

"Oh, very," he said. "Robert's reputation would have been finished. I would guess he planned to marry her anyway after she became pregnant. Instead, she died on the railroad tracks behind her parent's home. Robert had an alibi—with witnesses. The evidence pointed towards an obvious suicide. The prosecutor didn't call for a trial."

I sat there for a long time before I stood to my feet. "Thanks for telling me."

"Be kind to him," Joe said. "Things happen."

I stepped outside and left. The horses trotted up the street without much guidance from me, headed towards the house on the hill, towards my home, my husband, and my destiny. I now knew. I would never fill the shoes of Robert's loss, as he would never be Walter. We were together, two wounded souls who sought comfort in the loss and regrets of life. We both had dreamed of greater things and had been given each other instead.

Lamar took the horses from me when I arrived at the house. "Did they act up for you, Mrs. Matthews?"

"I grew up around horses," I said, "and they are well trained."

He grinned. "Mr. Matthews only keeps the best."

"He does," I agreed. "Have them ready for me this afternoon. I want to pick up Jackson today. You can take him for the rest of the week in the automobile."

"Yes, ma'am," he said.

I worked in the garden until lunch time, when Bessie called me in for sandwiches.

Mrs. Emmett was waiting at the table. "How was your morning, dear?"

"I dropped off Jackson and went to see Joe at the restaurant," I said.

"Oh." She helped herself to a sandwich.

"I could have asked you," I said, "but I wanted to spare you the telling."

She took a moment before she spoke. "Does this change anything?"

I shook my head. "Unless you count knowing for sure you will never fully fill another's place."

"You two were meant for each other. Don't doubt," she said. "Are you going to tell him?"

"I don't think so."

"You're wise. Live with this in your heart and love him, until he tells you."

I took my first bite of sandwich. "Has there been news lately from the community?"

Mrs. Emmett took a moment to collect herself. "I spoke with my contact a month ago. Nothing much going on other than weddings, children growing up, and old people dying."

"Community life," I said. "Was there another baby for Barbara?"

"Yes. A girl. Susan. They appear happy."

"I'm glad," I said.

Bessie appeared with a pitcher of chocolate milk, and I poured a cup.

Mrs. Emmett stood to her feet. "Working in the garden after lunch?"

"I think I will."

"You have a touch with plants."

"Were you afraid I would kill everything?"

Mrs. Emmett laughed. "I've never been afraid around you, not even for a minute."

"Thank you."

She left me, and I finished my sandwich. I took a glass of chocolate milk with me into the garden. I worked until three before I went down to pick up Jackson. I waited by the road until he came running out of the door with the other students. I went down to help him into the carriage. "Did you have a good day, sweetheart?"

"I love school." He beamed, so like Joy in his happiness. They were both Walter's children.

I hid my tears. "Lamar is going to drive you for the rest of the week. Do you mind?"

"I love Lamar," he said.

I gave him a hug. "You love everything right now, don't you?"

"I love Daddy and Mommy and Marie and Lamar and school." he chanted.

We drove home to the sound of his chatter in my ear. He ran into the house ahead of me to tell Mrs. Emmett about his day. Robert took him up on his knees after supper and listened for nearly half an hour.

"Sorry, he's really wound up," I said.

"We wouldn't have him any other way." Robert patted Jackson on the head. "What a good boy you are. Run along and play before your bedtime, otherwise you'll never sleep."

"Thank you for being kind to him," I whispered to Robert after Jackson left.

Robert pulled me down and kissed me on the cheek. He looked into my eyes. "How did God make someone like you?"

"I think the work took him awhile," I said.

We laughed together, gently, as the rain on the roof of our farmhouse. We were not like the lashing storms of spring which pass in an hour, but like the showers of summer come to stay the night.

He held me in bed until I fell asleep.

Chapter 39

Over five years later, the fateful day dawned with a slight rain falling from low clouds clinging to the horizon. I left with Lamar and Jackson in the automobile, to make sure the classes were in session. Mrs. Summers was out in the school yard in her raincoat to meet the arriving students.

"What awful news," she said, when I walked up holding Jackson's hand.

"I know. I thought school might be dismissed for the day."

"We should," she said, "but dismissing classes wouldn't help, I suppose."

"Everyone has been praying at the house."

"So have we." She gave Jackson a long hug.

"Everything okay?" Lamar asked when I arrived back at the car.

"Yes," I said. "Do you think Robert will volunteer?"

"Wouldn't know," he said, "but wouldn't surprise me. He'll do the country proud."

"Yes, of course." I climbed back in.

He placed the car in gear. "Has your family served?"

"My Grandfather was in the Civil War."

"North or South?"

"The North, I think."

He grinned. "Only a northerner wouldn't know."

"Sorry."

"There were honorable men on both sides. The conflict was a brothers' war."

"Unlike this one?"

"Certainly, unlike this one," he said. "There is no honor on the other side."

We arrived back at the house, and I would have gone to work in the garden but for the rain. I went instead into the empty living room and sat on the couch. A feeling of heaviness hung over the house and had since the news arrived yesterday of the surprise attacks on Pearl Harbor by the Japanese navy. Grandpa had gone to war, but the fight had felt distant and impersonal.

Here, the reality of the war was brutal, and in your face. I sat and wondered what the days ahead would hold for us. For me. For Robert. The president would give a speech at noon, and Robert wished to take in the whole thing.

In the meantime, I was hearing the voices of my childhood preachers. According to them, war brought nothing but trouble, fighting, dying, and in the end a peace which was always elusive. Only forgiveness, humility, and graciousness toward one's fellowman won the day. Those words felt weak in this place, a mere mirage on the horizon. I allowed the warnings to slip from my mind.

We gathered in the library for lunch, and Bessie brought in sandwiches. I tried to eat, while the others were glued to the announcer's voice on the radio. The clock on the wall ticked steadily onward. Twelve-thirty arrived and the announcer's voice died down. Robert moved closer to the radio, and Mrs. Emmett sat on the edge of her chair.

The voice of the president filled the room, "Mr. Vice President, and Mr. Speaker, and Members of the Senate and House of Representatives: Yesterday, December 7, 1941—a date which will live in infamy—the United States of America was suddenly and deliberately attacked by naval and air forces of the Empire of Japan …"

When the president's voice stopped, Robert began to pace the floor.

"What are you going to do?" Mrs. Emmett asked.

He didn't hesitate. "Enlist, of course. The air force probably. I can't fly planes, but I'm handy with my hands."

Mrs. Emmett's face was pained. "I wish you wouldn't. You're forty-two years old."

"I'm enlisting." His voice was firm.

"Men die, whether they're working on the ground or not." He faced both of us. "I'm going."

I couldn't find my voice to object, even if I had wanted to.

Mrs. Emmett sighed. "At least Lily's on your side."

I found my voice. "I am, but, at the same time, I don't want him to go."

He squared his shoulders. "I go for my country, for honor, for those who died yesterday, and for the fight against evil. We should have been in this war a long time already."

I reached for his hand—until he broke loose to pace the floor again.

Mrs. Emmett didn't say anything more, and I rose to leave the room. The two of them had loved each other before I arrived on the scene. They needed time together in this emotional hour without my presence. I would have Robert tonight, and until he left. I was his wife, and I would be his widow—if Robert was taken. There were plenty of widows at the moment whose husbands had died in the Pacific yesterday. There would be many more before this awful fight was over. I had no right to believe I would be spared. Yet, I prayed Robert would live to see Jackson grow into manhood.

I could no longer flee back to the community for shelter. They had their duty to their own lives, to their work in the fields, to their world view, and to the peace they made with each other. If I was there, I would disrupt and destroy. Here I could preserve and love. War had come. What I had grown to treasure was in danger, yet I must face the peril. I must be strong. I must support where I could.

Maybe I could help the war effort. Surely there was some material way in which women could offer aid. Did they not heal what was broken? There were nurses who bandaged torn limbs and cooled the feverish brow. I could be a nurse.

The rain had ceased outside, and I paced the garden for a long time, the droplets trickling from the leaves surrounding me. When I figured they had been given enough time together I returned to the drawing room. Robert was still pacing, and Mrs. Emmett was on her chair. "You're back," she said.

"I want to help with the war effort as a nurse," I said.

Robert's face brightened. "Lily! Why am I not surprised?"

"How is one trained?" I asked.

Robert's voice was filled with delight. "We can set you up for training."

"I suppose so." Mrs. Emmett turned to me. "A noble gesture indeed, Lily. I'm sure our country can use your help."

"Thank you."

Mrs. Emmett smiled. "You'll make a great nurse."

"I agree," Robert said, already at the library door. "With everything settled, I'm going into town."

The sound of the automobile soon puttered out of the driveway.

"I guess reality is reality," Mrs. Emmett said. "War is upon us and we must join the fight in one way or the other."

I walked to the window and looked out.

"Are you thinking about them this morning?" Mrs. Emmett asked.

I didn't look away from the window. "I was, yes."

"Do you want me to find out how everyone is doing?"

I shook my head. "They're fine, I'm sure. They don't go to war." I didn't want to think about Grandpa and how the community had used him.

"Yet war comes whether we like it or not," she said.

I turned away from the window. "How do I become a nurse? I'm serious, you know."

"I know you are, dear. I'll look into what's required." Mrs. Emmett stood to give me a hug. "You're such a blessing. I know the Lord sent you to us."

"I'm glad I'm here," I said.

As dusk fell, Robert and I sat on the edge of the bed after the house had quieted down, close, but not looking at each other.

"Did you sign up?" I finally asked.

"Yes. They took me without any hesitation."

My smile was strained. "Your aunt will help me with the nurse's training."

"I knew she would," he said.

"When are you leaving?"

"I don't know yet. They will tell me."

"You know I will miss you." I bit back the tears.

"And me you." He turned to look at me.

"You have been very kind."

He reached for my hand. "I want you to know about what happened before you came here."

I hesitated. "I already know. I'm sorry. I asked Joe."

He studied me for a long time. "Yet you still loved me."

"I never stopped. I couldn't."

"You're so beautiful inside and out," he said.

I forced a laugh. "Growing up they said I was pretty on the outside, but not on the inside."

"Then they lied. You touch the heart and soul, and you heal."

I nestled closer to him. "I'm glad I'm beautiful to you— inside and out."

He buried his face in my hair. "What did they do to you?"

"Does what happened to me matter anymore?" I asked.

"I would like to know."

The old coldness rose to chill my entire body. "The deeds are done and gone, and we're here."

He seemed not to hear as agony filled his face. "They had her body removed from the tracks when I arrived, but the blood was still there, everywhere. The engineer of the train said she never moved, lying there. I will be haunted by her death until I die."

I clutched his hand. "What she did wasn't your fault."

"I was the father of her child. Their death was my fault."

"She might still have done what she did."

"Maybe." He didn't look convinced.

"She loved you. I know what loving desperately feels like."

"Enough to kill yourself?" he asked.

"I'm not dead, but I felt like I was dying."

His face was still filled with pain. "There must have been another way—than to die on the tracks by your own hand."

I pulled him close. "God allows what he allows because he knows how to untangle our messes. I find peace with my surrender into his hands."

"What is your mess, since you know mine? I want to know."

I waited a long time before I spoke. "My father—well, my stepfather—came to my bed for most of my growing up years."

His hand tightened in mine. "How beyond awful. How did you survive?"

I took a deep breath. "How will we survive this war? No conflict spares the innocent, and neither did mine."

His face was close to mine, pensive and puzzled. "Yet you have borne your suffering with such grace."

"God takes away and he gives again," I said. "We bear the burden of the living, and the suffering of the dying. If we love in our pain, the grace given will be enough to heal any wound."

His puzzled look remained. "Why was I given you?"

"Why are we given anything?" I stood and undressed by the window in the moonlight.

He held out his hands. "You're a wonder. You're too good for me, such beauty and such sorrow."

I walked into his arms and kissed him. "They come together," I said. "We drink the cup to the dregs. God requires no greater burden."

Chapter 40

Almost a year later, I stood with my coat pulled tight around my shoulders, and my face turned against the wind blowing across the hillside beyond the big house. On the distant southern slope were the graves of Robert's parents. Below me were the familiar fields of the home I had grown accustomed to since my arrival here, pregnant with Jackson. Today, a light snow blew across them, the Christmas lights at the house turned out. The war had raged across the oceans for the last year, with bodies torn asunder by bombs and bullets, and loved ones taken. We could not expect our lives to remain untouched.

Jackson stood beside me, tall at twelve years of age, his figure erect, and his face full of sorrow . I reached for him and pulled him close. Mrs. Emmett stood beside us, the gape of the open grave at our feet, this hole in the earth, this piece torn from our hearts. The telegram arrived, and I had hurried home from Walter Reed Medical Center where I worked, my leave granted at once. America had gone to war, but America gave its citizens time to grieve. I mourned today, and would weep tomorrow, perhaps for the rest of my life. Because I will always have been the wife of Robert Matthews.

The wind stirred, and I let go of Jackson to stand upright. Minister Albright stood at the head of the grave with the closed casket in front of him, his body framed against the distant sky. He nodded to Mrs. Emmett, his face set, as one who had seen too much sorrow and could handle no more pain. I didn't blame him. Robert was not the first native son to arrive home in a casket. I was sure he would not be the last. The war had only begun to dump its deluge on a weary earth.

The military contingent was grouped further down the hill. The sergeant in charge had his back turned towards us, the contingent's faces grim, their weapons by their side. There would be guns fired today in honor of Robert Matthews. I had not protested. This was Robert's world and I would embrace every part. Even guns firing at funerals when peace should reign, voices should be hushed, and prayers alone offered under the open heavens.

Jackson stood proud beside me, and I would join him in his pride. I was glad I lived in a land where men believed in honor, in duty, in giving their all for their country. I had not clung to Robert when he planned to enlist or wept unduly on his shoulder before he left. We had loved and love was enough.

Robert must have known this time would come when he had walked out the door for the last time, as men sometimes did when eternity began to unfold in front of them. What else explained our conversation on the bed the night after the president made his speech. We parted with open hearts, which hid no shadow.

Minister Albright began to speak, "We have gathered here today, in the sight of God, and of these dear beloved ones, to bury a son we have all loved and admired. He was a man of conviction, a man who heard the call of his country and answered. We know and trust God has taken the soul of Robert Matthews into his arms. We sorrow, as those who have been left behind, who believe God weeps with us today. God knows our pain. God once walked this earth with us, and still does. We have not been left without comfort. Robert's widow, Lily, has requested the reading of the psalm which is so familiar to all of us—and dear, Psalms chapter twenty-three. 'The Lord is my Shepherd, I shall not want. He maketh me to lie down in green pastures ...'"

I listened to the familiar words I had heard my entire life. They were the same here as they were in the home community, and their comfort was the same. I did not understand, but this simply was, as my life was beyond explanation.

Minister Albright ended his words and the guns down the hill fired. I didn't flinch but pulled Jackson tightly against me as another volley thundered across the valley. The casket was lowered and settled into place. No one moved. I had requested this nod to my culture, and Mrs. Emmett had agreed.

The first shovel of dirt was thrown in. Taps played, the sound hanging in the air to haunt the entire hillside. Such mournful beauty was drawn deep from the soul, not unlike my own people who sang hymns composed by men in chains, with bodies bound in prison, with spirits reaching for freedom. Was this not what death did? The earthly was left behind in the dirt of the ground, while the heart soars upward to the Lord. I gazed at the heavy skies above me. This was the same song, the same desire, the same hope stirring in the heart of all mankind when the earth took what was not hers to possess. Someday, this travesty would be made right.

I placed my bouquet of flowers at the head of the dirt mound and turned away. I shook Minister Albright's hand and whispered, "Thank you, Reverend, for your kind words. They were a comfort to me."

"I'm sorry for your loss," he said. "Robert was a good man."

I nodded and moved on. Mrs. Emmett walked beside me with Jackson on her other arm for the trek down the hill and up the other side. Once we arrived, they helped me settle on the couch, as if I were feeble and old.

"Are you okay?" Mrs. Emmett asked.

"He loved me," I said, and the tears came again, "but I'm okay. Thank you for what you have done for us."

"When do you go back to Walter Reed?" she asked.

"Tomorrow."

"And after tomorrow?"

"There's the war," I said. "I'm committed, and things will get much worse."

"Are you staying here after the war?"

"I'm not going back to the community," I said. "At least not until Barbara passes."

"Let me give you my contact's address. I'm old. I may not be here when this war ends."

"Don't say such a thing," I chided.

Mrs. Emmett ignored me. "My contact is a chauffeur for the Amish and is more than willing to keep you up-to-date with what happens in the community. Now I should get busy. Are you sure there's nothing I can do?"

"I'm fine. I'll spend the day with Jackson, and he's yours when I leave tomorrow."

I waited until Mrs. Emmett was out of the room, before I stood and walked to the window. The last of the military squad had loaded their equipment and were on the way out of the driveway. I made my way upstairs and knocked on the door before I entered. Jackson was reclined on the bed and didn't look up when I sat beside him. I took his hand in mine. "Sweetheart, how are you doing?"

"I want to fight like Dad," he said.

"You can't. You're only twelve."

"They take young boys," he said.

I pulled him close and held him. He wept, great sobs bursting from his chest. "He loved you, Jackson. He loved you with his whole heart."

"I want to be like him," he said.

"You already are, dear. You're brave, honest, and true. You work hard in school. You will grow up to walk in his shoes."

"I will fight in this war," he said. "I have to."

I hushed him. "I can't lose both of you. You'll live with Mrs. Emmett, study hard and get ready for life ahead of you."

His body went limp as he gave in.

"We should talk about your real father," I said.

"I don't want to. He's not here."

"Not because he doesn't want to be," I told him. "Walter loved me as your adopted father loved you."

"I don't care."

"Someday you will. I will take you to him when the time is right."

"Robert was my father," he said.

"I know he was, and yet the truth doesn't hurt us. I want you to know the truth. I want you to know who I once was, and who knew me and loved me deeply. Robert would have wanted you to know."

"How do you know?"

"Because Robert told me."

He stood to walk over to the window. I joined him to gaze towards the distant grave on the hillside.

"I don't like this," he said.

"Neither do I, sweetheart, but life is not about what we like. Life is about what we have loved."

Section Nine—November 1945 to June 1977

BARBARA

Chapter 41

I bent low on the bedroom floor. The girl I helped dress was tall, her figure slender and beautiful. As Lily had been. She took my breath away, and this was the morning of her wedding. The house had been cleaned in the last few weeks—from top to bottom. Joy had waited for this day, through long years of war while Henry served his time in one of the conscientious objector camps in Pennsylvania. There, under government supervision, the men performed alternative war service by maintaining roads, fighting forest fires, and repairing public works. She could have rushed ahead with her wedding back in 1942. The reasons would have been plenty. Hostility outside the community towards the camps was widespread, and Joy loved Henry. She had wanted desperately to claim him as her husband before their long separation, but Joy had done what was right. Joy always did what was right. Where was the surprise anymore?

"Is something wrong?" Joy asked.

I stood to my feet. "No. I was just distracted." I brushed the folds of the dress through my fingers. "This is everything a wedding dress should be."

"Perhaps my dress shouldn't be so beautiful," Joy said. "After the suffering our people have been through by objecting to the war."

"Your dress is fine. You're the one who is perfect, not the dress."

Joy blushed. "I'm happy, but I hope Henry doesn't think my attire too extravagant."

"The day is real." I pinched her arm. "Wake up. Henry will love you, whatever dress you're wearing."

Joy turned sideways. "I suppose the dress isn't too much. I tried to find just the right color to suit the occasion. Not too dark, not too light. God has given me Henry, and I do love the man."

"Henry loves you." I assured her.

She stepped over to the bedroom window and pushed the drapes back. The sun had not risen yet. The first rays were a bright glow on the horizon. In the distance, the first buggies appeared with their lights dim. They were likely the cooks, and Henry's buggy was in the mix. Tonight, the man would see the beauty of my daughter, her womanly glory no man on this earth had seen yet. He would look and wonder that the Lord had made such splendor on this earth.

Joy and Henry didn't know the sorrow of my world. They were the first fruits of a new generation. After my rough start with Joy, I had done what I could to make things right. No one in our home had suffered the things my sister had suffered.

I walked over to the window to join my daughter. "You know Henry will be pleased with you tonight."

Joy's face flamed. "Do not speak of such things."

"We cannot live without the things which happen between a man and a woman," I said. "You're a woman, and a woman dies without love, without the kind of love Henry will give you. Love him, Joy. Do not be ashamed in front of him. Give him your heart, and all of yourself. Do not draw back from his joy or from yours. Henry is a man. You have the power to give him the desires of his heart."

"Mamm!" Joy exclaimed. "Pretty soon I'll be so red faced I'll be unfit to walk out in public."

I squeezed her arm. "Be bold with him tonight. I'm sure his heart is not as settled as yours. He doubts. The years in the camp have taken their toll. He planned on taking you as his wife before he left. He was wise not to, but the decision came at a cost. He will struggle with believing the Lord has made a woman like you, and to accept you're his. Do not take his hesitation as rejection. Remember!"

Joy covered her face with both hands, and I slipped from the room. I had said too much, but I couldn't help myself. The cooks were on the front steps and I hurried to open the door for them.

"Good morning." I whispered my greeting into the stillness of the morning air.

"Good morning." They replied, equally hushed.

Mamm was among them, and I held the door wide. They trooped in. I glanced across the yard. Henry was busy unhitching his horse beside the barn and would find his own way inside.

I hurried back to the bedroom. "There is no one else around at the moment," I whispered to Joy. "Go out and meet Henry."

Joy stood, frozen in place. I took her arm and led her out of the bedroom. Once outside, she moved on her own across the yard. I waited until the two forms reached each other, before I walked away from the window.

Mamm was standing in the kitchen doorway with Elsie and Mary beside her when I turned around. "Did Joy just go out?" Mamm asked.

"Yes, I sent her to meet Henry."

"She's in her wedding dress."

"There's no one around," I said.

Mamm turned away, her face troubled.

There was the sound of steps on the front porch and Elsie sang out, "They're here."

The two girls rushed forward to open the door. Henry stepped in, almost tripping on the threshold, his face red.

"Good morning, Henry." I greeted him.

"Good morning." He stuck out his hand, while the girls hugged their sister.

"Get back inside the bedroom right now." Mamm ordered. "Henry can stay out here with us until the rest of the wedding party arrives."

"Please." Joy begged. "I want to stay with Henry. I can flee if someone comes who isn't supposed to see me."

"Let them," I said.

Mamm shrugged and disappeared into the kitchen. I followed her. The cooks had almost completed the food preparation, and several of them were busy carrying the heavy kettles out through the washroom door headed towards the makeshift kitchen set up in the upper barn loft. I stepped forward to help but was shooed away.

I waited while they left with the kettles. Dawn had begun to lighten the sky outside the kitchen window, and I settled into a chair. I hadn't changed my dress yet, but I could wait. Walter was in the barn. There was no rush until he had helped the last of the guests unhitch and came inside. Walter took great pleasure in Joy's relationship with Deacon Miller's son. He had thought the conquest a worthy one for his eldest and greatly beloved daughter. Joy for her part could have dated any unmarried man from the community she wished. Her choice hadn't been the most handsome one, or the most dashing, more like the most solid and mature. I thought Henry had always been a little puzzled over his good fortune, as the man should be. Henry would never know what a wonderful wife he had in Joy. How could he? He had nothing with which to compare Joy.

"What are you thinking?" Mamm asked.

"About Joy and how things have turned out."

"I can't look at her without seeing Lily," Mamm said.

"The past is in the past, Mamm."

"My mind knows, but my heart doesn't. My sin grows larger with each passing day."

"Can't you forget for once? This is Joy's wedding."

Mamm nodded. "I'll try to enjoy myself for Joy's safe. The Lord knows the girl doesn't need me to darken her happiness."

"Just think," I said. "For a long time now, we have heard nothing about the Lord's judgment on our family. You have expressed your sorrow over how things went with Lily. You should move on."

"Daett never confessed anything before he passed," she said. "I've often wondered. Do you think he was welcomed into the pearly gates?"

"Worrying about Daett isn't going to change anything," I said. "I'm just thankful this generation is different. My greatest happiness is the knowledge things are changing for my children."

"Things have changed." Mamm agreed. "I wish what we did wouldn't have happened, though."

"We can't change the past," I said.

I motioned towards the living room where Joy and Henry's voices rose and fell along with the two girls. "We should be quiet. They'll hear us soon."

I stood and moved away from the table as more buggies came in the driveway. The living room was empty, so Joy and Henry must have fled to the bedroom. I went to the front door and greeted the first of the wedding party with a cheery, "Good morning. Joy and Henry are waiting in the bedroom, and someone will be serving breakfast in the barn, soon."

Henry's younger brother Abe and his girlfriend Carrie hurried towards the bedroom with their hands clasped. There would be another wedding this season, if I didn't miss my guess. Abe had also served his time in the conscientious objector camps for the past four years, as had a large portion of the young men from the community. Most of them had postponed marriage until the war was over, so they wouldn't leave wives and prospective children to fend on their own or burden the community with their care.

There would be many couples who planned a wedding this season—as many as could work the date in, and next year would bring a baby boom to the district. Joy's child would be among them, I was sure. Joy would raise the son I was never allowed to bring into adulthood.

Joy would be a capable mother and a happy one. She would bring children into the world who would make a better world than the one I had experienced in my childhood.

There was the sound of steps on the front porch again and I opened to door to greet Willis Wagler, the other half of the wedding party. Willis had been sweet on Elsie before the war and had brought her home from the hymn singing a few times since the men came back from the camps.

"Good morning, Willis." I extended my hand. "Elsie's upstairs somewhere. Breakfast is about to be served in the barn."

"I'll wait out there then," he said, and began to back away.

"No." I stopped him. "I'll get the others and you can go out together.

Willis nodded and waited. I stepped into the back hallway and hollered into the open bedroom door. "Everyone's here. Why don't you go to the barn to eat?"

"In my wedding dress?" Joy called out.

Henry stuck his head out and offered. "I'll bring Joy a plate, and we can eat in the kitchen."

"Okay," I said.

"You're such a dear." Joy sidled up to Henry, her face filled with happiness.

"No kissing in front of me," Abe teased, and everyone laughed.

Elsie appeared moments later. She greeted Willis with a bright smile, and they left. I took Joy's hand, and we made our way to the kitchen.

"You all right, Mamm?" she asked.

"Just happy," I said.

A slight smile crept onto her face. "Those things you said earlier. You were right."

"Just let him love you tonight in his own way. You'll be okay."

"I know." Her smile changed to a dreamy gaze at the blank wall. "I almost wish Lily was here."

"She can't be," I said, a chill coming into my voice.

Joy had been there during those nights when Walter had gone out with Lily. She had never said anything, but she had to know. I swallowed my pain. Why was I trying to instruct her on matters of the heart? My sister had taught my daughter better how to love than I had.

They said their vows exactly at twelve o'clock, as if Bishop Hochstetler, our new bishop, had timed the occasion. The picture they made standing there in front of the congregation, the young bishop with his long black hair and beard, and the young couple—Henry nervous, his beard still a scuffled attempt at what he would eventually produce, and Joy blushing, but so happy.

Walter was seated beside me, beaming. I figured he was seeing Lily in her wedding dress, the one he never saw, but should have. Again, I pushed back my dark thoughts. I kept my eyes on them until they said the vows, and Bishop Hochstetler pronounced them man and wife. I lowered my head and let the tears come. They trickled in drops onto the hardwood floor below me. The new had arrived, but the old haunted us. I glanced over at Mamm. Her pale, hollow look frightened me. There must be some way Mamm could let go of the past and join us in our joy of what lay ahead.

We didn't get to bed until well after midnight when the last visiting guest left the evening hymn singing. Henry and Joy were staying upstairs in Joy's bedroom, as was customary for the married couple's first night together. I undressed and I climbed into bed, while Walter sat on the edge.

"They're awful quiet," Walter said.

"They'll be okay."

"Henry will be good for her. He'll love her." He sounded worried.

"Forget about them," I said. "Come. I'm waiting."

"This isn't your wedding night." I could see his grim face in the dim light of the stars.

"I'm not an old woman yet," I said.

I lifted the quilt, and he finally leaned over to kiss me. In the darkness, he traced the shape of my face with his finger, until I pulled him close. I hoped Joy and Henry were too occupied upstairs to hear us.

We feel asleep within reach of each other, and I awoke with the faint blush of dawn on the horizon outside the bedroom window. Walter was still sleeping, since everyone was given slack on a post-wedding morning. I tiptoed into the kitchen. I hadn't heard any sounds from upstairs all night, but I figured I wouldn't have while I was sleeping. I was in the kitchen with my glass full of water when I heard them, the unmistakable rhythmic sounds of love in a bed. I didn't know what I expected to feel, surely not horror, but perhaps some degree of happiness. I stood there with my glass of water, and the rush of joy flooding through me caught me completely by surprise.

Chapter 42

The years went by swiftly, each one the same and yet different in subtle ways. This April morning, the spring breeze stirred outside our windowpane—the trees fresh in the yard with their green leaves. Another awakening had occurred from a long winter when snow-covered fields were the only view out of our kitchen window. I was bent over the kitchen sink with our youngest daughter Susan working beside me. Jane had married two years ago. Susan had turned twenty-two last month. My passionate daughter, conceived the night Walter first loved me, should have married at eighteen, but couldn't make up her mind who among her numerous suitors she should select. She stood frozen at the moment, a dish towel tossed over her arm, lost in her thoughts. Had she finally settled on a man?

I didn't disturb her but kept washing the dishes. I was beginning to feel old, and the dreams of the young were a balm to my weary body. Walter was working in the barnyard, bent over the wagon tongue to fasten the last of the horse's traces, ready for another day's work in the fields. I plunged my hands into the dish water, and Susan was jerked out of her reverie by the water droplets landing on her arm. She grabbed a bowl and busied herself wiping the surface dry.

"You're not sinning," I said, "thinking about him."

"Who?" She tried to sound innocent, but her voice trembled.

"I know what love is," I said, "once you really love."

Susan turned bright red. "Are you sure these things I feel for a man are right?"

"Who is this fellow?" I asked.

"You don't know?"

I laughed. "If you made me pick from the lot, my first choice would be Samuel Stoll."

She ducked her head. "I think he's who I want."

"Have you accepted his request for a date?"

"Yes, for this Sunday evening."

"Susan!" Now I was exclaiming.

Susan buried her face in the towel. "Oh, Mamm, what shall I do? I've so wanted this moment, and now …"

"You'll bake a special plate of cookies," I said, "and serve him lemonade or milk, whichever he prefers, and you will sit beside him on the couch and talk."

"Talk." Susan fanned herself. "My knees are weak already. What if I have nothing to say?"

"He's probably more interested in your company than in what you have to say," I said.

"Now I'm going to pass out."

"Don't worry. You'll find something to say. All of your sisters made out fine."

Susan didn't appear convinced. "There may be a problem—now I've decided on a man. Samuel was dating a girl in Allen County before they moved here. Someone said they were engaged, and Samuel broke his promise to her."

"They shouldn't blame someone for a broken dating relationship," I said.

Susan made a face. "I guess I feel guilty. I figure I'm stealing Samuel from some girl who deeply loves him. I mean, who wouldn't want to steal him? Samuel is quite a catch."

"You're doing nothing wrong," I said. "Samuel has to sort out whatever situation he has with the other girl. Things change with couples. We date to find out if this is the right person. Ask him, and Samuel will tell you. He doesn't seem the type to deceive."

"So, I shouldn't have turned him down?" she asked.

"If you are interested in the man, the worst thing you can do is reject him."

"Oh, Mamm!" Susan gave me a big hug. "Thank you. I'd best get busy with the cleaning. I don't want a single spider web anywhere in this old house come Sunday evening."

"There are no spider webs," I muttered, but Susan was already up the stairs.

I returned to the sink and finished the last dish with the towel Susan had draped over the kitchen chair. I called up the stairs when I finished, "I'm going over to Grandma's house."

There was a muffled shout, and I moved on. Walter was in the field behind the barn when I walked out the front door. He pulled back on the horse's reins as I hurried up to him.

"I'm going over to Mamm's house for a little bit."

"Okay." The reins hung loose in his hands.

"Susan's bringing Samuel home on Sunday evening. I need to speak with Mamm before she hears anything from someone else."

He nodded. "Our weddings do disturb her, but Samuel seems like a nice fellow."

"Did you hear anything about an old girlfriend in Allen County?" I asked.

"No, but I hope Susan wins. She's a decent girl."

"You're not much help." I scolded.

"All's fair in love and war, as the English say."

"I'd better go," I said, and tried to smile.

"Let me tie the team up at the fence, and I'll harness the horse for you."

"I can harness the horse myself," I objected, but he was already on his way.

I had my horse Macy out of the stall by the time Walter secured the team and arrived inside.

"Are you sure you can handle this horse," he asked. "She's new to you."

"I'll be okay."

"We're both getting old, you know."

"Our youngest daughter dating doesn't make us old."

"I guess not," he said.

He led Macy out of the barn, and I held the shafts up for him. He gave me a quick peck on the cheek before I climbed in the buggy.

"Thank you." I called out.

"Always an honor." He left with a quick wave of his hand.

I drove Macy out of the driveway at a brisk trot, to arrive at the Old Swartz homestead ten minutes later. Mamm was out on the front porch swing but didn't come down to greet me while I tied Macy to the hitching post.

"How are you doing?" I called, halfway across the lawn.

"I can still walk out to the swing."

I took her hand when I arrived. "Are you cold?"

"I guess I could use a blanket," she said.

I brought one from the house, and wrapped the cloth around her, before I seated myself.

A tear glimmered on her cheek. "This is so embarrassing, sitting out on the front porch in the springtime with a blanket. I should be working the garden."

"The weather is still cool, Mamm, and old people need blankets."

"I guess I'm old." She seemed to shrink into the porch swing. "How are things going at your house?"

"I came over to discuss something," I said. "I wanted to tell you so you wouldn't get upset. Susan's bringing Samuel Stoll home on Sunday night."

"I see," she said.

"I'm sorry Lily and I caused you so much trouble."

"I'm the one who sinned so grievously," she said. "You know I did. I never paid for my transgression."

"You don't think what happened so far was enough?"

"You paid your price. I never did. I made Lily bear my suffering."

"Mamm, please!"

"I lie awake at night," she said, "still hearing awful noises upstairs or worse, I hear nothing. The worst nightmare is the silence. Lily never made a sound. I can hear her stillness. She bore my wickedness as if her own. I'm not worthy to see the gates of glory, let alone enter them."

I held her hand. "Shall we talk about something else, Joy maybe? She's expecting another little one."

"I don't have much time, Barbara. Tell me what I can do to make this right? Is there any way I can pay my debt to Lily?"

"You don't have to, Mamm."

She stared at me. "You never made a fuss about Walter being with Lily there at the end. You were paying your price."

"Mamm, I didn't think in those terms."

"Yet knowing Lily was with Walter cost you a lot, didn't it?"

"Of course, he was my husband."

"You're avoiding the truth, Barbara. You knew what you were paying."

"Maybe?" I allowed. This truth I stridently avoided when I could.

"Now Walter loves you. Tell me what my price is? I must pay before I go."

"I don't know, Mamm. How could I know?"

Fear filled her face. "There is nothing with which to pay. Lily doesn't want anything I have."

"You don't have to pay. Lily understands."

"I wish Lily had screamed," she said. "I tell myself I wish Lily had, then I know I am looking for an excuse again. What happened was my fault, everything was my fault."

"Maybe you don't need to say anything more," I said.

"There must be something I can do. Why is there nothing?"

"Let's talk about Susan and her date on Sunday night," I said. "You can be happy with us. The wedding doesn't have to disturb you—if their relationship brings us to their marriage day."

"You came to tell me this?"

"I came to see you," I said. "Can I get you something to drink?"

"Water, yes."

I brought the cold glass from the kitchen, and she took a long sip, the tears heavy on her cheeks."

"Why are you crying?"

"I have to do something," she said.

"Mamm, stop talking about the past. Shall I stay the night with you?"

She shook her head. "Joy sends her oldest over to make supper for me. I don't need anything else."

"Perhaps you should speak with the deacon, tell him everything."

"Nothing will help now," she said.

I took her inside before I left and made sure she had food around to eat for lunch. "I'm going now."

She nodded and attempted a smile.

"How's she doing?" Walter asked after supper.

"I tried," I said. "Maybe you should talk with her."

"I'll see," he said, but I don't think he ever did.

Walter never forgot what had been done to Lily.

Chapter 43

Two years later, Susan's wedding day arrived. The first frost had fallen the night before, the crisp sheen still on the turning leaves. Another week and the golden brown and deep yellows of the fall season would be in their full glory. Susan had wanted a wedding in early November. Maybe because she wished to differentiate herself from her sisters who had married later in the month, but I knew better.

Susan was in a hurry, and I had no objection primarily for Mamm's sake. Susan had been through a rough spot with Samuel, and Mamm had suffered the most. There had been a former girlfriend, an Esther Byler. The two had been engaged. There had been a visit from Esther to the community which exposed the whole affair. Revelations followed. Samuel had not done his duty when he left Allen County. He had his excuses. He had been overtaken by Susan's charms, and had not made things clear to Esther. I had flashbacks of our scandal with Lily, but in my heart I knew nothing compared to Lily.

Susan turned her passion, not towards Samuel's transgressions, but towards helping him recover his reputation. She even accompanied the man to Allen County for a meeting with Esther and her parents. What was said, I was never told, but calm settled slowly over the whole mess. I didn't notice how disturbed Mamm had been until peace came.

"This was not Lily," I told her.

"My sin follows me to my grave." She intoned. I might as well have been speaking to the wall.

"Mamm, you have to stop this." I ordered. "Susan is going to marry the man. Everything will be okay."

"Lily should have married Walter," she said.

The words stung deeper than I expected. "You're just questioning everything. You don't know what you're saying."

"I must pay." She muttered. "There must be a way to pay."

"I'm sorry this happened," I said, "but this is not the past. This is a new day, and Susan is not Lily."

"I burned Lily's bed last week," she said.

Startled. "You did what?"

"I had to stop the silence, only she's still up there."

"Where did you burn the bed?"

"In the garden," she said. "Where I first met Lily's English father."

I went to look. There was indeed a tangle of wires on top of a pile of ashes. "Mamm." I tried again when I came back into the house. "You have to accept things. You can't change what happened. Can you at least be happy when Susan gets married?"

"I'll try," she said, but she looked dazed.

I left her. There was only so much I could do, and I was at the end of my wits.

Today, my last daughter was marrying, and Mamm would have no further agitation of her unpleasant memories. The yard outside was already filled with buggies, but I was not going to hurry.

"You're looking chirpy," Walter teased from across the bedroom.

He wrestled with his suit and slipped the coat over his shoulders. I stepped closer to adjust the straight cut collar and push his white shirt inside.

"You shouldn't say such things," I whispered in his ear. "I'm an old hag."

"You're not." He kissed me on the cheek.

"Are you getting married today?"

His eyes twinkled. "I guess we'll have to see tonight."

I playfully slapped him on the arm. "Soon you'll have me blushing worse than Susan."

He took my hand and we walked out of the bedroom. Our married daughters were gathered with their husbands and children, their gazes fixed on the stair well.

"They're almost ready to come down," Joy said.

"You're sure making an occasion out of the day," Walter said.

"Why not? Our baby sister is getting married." Elsie buried her face in her husband Willis's shoulder in her glee.

Footsteps sounded on the steps, and the door opened moments later. Susan stepped out in her light blue dress. My dress had been made from the darkest blue material I could find, in perfect sync with the church ordnung, but wedding customs had changed since my time. Deep down, I didn't mind these changes in the rules. Susan had chosen the perfect color. Only Joy had been given Lily's loveliness, but each of my girls had a beauty in their own right. Susan was even more gorgeous than when I had helped her dress early this morning by the light of the kerosene lamp.

"You're so lovely," several of the girls cooed together.

Susan blushed and hid her face with both hands. Samuel beamed beside her, unashamed of his happiness. There had been no talk as I had with Joy when I dressed Susan this morning. There was no need. The war years and their hardship were a distant memory. The young people seemed bolder now, more confident, and surer of themselves. Samuel would have no hesitation in bed tonight, if I made my guess. Susan for her part would undress without a moment's bashfulness.

The girls were hugging each other, and I joined the melee.

"My dress," Susan squealed more than once.

The sisters began to move outside with their families, headed to the barn for the start of the service. I waited with Walter until everyone had left, except the wedding party. I gave Susan one last long hug.

"You look beautiful, my little one," Walter said. "I know the vows haven't been said but let me be the first to congratulate the new Mrs. Stoll."

"Oh, Daett!" Susan flew into his arms.

"You're getting a good wife." I told the beaming Samuel.

"I know. Thank you for doing such a fine job."

I turned away, so he wouldn't see my tears, but he noticed. "I know a little about your past," he said. "I admire you greatly, and obviously your daughter. Thank you again."

I dabbed my eyes and took Walter's arm. We exited through the front door. Walter paced himself on the walk to the barn where we parted ways at the broad barn door. Men were seated on one side, and the women on the other. This was the tradition of the ages, timeless in its application even as the culture elsewhere moved on.

This community would always be my home, my place of rest. This was where I belonged, where I had lived my life, and where I would die.

I sat down, and the wedding party entered the barn. Every eye turned in their direction. Susan had her gaze appropriately cast on the floor, with her face flushed. Samuel had a slight grin on his face. His brother Lester led the way with his girlfriend Sherry beside him. The party swept in and took their seats across from the ministers. The first song was given out and the three-hour service began. I glanced over at Mamm, and she was trying to smile.

Bishop Hochstetler had the main sermon. "The Lord has been gracious to his people again," he said. "His mercies are new every morning. To each generation the Lord's grace is fresh and alive. King David wrote in the psalms, 'once I was young, and now I am old, yet I have never seen the righteous forsaken or his seed begging for bread.' I can say amen to those wonderful words. We have much we can look forward to on this earth. We live under the blessing of the Lord's hand. On the other side, the troubles of fallen mankind are many. The world rages in its fury at times, and even those who seek peace are troubled. Our past generation has lived through two of the world's worst wars, and now here we are with threats of war still being made every day. Peace is the only choice God offers his people, to live for others, to give and not to take. These are the perfections of the Lord's way which we in our frailness must seek to follow."

Bishop Hochstetler paused to clear his throat. "I wish to honor the Yoder family today. Walter and Barbara have been faithful members of the church from their youth. They have grown up among us and have sought to raise their family in the fear of the Lord. Today, the last of their daughters will take her vows with the man who has won her heart. Let us be thankful on this joyful day and rejoice with Walter and Barbara. Let us praise the Lord for the mercies he has given. God has brought the two of them through many troubled waters, but we see the fruit of their labor today, in this their lovely daughter Susan, and in Samuel who will soon be their son-in-law."

I stole another look at Mamm. She had her head down, and I couldn't see her face. Bishop Hochstetler concluded his sermon and Mamm still hadn't looked up.

"If you're still willing." He spoke to Samuel and Susan. "Will you stand before me for the sacred vows?"

They stood, and I pulled my gaze away from Mamm. The questions came quickly, answered by Samuel's confident voice and Susan's higher one. The words were soon finished, and the union made. Samuel and Susan were husband and wife. Heaven would never change their reality, and the earth was forbidden to try. Mamm was sitting up straight as Samuel and Susan took their seats and the last song was sung.

The service ended, and the crowd moved outside until the tables could be set up. When the guests came back in, the table waiters poured out of the makeshift kitchen in the back of the barn loft, and the food was spread out on the tabletops.

I took my place along with Walter at the head of the family table, with Susan and Samuel in the corner of the barn where the wedding party sat on either side of them. Mamm was supposed to sit beside me, but she had disappeared. I closed my eyes, listening to the sounds of happy chatter around me. I had so hoped Mamm would not be overcome by the day. Perhaps if we left her alone her grieving could be completed.

Walter whispered in my ear, "Where's your Mamm? They're ready to pray."

"I don't know." I mouthed back.

Bishop Hochstetler was on his feet again and led out in a prayer of thanksgiving. The eating began—fried chicken, dressing and noodles, vegetable sides, and coleslaw. After the main course, dessert followed—date pudding; cherry, pumpkin, and pecan pies; sheet cake; bowls of canned fruit; and celery sticks.

I ate slowly, determined to savor and enjoy each bite. This was our last wedding, and I would bring Mamm a plate of food later, wherever she had gone to lick the wounds of the past.

Walter squeezed my hand under the table. "You have done well, Barbara."

"You were a good father," I whispered back.

He smiled. I went to find Mamm after the meal concluded. She was upstairs in one of the bedrooms where the smaller girls played.

"Mamm, you have to eat," I said.

"I'm not hungry." She muttered.

"Come downstairs, and I'll bring in a plate."

She gave in with a blank expression on her face. I took her hand and led her down the steps. I left her on the couch until I returned with a plate of food. I stayed with her until she finished.

"I want to go home now," she said.

"Are you tired?"

"I'm weary of soul."

"Shall I come and stay with you the rest of the day?"

"And miss your daughter's wedding?"

"They're married." I tried to smile.

"One of Joy's girls will be over like usual. I'm okay."

I went out to find Walter and we hitched her horse to the buggy. She was waiting on the lawn when we finished and climbed in to drive away.

"Come. Let's be happy," I said. "I will visit her tomorrow."

The afternoon drifted on, familiar moments, followed by the flurry of the evening meal served at six. The young people's singing came next, completed by nine. The guests hung around chatting, discussing the day's events, and wishing Samuel and Susan their final congratulations.

Eleven o'clock approached when the last buggy left the driveway. Walter and I went into the house, but there were no signs of Susan or Samuel, and no noises came from upstairs. My passionate daughter would not wait until the morning as had her oldest sister.

"What do you think they're doing?" I whispered.

"Perhaps we should go outside for a bit," Walter said.

We did, and sat on the porch swing with the full moon over our heads, casting a soft glow across the front yard.

"You think they've quieted down?" Walter finally asked.

"Look!" I motioned beyond the shadows of the house, where Susan's form crept out of the washroom door followed by Samuel's, his hand firmly in hers. Under Susan's arm was a bedroll and Samuel carried pillows and a quilt.

Walter's laugh was soft. "Now I've seen everything."

"Hush." I warned. "They'll hear you."

The two didn't slow down but scurried across the yard towards the barn without a backwards glance. The wooden door opened and closed behind them with a soft click in the still night air.

"Those two aren't bashful." Walter mused.

"She's your daughter."

Walter laughed. "Perhaps we both share in the blame?"

"The haymow on your wedding night," I said. "Now I have heard everything."

He turned towards the barn, where faint cries came from the upper loft door. "We should go inside," he said.

I took his hand for our walk to the bedroom. We undressed but lay there for a long time, simply looking at the ceiling.

"Did Lily make love like Susan just did?" I finally asked.

"Please, Barbara. Let's not go there."

"I'm glad you were with Lily," I said.

"Barbara!" he said again, sharper this time.

"I mean what I'm saying. You healed a deep wound my sister carried." There, I had said the words.

I heard his breath leave him slowly. "How gracious of you."

I turned to touch his arm. "I'm glad you made love to a beautiful woman. You deserved someone like Lily."

He didn't say anything, but he held me. I was happy I was alive. Happy I was breathing.

I awoke in Walter's arms, to hear the rapid beat of a horse's hooves outside the bedroom window coming into our driveway. I grabbed my housecoat and had my arms in the sleeves when Walter opened his eyes.

"Who just drove in?" he asked.

"I don't know."

I was at the front door when Walter passed me still buttoning his shirt. I made out the faint outline of Joy's son James, the oldest boy who was still at home, seated in the open buggy door. I ran with Walter to meet him.

"What's wrong?" Walter called across the lawn.

"Just come with me," he said. "I'm not supposed to tell you."

"Who is this about?" Walter asked.

"Grandma," he said. "You must come."

"Did she pass away?" I asked.

"I was told to bring you." He stuck with his line.

I rushed back inside and dressed. Walter had our buggy ready when I arrived outside again. We dashed out of the lane with James behind us.

"What do you think happened?" I asked.

Walter didn't answer but drove Macy at a dead gallop for most of the way. There was a police car and an ambulance in the driveway when we arrived. I turned cold inside. How Walter knew something truly awful had happened, I didn't want to know.

Walter leaped down and tied Macy to the hitching post. He helped me from the buggy, and the police officer let us through with only a slight nod. Dr. Meyers was in the hallway with his bag packed, obviously ready to leave.

"There was nothing I could do," Dr. Meyers said.

Joy appeared and flew into my arms. "I'm so sorry, Mamm."

"What happened?" I asked.

She didn't answer but led me into the bedroom where Mamm's form was covered with a sheet.

"What happened?" I asked again.

Joy pulled back the sheet to reveal the stab wounds in Mamm's stomach. They had obviously been thrust upwards with considerable force.

"She was alive covered in a blanket when Miriam arrived this morning," Joy said. "Grandma told her to call Dr. Meyers, who called the police when he arrived, but Miriam didn't see her like this."

"Who did this?" I asked.

"Grandma told Dr. Meyers and the sheriff she had—by her own hand," Joy said. "They believed her. There will be no search for an assailant."

The undertaker came for the body soon afterwards, and Walter helped me clean up the mess. I expected the news to sweep through the community by the evening, but a strange calm settled in instead. I didn't try to keep the matter secret, but neither did I talk. No one said anything at the funeral about how Mamm had died. The sermons were preached as if an old person had reached the fullness of her years and passed away in peace at night.

The undertaker did an amazing job with the wounds in Mamm's stomach. You could see several thin red lines for a few inches, but nothing more. I wondered if Mamm had chosen to drive the knife in there to hide the wound, but I figured there was another reason, her desire to inflict on herself the slow agony of an inevitable death.

There was no way to reach Lily, even if we had wanted to.

Chapter 44

Twelve years had passed, and I visited the graveyard often to sit and ponder if Mamm had found the peace she desired so desperately. Lily would not have required such a payment. No one would have, yet Mamm had required the action of herself.

For us, life went on. Christmas time was here again. The yard was drifted deep with snow under a clear sky. Last week's storm was past. The Lord continued to give us good things, which I couldn't understand at times. The children knew little of our sorrow. For them, we must try to find joy in living. I prayed this Christmas day would be blessed and memorable. The county had made valiant efforts to keep the county roads open, so everyone should be able to make the journey to our house without an unreasonable amount of difficulty.

"Anybody here yet?" Walter hollered from the washroom door.

I jumped. "Don't scare me."

He slipped his arm around my waist. "Getting touchy in your old age."

I leaned into him. "You have been so good to me, and today the children are coming home. We're old, but we're happy."

He grinned. "Looks like I had best go help Henry and Joy unhitch. They just drove in."

I waited while Walter crossed the yard to greet Henry and Joy with a big smile on his face. Joy's two oldest children were married, and her teenage children would drive in later on their own, but her three youngest tumbled out of the buggy, their faces aglow with happiness. None of Joy's girls had her beauty, as if the mark of the past had been completely erased.

Two more buggies appeared in the distance. This joyous occasion had indeed commenced well. Walter and I were empty nesters now, and so must Lily be, out there somewhere. The community had almost forgotten her name, but I would never forget.

"Good morning." Cheerful voices hollered at me.

I waved back, and held the door open for them to tumble inside.

The youngest, Miriam, surveyed the pile of presents behind the wood stove. "Who made all this stuff?

"Walter did," I said. "I'm sure there's something in there for you."

"He made all of this?" The oldest of the three, Adam, asked.

"Walter worked hard," I said, "because this is a very special Christmas."

"Why?" They asked together.

"I don't know. This Christmas just is." I went back to open the front door.

Joy gave me a hug. "How are you?"

"Okay. The weather is beautiful."

"I know. The Lord has blessed us."

"Make yourself comfortable while I get breakfast on the table," I said.

"I should help." Joy followed me into the kitchen. "You'll have the house so full today the place will bust at the seams."

"Exactly what I want!"

"Henry says there'll be a hard winter, and perhaps another next year. He reads the Farmer's Almanac."

"We'll be okay," I said. "We always have been."

"I know." Joy left to put her coat in the bedroom.

Buggies began to fill the yard, with horses everywhere in stages of unhitching. Walter raced around the yard to help where he could, but his movements were more motion than action, which was perfect for this day. I wanted lots of motion, a joyous family time, everything going nowhere. We were not trying to impress anyone. We were just being together, which was how things should be.

"You okay?" Joy asked at my elbow.

"I'm fine," I said.

"Thinking about Grandma?"

"I wasn't at the moment, but yes."

"We must trust the Lord to make things right," she said. "Grandma couldn't forget Lily?"

I nodded and returned to the front door where I welcomed everyone in as they arrived. Joy stood guard to collect the coats, with frequent trips back to the bedroom.

"We have to get the presents open!" Miriam declared. "I'm not waiting any longer."

"Then let's," I said, and opened the front door to holler out. "Walter."

He came at a run. "What?"

"There are enough children inside to start handing out the presents," I said.

He didn't hesitate and left his boots and coat in the washroom. I posted myself in front of the wood stove. The noise level increased, as Walter gave the packages away. Loud thank yous were hollered out everywhere.

Paper was torn off, and several children began to set up homemade painted blocks in one corner, while others drove miniature wooden horses with farm implements across the floor. Walter continued to hand out the gifts. There were homemade dolls and dollhouses of various sizes for the girls.

I took in the chaos with my heart full of joy. These were my children, my grandchildren, and two great grandchildren. This was what home was like. This was what love produced, and what came from the blessing of the Lord.

I stirred in front of the stove—the trance broken. The girls were busy in the kitchen, and I joined them to help with the final food preparations. I had prepared part of the basics yesterday and the rest early this morning before the sun had come up. Joy directed several of the sons-in-law to pull out the long table and add the extra leaves. With the tablecloth spread, my girls came out with the dishes on cue and set the table while the work in the kitchen continued.

The noise in the living room increased, and the food continued to flow onto the dining room table—ham and bacon, eggs, pancakes with butter and golden maple syrup. I offered my help again, but Joy shooed me away. "Go sit while we finish."

I gave in and took the rocker beside the couch. The smaller grandchildren began to climb into my lap, while the others played on the floor in front of us.

"Time to eat," Joy announced.

Walter clapped his hands and silence fell. "We are very happy everyone could come this morning. You make our hearts glad in our old age. Now if Barbara will bring me the Bible, I will read the story of the real reason we're celebrating this day."

I stood to give Walter his German Bible. He opened the pages standing in front of the wood stove, the warmth heavy, and the room still.

Walter began to read, "And it came to past in those days, there went out a degree from Caeser …"

I listened to the words I had heard so many times before. They were like music, like a divine harmony playing in the air, the story of a young couple with no place to stay, a young mother who bore heaven's child, and the man who believed in her honor.

People said horrible things when they did not understand, but the story continued beyond the birth of the child. There were always those who believed goodness remained on the earth. Joseph had trusted his young bride enough to cover for her and stop the tongues from wagging. The child had been born in the manger with honor, with a father by its side.

I was not the only one who had found grace in my old age. I had to believe Lily had also found happiness, wherever she was. The Lord would not leave Lily to walk this earth alone, or Lily's child. Lily had borne Walter a son. I was certain. The two would meet someday, after I was gone, and the wound had been fully healed. How? I didn't know. What I had was enough tonight. Everyone was here. The Lord smiled upon us, and he had left the story of his own journey on this earth.

Precious seed was being planted in the young minds gathered at my house, as the seeds had been planted in mine. Those seeds would grow into a mighty crop, much better than the one I had produced, because the Lord had removed the poison from my life. They in turn, would give greater gifts to their children than I had been able to give.

"A truly good and precious story," Joy said at my elbow.

I nodded, as Walter finished and closed the Bible to hand the book back to me.

"And now for a song," Walter said. "Perhaps Joy can pick one for us this morning."

Joy began to sing at once, the old melody of "Silent Night, Holy night." The room rang with the German words, as they sang from memory.

"Now let us pray," Walter said when the last note had died down. He led out in a steady voice. "Our Father which art in heaven, hallowed be thy name ..."

When Walter finished, several of the girls jumped to their feet to rush into the kitchen. They returned with the rest of the steaming food and set the plates on the table. Everyone was seated, the adults at the dining room table and the younger ones in the kitchen. The last few had to sit on the floor beside the wood stove, but no one complained.

The girls served and I remained beside Walter by their orders. The meal continued. The happy chatter rose and fell around the table for over an hour. Walter closed with another prayer of thanks, and the children rushed back to their new toys. Most of the older ones gathered up their courage and made their way outside to play in the snow. They soon had a sizable snow formation of some sort erected in the front yard.

I insisted on helping clear the table and caught up on everyone's news while we washed the dishes. The adults drifted back to the living room, where I sat in my usual rocker with Walter in the other one.

"The king and queen in their domain," Joy said, standing in front of us. "I like you two like this."

"You were a great daughter to me," Walter said. "Thank you."

Joy kissed him lightly on the cheek and left again. After the breakfast food was cleared away, the girls brought out the homemade candy and goodies, their contribution to the day's events. They spread the sweets on the table, adding finger foods and further conversation, while around them a steady stream of people moved in and out of the house.

By late afternoon, the buggies began to leave. I pulled on my thick coat and stepped out on the porch to watch them leave. I waved as each buggy left, the children leaning out of the buggies to holler, "Thanks, Grandma. See you next year."

But there wouldn't be a next year quite like this one. I would let one of the girls host the following Christmas. They needed the experience, and they should begin the long build of their own memories. I would be there, but they would be in charge with their husbands.

Walter joined me on the porch as the last horse drove out of the lane.

"Should we go inside?" he asked.

"Just a few more minutes," I said. "I'm savoring the afterglow of the day."

"Come," he said. "The house is warmer."

I gave in and took his hand as we crossed the threshold together.

Chapter 45

Nine years later, the soft summer breeze drifted in through my kitchen window, and the smell of fresh baked bread wafted out into the living room as I hobbled across the room.

Walter lifted his head from his rocker and took a deep breath. "Bread. You're baking bread."

"Yes," I said.

"I'll have to eat some later." He struggled to rise.

I let him take his time, his movements made in jerks and starts. He steadied himself on the rocker arm.

"You should stay inside."

He let out a snort, "The farm needs my attention," and made his way to the front door. I let him go. He was not needed outside. He could not perform anything but the smallest tasks. His left arm was useless, taken out by a stroke last winter—the enemy had risen from within to strike at what was most precious to a man—his strength, his ability to control his body, his power to give himself commands and have them obeyed.

Summer was here again. This was the time when Walter used to hit the fields early and stay late and drive himself until he was exhausted. Those days were gone, and Walter was restless. I had expected he would be. Only the turmoil was worse than I had imagined, which added to a deep weariness in my bones.

I slept nights, but the tiredness didn't leave with the arrival of morning. There was no sense of relief like in the old days.

The urge to execute duties lingered in the recesses of the brain, the memory of energetic days un-erased. The habits of a lifetime had been brought to a halt while the mind was still alive.

Worse things could be happening. We could be unable to care for ourselves. I knew this and so did Walter. He restricted himself to the occasional protest. We had lived full lives. We had experienced much—too much perhaps, but we were alive, prisoners of our bodies, yes, waiting for the end which must come soon.

I watched through the window until Walter reached the barn and closed the door behind him. He needed the exercise, and I was thankful he could move about. There were decisions which should be made about our future, only Walter wouldn't make them. I didn't waste my breath with arguments. We were too old for conflict.

I returned to the kitchen and lifted the last of the bread pans from the oven. I set them on the table, tapped the loaves loose, and buttered the tops. The steam rose from the crusty brownness, the product formed to perfection by years of practice, the bread a display of beauty in its simplicity. Such was bread and the art of bread making—not unlike our lives. Until one day you were done, and the page turned.

I spread dry towels over my bread, four loaves where a dozen or more had once been laid out on the table. Even these would be threatened with mold before they were eaten, but I couldn't make less. Not yet, at least. I would try to eat more. I needed the nourishment, my bones were showing on my hips. Eating had been a problem of late. The simplest of tasks, the normal urges of the body turned into another enemy. Foes rose everywhere when the dusk of life fell. They quickly outnumbered friends. Once fertile fields were transformed into hostile camps inhabited by invasion forces.

I left the kitchen and made my way to the front door. There was no sign of Walter. He would stay outside until he could barely crawl back in, but I would not take this small pleasure from him. Pain was joy now, a strange turn of events, but true. One could consider any feeling a sign of distant life, reduced to a memory of abundance and bustle.

I stifled the urge to grab my shawl draped over the top of the couch. This was summer, winter was past, and yet the cold lingered, caught in the marrow of my bones. I didn't admit this to Walter or to anyone else. If worn, the shawl would reveal my secret. So the shawl stayed behind, and I shivered. The sun would warm me once I was outside. I would leave the buggy doors open. I would welcome the rays. My body failed me, but the sun was there to help, the one friend left in the sky. He still beckoned with promises and gave strength for what must be done. I wished to die when the sun was in the sky, perhaps at high noon, but I had no right to request the time of my departure.

I might be required to cross over in the night, led alone by faith, with no comfort, and no hand to touch mine. Bleakness would be what I deserved, for how I had lived my life, for how I had banished Lily. I was the strong one, yet I had given way in the moment of highest crisis. I could not live with Lily raising Walter's child down the road from me. The bitterness would have spoiled our lives and destroyed the one thing we both loved—Walter and his son. Lily had made the choice for me, and the decision had been right. The years had proven the moment. Now the day drew near when Lily would return. I would not be here. Lily would know when the moment came—somehow in Lily's way, but I must prepare the road. I must say the words which needed saying. For this much, I had the strength.

I crossed the yard and entered the barn. Walter stood by the empty stanchions, his gaze fixed on the concrete floor.

I approached to slip my arm around his waist. "Don't torture yourself like this. Emery does the chores and takes care of the place."

"I know," he said.

"I'm going over to Joy's place."

"I'll hitch the horse for you," he said.

"You can't throw on the harness."

Pain etched on his face. "I can try."

I looked away. "Okay. I could use your help."

We made our slow way towards the stall, where Basha, our new driving horse Walter had brought home from the sale barn early last fall before the stroke, neighed a greeting. In the old days, I would have renamed the mare something decent before Walter had the horse off the trailer, but these were not the old days.

The modern ways were everywhere. The roads crawled with English automobiles, the dust stirred by rubber wheels, their speed worse every year. To grow old was one thing, but to grow old in the midst of such trauma was more than a body should be asked to bear.

I would not last much longer, but Walter might. The life I left for Lily wouldn't be much, a pittance compared to the passion which once passed between my sister and Walter, but I could not give more. I had done my duty. I had lived my life with Walter, borne him children, and loved him. Walter was my husband. Heaven would understand and forgive me for taking what didn't belong to me.

Walter banged on the stall latch to open the door. I winced. Walter was too taken with his own efforts to notice my pain. We were two old people who should be in bed instead of working in the barn harnessing their driving horse to the buggy. I should call Emery who worked somewhere in the back fields today, but Walter wouldn't like the fuss, and this, a little of what Walter wanted, I could give him.

Walter reached for Basha's halter with his good hand and led the horse out of the stall. I lifted the harness from the hook on the wall and slid the contraption over Basha's back. Walter stayed at the horse's head until I had the straps fastened. In the old days, I would have stood at his place. Walter accepted his fate, but the agony on his face was plain to see. I said nothing as I followed him outside and held up the buggy shafts. He guided Basha underneath and took his place again. After I was done, he tossed me the lines with his good hand, and stepped aside.

I took off, and waved, but Walter had turned his back, on his way back to the house, his shoulders stooped. I jiggled the reins and Basha trotted along at a brisk pace. The usual automobiles whizzed past, and I stayed half in the ditch where possible. No one else in the community drove like this, but I could not overcome the instinct to flinch.

Joy was on the front porch when I drove in and hurried across the yard to tie Basha to the hitching post.

"Mamm!" Joy scolded. "What are you doing out today by yourself."

"I need to talk," I said. "Can I sit with you?"

"Of course. Is Daett worse?"

I shook my head. "He helped me hitch up."

Joy sighed. "Why don't you two move into the dowdy house? Life feels dangerous with you over there by yourselves."

I seated myself on the porch swing. "I know you speak the truth, and yet you cannot put your Daett in a dowdy house when I pass. You would make the wrong choice. He wants to live in the house we've had together, where we've always been."

"Everyone lives in a dowdy house in their old age," Joy said.

"Stop trying, dear." I patted my daughter's arm. "There are a lot of things I can't explain, or rather don't want to. Let him die in his own house, Joy."

"You know you can't fight things, Mamm. Sometimes they just are what they are."

"I know, but I can do what I can. You have to take care of Walter at our place."

"And why is this?" she asked.

"Lily is coming back," I said.

"Mamm!" Joy scolded. "I know I once lived with her and still love her, but she doesn't belong here."

"Her coming back was part of our plan," I said. "Lily will know when I pass, and she will return."

"What in the world are we supposed to do when she comes?" Joy asked. "First, you tell me you're dying. Now you say Aunt Lily will come back. I'm going to feel terrible telling her she has to leave again."

"Which is exactly what you must not do," I said.

"Is this some kind of restitution? If Aunt Lily comes back—much as I liked her, we are not in the past anymore. I have the reputation of my children to think about."

"I don't know how you will handle her," I said. "I'm too tired to plan everything. Take care of Walter for me, and I think Lily will do what is right. I trust her. I know I shouldn't, but I do."

Joy was silent as the porch swing squeaked above us.

"I know I have no right to ask," I said, "but I'm asking."

Joy reached over to squeeze my hand. "You have every right to ask."

"You will let her stay then?"

"I will, but I'm not telling Henry. Not until she comes at least."

"There is one more thing," I whispered.

"Mamm! Please."

"There are several notebooks in the top of my dresser drawer. Give them to Lily when she comes."

Joy said nothing for a very long time. "Why are you doing this to yourself?"

I rose to my feet. "I should be going. Walter is alone in the house with the bread. He might have all the loaves eaten by the time I get back."

Joy followed me back out to the buggy. She untied Basha from the hitching post while I held the reins. I took off with a quick wave out the buggy door. My daughter was still in the front yard watching me leave, when I glanced over my shoulder. I drove down County Road 1200 and let the reins out until Basha moved along at a steady trot. I stayed out of the ditch even when the traffic on the road shook the buggy with their passing air blasts. I saw Lily's face and Walter's in the clouds, both of them young, gazing at each other.

Walter came out of the house when I pulled in the driveway. He held the bridle while I unhitched the traces. I let Walter take Basha into the barn and entered the house. The stillness hung heavy, the aroma of bread from the kitchen full in the living room. Walter had closed the window, so the summer's chill must also have reached him. I entered the bedroom and knelt to pray. The words didn't come. They were like a weight on my chest. I looked up at the window where the rays of the sun streamed past the window drapes. The quilt beckoned, the softness a hollow of warmth and security. I took off my shoes and lowered my head on the pillow. I brushed the wrinkles out of my dress. There was strength flooding into the window, a cloud of brilliance, like an ocean opening with waves and waves never seeming to stop. I hoped this was how I would be allowed to pass over.

"Barbara," Walter called from the front door.

"I'm taking a little nap," I called back.

He muttered something which I couldn't understand, and I drifted off to sleep.

Section Ten—October 1977 to January 1978

LILY

Chapter 46

I drove north out of Loogootee on Route 231 and near the Crane Naval Center turned west towards Odon. I soon left behind the forested glory displayed along Route 231 for the sparse trees dotting the farmed fields. The bright gold and yellows mingled with the darker brown of the autumn colors soothing my nervousness. At least I had arrived back in the community at the peak of their Fall glory.

I clutched the steering wheel until my fingers hurt. My car sat low on the road, a simple Chevy Impala purchased new last year, dark-colored and appropriate for this visit. I was the one who would be out of place in the community, a woman lost in time, coming back to where she didn't belong. I should never have come. There were too many years under the bridge, yet I had come. I couldn't stay away. Not from Walter.

Jackson didn't know where I had gone, and he didn't need to know for another few weeks. He had married in his mid-thirties, fifteen some years ago, and lived with his family in Arlington. Jackson worked for the government in some obscure job I couldn't understand. Or maybe Jackson didn't wish to explain. The work was honorable and worthy and needed. Jackson checked on me at the big house on the hill at irregular intervals. I would tell him where I was when the time came.

I slowed as the first houses of the small burg of Odon appeared in front of me. If I was rejected and turned away from the community, Jackson would never know. I wouldn't blame Walter if he sent me packing. I was no longer the dashing beauty of yesteryear, nor did I have a claim on him. Time had done its work. I had loved, and I had waited, and I was what I was.

First things first though—the graveyard, a part of the past which was not here when I left—my sister's passing. Joy would have the headstone up by now. If not, there would be a wooden marker of some sort over the place where Barbara lay. There were the others, Mamm and Daett, and Walter's parents. Mrs. Emmett's source dried up before those events. I had been left with the daughter's commitment to notify me of Barbara's death, for which I was thankful.

I drove through Odon and turned south at the light. The fields open again beyond the last streets. Familiar places, houses I knew, changed in ways I couldn't place at once. New paint, new siding, a barn with a metal roof instead of slate, a new addition, and in some places everything was different.

What did I expect? Fifty years had passed, almost to the day, since I fled this place with Walter's child inside of me. Fifty years didn't leave things untouched. Fifty years were a lifetime in other places. I was a fool to come back. I could have sent a card, and so broken the silence. I could have wished Joy and her sisters well and expressed my sorrow at their Mamm's passing. Yet, as always, the easy way was not my way. I must see Walter. Barbara had promised, and my sister kept her promises.

I held my head down as I passed within sight of the old home place. No buggies were on the road this time of the day, and they wouldn't recognize me anyway. I was not desperate, hungry, and longing for what I could not have. If I had been unhappy, I would have come back long ago. Desperate people did the irrational. The choice I made to return was made because the time had arrived upon which Barbara and I had agreed. The paper on the box must be unwrapped and the strings to the bow cut. Duty brought its peace. I had done my duty these fifty years. Walter could do what he wished about my arrival.

I slowed and turned west again. I came to a stop by the iron fence surrounding the enclosed graveyard and climbed out. The brisk autumn air moved across the open fields. I pulled my sweater tighter over my shoulders and opened the creaking metal gate. Gravestones with familiar names were everywhere. I moved among the ghosts of the past. My eyes searched the ground. I found their names on the far, right-hand side. Mamm and Daett were a little distance away from Walter's parents. The years had replaced the broken sod with a lush cover of green. I knelt and ran my hand over Mamm's headstone. I should weep, or say a prayer, but nothing came.

I moved on to find Barbara's grave, the headstone in place, a dark gray marble slab with the simple words, "Barbara Yoder, beloved wife and mother."

"Sorry I wasn't here," I whispered.

I couldn't have come, even if they had known how to notify me. The disruption at the funeral would have been too severe. These were Barbara's people, and she knew them. They needed to know who was who, and who came from where. The story would have robbed Joy and her sisters of their time of mourning. I knelt and the tears came. In little trickles at first, then waves of emotion racked my body. Time slowed as the sun climbed higher in the sky, and I waited. I waited long. What did another hour matter, or another year, or another time? Our minutes were almost out of the glass. No one could stop time.

I moved slowly and climbed back into the car, the roads empty in either direction. I drove north again and pulled into Joy's driveway. This was the place to begin, not at the old homestead. Joy would know the next move and whether I was welcome to continue the visit. I parked beside the barn and opened the car door. The barn has been painted a few years ago, the roof brisk with brightness, the fences freshly washed. Henry kept things up well. My childhood was spent at a place like this, the hopes of my youth vigorous, with my expectation of life's unspoiled beauty yet to unfold.

I glanced into the barnyard. There was no haystack. Why should there be one? My mind was playing tricks with memories from long gone. I waited for what could not be, for something wonderful, for Walter to appear. I looked back as the barn door opened and the bearded face of a man comes into focus. "Henry?" I guessed.

The questions flashed across his face. "Who are you?"

"Lily," I said.

The name didn't seem to register. Why was I surprised? Henry came into the family after I left. He couldn't have been more than Joy's age back then, a stripling of a boy, now a man.

Henry cleared his throat.

I pasted on my best smile. An old woman couldn't be threatening to this tower of a man. "Could I see your wife, Joy?"

"Oh." Comprehension dawned. "You must be one of the ladies who buy from the garden in the summertime. There are a few pumpkins left, but not much more."

"I'm Joy's aunt," I said.

He stared and his gaze shifted to my car.

"I really am," I said. "Sorry for the shock."

"But you …" He searched for words. "I did not see you at the funeral."

"I wasn't there."

"I see," he said, but he didn't. He hadn't moved, either.

"Can you tell Joy I'm here?"

"I guess," he said, then seemed to change his mind. "The front door is up there. You can knock."

"Thank you." I gave him a bright smile.

His capitulation had been a great one. The men here were the guardians of the home. He had given me, a strange woman, with strange claims, the green light to speak with his wife.

He stood and stared after me as I made my way up the familiar walkway. The porch steps had been changed along with the porch floor and the swing. There was new siding on the house. I knocked and the door opened.

"Good morning." Joy spoke cheerfully.

"Do you know who I am?" I asked.

Joy stared for a moment. There were footsteps behind us, and we both turned. Henry had followed me to the house and stood at the bottom of the steps, his bearded face turned upwards.

"I'm okay," Joy said, and grabbed my hand to propel me inside. She motioned towards the couch. "Sit."

"I can leave," I said.

Joy shook her head. "I was expecting you. I just hadn't told Henry."

"How is Walter?" I asked.

"Holding on by a thread."

"He is ill?"

"Daett had his second stroke when he found Mamm passed away in their bed. There isn't much time for whatever you two have to make right between yourselves."

"I had hoped, perhaps, there would be more time."

"He can't talk much," she said, "and doesn't get out of his wheelchair."

"Can I see him?" I asked.

Joy didn't move. "How did you keep track of things in the community?"

"My husband's aunt kept contact with one of your drivers who hauls the community people around, a Mrs. Fields."

"She's been dead for years."

"I know. Her daughter agreed to notify me of your mamm's passing."

Joy appeared satisfied. "Let's go then."

"You will drive with me in my car?"

Joy shrugged. "Why not? Most of the young generation never heard of your excommunication. Time has passed, what—?"

"Fifty years," I said.

Joy led the way outside, to holler towards Henry who stood at the barn door. "I'm going with her to Daett's place."

He nodded and disappeared into the barn. We climbed in to drive the short distance along the familiar County Road 1200.

"Do you notice much change?" Joy asked.

"I see the community from fifty years ago," I said.

"You won't know Daett, I'm afraid."

"I'll know him," I said, and slowed for the driveway to park by the barn.

We climbed out and walked up the sidewalk together.

A young woman opened the door for us. "Mamm?" The question came with raised eyebrows.

"Miriam." Joy addressed the girl. "This is Aunt Lily, and this is Miriam, my youngest girl."

"Good morning," I greeted her.

The wrinkled brow remained. "Aunt Lily?"

"I know, dear, we'll explain later." Joy led the way forward.

The wheelchair was turned away from the front door, a quilt hung over his back, the head above the frame, white haired and shriveled. I moved slowly and placed myself in front of him.

He looked up, puzzled at first, before the smile formed. "Lily."

"Yes." I got on my knees and took his hands. "Walter." The tears came.

"I have been waiting for you," he said.

I embraced him. The thin frame of his bones pressed into my hands. Only the eyes were the same, with the intensity leaping upward.

"Are you staying?" he asked.

I touched his face. "I'm never leaving you again."

Chapter 47

Three months later, I was still here. I had called Jackson and told him my whereabouts. My morning routine was to carry Walter's tray of food into his bedroom. I wasn't permitted entrance during the night. Miriam was vigilant, under strict orders from Joy. Even the appearance of anything inappropriate must be avoided, so I stayed upstairs in the spare bedroom, while Miriam slept on the couch. I was too old, and Walter was too crippled, for any naughtiness, but things are what they are. Miriam's older brother Lonnie slept upstairs in the bedroom across from me and made several trips down at night to check on Walter. Miriam kept the household running in the daytime, and I helped where I could.

I held the tray in one hand and pushed back the bedroom drapes with the other. The sunlight poured in.

"Good morning," I greeted Walter.

He grimaced at the bright light.

"Do you want the drapes pulled again?" I asked.

"Bright is good," he said, and attempted to sit.

I helped him up. "I have your oatmeal ready."

A smile crept across his face. "You look good this morning, a sight for sore eyes."

"I'm an old woman, Walter."

"You will always be beautiful to me," he said.

I kissed him lightly on the cheek. Miriam wasn't around to stop me. He took a bite of oatmeal as I held the bowl for him.

"Are they coming today like you said?" he asked.

"Yes."

He stopped chewing and studied my face. "What does he look like, my son?"

"A little like you when you were young, handsome, and quick on your feet."

He grinned. "Which means I'm not anymore."

"You're still handsome," I said.

His laugh was weak.

"Are you well enough to meet them today?"

He nodded.

"I think you should eat all of the oatmeal. You'll need your strength."

He didn't protest and I scraped the last spoonful from the bowl.

"I'll be back," I said, and left for the kitchen.

"How's he doing?" Miriam asked.

"Fading fast, I'm afraid."

"Mamm claims he's holding on for some reason."

"I agree," I said. "Jackson could have come sooner by himself, but I wanted the whole family."

"This Jackson has two grown children?"

I smiled. "He does, both boys."

"How are things done in your world?" Miriam was looking at me. "Mamm keeps us close to home."

"Which is for the best, believe me." I gave Miriam a quick pat on the arm. "Can I help with the dishes?"

Miriam motioned towards the towel. "You really did live here in the community, many years ago?"

"I grew up in what was your Great-Grandmother's house."

"Mamm said so, but you don't look Amish." She gave me a quick glance.

I hid my smile. "I left a long time ago, like fifty years."

I got another glance. "Mamm won't tell us anything about those days."

I couldn't help thinking how dangerous Barbara would find this conversation. "Maybe she doesn't want you living back there."

"Were your lives strange or scary?"

I lied a little bit. "Just two sisters growing up together."

She obviously wasn't buying the line. "You're not telling me either, are you?"

"I guess not." I dried a bowl thoroughly.

"Do you have maids where you live?" She tried another tack.

"Actually, we do."

"Do they cook for you?"

"Yes." I was relieved by the appearance of much safer ground.

"How can you cook after fifty years of maids?"

I laughed. "Some things just always are. You don't forget them."

"Why is this coming of your son such a big deal to Walter?"

I gave her a glare. "You don't quit, do you?"

Miriam grinned. "You can't blame me for being curious. Has Walter met him before?"

"Not really," I said.

"Doesn't Walter know he's your son?" She was quite nimble on her feet, I had to admit.

"We'll just go around in circles all day, sweetheart. I'm not telling you. You can ask your mamm."

Miriam made a face. "Mamm's lips are sealed."

"There we go." I gave her a stern look. "Some things are best not said."

"Why do you adults have so many secrets?"

"Maybe you can have less of them."

"My life's pretty boring." She wrinkled her face.

"You can be very thankful."

"I don't think boring is good."

I smiled. "You'll marry someday and have a husband and children. Life will get interesting enough."

Miriam's neck reddened slightly.

"Any man making eyes at you?"

The redness moved into her face. "I'm not talking."

"You want to marry him if he's the right man."

"Mamm had to wait four years to marry Daett," she said. "There was a war. Do you have lots of wars out there?"

"My husband Robert died in a war."

"I'm sorry. Was he Jackson's father?"

"You're a curious little miss," I said.

"Do you always talk like this, with nothing being certain?"

I gave her a smile, but Miriam was looking out the kitchen window at the automobile pulling into the driveway. Lonnie had cleared a path to the barn earlier, and a smaller one up to the house. We couldn't do much better with the constant storms this winter. Hardly a week passed before another one moved across the state. The weather was clear today. A matter for which I gave thanks.

"They've arrived." Miriam declared, and leaned over the sink for a better view.

I hurried back to the bedroom. Walter sat propped up on his pillows, his face pale. His eyes lit up when I appeared.

"They're here," I said.

"He doesn't know he's my son, does he?" he asked.

"I think Jackson has guessed, but we shouldn't say anything to the others."

I left him to open the front door. Miriam stayed in the kitchen, bashful no doubt with this car full of English people at her doorstep.

"Mother." Jackson greeted me with a hug and a kiss, as did Ashley, his wife.

"Hi." Both of Jackson's children gave me smiles.

"Thank you so much for coming." I stood back to let them in. "I've waited so long for this, and so has Walter."

"The trip took a while to fit in with Christmas and the holidays," Jackson said.

"I understand."

"Who is this old man anyway?" Allen, Jackson's oldest asked. "Dad was kind of vague, something about your background."

"Walter is an Amish man, and you're in Amish country," I said. "He's someone from my past who is very dear, and I want you to meet him. Think of this as a favor to your grandmother, an old eccentric woman."

They chuckled.

"I didn't know you knew Amish people," Raymond, the second son said.

"I don't talk about them often."

"Like never to us," Allen said.

"Your father knew. I'm just grateful you came."

"This is awful mysterious," Raymond muttered.

I led the way past the kitchen and paused. "This is Miriam, who helps with Walter's care."

Miriam gave a little wave from the kitchen sink, looking wide eyed, saying nothing.

"An Amish woman," Allen said once we moved on.

"Hush!" Ashley whispered. "She can hear you."

I hid my amusement and entered the bedroom with the troop behind me. Walter's eyes were bright with tears.

"This is Walter," I said. "And this is my son Jackson, his wife Ashley, and their two sons, Allen and Raymond."

"How do you do, sir?" Jackson offered his hand. "I'm glad to meet you."

"Good to see you." Walter clung to Jackson's hand for a moment before the grasp slipped from his fingers. Allen and Raymond also offered their handshakes, as did Ashley.

"You must be very dear to Lily," Ashley said. "We're glad we could come."

"Thank you so much," Walter said. The tears glistened on his cheeks. "You were very kind to come, and your sons are very handsome young men."

Allen and Raymond laughed. "Maybe we should take him out with us on Saturday nights."

"Boys." Ashley chided. "Mind your manners."

"How do you know our grandmother?" Raymond asked.

Walter took a moment before he answered. "We go back a long way. I know your grandmother from the time she used to live in the community."

"Never heard the story." Allen looked at me.

"You had other things on your mind, dear, and this was a long time ago," I said.

"I'm glad you have come." Walter filled the silence quickly. "I only wish I could have seen more of you in my lifetime."

"Maybe you boys can step outside a bit, while I talk with Walter," Jackson suggested.

"There's a cute Amish girl in the kitchen." Raymond grinned. "Do you think she'll talk to us?"

Jackson glanced at me.

"Why not," I said.

The two left, and Jackson moved closer to the bed. "I'm also sorry, sir, I didn't get to see more of you in my lifetime."

I touched Jackson's arm. "Ashley and I will step out for a minute."

Jackson nodded and Ashley left with me.

"Am I reading things right," she asked. "Is this Jackson's real father?"

I sat down on the couch before I answered. "I suppose there's no harm in knowing. Yes."

"What a story." Ashley's eyes were wide.

"Not a tame one, but an interesting one, I suppose."

"Why didn't you marry the man? Aren't they honorable in these communities?"

"He was married to my sister."

Ashley let out a long breath. "More than interesting, I would say."

"Too interesting, believe me."

"Was your sister some looker?" she asked.

The memories flooded back for me. "Barbara was the plain one," I said.

"So, you didn't want him?"

The tears came, and I choked. "I wanted him more than I wanted life itself."

"I see," she said. "A story indeed."

We fell silent to the sound of the young people's chatter in the kitchen.

"Sounds like your Amish girl can talk," Ashley said.

"We can talk." I forced a smile. "Shall we join them?"

We stood and entered the kitchen. Allen and Raymond were seated at the table with sandwiches and glasses of orange juice spread in front of them.

"Dinner." Allen hollered. "Can the Amish girls ever cook."

"And you can eat," Miriam said from near the stove. Her face was several colors of red.

I motioned for Ashley to take a chair. "You might as well stay for lunch. Jackson may be awhile.

Ashley was easily persuaded, and Miriam served the food. She insisted I eat with the others. Ashley didn't say much as Allen and Raymond continue to ply Miriam with questions about the community. Jackson appeared after a while, sober-faced, and sat down to eat without a protest. They left when

Jackson finished. I waited until they had made their way clear of the snowy driveway before I returned to the bedroom. The sun rays burst through the window with a fierce intensity and I pulled the drapes before I approached the bed. Walter appeared asleep, exhausted no doubt, from the day's events.

I'd begun to tiptoe away, when I stopped. Something wasn't right. I moved back to the bed and touched Walter's hand. The coldness seeped into my fingers, and I jerked back.

"Walter!"

There was only silence, and I saw nothing move. His breathing had been shallow of late, but not like this.

I touched his face, where the warmth lingered.

"Walter!" I called again and shook his shoulder.

There was no response. I stepped back, my hands on my face. I waited, and slowly peace came. This was right. Walter had not died alone. Barbara had come for him. I stifled a sob and went to find Miriam. The girl turned ashen-faced when I told her. She rushed into the bedroom to verify my observations.

"Go tell your mamm." I ordered.

Miriam followed me to the barn where I helped her harness the horse and hitch him to the buggy. Miriam climbed in, and I handed her the reins.

"Will you be okay while I'm gone?" she asked.

I nodded. "I will wait for your mamm."

I returned to the house and heated water on the stove—plenty of it—and filled the bowl. With a bar of soap and a washcloth, I carried the water into the bedroom and began to work. I undressed him and washed him—his feet, his hands, his face, his legs—with great care, with tender motions, and with tears nearly blinding me. I used my hair to dry the skin on his face. I held him close and rocked him. I willed the warmth to return, but he belonged to Barbara again, and not to me. I found his white shirt and his best suit in the closet, his cleanest underwear in the dresser drawer and began to put them on. I finished and had my suitcase packed when Joy pulled into the driveway with Miriam on the buggy seat beside her.

I met Joy at the front door. "I washed and dressed him."

Joy didn't answer, but we embraced. "You're not staying for the funeral?"

"Some things are best left alone," I said.

"Will we see you again?"

I shook my head. "You will bury him beside Barbara?"

"We will, and you, when your time comes?"

"I have a pretty hillside."

"They did learn to love each other," Joy said.

I smiled through my tears. "I'm glad."

"I figured you might be leaving." Joy held out a brown bag. "Mamm wanted you to have these."

I raised my eyebrows.

"I haven't read them," she said.

I took the bag. "Goodbye, then."

"May the peace of the Lord go with you," she said.

"Thank you, and thanks for letting me stay these short months."

"You can thank Mamm."

"You're very kind," I said, and went down the snowy walks with my suitcase in one hand and the brown paper bag in the other.

About the Author

Jerry Eicher has written and published over thirty works of Amish romantic fiction, along with his childhood memoir, *My Amish Childhood*. He lives in Virginia with his wife Tina. They have four children and seven grandchildren

Made in the USA
Monee, IL
15 March 2021

62851814R00213